HIDDEN VICTORY

for Mary,

with my priestly blessing.

Herbert F. Smith S.J.

Books by Herbert Francis Smith

Living For Resurrection
God Day By Day
The Lord Experience
The Pilgrim Contemplative
How To Get What You Want From God
Hidden Victory

This book is available at a special quantity discount in bulk purchase for educational use, parish fund raising, premiums and sales promotions. Contact the distributor: Bonny Books, Inc., 180 Sweeney Street, North Tonawanda, N.Y. 14120 (716-692-8756).

HIDDEN VICTORY
A Novel Of Jesus

by
Herbert Francis Smith, S.J.

First Edition 1984

Saint Joseph's University Press
5600 City Avenue
Philadelphia 19131

Distributed by Bonny Books, Inc.,
180 Sweeney Street, North Tonawanda, N.Y. 14120
(716-692-8756)

Cover: Shroud of Turin photograph © 1963.
Holy Shroud Guild, Esopus, N.Y. 12496

Imprimi Potest: Joseph P. Whelan, S.J.
                 Provincial, Maryland Province

Nihil Obstat: James McGrath
                 Archdiocesan Censor

Imprimatur: John Cardinal Krol
                 Archbishop of Philadelphia
                 January 10, 1984

The Nihil Obstat and Imprimatur are official declarations that a book or pamphlet is free of doctrinal or moral error. No implication is contained therein that those who have granted the Nihil Obstat and Imprimatur agree with the contents, opinions, or statements expressed.

Printed in the United States of America
89 88 87 86 85 84   5 4 3 2 1

Library of Congress Cataloging in Publication Data

Smith, Herbert F.
   Hidden victory.

   Includes index.
   1. Jesus Christ—Fiction. I. Title.
PS3569.M5373H5 1984 813'.54   84-3452
ISBN 0-916101-01-0
ISBN 0-916101-02-9 (pbk.)

DEDICATED

to the land of Israel,
of which I have dear memories,
and to the people there and at home
who made this book possible.

ACKNOWLEDGEMENTS

To name all who have helped with this book is not feasible, but to mention the following is a welcome obligation as well as a kind of recall of the novel's genesis: in Jerusalem, Dr. David Flusser of Hebrew University, Fr. Frederick Manns of Studium Biblicum, and Fr. Jose Espinoza, S.J. and the students of The Pontifical Biblical Institute; in Galilee, Sr. Mary Olivette, C.S.C., of Mater Ecclesiae Center, Tiberias, and Fr. Jerome, O.S.B., Sanctuary of the Multiplication of the Loaves, Tabgha, Sea of Galilee.

Dr. and Mrs. V. Michael Vaccaro of Hahnemann Medical University read the ms and offered valuable critiques. Many others proposed revisions, some of major importance: Fr. John Hardon, S.J., Mr. Alan Ameche, Jr., Mr. and Mrs. Alan Ameche, Sr. Marie Cornelia, S.S.J., Fr. James E. McGuire, Dr. Joseph Gambescia, Mrs. William Albertus, Mrs. Lois Flatley, Sr. Agnes, S.M.G.

Jesuits at Saint Joseph's University contributed their many talents: in theology, Frs. James Neville and Martin R. Tripole, chairmen past and present of the theology department, and Fr. Henry Hammet (R.I.P.); in proofing and refining, Frs. Michael Smith, Lawrence R. McHugh, and John Carboy; in literature, Fr. Francis Burch, who gave brilliant guidance in the writing of the novel, and Fr. Joseph Feeney, in the final editorial work.

The tireless, skillful work of Carol and Kevin McLaughlin at Saint Joseph's University Press are memorable, as is the support of Catherine McInerney, and the prayers of my Carmelite and Poor Clare friends. Finally I name my brothers George and Robert, and friend Alan Ameche, businessmen, whose Bonny Books, Inc., plays such a crucial role in marketing this book. To these dear friends and colleagues, and many others, my gratitude.

INTRODUCTION

This is a historical novel. It can be entered at different depths, as adventure, history, or revelation.

The novel is solidly rooted in the four Gospels. The theme is drawn from Mark's "Gospel of the Messianic secret," the inner depths of Jesus from John; the Infancy accounts from Luke and Matthew. Interpretation is founded on a solid contemporary theology of Christ, which sums up 2,000 years of faith and meditation.

Descriptions of the social and religious environment, the land, and the flora and fauna are based on accepted research works and on the Holy Land today, where the author dwelt and traveled while writing the first draft.

What little is known of the twelve apostles is adhered to, but imagination has fleshed it out. Certain minor characters are figments of the imagination. Incidental dialogue and minor events are fabricated to give flow to the drama.

In brief, the author has done for the reader what scholars and contemplatives have long done for themselves—filled in the chinks of the Gospels. The reader interested in the substantive roots of the novel should consult the Appendix of Scriptural References to compare the various episodes with their Gospel foundations.

Jesus is, in the words of St. John of the Cross, "a rich mine with many pockets containing treasures—however deep we dig we will never find their end." This novel attempts to dig deep. Whether it digs out the true ore is yours to decide.

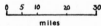

CONTENTS

Cover photo of the Shroud of Turin is used with the permission of the Shroud of Turin Guild. Cover art work by Carol and Kevin McLaughlin.

Part One

MISUNDERSTOOD SON

1

This drench of blood stains my tunic—as if it matters—
yet every blade of grass matters tonight—I go to die! Those
olive trees snake into the mist under that paschal moon
vanishing in smokings—cold moon chilling my bones. The
blood runs before the nails go in—I go to my fate.

Your Son, out of Adam and Abraham, Jew of Jews—must
he die in nightmare? Scion of the chosen race, come in body
life—why take my life? Howling Satan tramples this fat
grape—the red juice running. Father, you make all things
new. Make for them new hearts that will never shut me out
—unshutable hearts!

Despair stalks—I can't outrun it. Why? Eager I was at your
sending—enduring the angry buzzings and white-hot stings
—embracing all. Why then this refugee of the night—memory
writhing like a beast at bay—seeking escape?

Must I think it all through again? Be buried under memory's
mountain? And foresee the doubters to come after? Asking
why I didn't save the Baptizer—and squandered my supposed
powers on trifles—a jar of wine! Not understanding my
experience—the impossibilities I faced—impassable mountain
peaks. How shall they see it—that for what I am and teach,
there are no words? And that my hearers—for fear—for
burden—did not want to know.

What flesh and blood has the courage to follow all the way?
Up, out of the swamps of sense, to faith's misty peaks?
To where this soul, awash in its mystery, sails its shoreless
Sea. Seeing this body, who believes what I see—that I AM?
Yet why are they blind to my signs—greater than the sea

3

—and to my self-giving—outbounding the heavens?

I grasp for consolations—seek escape in happier times. She of Migdol—at sight of me sensing my truth beyond her reach. Young John—seizing at first meeting upon the vastness of my presence—dedicating himself to exploration day and night. Peter—plunging after me down many a fearful landscape. Committed more in heart than understanding—yet, in the test, speedier than the mental fleetfoots to grasp at least the half of me.

That episode in the Temple—I was twelve—why does it parade across my memory now? Because they didn't reject me then—even saw promise in me? So little they saw—only the shallows on my shores—it was prophetic of the failure to see closing on me now like an army of the blind.

A day of beauty? A day of grief and forebodings that sounded an ominous drumbeat of this dark future! It set my blood to pounding when that poor old pilgrim was hurled to the Temple stones with a Roman curse ringing in his ear.

We weren't ready, so peaceful were the seven days of Passover, and our passage down the Mount of Olives for the morning sacrifice. How the city lay aflame in the rising sun, so that Joseph paused on the heights, to gaze across the valley at the Temple where the white smoke rose.

"Always," he pondered aloud, "the Temple reminds me of your mother." Touching her hand, he sought her eyes, and they exchanged that glance of love which never died. "At her birth a quarter of a century ago, Herod decreed its rebuilding, so it grew with her."

Then she, too, reminisced. "My father used to let me toddle at his side when he went to watch the workmen fitting the great stones. A little north there, near the sheep pool, I was born. Only later did the political turmoil drive us to the quiet and safety of Nazareth."

Turmoil. It beats upon me. It was back, then, throbbing in the air, when we saw the fallen pilgrim, and the people shrinking from the angry soldier. We sprang to his aid, the Roman glowering, the old man mumbling, "It was an accident —bumping into you."

"Careful," came a hoarse warning from a fellow countryman. "Freedom fighters got two Romans in the night."

4

The occupying forces everywhere, foreign phrases rolling from their tongues—was my word less foreign to my people?

How Ab's violent words were to chill my blood that morning. I'd just found peace in the face of that old rabbi, Elijah. A little man with billowy white beard. Face drawn fine as an artisan's gold leaf. So fine, it hovered as on vision's edge. Poised for the final purification that would send it vanishing into spirit's realm.

Peace—my mother lost hers at that whisper of death in the night. How she clung to my hand as we threaded through the milling throng. "We don't want to be separated." Her voice so grave—"We leave for home within the hour."

Joseph speaking of other horrors. "A fine turnout of pilgrims. More than the year of the Temple massacre."

"You never talk about it," I prompted.

"Not with young boys. Inflames their imagination. But you'll soon be a bar mitzvah. Besides, I didn't see it myself. We'd fled danger—gone into exile with you in our arms."

"I know—Herod's slaughter of the babies." He eyed me, surprized, and I explained. "Our priest-kinsman spoke of it, and of how they hid my cousin."

His eyes fogged with stormy memories. "Herod—insecure old man—was obsessed with the notion he'd lose his kingdom to some new-born destined to it. Just one instance of his mad fears."

"He was always afraid of being dethroned then."

"He got the idea Mariamme—the most loved of his wives— was plotting his overthrow. Killed her. Wandered his castle bellowing laments—then strangled his and her two sons on the same charge."

"You started to talk about the massacre."

"That sprang from another of his follies—though he died before it happened. Always the puppet of Rome, he mounted the Roman Eagle over the Nicanor Gate." He indicated the immense bronze rampart.

"We don't allow secular power-signs in the Lord's sanctuary."

"Exactly. But once Augustus Caesar got his first taste—it was in Pergamon—of being worshipped as a god, it was hard stopping him. The golden eagle, it seems, was the opening move toward emperor worship here."

"Never!"

"Amen. Bold youths hacked it down. He burned them alive—but dared not restore it. He died, and the people demanded reforms of his son, Archelaus. He gushed promises—and crammed the Temple with soldiers. The people stoned them. He loosed his army. Three thousand died."

His grim memories poured out of him like blood—and pour out of me in this wild hour. The wildness was back then. Word of the freedom fighters' deed set blood boiling with rebellion. The crowd writhed and pulsed with dangerous intent. Temple police, driving through, sprayed people aside, divided us. Impossible to find one another. Had to wait the crowd's thinning. I went to the court of men.

The sacrificial rites! Silent lambs slashed at the throat, blood pouring into silver basins, splashed against the smoking altar. Imperious trumpet burst. The colors of magnificent regalia, jewels flashing, attendants fawning, the revered high priest parading past, disappearing through the embroidered veils adorned with flowers of purple.

Those savage mysteries. I thought of the rabbis discoursing on such things. I went to hear them. What distress for my parents—they mindful for the next three days only of the dangerous unrest, I of the purpose driving me fiercely. Longing for my people's freedom. Father, I pondered my mission amid violence and bloodshed. How quell it before the drive for independence won out or was crushed out?

Surging up, in that hour, out of the bones inherited from Abraham, came the call to serve you, Father. I responded.

The lofty Portico of Solomon. Disciples surrounding old Rabbi Elijah and a younger man—it was there Ab erupted.

"So you see," the veteran was expounding, "we're not all of one mind about the coming of a Messiah, or his identity—or even what his advent will portend. We Pharisees hold that a Davidic Messiah is promised. He . . ."

"Rabbi Elijah," the younger man broke in, "I expect a priestly messiah as well. How he's needed, now that the legitimacy of the reigning high priest is at question!"

"Rabbi Joram, you suppose the Messiah will walk the paths of this age, I that he'll usher in the age hereafter—

6

burning away corruption, burying sin and death, making us shine as stars. No sacrifice then but that of praise."

How their Anointed listened to their expectations! How he examined the speakers! Joram was Elijah's contrary. Young, heavy of flesh, florid of face, he displayed no kinship with spirit save for shrewd intelligence flashing from observant eyes.

"After all," Elijah was going on, "our destiny's a spiritual one."

It was then Ab stood forth to curdle my blood.

Bounding up, a towering giant of fiery orb. A mighty beard seared by a livid scar. A commanding face, softened a little—yet promoted in menace—by full strawberry lips.

"Bah! You bookish people—all the same."

Joram recoiled. Elijah tranquilly addressed the imposing figure in his fine, thin voice. "Your problem, son?"

"My problem? Your problem! Forever prating of afterlife— never seeing what's before your eyes—that if you served up God on a silver platter in a crystal temple, the people'd be too busy to come—except maybe to sightsee the temple. Home and homeland is their god."

"Please . . ." Joram's weak protest drowned in the outburst.

"You spin out a Messiah hung up on priest and sacrifice and life beyond. We demand a sword-slinging David to leap a throne so a man and his family can live free."

"Son, we believe in a Davidic Messiah, but we're teaching you what the Scriptures say of him."

"Teaching me? I, Ab, teach you our daggers and swords must spill blood and guts before a Jew can sit a throne."

"You zealots think to force the Lord's hand. Can't be done."

"The Maccabees did it."

"The Maccabees?" The rabbi's fine eyebrows rose. "Desecrators of the high priesthood—seizing it from the Zadokites. Plunderers of the line of David—illicitly wearing his crown."

"Bah! Technicalities of book people. Barabbas, come." Ab seized the hand of a ruddy-cheeked boy coined in his likeness and stomped away.

"And after that," Elijah droned, "the Romans plundered

7

the Maccabees, and our kingdom was gone again." He added in an undertone, "Those terrorists will destroy us all."

The revolutionary wheeled. "Haven't fake Christs come before? How tell the real one? When he splits Roman heads for kindling wood, and burns up their army in the fire. Then we'll know—not before!" With that he was gone.

Black clouds churning, the air cold—but not that chilling my blood. This dark garden loomed up then. This dark future was written beforehand—not in the stars, but in the seething violence of men's hearts. But not all. How her heart opened to me after three days. I taste its sweetness now.

Heavy silence—we stared at the rabbis. Joram eyed the gathering crowd and the glowering troops. "Rabbi Elijah," he bawled, "what unsettling fare for youngsters." He lifted his gaze above the disappointed faces. "David writes, 'Don't be troubled about wicked people. Be not envious of wrongdoers.' Well he knew that the prosperity of the wicked is fleeting. By the Lord's care, the children of the just never beg bread. No evil befalls us unless we sin."

The poorly-dressed students looked sad; the well-dressed, smug. My indignation flamed. "Why, then, Rabbi Joram, did Jacob have to send his sons to beg the sale of Pharoah's bread? You yourself questioned the legitimacy of the high priest. How can you, by your norm? He's prospering. Will he soon be poor? And the common priests suffer want. Why? Are they not devoted to the people and their sacred trust?"

"Boy—dare you call me wrong?"

Elijah smiled at me sympathetically, then intervened gently. "Rabbi Joram, questions are the learner's prerogative, as we know. Permit me to explain to the boy. You don't intend to be taken altogether literally. We know that at times God tries the just, as the Psalmist himself explains elsewhere. And he teaches that the unjust are sometimes allowed to prosper like hoary old oaks— but the day comes when they are chopped down. It's the just who will see a long life."

"You're kind, rabbi. If long life is assured the just, how does Isaiah foretell the Servant of the Holy One who shall suffer unjust condemnation and go to an early grave?"

"Elijah stroked his beard gravely. "Child, where have you learned your Scripture?"

8

"From my Father."

"How does he explain this suffering servant? Is God unjust then?"

"Isaiah explains. His servant, who atones even for his slayers, will see his offspring in days prolonged."

"And the meaning of that, boy?"

"The resurrection."

Joram stared. Elijah nodded. "Yes, we Pharisees teach the resurrection. But we don't let it undermine the expectation of present advantages, especially since some of us"—he glanced slyly at Joram—"are overly fond of them."

In the listening, in the learning, in the stirring exchanges, I discerned the call to remain. The caravan set out without me. My parents joined its swollen ranks, expecting me to do the same. Behind I remained, asking and answering. Sleeping at night in a hidden corner, and taking what food I could.

On the third day, when Elijah invited us to rest, I looked about. She stood there, staring at me, eyes wide with shock. "My child. Why have you treated us this way?" Her gaze, taking in my thinner face, descended to my stained and rumpled cloak, and her voice softened. "Imagine our worry, searching for you—afraid for you."

On that face, a worn expression never seen before. Eyes that looked older. Staring eyes, trying to regain accustomed focus, after long gazing into vacant space—or something worse. Dry lips, puckered to a smallness, looking bruised. Pale cheeks, as though some swordthrust had drained the body's blood.

In the eyes, most of all, the wound. Of unknowing. Know and understand she must. Lest her power to love—her life—be itself wounded and diminished.

I could do nothing but look, silently communing, into her eyes, commiserating, waiting for the time of words. Soon the storm-tossed brow was subsiding, the last breakers of distress pattering up on the shore from a tempest now past. Beyond reappeared the tranquil sea of her life, sparkling with the rays piercing the clouds.

How respond to her plaint, lucidly and in a word? How say to her keen intelligence what, grieving and bewildered, she must yet remember? That it is the unique identity of our people to hear at any hour your call to be led afar, like Abram, with no man's permission. And at any cost, as he went with fire and wood and son to offer sacrifice. That even striplings are summoned by the inner voice, as was Samuel. That in her grief she had failed to be mindful of her own girlhood call to abandon the way of the earth. Would that not have helped her grasp my case? My summons to be where I had remained, to your purpose.

In the very soaring of the Temple, in the ascent of that edifice to the heights, hiding and hoarding, within its most sacred little chamber, your dwelling, I had found a kind of kinship. In myself, too, soaring indefinitely beyond the Temple, reaching to my Father's heart, and there abiding, the Holy of Holies was hidden. And so, gently, I said what she had need to know.

"Searching? For me? Did you not know I had to be in my Father's house?"

It was touching to see her face tell of her eagerness to extract from those words their balm. But healing did not come—not then and there. The nourishment would take long digestion. She had sensed the hidden consolation, and remained still shaken, rocking in the crosscurrents of sorrow and joy.

Her earnest pondering of my words made her own sound anew in my ear—"My child, why have you treated us so?" And my heart separated it into the colors of many questions— "Do you part from me with such ease? Take leave of me in this troubled land without a word to ward off my dread? Give such obedience to your Father in heaven, yet owe nothing to your mother on earth? While still a young boy, with my mother's heart bound to every hair of your head? With trooping devils of worry raising terror in my nights?"

Burdensome the clouds that hang dark between mind and mind. Hearts lashed together by love's cords, yes, but minds? They travel their paths like sister ships on the Great Sea, where troubling mists sweep in, obscuring all contact.

I suffered for her. She, sensing this and, by an admirable effort, breaking free of her grief, did a thing sweet and memorable. With her eyes upon me, filling with a joyous love as though finding the perfect solution, she opened her lips

10

and as simply as though saying everything, said, "My son." And we fell into one another's arms.

What became manifest in Joseph likewise consoled me. With troubled face he had observed, in silence, our near-silent exchange. Now, at once, he looked cleansed and purified of all unrest, as by some wave from the current of our interchange washing over him. His face lit up in its far-spreading smile pacific. Striding over, he embraced us embracing. Then he drawled, in the Galilean dialect which sounded strange to me after days with the fleet-tongued rabbis, "It's a thing of the past."

Rabbi Elijah, beaming at this issue, stepped forward and touchingly expressed the fondness he had conceived for me. Rumpling my locks with frail hand, he took delight in telling my parents that I was a precocious boy.

Joram studied me through slitted eyes. Similar eyes I would see in my home town when, through some tale-bearer, word of the misunderstanding reached it. The store-keeper, for one. His stage whisper rose one day as I departed —"It's that brazen son of the carpenter."

Yet as a boy I acted always to please you, Father. Not less so because I did things with the leaping enthusiasms and impulses of the young, and not with the weighed and measured patterns of manhood. Who would want it otherwise? Growth has its times and its seasons.

Memorable, that trip home, joyful with our reunion. Three days we travelled, treading the ripening fields and skirting the barren mountains. We covered some of the same ground as those early wayfarers, Abraham and Jacob. We trod the chalky soil of Judea, where tall pines grow, passed spreading terebinths, and scrubby oaks stunted by gnawing goats. We admired the showy lilac flowers. Into the warm and sheltered Jordan rift we descended, alert, because of the smallness of our number, for the danger of the wild ass, the cheetah and the viper. The journey was hard but pleasant, with not another word spoken about our separation. Then the relief of hanging up our cloaks in our own little home, eating at our table, and sleeping in our accustomed beds.

As the days passed, that hour of misunderstanding, appearing all loss at the time, taught me to feel more readily the

11

sorrows and joys of others, and I found new favor in our town.

In the course of that year, sprouting into manhood, I looked both backward and forward. Pondering my origins and my destiny, I was preoccupied with the consequences of my meaning and my task. So passionate was my devotion to you, Father, that it led to the wounding of Joseph once more.

2

Years ago, ungovernable mysteries had engulfed Joseph. A flood roaring into his youth. Shifting the foundations. Torture he found it to think of having to speak to me of those intimate affairs one day—when I had grown. Yet he managed. When the time was ripe.

The highlands of Nazareth. My body growing apace with other children's. Human experiences—boyhood friends—contests of strength—climbing the tallest tree of the loftiest peak to see as far as eye can see—the Great Sea in the distance. Hastening home to relish mother's cooking. Tender with her always—cherished and cherishing. Mastering the lessons at school. Learning the carpenter's trade.

Nazareth. We children tending sheep with the shepherds—gathering the crops in season—caring for the livestock—learning early the facts of life. And life in the town—colorful weddings—drunken brawls—shouting matches of husbands and wives. Doors creaking in the night—political terrorists—other unholy alliances.

Judas the Galilean searing the sky. False messiah. Raiding the armory of Sepphoris. Rebellion against Rome. Uproar, infighting, assassinations, pillage, tumult of every kind. Joseph anguishing—become involved? In madness. Hopeless. Foredoomed. Mother's grief-stricken face. Swarming of the Roman armies. Sepphoris—nearby—flames in the night. Inhabitants sold into slavery—relatives among them. Dead bodies in our streets. Widows in mourning. Mountainous taxes. Famine. Standing in long lines for a handful of grain. The hobbling sick and the poor. Uncle Yeshua growing rich by shrewd farming and tight-fisted greed.

Deeds noble and ignoble. Two boys squaring off to defend honor offended. One proposing a wrestling match, the other, fists—scorning to roll in the mud. The smell of fear—relieved when the form of combat couldn't be agreed on. Honor deemed preserved by the stand-off.

One more youth growing up in a rustic town—a violent land. Yet never a time I did not know myself missioned into the world—your Son sent into flesh.

To Joseph always intensely devoted—yet always in tension. I a restive young colt—two halters circling his neck. Feeling the tug of one master here, the other there—rearing and whinnying lament even when standing and grazing. For even when the reins were slack there was pain from the future—anticipation of the time when one master must be distressed. No colt should suffer two masters. How two fathers? Longing for the hour of bar mitzvah. Joseph would slip his halter. Acknowledge me a son of the Law. Subject in my own right and conscience. No longer satellite to his.

At last the hour—the day after my thirteenth birthday— the joy of the short walk to the synagogue. The pride of my parents. The bracing air—congratulations of the townspeople converging from all directions—fields rich from the winter rains—oranges ripe for plucking. Stepping out of the bright light into the darkness. On my cloak, newly sewn by mother's hand, the four fringes. Containing the parchments—the prescribed Torah passages every adult male wears.

Intoning of the Shema. Your Son covering his eyes. Entering deep into the words. "Hear O Israel, the Lord is our God, the Lord is unique. And you shall love the Lord your God with all your heart, with all your soul, with all your strength. And these words of my command of this day shall be in your heart . . ."

Hezekiah, head of the synagogue, speaking. "In this town of five hundred souls, who does not know each of his neighbors? This week we greet as bar mitzvah the son of Joseph the carpenter."

13

Clapping and cheering and well-wishing. Hezekiah addressing me formally. "Yehoshua, I summon you to the reading of the Torah." Procession to the Ark. The Scroll of the Law in my hands. Reverence like waves of incense. On to the lectern. The ringing of the cadenced prayers. Unrolling the scroll. He indicating the reading. "But first, your prayer, bar mitzvah." My voice raised.

"Father in heaven, I praise and thank you for admitting me into the covenant of circumcision. And for shepherding me, as you promised Abraham, Isaac and Jacob. Today in manhood I shoulder the Law. Incarnate it in my body. Let my life say to the Chosen People and to the Gentiles, 'The Lord is our God, the Lord is unique.'"

Murmurs of approval—buzzings at the eloquence of a carpenter's son. Hezekiah rapping sharply—"The reading!" The appointed passage flowing from my lips. Murmurs and buzzings redoubled. Hezekiah barking for silence. "We didn't expect a workman's child to read with polish. Well, don't exaggerate his accomplishment. The poor try harder, you know." His irritation evident—a nobleman with an ungifted son. "Joseph, come, make your paternal prayer."

Joseph at my side. Composing himself with bowed head, then beginning. "God of our fathers, into my hands thirteen years ago you gave the firstfruits of my wife's womb. Today my heart resounds like David's harp. I return him with pride, a son of the Law. I return him with a reverence and love only you and his mother can know." Silently, back to his seat.

"Yehoshua"—Hezekiah rasping again—"the reading from the prophets." And hoarse in my ear, "None of the uppityness I heard you showed Rabbi Joram." He unrolling the scroll of Isaiah—reaching the appointed text I'd prepared—spinning the cylinder beyond—stopping at random. "Read here."

Recognizing the passage—looking at my mother. Her face, radiant with pride, lighting with a smile. Joseph struggling to show less than he felt.

"Read, read!"

"Again the Lord spoke to Ahaz, 'Ask a sign of the Lord your God. Ask for something as deep as hell or as high as heaven!' 'No,' Ahaz demurred, 'I won't test the Lord.' And the Lord responded, 'Hear now, you House of David. Have

14

you tired of wearying men? So now are you bent on wearying my God? Well, the Lord himself will sign you a sign. Listen well when I say it—a virgin shall conceive and bear a son, and shall call his name Immanuel.'"

Following the custom—reading the Hebrew text—translating into the vernacular. Mother's face—wonder and reverence rolling in waves—Joseph covering mouth and beard—indescribable look of eyes staring. The colt in his hour of freedom—one halter slipped—cavorting for joy.

At the door of our home. "Father, a matter I'd like to discuss." Mother's bemused smile—"The Bar Mitzvah has secrets already?" Her hands thrown up in mock helplessness. She entering—the door closing on the oil lamp flickering dimly.

North the village well where women and children congregate—we going south—walking long before I broke silence.

"I've always tried to show you filial reverence—addressed you as father."

His wordless nodding.

"Children all about, romping with fathers, chanting with passion, 'Abba, Abba!' I wanting to shout with equal abandon—and not wanting. In my heart, reserving that name for the One."

Mutely, gently, laying his hand on my shoulder. Searching, waiting, finding words. "When I say, 'Son,' neither is my delight unpained. Yet mine you are, my own wife's child, born to me within our bond."

"Today in the synagogue, Isaiah. The source of our joy—and our pain."

His voice wounded. "You heard my prayer. Today I restored you to your heavenly Father."

"You know my filial love—always."

His hand raised for silence. "Perhaps I've waited too long. To give you an account. Yet men don't discuss such things with children."

The rush of vehement feeling in those words. Sweeping away the fallen leaves of the years. Unclogging the channels of our communion. We had stopped—he began walking —silent—gathering his thoughts. A shepherd waving and

15

halloing—we mounting the brow of the high cliff—sinister it would loom in my future. He recounting there my human origins.

3

Hills and mountains surged up around the bluff where they stood that blustery December day. Too absorbed they were, in their communion, to heed the icy wind whipping cloaks and piercing to the bone. As the man summoned up his memories, the boy studied his appearance. He never tired of that face—fairly uncomplicated, if you didn't probe deeply. Clean-cut, virile. Strong of line, weatherbeaten of cheek, firm and sure of expression. Telling the acute observer a further story by what was absent—no defacement of the warrior, no crow's feet around the luminous eyes, no lines across the wide brow. A face at home with, blending with, field and forest, by its naturalness of tone. Nothing out of the ordinary seemed to register in its spaces—or be registered as history—until you learned its language. And then you began to grasp that what looked to the uninitiated like a placid record of non-events was something much rarer—was the tranquillity of supreme maturity. Not yet thirty, he was the most mature man the boy had ever known.

He himself was advancing in natural wisdom. Exercising his human powers. Learning to feel with the heart. Questing and searching for so many things—how to interpret look and gesture, how to understand people and turn their thoughts to life at its core. How to win them over. In brief, how to accomplish his mission. This father of his left the impression he had found his answers long ago. Now he moved through life like a seaworthy ship crossing a placid ocean, a ship so well engineered that it feared no storm. If it must roll and pitch when they came, it would roll and pitch with the same security it enjoyed in untroubled waters. What long apprentice-ship, what wild weather, had engendered such a veteran of

16

the sea of life? There were no scars to tell.

Though his observation of Joseph in daily life—and occasional crisis—had confirmed this reading, he had still more to learn. He learned in times like this, when deep currents stirred within, and a trace of their progress moved across the tranquil features. The black of the eyes grew blacker, as though intensifying the capacity to absorb floods of light. The more intense gaze, echoed in the hunch of the shoulders, bespoke inner contact with unfailing sources. The occasional slow blink registered acknowledgement—"Yes, I understand."

This attunement, this blending of self with inner and outer realities, was what could be learned from the man, and learning he was. Learning fast, with his own inner resources to draw on.

The man stretched out a hand, as if catching the first threads of his account—or signalling his readiness—and began.

"I've taught you to observe the saplings from the time they are seedlings. To learn which will be your fruitful ones long before they bear, and cultivate them. We do that with people. I fell in love with your mother when she was very young. Joachim approved—it was evident. About her attitude— something made me wonder. I was tempted to ask him for her at once since, before twelve, he could engage her without her consent."

"Grandfather would give her to none without her consent."

"Temptation"—there was a twinkle in his eye—"is what we resist."

"And she was resisting you."

"True, I'm afraid—but I was convinced she loved me, and waited with confidence. Awaited a shock. When she came of age, I began courting her in earnest. And met resistance. Casting about for a reason, I decided she was testing my love. I tried extravagant ways to win her."

"How you've succeeded!"

"How I failed—then. Once spent a whole day gathering wild flowers. When she came out early to milk the goat, she found, spelled out in blossoms, 'Mary, I love you. Joseph.' Except, that is, for the letters the goat had eaten. She was touched. Sweet to me, but reserved still. Taking it for maidenly reticence—I should have known her better—I asked her

17

father for her hand. He put me off. It was confusing. I was sure he and Ann approved, and convinced she loved me—you can't hide these things. Driven to boldness, I asked her. She said bluntly she wouldn't marry me. I was stunned, but"—he smiled—"not so stunned I didn't pursue my love."

"Knowing mother, I'd say it looked hopeless. Knowing you—not hopeless."

"You do know us both. Convinced we belonged together, I tried persuasion. Could see no obstacle. Told her that. 'Only if you tell me you don't love me,' I vowed, 'will I ever leave you alone.' At that she broke down. Cried. 'Don't,' she begged, 'make it so hard for me to go the way the Lord calls.'

"I was mystified. 'Can you tell me what that is?' She whispered, 'I'm not to follow the way of the earth.' Stunned, I fell silent. Until I recovered, and asked, 'What convinced you?' She told how, as a little girl, she met Anna the Seer in the Temple, and said, 'Ever since, I've felt called to live like her.' But I objected, 'She's a widow, Mary—not a virgin like you.' She only replied, 'As she lives, I feel called to live always.'

"I resisted. 'I don't find this way in the Scriptures. We're told to increase and multiply.' 'Why Joseph,' she returned, 'didn't Moses separate long from his wife to do the Lord's work? And tell me, did Jeremiah ever marry? Don't the Essenes practice celibacy to hasten the Messiah's coming? Don't even the goyim have their vestal virgins?'

"But I wouldn't give up. 'Mary, every Jewish maiden longs to be the one who bears the Messiah.' At this, she was merry. 'Me? Joseph, if I had doubts of your love, that would spank them and put them to rest. I don't conjure up such a thought even in my dreams. But'—she grew solemn—'on behalf of the elect mother, I dare to be a barren womb pleading. Crying, O Holy One, no womb in Israel is more full than mine until the one you choose is filled with the One you promise.' She looked at me earnestly. 'I believe you can understand, or I couldn't have loved . . . What is it? Your eyes flame like Hannukah lights.'

"'Mary, listen. Once I was set on consecrating my life that way. Rabbi Uriel opposed it. I decided it wasn't from the

18

Holy One. But think—if you live alone, suitors will pester you. If together—you, my wife, a barren womb—both of us . . .'

"That brought fear to her eyes. 'Dare any two—young—share a home—when they've forsaken the way of the earth?'

"The logic of it crushed me. 'I'll not pressure you against your conscience.' We fell silent. A deep pool of quiet gathered in me, and a certainty of how hard it would be for her, and so I said, 'Mary, trials and temptations will press on you in any way you live this life.'

" 'If only I could join the Essenes.'

" 'You can't. They reject the high priest. And Temple worship.'

" 'I know.'

" 'I won't say any more. Except that I'm going to consecrate my life too—convinced now that the Lord was drawing me. And that you should think over my proposal.'

" 'I must think—think of everything.'

"The following week we announced our betrothal."

In the long silence that followed, the man studied the boy's face. Glowing features of softly molded firmness—seen only in the young. Evoking images of budding things. Down on cheek and chin—awakening manhood. Not the uncomplicated face of a simple country boy. Lofty forehead. Lean contour of the jaw. Strong cheekbones. The penetrating gaze of shining pupils set in white orbs. Sturdy body, graceful carriage. Sparkling alertness. Keen intelligence.

Lashes straight as the teeth of a comb—raised high in expectation—over deepset eyes. Reminiscent of his mother's, but more intense, more searching. Reaching out in such a summons to communion as to wake the very stones. That habitual look—it hinted of a life within incubated of passion—of joy and sorrow and promise beyond knowing. Lips prominent yet refined, the lower straight and firm, the upper dipping at the center, lifted out from the white teeth. In a way that bespoke an eager inquisitiveness furthered by the upward tilt of the head. At the moment, those lips were joined in a firm line expressing the same concentration as the eyes.

His whole presence projected a gentle sensitivity fused

with the sappy toughness of youthful strength. The ruddy cheeks added an aura of flaming life. His whole aspect radiated that natural sacredness of young bodies. Lifting the spirit to reverence, anchoring the heart in comeliness.

Joseph protracted the silence. How find the words to convey what he must without offending that open gaze? He stood unmoving, fashioning the account from searing memories. Staring into the distance. Reliving that wild hour of his mindless trek. Down from the heights of Nazareth. Driven by the shocking sight which changed his life and—he now believed—the world.

Joseph was a man of character, of unshakable devotion to those he loved and believed in—his God, his intended bride, his people. Yet that hurricane of a day had whipped him about like a sapling. Exposed him to conflicting loyalties—threatened to break him. His thoughts went back now to that day.

Early morning—the news of King Herod's latest madness. The outcome of the charge of conspiracy leveled against his sons and heirs, Alexander and Aristobulus. His foreign overlord in Rome—Emperor Augustus—had counseled discretion and leniency. Herod's "leniency" had been reported. The two boys had been taken to the fort at Sebaste, and there strangled. He was carrying the terrible news to Mary.

Hand running over bearded cheek and big cheek bones. Tall figure hunched forward reflectively. Long legs sweeping out in great strides. Hand probing the lean, firm line of the jaw. Much to think about.

Herod had long since murdered his wife Mariamme, the mother of the two boys—no wonder he feared them. He had been driven by a wild suspicion planted by his sister, Salome, the real mistress of intrigue. Herod had professed a passionate love for Mariamme, and had never had cause to suspect her of marital infidelity, but she had met her death at his hands all the same.

Mary would be so grieved by this further sadness for their people. At the thought there crept back into his mind what he kept throwing out, what he refused to believe he had seen, what his carpenter's eye kept insisting on nonetheless—signs she was carrying a child. Rather would he believe he was

20

losing his eyesight or his mind—he would not lose faith in her! He had seen her for the first time in over three months just yesterday when she returned from visiting her kinswoman Elizabeth. A marvel that the old woman had borne a child after all those years of sterility. He smiled—perhaps Mary had just eaten too well at Elizabeth's table. He was glad for the opportunity to pay her a visit this morning, terrible as the news was.

What he first beheld was her stunning beauty, enhanced by the delicate flush of the cheeks. What he saw next in the graceful form clothed with a light pink tunic in the light of day he could no longer deny—he had seen too many women with child. He stared at her face, but could not decipher what he saw there. A fleeting pain sprang into the eyes when she perceived his look, and then a great wave of pity swept her face—but no remorse, no guilt! He could almost swear he even saw a triumphant joy hidden deep and unreachable, and this redoubled his consternation. The eyes of her father were on him, bleeding out a suffering that added the more to his own. Hardly knowing, he turned on his heel. He found himself running, plunging, tumbling down the steep slopes of the town. If only they'd followed the way of the earth—shortened their engagement period if she wanted a child! Then what a joy that sight!

He tried to pray, was sucked down into a whirlpool of streaming thoughts. Why so soon abandon her call to chastity? Tender she was, but never weak—no, sturdy as oak, solid as bedrock! Why then betray him? Why play the harlot even with God? Impossible! But if violated, why not tell him? In that hour his ordered, intelligible world exploded into a slatternly waste mocking his quest for meaning. A filthy tide of godlessness bubbled up miring him, sinking him in its quagmires, choking him with misty fumes, he bellowing to God for deliverance.

All that day and into the night he strode by road and wasteland, over dale and mountain, unfeeling, eating nothing, witless. Under the stars he was in the surf, wading out into the Great Sea. Even the cool, salt spray did not call him back, but when the water reached his neck he turned and waded north toward pagan Tyre.

21

At last the whirlpool of his thoughts dried up, his mind numb, and so too his body. He staggered onto the wild beach to fall spreadeagled on the sand. What course? The Law called for the stoning of his Love! For what? For playing the harlot! How dare he say it—think it? No! She was pregnant! Yes! His mind tore. What am I to do? O God, hear me! Then he sorted it out. She was pregnant, not by him. For a just man, there could be no wedding, but surely he need not—must not—expose her to punishment, not knowing source or circumstance. He would hush up the proceedings, do what else he might. At that a few shreds of peace settled around him, and he slept. He sat up wide awake in the night, remembering what the angel had said, experiencing a joy so immense it shrunk the Great Sea beside him. He leaped up, hurried home, took Mary in his arms as the dawn broke, and told her he knew.

When Joseph had sorted these turbulent remembrances, he turned to the boy. "You must realize I told you the details of our engagement only because of what next happened." The boy nodded. "That has to do with your origins, which you had a right to know—at a suitable age." Again the accepting nod.

"Your mother and I announced the usual year-long engagement. Several months later I found her with child. I couldn't believe, I couldn't deny. How describe my turmoil?—I won't try. A betrothed woman who proves unfaithful is to be stoned."

"You didn't think that of my mother?"

"What sane thought could I think? I decided the Law required of me only that I end our engagement."

"The equivalent of divorce!"

"Yes, that's the Law. I planned to draw up a bill of divorce. What else could I do?"

"Ask an explanation of her."

"I refused to consider that—for what it seemed to imply. Yet my not asking troubled me too. It seemed like a judgement—like assuming she had nothing to say for herself."

"Perhaps only inability to imagine what she could have to say."

"I hope you're right. Anyway, after my decision, I slept—

and woke in the night with a message I couldn't doubt. I was to marry in good conscience. 'It is by the Holy Spirit she conceived,' the angel told me, and said, 'Call him Jesus. He will save his people from their sins.'" He fell silent. At length the boy spoke.

"I've ever been aware that I AM—aware of my descent to the mission awaiting me. Aware of Isaiah witnessing to it."

"And I stand as witness."

"My mother?"

"The sole human witness of what actually happened. When I told her I knew of it, she described the messenger's visit, and how she found herself in the way of woman."

"And you had found your solution."

"We wept and laughed together. Joachim came barging in."

"I'd expect the whole family to barge in with him."

"We announced we planned to marry at once. Under the circumstances, you can imagine how it pleased him."

"Any fuller description by mother?"

"The angel started by praising her—it made her afraid. He calmed her. Announced she was to bear a child. To be called Jesus, Son of the Most High. Destined to inherit David's eternal throne."

"With her plan—that frightened her more than the praise."

"Oh, she was cautious. Asked how that could be reconciled with her call to perpetual maidenhood." He smiled. "Whether by suitors or messengers, your mother's not easily misled."

"You're telling her son?"

"She was reassured. God's Spirit was the solution—no human father. He must be called 'Son of God.' She said her yes."

"And waited for you to see."

"She didn't think it right to tell me—ask such faith of me. Left it in the Lord's hands. We were married at once. My wife came to live with me."

He spoke the final words with pride, then added, "But there is more you must know."

There are human events so delicate, so sacred, one is reluctant to desecrate them with the touch of words. And so Joseph looked at the boy as to find in him the way to loose what was lodged in the channels of his mind. He looked at him and looked back to the moment of the first sight of him and the thoughts and spinnings of the soul evoked in that sacred hour—how in the icy air he had gathered wood from the earth for the fire and the water while his mind gathered to his bosom the soul of that event for which he was making his votive offering of preparation. O holy event! Holy not solely in who the child was. Holy because out of the sacred fire of a woman's love new life was emerging as it had emerged in endless cycles of love's gift to itself.

Birth, that abyss of mystery. Event ever new—the springing fountain of the future, the burgeoning seed of tomorrow. Woman's mystery overflowing, life's ecstasy, a child's bursting with cries and alarms into freedom's dawn.

They had expected the sacred event to transpire in Nazareth, but it was not to be so. His hand trembled on the wood when the sacred prophecy flashed to mind. Away in Rome Caesar Augustus dreamed his might had worked their departure from hearth and home by his decree—while the Almighty had decreed it ages ago. "You, Bethlehem, out from you shall issue for me one to be Ruler in Israel whose origin hides in the hoary past, in days of yore." The Lord of history— they were in his hands.

The blue in the cheeks of the boy at his side on the cliff brought him back. Chilled to the bone. Compassion broke the jammed words free at last.

"I want to speak to you about your birth."

"There's something my mother omitted."

"Yes."

Man and boy had warm memories of how his mother used to tell him the story of his birth. She told it so sweetly he begged to hear it over and over until the telling became a ritual.

"When your kinsman John was born, and I returned home to Nazareth," she would begin, "I had two gifts for you, and you hadn't yet come into the world. The first was a little priest's tunic Elizabeth sewed for you. 'Why a priest's tunic?' our relatives asked. 'You're of the kingly line, not the priestly.' 'And besides,' they objected, 'how does Elizabeth know it's a boy?' 'You must ask her,' I'd reply."

"And the other gift?" he always inquired, clutching more tightly to his breast the little carved lamb he used to cherish.

"A lamb," she would answer, "which Zechariah the priest carved for you to offer when wearing the linen tunic. Oh, there it is!" And she pointed, and they would smile at one another.

"All our kinsmen were bringing little gifts for you," she continued. "So many were awaiting your arrival, so many would come from afar when you were born. Your grandparents Joachim and Ann planned to make the trip from Jerusalem. That's where I was born, you know." He would nod sagely.

"They were all waiting with bated breath. That's because birth is a mystery. You see, every birth is the past and the future of us all. In every birth mankind is born anew." He watched her with glistening eye, fascinated by the power of words, captivated as they marched by like Roman soldiers on parade, their armor clinking and flashing in the sun.

"I was surprised by you," she would say, and as part of the ritual, pick him up and hug him. "I didn't think I'd ever have a baby. Some mothers think that, you know."

"But that's not what the priest said when you married," he would remind her.

"No, he prayed, 'May you grow into thousands of myriads, may you have nations of children.' That was just after Joseph said, 'She is my wife, and I am her husband from this day forth.'"

"You forgot," he would remind her, "about the little crown Uncle Yeshua brought me because King David was your forefather."

"Oh! But I was thinking how you never got to wear your little linen tunic at all, what with our rushing from Nazareth before your birth, and our return so much later it was too small."

"That's why I was born in David's town."

25

"Emperor Augustus ordered all the people to be counted in the towns of their ancestors—that's called a census. So we went south, past the region of Dothan, where Jacob's son Joseph searched for his brothers. You remember, they were jealous of him, so they sold him into slavery, and he was carried off to Egypt. And then what?"

"He saved the whole world!"

"That's right—from the famine. In Bethlehem there were so many people I got upset because I was going to have my baby any moment, and we couldn't find lodgings. Your father remained serene as early morning before anyone's up. He's always been that way—except once. Maybe he'll tell you about that some day. Anyway, he said, 'Mary, don't worry, we'll find a place because of King David.' 'What do you mean?' I asked. 'So many hereabout claim David for ancestor.' 'It's not that,' he answered. 'David gave Chinham land near Bethlehem, and he built a spacious inn. It's still here, so there should be plenty of room.'

"Why did David give Chinham land?" the boy always asked, he so liked to hear the story.

"Because Chinham's father, Barzillai, helped to save King David's life and kingdom. You see, David had a handsome son named Absalom. When Absalom saw he could win over the people, he did something very evil. He stole the army and the kingdom and marched against his father. With Barzillai's help David escaped, and then David's army defeated Absalom's army. David forbad hurting Absalom, but they killed him anyway, and he wept his heart out. Later he rewarded Barzillai by giving his son Chinham the land near Bethlehem. Only, the inn he built there ages ago was overflowing with people when we arrived."

"And you couldn't wait."

"No. But Joseph said, 'Don't worry, I know a place that will do.' He took me to a cave in the Field of Ruth. She was your ancestress, you know. She married Boaz, the great-grandfather of David. The cave was full of people, but Joseph was still calm. 'There's another cave, less well-known,' he assured me, 'but a little harder to get to.' He pointed way up the hill of Bethlehem. There we found only the animals, so we stayed. Berenice the midwife helped me,

and you were born. It's a good thing Bell—that's Berenice—
was there, because your father was marching around like a
wooden soldier. Most men aren't too good at births, you
know. You gurgled and bleated for milk, and I fed you at
the breast—but I've weaned you from the breast since."
"Sure." The child would shake his head in agreement.
"That's for babies."
"One day you'll have to be weaned from your family
and go out into the world and stand on your own two feet.
You will, you know. Every man and woman has to."
"But not yet."
"No, not yet. I'd hardly fallen off to sleep when shepherds
came to visit. They brought you a little lamb as their gift.
Some day Joseph will tell you more."
Thus would conclude Mary's account, which ran through
the mind of man and boy as Joseph began. "Before I took
Bell the midwife to your mother I said, 'Bell, in preparing my
wife you may see what you haven't before.' 'Joseph, I
delivered you a few minutes' walk from here,' she lectured
me, 'and many another before and since. Don't worry!
There's little new to see.' 'Promise you'll say nothing,' I
insisted. 'You make no sense,' she snapped, 'but I promise.
I'm no gossip.'
"Bell prepared your mother, and I built up the fire for
hot water. Bell gasped, rushed over, drew me out of the cave,
alarmed and angry. 'I don't know what this is,' she cried,
'but any midwife would know Mary's not going to have a
baby. And you, her husband, should certainly know. She has
yet to do her duty as a wife—she's still a virgin!' 'Bell,' I
insisted, 'she's carrying a child. Didn't I try to prepare you?
Now go and help her.' 'Abraham and Sara!' she gasped,
'What is this?' I guided her gently back to your mother.
"The hours dragged like stubborn mules. After midnight,
one great peal from your mother—of agony or ecstasy, I
never knew. Then a baby's crying, and Bell's summons,
'Come see—a beautiful baby boy!' As she bathed you she
turned her face to me, eyes wide as the Jordan sweeping into
the Salt Sea. 'Abraham, Isaac and Jacob—only now do I
believe you!'
"Your mother crooned nursery rhymes while she nursed

27

and fondled you—she was never more lovely. 'My husband'—she turned to me—'now that he's been fed, take your lovely son, for what is mine is yours, and yours is mine. Support his head, like this; he can't do it himself yet.'

"At once Bell was giving me orders. 'Here, give me the little fellow to anoint and wrap snug in swaddling bands before he catches his death of cold! No doubt about it—he favors his mother. Now we can all get some rest.' She laid you in the manger which I had made into a crib, and left, and your mother slept. I laid another log on the fire. It was a bitter cold night, and the few houses nearby were dark—all was dark but our fire and the stars.

"A noise woke me. Three boys and a man—shepherds all —stood by. 'Shalom, shalom,' I greeted them. 'Come, warm yourselves. Have your sheep strayed?' 'We came to see the Messiah child just born!' the boy Kenan sang out. I stared in silence, then, 'I'm Joseph. Did the midwife tell you of the child?'

"Mary called sleepily, 'Who is it?' and when she heard she said, 'Enter, and welcome! Joseph, bring me the baby. I hate to disturb him, but if they came—how did they know?'

"'We're shepherds, lady mother'—it was Kenan who spoke—'We were in Ruth's field guarding our sheep. Or I was, while the others slept. From Bethlehem I saw this bright light coming far above the new-fallen snow. I shouted, and the others came. The light rested on the hill hard by us, and the light faded, and there stood a man in white. He told us to calm our fear, that he had news teeming with joy. 'Your Saviour and Lord has been born at last. Go to him in the cattle cave on the upper ridge. He's lying in a manger.'

"The old man with him murmured, 'My wife never bore, so I cherish Isaiah's promise, "A child is born to us, a son is given us." The angel made me remember it.'

"'What's your name, shepherd?' your mother asked. 'Enoch, lady mother.' 'Enoch, hold the son born to us all.'

"The shepherd Mahalel said, 'Lady mother, our flutes play the psalms of David. May we play, "The Lord is my shepherd?"' They played, falling on their knees.

"They asked to come again, and departed. From a distance

Mahalel's clear voice rang on the night air.

Mary's little boy is born
Shepherd of us all.
Shepherds trip across the hills
At their Shepherd's call.

Joseph paused. "That's what I had to tell you."

They looked at one another with deep feeling, and impulsively the boy threw himself into the man's arms.

On their way home, the father laid his hand on the boy's shoulder. "Your mother," he announced, "has something more to relate."

5

She had made light of it in a fond way, but the serious look of her son going off with her husband had an effect like pulling the cork from a bottle. All her memories were spilling out. And that must be happening to them too. Talking about the matters which meant most to them.

Seared into her soul was the look of Joseph when he first saw and grasped her condition. That day, when he bent his tall frame and entered, it was evident he was bearing some sorrow—informed of some new evil in the land. He had always shown the intense patriotism of the Galilean.

She wrested her attention back. Had to prepare the meal. She moved the jar of powdered locusts out of the way. Not the tastiest of foods. Thankful to have no need of them today. Last summer's swarms of the migratory grasshopper—an unpleasant opportunity. Gathering them in quantity. Pulling off heads and legs until fingers were sore. Drying them in the sun, grinding them in the handmill. A blessing to have them, with the high taxes and the price of meat. Mixed with flour and made into biscuits, they provided good nourishment.

She reached for the pitcher and went out to milk the goat. The creature baaed a greeting without interrupting its grazing.

As she worked, she gazed at her home. It always gave her pleasure. She had helped gather it stone by stone from the fields. The wattled and thatched roof which gave it such a soft look was no proof against hard rains—but then they were infrequent. Grass and a sprinkle of winter flowers hugged the walls. A little house—hardly fifteen feet long. The ten-foot width abutted the face of a cliff. Inside, a cavern extended the space a little into the naked rock.

Remembering Joseph entering that day. His greeting to her. His eyes widening with gladness when they met hers— her grave eyes. She knowing he would see now. Worried—yet thrilling with pleasure, the way his manly features melted.

"Shalom!" Burly Jason, the smith—their nearest neighbor, who fashioned Joseph's tools—called the ancient greeting as he tramped up. Staring at her—she not knowing why. He beholding the snowy woolen cloak draped gracefully over the gently swelling breasts. The blue apron fastened around her slim waist accenting the flare of the hip. Her tunic, the color of a pink rose, the dye of pomegranate bark, peeking out at ankle and neck.

So harmonious was the beauty of that face that it took an effort to concentrate on eye or lip. The flowing, melting wholeness presented itself as one loveliness. It seemed a desecration to dissect it into elements. Yet eventually his gaze descended the declivity of the ivory brow to concentrate on the expressive eyes. Luminous whites. Big, dark pupils that sparkled. Prominent, full lips curving in a smile beneath the firm line of the nose and the dimpled channel beneath it. Locks of glossy dark hair peeking out from the wine-rich cloth draping head and shoulders.

Jason was captivated by the bewitching air of a singing, dancing liveliness she projected without ever an unbecoming gesture—indeed with a modest comportment beyond reproach. The more captivating because the alchemy by which it was created was beyond him. Not accounted for by the effortless grace of her carriage or her charming smile. So noble, he could well believe she was descended from the line of kings. Something about her he couldn't read—the limpid spiritual qualities and emotional sensitivity of her features were beyond his ability even to name.

A lucky fellow, that Joseph. His own slatternly wife—if at least she'd keep neat and clean. His step faltered in his absorption. When she gazed at him inquisitively, he waved self-consciously, and started off.

"Jason, my husband's axe needs sharpening."

She went to the little shed while he waited. The bench was strewn with tools—saws and chisels, a plane, a hammer, a drill and a compass. Two axes leaned against a wall. She examined them, selected one, and took it to him. "This is the one. They dull fast, the way he uses them. How is your wife?"

He froze, feeling guilty—had she read his thoughts? "Less than passing good."

"Sorry to hear it. I'll drop in on her. Jason, pluck some of those lovely winter flowers. Surprize her with a bunch. To chase the blues away."

He nodded dumbly, gathered a handful, and tramped off with the tiny blossoms dangling from a huge paw. She took her pitcher inside. The single room, of bare stone, was sparsely furnished—a table, a few chairs, a loom, a chest of drawers, and abundant shelving. Mounted on the south wall was a saffron cabinet housing their precious heritage, the scroll of the prophet Isaiah. The pile of rush mats which served as bedding, doubled for seats. A few feet from each end of the room hung the curtains drawn at night to provide the privacy of bedrooms.

They would have preferred a wooden house, for its dryness and coziness, but such was the sparsity of trees in the arid land, and the endless labor of working wood with poor tools, that it was out of range. Craftsmen like her husband were as much masons as carpenters, since fieldstones were free for the gathering.

The palm-bark soles of her camel's hair shoes whispered over the clay floor as she went about gathering the ingredients for their meal. The low ceiling—Joseph could barely stand tall—fell lower where it merged with the cave. The latter was storage space for jars of water, oil and grains, a goatskin of wine, and cheeses, dried fruits and nuts.

She reached for the jar of barley kernels, changed her mind, and selected the precious wheat. Pouring a measured

31

amount of grain into the small handmill, she began grinding.

Her thoughts drifted back to his resonant voice caressing the greeting of peace. His eyes widening with gladness when they met hers. She thrilling with pleasure at the way his manly features melted. The happiness in his cry, "So good to have you home again." Generous mouth widening in a youthful grin. Black beard lifting as he raised his head higher. Strong arms flying out with open hands in a gesture of embrace. Then he saw—the way her tunic no longer traced out the graceful lines of maidenhood. A club might as well have struck him full in the face.

Struggling those weeks to spare him this. Tossing and turning in the night. For some way to break the news. Finding none. Ask him to believe such a prodigy? When her witness was also her defence? What the Lord had done, only the Lord could witness. And three months absence—such fertile soil for the imagination. Though her motherhood had preceded her departure.

Father. He'd seen at once—on her return. His evident grief—that they hadn't awaited their marriage. As he surely thought. He witnessing the look on Joseph's face—it spreading to his like contagion. What thoughts then? And her mother. The sorrow in her eyes there was no assuaging.

How the gossip of the village women hurt. They would suddenly fall silent as she approached the village well, looking at her knowingly. Sometimes she overheard remarks. "We thought her such an innocent," one sniped "—you never know! Wouldn't you think at least Joseph could keep himself in check." The woman had professed embarrassment on seeing her, but her satisfaction was only too evident. Of course, some had been kind, and some of the men too, but others had smirked, and stared with insolent boldness.

She was barely a woman at the time, but through the experience and the sorrow she matured almost too quickly. And learned so much about the flaws and unreliability of human judgment—both she and Joseph had trained their son to take such care. What had borne her up was the child in her womb, and the Lord's favor.

The next day Joseph had rushed in unannounced with the light of understanding, and then what happiness! Soon

32

thereafter they were married, and settled down in their own home. How mysteriously beautiful to have a new life stirring within, awaiting the day when marriage overflows.

Delivery came in a storm of joy that never abated. What joy hers, what peace! How describe it? A halcyon morning when the world, delirious with sweet pleasure, lays stretched out in hushed sleep like a little child as crimson dawn steals into the heavens. Mists hang like clouds of incense over the temple of the earth, and cattle stand motionless as hill and mountain. The promise is that soon the child will awake and leap laughing across the meadows with his dog as the birds of the sky intone the ecstasies of a new day.

Of course, troubles and terrors enough came, too, with her son—the danger for his life, the exile in Egypt, the hard journey home, the struggle of life in a tax-poor country. But if these burdens were great at times, it was because they threatened so great a joy.

When their son began to mature, so difficult it was to know how to treat with him of his origins. "How much should we tell him?" she used to repeat to Joseph. In their discussions they drew lessons of caution from families round about—from parents who filled small heads with harmful religious nonsense. Children need help to sort fact from fantasy, and time to grow up to spiritual realities. Teaching them to live their religious lives on a footing of miracles and wonders—as well encourage them to run full tilt down the icy pinnacles of Mount Hermon!

But of course part of the problem stemmed from the times they lived in. The prophet Daniel bespoke seventy weeks of years before the Messiah's coming. Those 490 years had elapsed shortly before her birth, so the present fever of expectation was justified. The problem was the people were only too hungry for portents and prodigies that exalted sign over substance, that clung more to miracle than to the promised Messiah. Children must be shielded from such childish preoccupation. Had the parents of Judas the Galilean put thoughts into his head that sent him rampaging through the province a pretender-messiah? He had generated a trail of blood and disaster for his people.

They had refrained from giving their little boy premature

accounts of the divine events attending his origin. To know was his right, but to decide when was theirs, and they had agreed it would not be before his bar mitzvah. Now their son had proved that he, too, possessed deep thoughts, and had chosen the same moment to broach them. Whatever they were, Joseph, she felt, was now inducting him into the mysteries heretofore hidden from him.

She scraped the flour together into a bowl, poured in water, and kneaded, breathing a prayer of gratitude for Joseph's eminent good sense. He was so anchored in it he kept you from being swept away by even the most stirring happenings. This had the effect of deflating self-importance in the bargain. To his guidance she credited much of the solid judgment her son showed. Only once in the twelve years had he jolted them by his behavior—and that was this year at the Passover. After heart-deep pondering, she concluded he was guided by higher counsel than man's.

Certainly he had been an apt pupil for Joseph. Fondly she recalled the day he had rushed into the house with a frown. He was nine, and his keen intelligence registered in the alertness of his whole carriage. He ran up to her and kissed her.

"Imi—my mother," he burst out, "is it true there is a river that stops flowing on the Sabbath?" His boyish voice rose with indignation. They were standing by the window, and the streaming sunlight limned his comely profile and fell on the white of an eye, setting it to glowing as with a deep inner radiance. The child's curls tumbled out from under his turban—the men wore their hair shorter than the women, but longer than the close-cropped Romans. When a little girl, she too had curly hair. And those features—the golden skin, the great eyes, the clear brow, that certain contour of the ruddy cheeks, the facial harmony—all were hers. There she stood, outside of herself, separated from herself, possessed by another in his own way. A melting sweetness absorbed her until she gasped as one forgetting to breathe, and such a painful longing pierced her she wanted to crush him to herself.

"Mother, aren't you going to answer me?"

At his words—which struck her as his declaration of

independence from her own preoccupation—she felt her train of thought dislodging like a silvery film slipping from a wintery roof. She smiled at the contact restored with the self-possessed little boy.

"Tinoki—my child—I'm certainly not going to neglect you. Who told you there is such a river?"

"Cousin James. Is it true?"

"I think your question deserves more than a yes or no. It's one you and your father should thrash out. He's delivering a plough to your Uncle Yeshua. He'll return soon. And now we'll grind the barley."

At the sound of Joseph's footstep, the boy ran to him with his question, and heard one in return.

"Who told you there's a river that stops flowing to honor the Sabbath?"

"Cousin James. Is it true?"

"What's its name?"

"The Sambation."

"Where is it?"

"He couldn't say. Somewhere that way." He waved vaguely toward the south.

"Why do you ask if it's true?"

"My Father doesn't do things that way."

"What do you mean?"

"He creates rivers to flow every day. They don't need the Sabbath rest. They don't tire."

"Son, come and sit down. I'm tired." Joseph poised the child on his knee. "Is the story of the Sambation perhaps just a way of saying that the whole land of Israel is holy?"

"That's not all James was saying!"

"Once in the Holy City I saw the Wadi Kidron in spate, but on the Sabbath it dried up. The rabbi said, 'Even the Wadi Kidron obeys the Sabbath better than the people.' Was that true?"

"It's true it stopped flowing because you saw it. Some would say it just happened. I think my Father intended it as a Sabbath lesson."

"Then was what the rabbi said true?"

"In a way. The wadi did what it was made to do because it had no choice."

35

"Might the story of the Sambation be a similar story, meant to say the rivers set us a good example, always doing God's will?"

"But if the rabbi said the Wadi Kidron stopped running every Sabbath, it wouldn't be true, would it?"

Joseph laughed. "No, it wouldn't. So the story of the Sambation is different. It's a 'once upon a time' story. We can safely consider it a made-up story to point out that rivers do what God made them to do. If he had made them to stop flowing on the Sabbath they would—and we should do what he created us to do."

The boy nodded in satisfaction. "But that's not the way my cousin told the story. When I didn't believe it, he said he'd find the Sambation and take me there and duck my head in it!"

"Tell him," Joseph laughed, "that if he finds it and the story is true, you'll let him—on the Sabbath."

The boy grinned. "I'll tell him."

Mary smiled at the remembrance. With the clay lamp she lit the pellets of dried vegetation in the brazier. The warmth was agreeable, though she was clad in cloak and apron. The house was always cold in winter. On the table she laid out the wooden bowls and earthenware mugs, went to the outdoor oven, and lighted a fire of the dried chips and shavings from the workshop. Soon she had fish steaming on the stone slab.

In her mind she justified once again the feast they were having despite their poverty and their plans. The ceremony of bar mitzvah had to be honored and impressed as a milestone in every boy's journey to manhood and full service of the Lord. How important then for her son! She recalled the day a few years ago when they had made their special plan for him. Arriving with a wagon load of logs, Joseph had frowned on hearing of the firewood she had given Nathan, their poor neighbor.

"Mary, I'd have made him work for it, as better for him and for us."

"Why for us? We're not that poor."

"I think we are. Something has been troubling me."

She sat beside him and took his calloused hand. "What is

it?" He returned a searching look before answering.

"We know our boy's the Awaited One."

"Of course."

"Then we have to prepare him as best we can for the work awaiting him." The words came with intensity, almost with desperation.

"Joseph, what's he to do? And if we don't know that, how can we do anything special to prepare him?"

"Dearest, one day he must deal with the rabbis of Jerusalem. For such a task, schooling in Nazareth is not enough."

She sighed. "I thought of that—and considered David, called from his flocks. He had no learning."

"Those were simpler times, before there were rabbinic schools. You know how the Judeans mock our dialect."

"I have worried over that—and their great learning."

"Mary, we should send him to them—to the school of Hillel—soon after his bar mitzvah."

"Joseph, for that we *are* too poor."

"We must save every penny. Even a year there would help. If the rabbis don't respect him, how hard it will be!"

"Then we'll try. I'll save, and put my hand to the spindle more often to produce surplus cloth we can sell. But Joseph, we can never say no to the hungry and the needy."

"Never, dearest. But when they can work to earn what they need, we'll require it."

It was sweet to call up these memories of how her child had grown at her side, and stood at her knee as she taught him—yes, and worried about how much to tell him. And yet, at times, when he looked at her in that profound, absorbed way, out of those bottomless eyes, the worrry seemed silly, and her teaching but a wonderful game. And then would come the strangest sensation—that it was she who was being allowed to learn, and that he who listened was teacher. At such times she felt herself like the little girl she once was, thinking to explain some matter to her wise and kindly old grandfather, who nodded with infinite patience, and let her ramble on. Was it just her imagination gone wild? Or was she indeed probing something wilder, stranger, beyond grasp—reaching up for a night star? The angel had said, "He will be called son of the Most High." What did it mean? Was the alchemy behind those strange episodes the angel's words—or in truth the son on her lap? Certainly, at times she felt the impulse to ask him the questions!

She heard the familiar voices approaching, and whispered, "O it's too deep, too deep. Let it alone!" She composed herself, and wondered if she would be called on to add to her husband's account of their beginnings.

6

She flung open the door in welcome, eager to sit with husband and son at table—yes, and to ponder with them the Lord's workings. Their boy, at times, gazed with them into the impenetrable light. Then, by some word, he would flash into its glowing center. Leaving them to gape and wonder— did he, the crux of the mystery, struggle to probe it? Or only ray it forth?

This little home. Bursting at the seams with life. Filled with love's deep sorrows, deeper joys, and bell-sound laughter. And now this celebration—an hour of love always to be cherished.

The embrace of each, the press of her lips to wind-chilled cheeks, the opening banter. "Your father-son outing gave me time to prepare a feast." Indeed, the room was filled with the fragrance of herbs and spices—which, generally, she used sparingly. Not that she didn't stock in her larder the leeks, shallots, mustard, caper, cumin and rue, coriander, mint and wild rosemary dear to her people. Just that she believed in simple foods, in keeping with the tradition that to eat was literally to "break bread" together—bread and wine being often the substance of a meal for the poor in the land.

She searched their faces for the results of their interchange. Reassured, she pursued her theme. "Perhaps it's a hint we've been eating too plainly?"

"It worked, son." The man's stage whisper evoked her ready smile. "Except that you didn't give us time to stop

38

at the grill and sample that savary fish."

The boy inspected the table, drew in a whiff of the steaming lentil soup, cast his eye over the bread and cheese, honeycomb, roasted almonds, and purple wine. "Today, father, we won't have to slip off to a neighbor afterwards—for supplements."

"Not my bar mitzvah. But if my husband lets the fish burn, it'll be a separate case."

"I'll tend them," the boy offered.

"You're blue with cold. Stuff the window, then warm yourself at the brazier—tending the pancakes."

Her husband soon returned with crisp brown perch wrapped in leaves. They performed the ritual washing of hands, and sat at table. "We bless him whose bounty has filled our lives with good things," Joseph chanted. "Blessed are you, Lord God, King of the universe. You bring forth bread from the earth."

He served the food, and sampled it. "Tasty fish. I'm a better cook than I was aware."

"No doubt," his wife agreed. "The fact that Uncle Tobias brought them fresh from his fishing trip to the Sea of Galilee can have little to do with it."

"I didn't know he was a fisherman."

"He wasn't. For his birthday his wife gave him a fishing net—a hint." Delicately accenting the last word, she raised her head, and looked at him expectantly.

"I explained to our son how we got started as a family."

The boy nodded. "With his usual economy of words."

Her sweet peal of laughter rang out. "And all the more clear for it. Did you mention Elizabeth?"

"I thought you'd want to tell him about that."

"You are a mindreader, my husband. It happened this way. From the Lord's messenger, I learned she was carrying a child. I asked father's permission to visit—not giving the reason. He couldn't locate a trustworthy caravan. Then the problem solved itself. Her brother, Thomas, arrived with the news she was six months pregnant, and asking for my help.

"Thomas got sick just before we reached En Kerem. He sent me the last few miles with a friend. I ran up the path, burst in, flew over and kissed Zechariah. He made excited

39

gestures, but no sound. You know how he was struck dumb."

"Yes, but he's made up for it since."

"He seized my hand and hurried me out of the village, up into the green valley. The wheat ripening in the sun. Trees blossoming. Fields full of promise. Up to their summer cottage. I ran—flung open the door. She was kneading dough at a little table. I called a greeting.

"She turned heavily, clutching at her child-filled waist. Leaving handprints of flour on the purple cloth. Laughing with delight. Crying, 'My baby's jumping with joy at your greeting.' Eyes opening wide. Sinking to her knees. Touching my still-slender waist—it was the first week. Crying, 'Blessed Mary. Blessed among all women!' Tears streaming. 'To what do I owe the honor of this visit? The mother of my Lord comes. Happy, blessedly happy you, for believing the Lord's word.' And we embraced.

"And that," she concluded, "is what I thought you ought to know. Now that you're a grown son, my dear little one."

"And the rest of the story?" The boy's eyebrows raised. "The rest?"

"Your grown son has other sources than parents."

"Such as?"

"Priest relatives."

"Oh."

"Zechariah spoke with me at Passover. 'Son,' he said, 'you're twelve now. My health's failing. There's a family and priestly matter to take up with you. Can't chance delay. Have you been told of your mother's prophecy?'"

"Prophecy?" Joseph sat up straighter.

"Yes. He said that after she exchanged greetings with his wife, mother did a kind of liturgical dance. 'Reminiscent of Miriam,' he said. 'Accompanied by an impromptu canticle. Put me in mind of Hannah—Samuel's mother.'"

'Whose song we've sung all over our lives," she interposed, but he went on.

"He told me how she pirouetted, singing, 'O Elizabeth, God is great. How happy my spirit in my God-Savior. He's fastened his gaze on me, his lowly little girl slave.' They embraced while she chanted, 'Every race, every age, will

40

cry, blessed Mary! They will, they will, because of what our mighty God has done for me.' There's more, but that's the part about the prophecy."

"I never heard about this dancing," Joseph murmured. She smiled. "That was when I was young and frivolous."

"And that prophecy," he pursued. "Famous. I no longer feel needed."

"Needed? Without you they'd call me infamous."

"When fame comes, the famous forget . . ."

Tenderly, she took his hand. "'If I forget you,' she quoted, 'may my right hand be forgotten.'"

"Perhaps I should add a humbling note," her son said. She turned to him alertly, eyeing him with that disconcerting devotion which had nothing to do with the question.

"Oh?"

"Zechariah's preserving your canticle for posterity."

"You said humbling."

"He told me he'd have to improve it liturgically. Re-touch the too-youthful expressions. To do you more honor."

Her face registered a complex of humor and endurance. "Ever the way of a man. I may just have a word with him."

They recalled many happy memories around the table that day. And stored up new ones to cherish forever. The day would remain special, yet its deepest richness lay in its communion with the whole stream of their life together.

After a reflective pause, the man reached out his hand to his wife, and they turned to the boy. "Son, today your mother and I have experienced the worth of our lives. We've kept our trust. Presented to the Lord a worthy son of the Law." He grasped the boy's hand. "We know you will do what he requires of you."

They ate their dessert of figs and sipped their sweet wine in silence. The woman watched the light and shadow from the three-wicked lamp playing across their faces. Both lighting and concealing their features. So like the drama of their lives. Each so exposed to the other, and yet so hidden in personal mystery. Would ever a day come of comprehending what had taken place in her body? What was transpiring under her roof? What seemed too sacred for words? The spirit might but kneel and reverently touch its fringes, and only

41

dream of what lay beyond.

After they had satisfied themselves, they sat together a while in silence. She treasured such moments. They communicated more than words.

When the boy spoke, his voice came as a surprize—she wasn't yet used to its drop down the scale to manhood. "I'm grateful. For everything up to this day. And for what you've told me of my Father's plan."

"One thing more." The man rose and went to the saffron cabinet. Reverently, he removed the scroll of Isaiah, and laid it in the boy's arms. "For our bar mitzvah gift. Our most precious heirloom."

The boy's eyes shone wetly. "I'll study it. Engrave it in my head and heart. It'll never be lost."

"We know," his mother said. "It'll be lived."

"I too have one thing more to do today. When three stars appear, help me to offer my Father fit praise. And to ask strength to bear what must come—for us all."

7

The years had passed at last, and brought me to my new beginning. Beginnings—those birthings of man's deeper self. Singing songs of promise—or who would leave his yesterdays?

Beginnings—they carry one on the current of expectations —and of dread. Will the sweep of the stream turn treacherous, plunging down cataracts to stillbirth?

Thirty years had passed since I was roused to mortal consciousness. Now was the time to fulfill your Emmanuel promise. Joseph had fathered my growth, kneading me into his likeness—as my mother nurtured me to hers. Patterns and guides. Fitting me with hard work for the years ahead.

The years went slowly—and yet, when the parting came, how swift they seemed gone—since the day of my bar mitzvah. Well I remember its close. Three stars appearing. Conjoined hearts chanting the Shema. No intimation my parents had that our little isle of joy was to sink in a storm of sorrow. Winter softened into spring—opening the jaws of a plague. Tending the sick, burying the dead, feeding the orphan and widow—until the sickness fastened on Joseph. With all our care, sinking ever lower. The final hour coming. He seeing mother's tears, she his worshipful gaze. Kneeling beside him, his hand in mine. His last whisper, "My Lord and Messiah." Eyes closing, leaving us. We wept. The long grief of walking in the steps of his absence. The plan for schooling in Jerusalem forgotten. My hand put to the carpenter's trade. Devoting my body to labor—earning our sustenance. Cherishing the honor of working with you in the continuing task of creation—the labor which constitutes history.

Experiencing the pain and joy of producing what intelligence fashions to contribute to man's dominion. Tables, ploughs, houses—fashioning the fashioner into the creator—your likeness.

The carpenter's trade—working on while the blood in my veins grew fiery to stride to my new beginning in the troubled land. No warrior ever awaited more eagerly the trumpet call—to leap upon the enemy of human nature and hurl him to defeat.

What the trumpet would be I knew—what Isaiah foretold —"A voice bellows in desert land, Prepare the way of the Lord"—and Malachi too—"Behold I send my messenger preparing the way . . . Elijah the prophet."

What release when reports flew across the land—the voice was heard. Blaring over the Jordan. The preacher baptizing in its flow. Joy that the voice was John's—my fearless kinsman—companion of my childhood play.

For my mother's care I had arranged. "Cousin James will carry on the trade."

"So your time has come."

Yes, her home duties were discharged. How rich she and Joseph had made me. Such family life—truest of human joys. Surpassed only by life with you.

"I have a gift." She tugged at the sticking chest. "A seamless tunic I wove for you."

"Mother, I take nothing but the clothes on my back."

43

"So it will go on your back then. Leave yours. I'll see that a poor man gets it."

"Let me have it."

"Ah, here it is. Woven in is a wisp of shearings from a firstling. Given at your birth by the poor shepherds. A reminder never to forget the poor. 'May he defend the cause of the poor,' was David's plea."

As I changed garments she called, "Don't miss Beth Ann's wedding."

"Mother, are you forgetting my responsibilities? Do you remember the words of old Simeon you quoted?"

"'You will bring the Gentiles the light of revelation, and shine as your people's glory.'"

"The part about himself."

"He rejoiced to be bought free of slavery—a free man at last."

"Don't you realize I'm not free? At night, waking to the clank of the chains of my mission. Tossing and turning until I carry it out."

"Yes, of course I realize. Try to make the wedding."

The parting embrace, the kiss, the exchange of looks no word can describe—sole signs of the forest of our intertwined roots. She—the single living soul who had divined that I AM. Yet she maintained the tenderest familiarity. To leave her was to engage in loneliness for companion.

On my solitary descent of Nazareth's slopes—flooding memories. The harvest festivals of my youth. Joyously celebrating the loved Feast of Booths. Young maidens dancing in the fields. The faces of the youths flashing with delight. Their comments ringing as the girls removed their veils and executed their graceful rhythms. Folk songs of sorrows, joys and love. Young hearts stirring. Many a youth's attention swirling down a narrowing vortex to one. Many a parent entreated by a son to approach a chosen maiden's father and seek her for his bride.

Resisting the appeal of married love. Learning obedience to the way suited to my mission. Since Adam and Eve, man and wife bodying forth the divine image—but how often failing. Jacob laboring seven years for his Rachel—how well I understood.

In my ear the song of the maidens, in my memory the lovely neighborhood girl with whom the currents of life brought me to share so much—but in my heart the desperate cry of the nations. Hopeless save for the one you have sent.

Others had prefigured my path. To serve you and your people, long had Moses lived unmarried—and like one unmarried. And by your love bewitched, Jeremiah. Serving, ever serving—forsaking the way of the earth. Now, the Essenes. And the occasional rabbi who weds only the Torah.

My heart—remaining open as the shores of the world to the seas of the peoples. Embracing none in a fashion that would hinder the coming of all.

The maidens failing to comprehend—how many understood Jeremiah's call? Not recognizing in me the Shechinah—the Divine Presence—calling all peoples to the wedding of the great King's Son.

Great the struggles of life. Mighty the clash within hearts. Holy the love of man and wife—yet subdued it must be to the love greater still. When the choice must be made, never to be preferred to you.

Where the race whose passion drives it up Sinais of faith to see your face uncovered? Where the hearts afire with love for their one unfailing Good?

Where the men who for the sake of the Shechinah—the Divine Presence—forgo the shechenah—the woman's presence? Where the youths and maidens whose love for you burns down to their vitals in the night, and flames out from their lips in fiery praise of your glory?

My task—to awaken them—send them trooping through the world in witness.

Lifting my voice, I promised—"I will father the race of lovers. Draw spouses to love you in their love and above it. Summon, from this place and that, boy and girl to leave father and mother and espousal—to espouse God alone. With my call—'Solemnly hear me. None who leaves home or parents or brothers or sisters or wife or sons for the sake of the kingdom of God will fail to receive greater in this age, and in the age to come, eternal life.'

"I will enkindle the depths of their earthiness with yearnings, and inflame the stars of their heavens with love. For this

I came. To it I go forth."

Bondsman to time no longer. Unharnessed by the sign that was written. Erupting from the years of my waiting. Down from captivity I sped, in the power of my devotion to you.

Part Two

THE MASTER

1

Down from the quiet of Nazareth I went—into raging battle. I went to build—and met the enemy who destroys. I went sharing the common urge of man the creator. He is seething to beget—driven by godliness of mind, fueled by imaginings of what can be. He labors to call down to earth those spinnings of the mind—and how often fails. He sees his plans disperse like vapors in reality's hot sun. Yet were his plans the illusion? Or his courage?

To shape the earth to one's plan takes courage. A man charges out to do it—and brakes before the cauldron of life. Sees it stewing with its own stubborn will, and the churning will of the people. It takes heart to stick even a hand into the steamy brew.

Where begin? How calm the anxiety of finding no beginning?

Down the cliffs of Nazareth I came, down the caravan route of the centuries—one begins by beginning.

The labor awaiting me—so new, so nameless. It must begin where it had begun—with my kinsman. Hawk's gaze scanning every visage, he was poised to proclaim him whose way he prepared by his volcanic eruption. Leveling mountains of resistance, filling gorges of ignorance. Now he must recognize me.

Long he had kept me waiting—banking the fires of zeal burning at my will to resist. Not before thirty, intoned the sages, was a man ready for the Song of Songs—but sooner, sooner, I would have wooed my bride Israel with songs of redemption.

My song was beginning. And anxieties. I pondered my

49

hoarded strengths. No possessions holding me hostage, no wife but she claiming me as debtor. "Father, I'm free, free in my devotion to you. Fail I cannot while willing your will."

Beyond Nazareth, the Plain of Esdraelon dark and fertile. Ready for seed in the first fall rains. My head resting there the night. Overhung by Mount Gilboa burnished by the glow of the moon. Where fallen Saul, arrow-pierced, despairing, lifted his hand a millenium ago to take his life. The grievous end of Israel's first king.

Now came I.

The next day, Jacob's well near Shechem quenched my thirst—between Mounts Gerizim and Ebal where Joshua, son of Nun, proclaimed the blessings and the curses. There I, Yeshua, gave thought to the new proclamation.

Evening followed at Bethel, where Jacob slept. I pondered his dream of heaven's ladder and the angels—my body on the earth, my presence at your side.

Spinning in a whirlwind I fell from the skies, flesh shredding, flying to heaven's four corners, drifting to earth. Out trooped the peoples and devoured it conscious still with my consciousness—my ecstasy. And agony—pigs too slobbering over me.

Bathed in sweat, I woke.

Of old, finding the fallen manna, they had cried in wonder, *Man hu*—what is it? Now a new manna—and new questions.

East, then, across the tortured desert traversed by Joshua, conqueror of the land—east to Jericho, east across the Jordan to Bethany and John and the gaping throngs.

"Is John the one?"—they whispered, lest the Romans overhear. He teaching, wild and wiry and thunder-voiced.

"You've got an extra coat? Give it to the dispossessed. A surplus of food? Share it with the hungry!"

"What must repentant tax collectors do?" a voice bleated. Hisses from the crowd—narrowed eyes turning to the hated Jewish collaborator with the badge of his office.

"Stop overcharging." Grumbles of the disappointed crowd. Encouragement of a strapping Roman soldier. His cavernous voice like a rumbling of the earth—"What must soldiers do?" Hostile eyes staring at the hated uniform. No sound but the song of birds.

"Stop exacting bribes. Stop accepting them. And you

silent ones—do you deem it enough to be Abraham's children? Take warning, offspring of vipers. Spew the evil from your hearts. Bear good fruit—lest your roots in Abraham be axed! For from these stones"—flying hand designating Roman soldiers—"from these God can raise offspring to Abraham!"

Currents of enthusiasm and disenchantment building in the throng. "He's the prophet." "Who can accept this?" "He's Elijah returned." John, hearing, leaping to a boulder's crown, waving wild arms over unkempt locks, eyes flashing in the burning light.

"Listen! Hear! I'm not the prophet, not Elijah, not Messiah. Just a voice shouting, Prepare the way! For One is coming. With Holy Spirit and fire—his baptism. His wheat he'll garner, the weeds consign to fire—forever."

He baptizing, I in the queue until first. He reaching to grasp the man behind me, and striding into the stream. "May this water wash away your foulness as of old it swept away our captivity, and the leprous unbelief of Naaman, pagan."

I confronted him. "I would be baptized."

"By whom? Not by me—by him we both await." In a hoarse whisper, "To your presence before birth I leaped."

"Do it."

"Does stagnant pond wash heaven-fresh waters? No!"

"Yield."

Stubborn, he searched my eye—then nodded. Impulsively, we embraced—dear kinsmen, friends since boyhood.

Hairy hands on my head, pressing me beneath the waters. He leaping, pointing, roaring, "Look! The heavens tearing open—dove descending—his baptism snatched from me!"

Excited people running. John bellowing—"May there be a washing here, where Joshua baptized into the promised land. Jordan, be washed! Stream to wash the world's waters for the Spirit's use!"

"Listen!"—the strapping soldier roaring—"A voice from the sky!"

The *bath kol t*hundering, "This—my only Son."

Divine fire of the Dove ravishing. Stormed with gladness. Lifted before the people by this testimony.

Cries of wonder kindling conflagration around me—far away—I was with you. In danger—from their enthusiasm. The Spirit seized me, drove me. Leaping from the water— running. Bellowing incoherently, they vainly followed me— a wind speeding into the desert.

2

Gazing down from my airy mountain perch, I pondered the hour just past. Below me the Jordan flowed placidly— unlike the frenzied currents of the throng that pursued me, excited by the *bath kol.* How they would have liked to wrest me to their expectations. How lead them to yours? Moses failed.

Shimmering below, the rim of the Dead Sea, where surged Mount Nebo. There upon its peak Moses, craning his aged neck, had to make do with a hungry gaze into the land forfeited by his doubt.

On the sea's nearer side rose the cliffs housing the Qumran Essenes. Jews, broken with Jews. Hating the corrupt high priests. Despising the common people. Calling for salvation—alienated from those through whom it comes. How shall they receive me?

Directly below, in Jericho, Joshua won his victory— with the aid of violence. The new victory must be different—man's spirit conquering creation, through the Son of Man.

My troubled people will peer out at me as from fortresses beseiged. Searching for a savior-king to rescue from poverty and from Rome. How many cry like David in the night, for release from Satan, sin and death? Clear their desires— and their demands. Had I not, in that hour, seen your sign— and seen the danger of signs? It set the cauldron of the people boiling. Before leaping in—how necessary to arm myself with the firm will to do your will. At the head of Life's book it's written—I came to do your will.

Days of fasting, thirst, and prayer. Endless thought. The density of my body attenuating. Heart burning brighter. The adversary came.

"Why here temporizing? Why not where you're needed?"

"Where I need to be, I am."

"Scheming, are you, to lure your people with vapors? Knowing you'll fail—losing your nerve?"

"Here to do what I must."

"Oh? Neglecting the unemployed father, the mothers with no crust to hand the children? Forgetting tramping foreign boots and tax-poor wretches? No pity? No plans to foster wealth like Solomon's?"

"The affluent I know are the poorer for it."

"Idealistic prating. Not very human after all? Not a compassionate man?"

Stinging charge—but he pressed on. "From the practical side, where will it get you with your earthy people—say your Uncle Yeshua?" He, thinking me his namesake, took a proprietary interest in me. I loved him—he loved his vast holdings. "Would he approve your plans, be led by them?"

"Men must be led against their selfishness."

"Selfishness? Be honest—call it human nature. Its needs are real—food and pleasure, the inventions of what you call God."

"I will lead men against themselves."

" And end leading only yourself? Learn the ways of the great. Caesar Augustus, lord of the world since your teens, subsidizes food and fast living. Some call him a god."

"Caesar's ways lead to Caesar's ends."

"You learn nothing from magnanimous Caesar? He feeds his people. Do the same with those uncanny powers you modestly hide. Start a great reclamation project of this ungodly wilderness."

"For God."

"I'll ignore that infantilism. Listen—my project will make you one of the great ones, remembered forever."

"Let men be remembered for themselves."

"Unreal. Consult your empty stomach. Learn to abandon that philosophy."

"Each needs the other's gift of self. With that, all else

53

comes."

"Ha! Rejecting your own creed? Virtual polytheism. Pretending men are not self-centered boors, but gods."

"It's written, 'You are gods, sons of the Most High.'"

"Written, written—prophetic pipedreams. Childishness. Get on with life, with what *you* can do!"

"That I intend to do."

"Do mighty things. Cast off your shackles, your delusions of 'doing God's will.' You have dreams to carry out as your own man."

"No man's his own."

"Spare me, please. Recall the great ones who were their own—unhampered by any creed. They worked their wills, and are remembered. Now to the project. Look around you— the land grows stones, not bread. Reclaim the land. You've discovered some secret power. Do what the prophets could do only in symbol. If you could make a voice sound from the sky, you can turn into reality their pious legend of bread from heaven."

"It's no legend."

"So the gullible say. But on to the project. Use your power —change stones to bread. One master stroke will provide bread, entertainment, and religion. Be nominated god-hero forever! And feed yourself first—you skeleton. Like so many of your people. Do you have a human heart or not? Turn that stone to bread!"

How I wanted to. And could. Can hungry men think beyond their stomachs? With bread assured, would they not turn to their need for spiritual food? Was I heartless?

Thus he pressed upon me false and tempting thoughts, and tearings of grief. I fought to bring my own purpose to the fore. Had I come to give bread that prolongs mortality? To give life a mere reprieve? Or to give living bread—give Life?

"Men have hands to earn their bread. Take away their need—and you give them stones. Men are more than their stomach. They live by bread, yes, but they live, too, by every word from God's mouth."

He knew he'd lost a skirmish. "You mean people want more than material things? True. What they need is the vision—"

"Of truth."

"Of reality! Through total experience—the probing of all knowledge. Eve was right. Knowledge of good and evil is the stuff of gods. Experience, then judge. What are goodness and badness but creatures of time and circumstance, products of the situation? Chuck the values Moses froze in a dark age. Experiment with life. Is blind acceptance of the old tales wise?"

"Faith in God's word is blinding vision."

"Faith? It's neither knowledge nor experience—it's a leap from life!"

"Life is to know God. Faith knows God by God."

"Your myth of cosmic paternalism again. So you will enforce Moses' 613 fossil laws? Fine. Preach your taboo-narrowed lifestyle. Breed a world of manikins on life's shelf."

"I'll call the world to obedience."

"Obedience? On second thought, your simpletons won't fill the shelves. Like Eve, the strong won't succumb. Like Adam, the weak will be sucked into their wake."

"They're free to choose. Life or death."

"You try my patience. If you must play the game of religion, do it in style!"

Seized beyond human power—and none other would I use in my own cause. Sped in a whirlwind. Falling to Jerusalem. Poised on a pinnacle of the Temple. He roaring—"I too have power! Enjoy its taste? See the self-important clerical ants below."

"They are worshipping God."

"Worshipping? Programmed ants. Mumbling rote ancestral incantations. Offering rote ancestral butcherings!"

"Offering as Moses commanded."

"Outdo Moses. He worked prodigies to please the people. Work greater ones. Stand their hair on end. Jump. Descend shouting you're the Messiah! You are, aren't you? Cry it to the winds."

Wonders Moses worked. Could I do less and be accepted? Would they have accepted Moses?—nearly killed despite his signs. If signs then, why not this one, before priests and people? Before the high priests—forcing them to believe both in signs and in me. So economical. One sign to compel the belief of those in power, and I need work no more. But wait! Did Moses' signs promote his glory? What! Am I delirious with fasting? The Son of Man came to be the way. "The sign appointed is lowliness."

"Teach lowliness then—remain a simple mountain man for life."

"I teach what I learned from my Father."

"I'm teaching you what you must learn."

"You are a liar."

"Oh? You wish scriptural confirmation? 'He puts you in charge of angels, to guard you against so much as a stub of the toe.' You doubt David's prophecy? You don't trust God?"

"Scripture also says, 'Test not God's providence.'"

Satanic violence seethed, hurling my imagination up some cosmic peak.

"Look at the prize—kingdoms and kingliness. Behold Caesar Augustus, Emperor of Rome and the world. Of power such as I offer you, he only whimpers in dreams. Seize and mount his throne—swell it to Hermon's height! Destroy his heathen influence. Bring true religion to your people and the world. Outshine Alexander the Great. For him armies died. For you men will die when his memory's dead. Behold the world and what your greatness can bestow on it. Desire it!"

"For the world's sake I will do much."

"Then acknowledge me. And my power to give the world or withhold it. My mark's on men. You're a skeleton worrying what to do about it. I'll tell you—kneel to my leadership. Our power will surge around the world!"

"To no creature do I kneel."

"Drop the charade of religion! You and I are the only gods. Play the man and be a god! Create with me a god-like world beyond religion's power. You've power—I have more. Fall and adore my power. Adore your lust for power. Don't deny that lust to me. Aspiring—aren't you?—to unheard-of titles. Fall, adore yourself and me. Let the old gods die!"

Such an eruption of my anger that he staggered and fell back. "Away! Out, Satan! Man's God says, 'The Lord your God adore, him only serve.'"

His presence dissolved. Trembling in every limb I was—

but not from fear. My voice raised, I chanted to the end the Shema Israel—my sword and victory. Sending up my prayer for all tempted to throw over their innocence to know as gods—and no longer know innocence, in which they are as God.

Power radiated unbidden. Angels descended to tend me. Wild beasts crept up, huddled at my feet, received new names. Sweetly I laid my hands on them in blessing. Comforted. Finding peace.

Out of trial, out of obedience—my way confirmed. Not riches, honors, and the pride of power. Girded must I be with poverty, humiliations endured, and the lowliness of obedient love.

My followers too must gird this way—a hard saying. Not strange Isaiah foretold they would not take it in— "Listen with care—listen in vain! Watch like hawks—learn nothing!"

Near my town—the tomb of Jonah, loved of Galileans. The Ninivites overturned his prophecy by repentance and piteous bleating. If my people would but do the same, to banish the terrible way Isaiah inscribed in words of blood— "The Lord saddled him with the guilt of us all . . . If he sacrifices his life as a sin offering, he shall see his offspring in a long life."

You placed the issue in my people's hands—and kept it in yours. Through success or failure, you assign me the victory.

Strengthened, I went to the task.

3

Humming a tune, John the son of Zebedee strode beside the river on the path to Bethany beyond the Jordan. That John was only a teenager was evident in the youthful face, the lithe body and the free-swinging gait. A first glance suggested that time and event had left no more trace upon those open features than voyages of old upon today's placid waters. Not a line marred the fresh skin, not an indentation disturbed the tranquil curving of flesh into clear brow, blooming cheek, and graceful lips and chin.

Closer inspection of the sensitive face required a modification of first impressions—the force of the daily cycle was infusing those features with a medal-like firmness and character. The transmutation was furthest advanced in the lips, which might have been carved from cherry marble. There was a chiseled look about the beard, though it was somewhat softened by the fineness of the hair.

Most striking were the eyes, and here the impression that time and event had left no trace must be altogether abandoned—must, indeed, be reversed, challenging the observer to match the ageless wisdom those orbs flashed. To peer in was to evoke a sense of plunging into bottomless depths from which there would be no emerging. Yet if they allured inward, they on their part gazed so intensely outward they seemed to be communing with the universe as with a sentient being—and probing beyond it to the far side of eternity. It was the gaze of the mystic, the seer, the genius, the lover—of one who sees great and noble deeds yet undone, and shall never rest until done they are.

Even now the youth was striding in a half-run. He was in no hurry—just enthusiastic about rejoining the Baptizer. He was passionately devoted to the man for patriotic as well as religious reasons—for if the mysterious personage whom the holy man was poised and impatient to point out proved to be the actual Messiah, that meant liberation, and soon, and he would be part of it, sword flashing.

That image pleased him, both as a Galilean and a son of Zebedee. Galileans considered themselves the country's patriots. Their province was a boiling pot of plots and plans for rebellion. The sophisticated Judeans were considered too practiced in compromise to deserve the name of patriot. His father had lost a brother long ago in the uprising of Judas the Galilean, and that had stoked his rebellious passions for good. His stories so stirred his son's imagination that he felt almost as though he had witnessed the Galilean firebrand's daring exploits himself.

He and his elder brother, James, had teamed up with their father to sail a fishing boat on the Sea of Galilee. He and James had come on the Baptizer early, on their return from taking a donkey-load of fish to the Holy City. They'd stayed an unforgettable month, hearing him preach, receiving private instructions, assisting at baptisms, and getting a taste of his austere way of life. Since then he'd become famous. Like all John's neophytes, they had been sent home with the instruction to work only as much as the support of their families required, and otherwise to devote themselves to spreading the message, "Repent, the approach of the Expected One is imminent!" This balance of manual and spiritual activities accorded with the Jewish tradition that only such a life throttled sin and led to salvation. The youth, as yet unmarried, was working for his father. His father was not enthusiastic about John's return to the Baptizer. He felt the man was moving too slow to please a real patriot.

The Baptizer was a mystery man who stirred John's blood. Hurtling around in his hairy mantle, thundering warnings and pronouncements, off alone in deserts, fiercely austere, he was the reincarnation of the prophets of old. He was even thought by some to be Elijah returned. Elijah, according to one rabbinic tradition, had been a priest like the Baptizer, who taught along the bank of the very river from which Elijah had been spirited to heaven in a fiery chariot. The stumbling block was that his parents were known, though now dead. Even so—some had averred that Elijah was destined to return by transmigration of his soul into a mother's womb.

Whatever his father thought, the Baptizer's rate of stirring up the people was terrifying the rulers, especially Herod in revolt-prone Galilee. He was already threatened with war by the king of Arabia for divorcing his daughter to marry Herodias, the wife of his brother, who was also angry with him. There was even a rumor that John had been dragged before the Jewish Supreme Council and ordered to quiet down before the Romans stepped in.

As the youth approached the Bethany ford, a figure emerged from a path cutting through a dense thicket on the opposite bank. At once his keen eyes recognized that figure, sculptured like a Greek god. "Andrew!" The two broke into a run, leaped into the river, and embraced midway in its waters.

"You don't know how good it is to see you!" The inflection in Andrew's voice made his companion back off a pace and scrutinize his countenance. It was youthful, comely, manly, bronzed and vital, but there was a worried look about the eyes.

"The way you say that," he returned as they climbed the bank, "tells me that things aren't going too well."

"He's changing before our eyes." The tone conveyed patent anxiety, and that was unlike Andrew. "Neither Simon nor any of the others understand what's going on." Simon was his older brother.

"Changing? What do you mean?"

"You know how he's always been?"

"Firm as Mount Zion, forceful as a blacksmith's sledge, unassailable as the Antonia."

"Exactly. When I stepped aboard, he was unsinkable. Now he's in a storm, the boat's creaking, groaning and shipping water, and in his voice I hear planks splintering."

John whistled softly. "That bad?"

"Worse. You know how we used to sit on the lake at sunrise and gaze at snow-capped Mount Hermon, towering over the other mountains, breaking through its wreath of clouds like a vision in scarlet and white. His face used to remind me of that—only softened by some inner vision."

"And now?"

"The snow's melted; there's nothing but stones and mud."

"You're coming on strong—in riddles. Tell me exactly how he's changed."

"I can't pin it down, and that's why I'm glad you're here. You're better at piecing things together."

"There must be something definite you can tell me."

"He used to look wild, the way a forest is wild, wild and peaceful. Now he is wild and restless."

"What does he *do* that makes you say that?"

"He'll be preaching or baptizing, and without warning shout, 'I must pray! We all need more prayer, to understand! To understand! Come back tomorrow!' And off he plunges

60

into the thickets, and we don't see him 'til dawn. His fasting's gotten so bad he's down to skin and bones."

"How's it affecting his disciples?"

"Some are confused, some leaving. And I can tell you how it affects me. I was as awed as if he were Elijah himself. Now I feel sorry for him, want to help him, and don't know how."

"When did this begin?"

"About six weeks ago."

"Anything unusual happen then?"

"Only one thing we can trace. People say a man looking a little like John—only more like Mount Hermon—came for baptism. They disagreed about something, and sparks flew. John baptized him, then shouted, 'Look, a dove descending on him!' Some say there was a voice from heaven, others that it thundered out of a clear sky. The man raced off, and nobody's seen him since."

"Not much to go on. Have you questioned the Baptizer?"

"Have you grabbed a tiger by the tail?"

"No, but I might. Where is he?"

"Come on." They hurried up the path between tall reeds and pines and myrtle thickets, and broke into a clearing. The prophet was seated there, staring. His appearance shocked the son of Zebedee. Andrew had not exaggerated.

"Baptizer!" The prophet looked up, leaped to his feet, and ran to embrace the youth, who wrapped his arms affectionately around the scratchy mantle, then stepped back and blurted, "You look like you've walked through hell!"

"Yes."

"Your disciples are confused. You ought to tell them what's happening"—John always spoke out in that perhaps presumptuous frankness of markedly innocent youths with mettle.

"The message had to come clear first. But now I will tell you—I've seen the one we awaited!"

The youths fell back, staring in amazement at the somber face. At length John spoke. "Baptizer"—he refused to be called rabbi: 'Your Teacher is yet to come'—"are you sure?"

"Didn't I say so?" The thunder at least was in the old, familiar vein. "The sign was unmistakable!" Calming, he looked at the youth with compassion, and spoke in a voice uncharacteristically mild. "Son of Zebedee, that was never

61

the problem. Never doubt my conviction or a jot of my witness. Nothing I ever said needs correcting."

"Then where's the joy! Why stagger around like a stunned ox?"

"What's afoot exceeds our hopes; what needs saying is beyond words—and about that you must wait to hear from another. What needs changing is what I left unsaid, but perhaps implied—for it is what I hoped. John, John, we thought the whole world would be changed in a day."

"Can't you be clearer?"

"Looming is suffering undreamed of—and glory! Prepare flesh for pain, patience for stretching, mind for tearing, heart for swelling beyond bearing! No more! I am stormed even now by revelation turning my world to heaven and to hell!" He turned and strode away.

"Wait!" John implored, pursuing. "Is he the prophet or Elijah or the Christ?"

The anguished question reflected the indeterminate nature of the Baptizer's prophecy. The Israelites were expecting the three ambassadors of the Lord just named, and in speaking of the "one who is to come" the Baptizer had never specified further.

Turning, the Baptizer bellowed, "I was looking sharp for the sign, and it came, and I'm not worthy to unloosen his sandal!" The youths came to a jarring halt, surprized. This man berated Pharisees for demanding excessive reverence, but even they taught expressly that no disciple need remove his master's footgear.

"Will we see him?" John called.

"When he returns."

"What shall we do?"

"Follow him."

Those were the last questions they ever asked him, for at that moment he jerked his head up sharply as though listening. "Come!" He raced for the river and the youths spurted after. The waiting concourse hailed him but he ignored them, leaped onto a promontory overhanging the water, and stood transfixed, staring at the figure in white descending the slope on the opposite bank. His face filled with light, he leaped down shouting, "It is he for whom I prepared you.

Look, and may God help you see! Him I baptized, and the Spirit descended on him. Others the Spirit touched"—his head spun, eyes resting fleetingly on the two youths—"but on none but him did it abide." His thunder was audible half way to Jericho. "That was the sign! 'When the Spirit descends and stays,' my Sender said, 'he is the one who will baptize with the Holy Spirit.' Now look on the Son of God, the Lamb who takes away the sin of the world!"

The son of Zebedee gazed for the first time on the face of Jesus. Its intensity of presence erased all else from his consciousness. Afterwards, to ask him for a description would have been in vain. It was not the features he would remember so vividly, but the presence and personage they radiated, and for which they could claim only fractional credit. For the difference in this man was not in his face, but in the impression created by his face—oh, the wonder was still more subtle! If all the faces John had ever seen were collected together like a hoard of precious stones, it would be as if the flaming sun should strike his alone until it burned with hypnotic brilliance, only the terrible brilliance originated not from without but from within.

Devotion surged in John's heart, turmoil in his mind. Who was this? He had heard holy men called sons of God before, but why call him a lamb? He didn't look like a lamb—or if he did, then like a lion as well! His strength and power were as pronounced as his nobility and comeliness and magnetism. He attracted you at once, but induced as well a pulse of awe.

Long had the youth awaited the day the prophet would point and thunder, "The awaited one, the Christ!" And now there was no Christ, only a lamb. Lambs were slaughtered and bled in droves in the Temple. Not a pretty sight!

The man reached the bank, turned, and disappeared into the thicket. The youth leaped into the water and splashed wildly across. His friend stood transfixed. The Baptizer thrust him forward. "Go, blessed one, and storm heaven you will be accepted!" Andrew lunged into the river, sending up a great spray as his powerful body half ran, half leaped to the far shore.

The two plunged through the trackless thicket after the man, oblivious of the thorny bracken and vicious thistles

63

which deterred others from following. They thrashed their way through the brush and came to an open place on the bank. There the Lamb stood. He turned with composure and looked at them. They braked their pell-mell advance and froze, returning his gaze, panting from their exertion, their hearts beating wildly.

"What are you seeking?" For the first time they heard that magnetic voice with its qualities like the face. An interminable silence ensued. John's lungs were bursting yet he did not breathe. What did you call this—this lamb? It was his friend who spoke.

"Rabbi, where do you live?"

In the ensuing silence, the eddying water and song of the birds gained more and more prominence. The youths stood utterly helpless. They had knocked on an impregnable door. If it opened they would pass through, onto a new path for which they longed beyond understanding. If it did not open . . . Like statuary in some rustic park they remained poised.

"Come and see."

At three in the afternoon of that warm November day they received his invitation. Seven words he had spoken, and their lives were changed forever.

4

The simple events of those first hours left a golden etching in Andrew's memory. From the first moment he experienced such total commitment to the Master that he was tasting his whole future. He was supremely conscious of entering on that rare wholesomeness, the friendship of selfless comrades devoted to a sacred cause.

Nor was that all. In the presence of this lordly man he found joy in the commonplace, and that is bliss, that is beatitude. It is life divested of accretions, stripped to the skin, feeling itself warm and golden in the sun.

Andrew lacked the intellectual gifts of his friend, but he had his own endowments. A man of profound intuition, and feelings that ran deep, he was sensitive to those unseen currents which are the real sap of life.

The young men followed the Rabbi farther into the thicket fronting the river. Passing a stand of reeds, he turned onto a little-used footpath which led to a small clearing and a booth of reeds. Here he faced them. "For the moment, this is where I stay, and you with me. But now it's time to gather food for our supper." Andrew spoke up in his self-possessed way.

"Rabbi, the Baptizer taught us to trap locusts, find edible roots and berries, and select bark from the right trees."

"Set about it, Andrew. By the fallen tree upstream you'll find honey. John, we will enlarge our shelter." Andrew went off, while Jesus and his companion began gathering reeds and rushes. When they had completed the task, and added two beds of leaves, John drew a hook and line from his tunic.

"Rabbi, I come from a family of commercial fishermen. Shall I add to our supper?"

"How old are you, John?"

"Seventeen. I've fished the Sea of Galilee since I was a little boy."

"Do as you suggest."

The youth scouted a likely spot, and cast in his line. He was pleased his new leader had put his hand to building their shelter. The usual rabbi would leave it to his disciples. Unlike the Baptizer, he mused, this new master agreed to be called rabbi, though he certainly could not claim the distinction officially, if only because he was too young—the requisite age was forty. Did he even have the extensive theological training and certification legally required for a title which means "my master, my teacher"? Certified rabbis were scribal theologians, official interpreters of Scripture and tradition. Of course, the title was just now coming to be reserved to men in possession of these distinctions.

When he returned he found his two companions crouched by a fire emanating the acrid smell of kindling wood and the aroma of roots roasting. "Rabbi, the fishing's not too good," he said ruefully, holding up two small fish.

"If my brother Simon were here, we'd have all the fish we could eat," Andrew asserted. "And if there's any doubt, ask him!" John's laughter rang out. He knew Peter, and his fisherman's pride. The Rabbi responded with a smile—and a word that made the two youths examine him searchingly.

"He will be catching a few for me. Where is he?"

"On a mission for the prophet. He's due back tonight."

Jesus and his first disciples prayed together and shared their meal as the sun slipped behind the mountains rimming Jericho and, with that swiftness characteristic of Israel's mountainous land, night and the chill of November fell together.

"My disciples"—the words were solemn—"you have begun with me. Never look back." He rose. "I will pray a while. Retire, if you like."

The sun rose on the Sabbath. Andrew found Simon, rendered a terse account, and asked, "Who do you think he is?"

"I'll come and see," pronounced Simon authoritatively.

Andrew stared at this elder brother, trying to imagine how Jesus would see him. His imposingly big and brawny body was topped by an impressively massive head with a broad, weatherbeaten face, still young. His headcloth, riding well up on the forehead, exposed thick black locks and the prominent brow, which was set in balance by the expansive cheeks and heavy black beard surging from the jaw. Abundant energy played in the brown eyes and the upward curve of the firm lips. His straight back bulged with massed muscles at the shoulders. The powerful arms which swelled the sleeves of his tunic ended in big, calloused hands. He had the formidable mien of a man of action and leader of men, but his somewhat intimidating aspect was all but neutralized by the ready twinkle of the eyes, the slightly untidy aspect of the beard, and the mobility of the features. These communicated an easiness to his bearing which conjured up the impression—and Andrew knew it to be true—that endowed with natural authority though he was, he would make an appealing leader because he didn't overgovern himself. Children were able to read off this gentleness of his at a glance, for they flocked to him like flies to sweets.

Simon, currently poised on the balls of his feet to set off

on his bouncy walk, blurted, "What're we waiting for?" and his brother led him to the others, where he barged right up to the master.

"Rabbi, I'm Simeon ben Johanan!"

He was surprized at the Hebrew form of his name coming out of him. He liked and used Simon, the Greek equivalent. He had intended to add, "From Bethsaida of Galilee, though now living in Capernaum; a fisherman by trade." Instead, he stood mute and waited. A frog croaked and plopped into the water. He began to fidget, his feet generating crackling sounds in the brush.

"So you are Simon, son of John!" The words came as from a man who has just made a discovery. "From today forth your name is Kepa." Thus originated—in Aramaic— Simon's new name, Peter—Rock.

"There is no such name!" Before the words were out, he saw by the Master's look that he had made a mistake, and in the same breath added whimsically, "There is now!"

The new name surprized John. In his opinion, it fitted Andrew better. Impulsive, precipitate Simon was inevitably forced to change his mind and his approach with some regularity. His brother was the opposite.

The brother mulled things over along similar lines. "But it's true," he conceded, "that with that look and that mountain of a voice, he gives the impression of a rock." Also, Simon was the dominant personality. "But as to that"—he smiled inwardly—"my brother has more than met his match for the second time this year." Simon had first met the Baptizer recently.

Simon was the most surprized—because he knew his own impulsiveness, and because the name was a dash of cold water waking him up to new possibilities. Here he had been accepting himself as an unchangeable clod. Now, in a flash, the gray barrier of unenlightened rigidity was leveled to the ground, exposing new vistas of growth awaiting him, calling him. He liked this man—he didn't waste time!

The next morning, Sunday, Jesus asked questions about the prophet's remaining disciples. Peter concluded with, "There's also Philip. He's a little old—almost thirty—and awfully attached to his father's farm and the horses he raises.

67

He'll inherit the farm."

"It's just outside of Bethsaida," Andrew supplied. "Only after a lot of urging did he come here with us."

"I'll see him, alone." With that, the Master waded across the ford. When he returned, with Philip in tow, he announced, "We leave for Galilee." This surprized them, but they said nothing. Before departing, he forded the river once more, drew the Baptizer apart, and spoke with him. They embraced, and he returned to his men. It was the last time they saw the prophet alive.

As they mounted the steep path out of the Jordan Valley, the prophet was raising his voice to the full height of its fearsome power. "Who has believed our report? Despised, rejected, oppressed, afflicted, opening not his mouth, a lamb led to slaughter for our sins! His way I prepared, but who hears? You vipers' brood, be warned! Bear fruit or your roots shall be axed and in the fire you shall end. Rather let him baptize you in Spirit and fire!"

That stormy outpouring swirled around the ears of the four, curdling their blood. What did the ominous words mean? They wanted to ask their new Master, but didn't. From the beginning it was hard to ask him questions, almost as if it were an offense. Was it because what he wanted them to know he made known without questions, and in other matters he required them to draw their own conclusions among themselves? Many months later, John would give a different reason—"To stand in his presence and ask a question is like standing in sunlight and asking for a lamp."

They went north all that day, traveling hard. On either flank lay unbroken arrays of jagged mountains. For miles the only crop was jutting rocks, pocked and striated by the eons, like time-worn statues of old men, grey and furrowed with age, squatting, waiting, as old as the world.

Peter stared at the stony landscape and mused aloud. "I wonder if there is any truth in what the rabbis say—that when God created the world he made three bags of stones, distributed one around the world, and dumped the others in Israel."

"This much is true, Kepa," the Master said, "that from now on there is one more Rock in Israel." They laughed

68

at Peter's expense, but Peter laughed too.

Mile after mile they journeyed along the Jordan rift. Hardly a blade of grass did they see, except close to the shrunken river. Fall rain would soon bring new vegetation, but from May to October there is no rain. The dark mouths of caves pierced the ancient cliffs, concealing the unseen eyes of the robbers who infested the route. That night they found a cave, ate the little food they had, and fell into an exhausted sleep. At dawn they set out.

"Teacher, I don't know where we're going," Peter blurted out, "but in this direction we'll reach Capernaum by nightfall, and could sleep at my place."

"Andrew said you were living with your mother-in-law."

"Yes, our fishing business is prospering in the town." Capernaum lies along the northwest rim of the lake: Bethsaida, Peter's family home, is a few miles to the east.

"Our next obligation," Jesus said obliquely, "is to attend the wedding of my kinswoman Beth Ann. Festivities begin tomorrow."

Peter beamed. "Attending the wedding of a kinsman is one sacred obligation I've yet to fail in—or fail to make merrier."

"Rabbi," Philip cried, "if you'd come and stay the night in Bethsaida with my family, I'd—"

"Why go that far out of the way?" Peter demanded.

"You didn't let me finish. Rabbi, I'd like you to meet Nathanael. He's a disciple of the Baptizer, and a good one."

"What is his trade?"

"He's a dresser of trees. Originally from Cana, he settled in our fertile region, and bought an orchard."

"Bethsaida it will be. And now I wish to pray." He strode on ahead, and walked alone. John turned to Peter.

"Simon, at sunset tomorrow Wednesday begins, and that's when maidens always marry, but widows never. Why is that?"

"The theologians require it for a virgin, so that if the groom finds his bride is not, and demands a divorce, he appeals to the court the next day, since it sits on Thursdays."

A sudden blast of wind threw the men off balance. "We're in for bad weather," observed Andrew, staring at the scudding clouds.

"I'd call it good weather," Philip disagreed. "We need rain."

69

"I wasn't thinking of hay for your horses," Andrew laughed. "I had unsheltered travelers in mind."

By the time they approached the southern reaches of the Sea of Galilee, sheets of rain were driving down, and white caps foamed on the beaches. They crossed the outflow of the Jordan, and continued along the western perimeter of the lake for several hours. Heavy rain obscured the far shore, some eight miles away. Night had long since fallen when they reached Philip's house cold, tired and hungry. After a loan of dry garments was provided, they ate a hastily prepared repast, and dropped exhausted on the mats laid out.

Like a general reviewing crack troops, Nathanael was striding through his orchard, admiring the expertly tended trees. Washed by the storm of yesterday, the leaves had cast off that leaden look and regained their sheen and brilliance. Still, he was too distracted by other matters to enjoy his orchard to the full this morning. He had to hurry. He was due to leave for his cousin's wedding. And he couldn't get that other matter out of his mind either, that long overdue decision. Should he, a dresser of trees, undertake the hard studies of the Law and earn the rabbinate, just to be more sure of recognizing the Messiah when he came? Though barely twenty, he was already a master of orchards. What made him think he could become a master of the Law, and a master of men? Why not leave well enough alone?

He plucked a few of the late figs, sat under a tree, plumped one into his mouth, and enjoyed the sensuous pleasure. "A wonderful tree, the fig," he ruminated, "giving fruit ten months of the year. How many people make their rabbi a like return? And here in this garden spot, where the melting waters of snowy Mount Hermon never fail to reach me, how can I ever know want? No, I'd best keep my bird in the hand." He spoke the last words aloud, as though trying to persuade an invisible audience.

"Nathanael, is that you? Philip here!" The voice came from the gate.

"Over here, Philip!"

His friend trotted over. "I'm in a hurry," he began unceremoniously, "but you have to meet our Rabbi. The

Baptizer witnessed to him. He may be the prophet Moses promised."

Nathanael looked skeptical. "What's his name and town?"

"Jesus ben Joseph. Nazareth."

"Nazareth? Ha! Can anything good come from Nazareth?" Philip gaped. He hadn't so much as given Nazareth a thought—that little town west of the lake, isolated by the mountain on which it perched. No doubt Nazarenes, like most mountain people, were considered ignorant, self-opinionated and lawless. Bethsaida, by contrast, was a center of business and culture, one of some ten cities of fifteen-thousand-plus which ringed the Sea of Galilee, making it the major population center of the land. Then it came to Philip that his companion's home town was close to Nazareth. Small-town rivalry could lay behind his cynicism, though he was always a bit cynical.

"Come and see."

Jesus gazed at Nathanael until he felt naked to the roots of his soul. "I see before me an Israelite without guile."

"How do you know me?"

"While you were under the fig tree I saw you."

Nathanael stared, speechless. That topsy-turvy decision under the fig tree! His mouth opened but no words came. Finally, as though alive on its own, his tongue said, "Master, you're the son of God, the King of Israel!"

"You believe because I saw you under the fig tree. You'll see a good deal more. Believe me, you'll see heaven opened and God's angels making a highway of the Son of Man!"

They were stunned. Peter, feeling he had to speak or suffocate, burst out, "Master, shouldn't we eat and go? We must hurry!"

At their repast Nathanael said, "Master, I was about to leave for my kinsman's marriage in Cana. Would you join me?"

"The wedding of Jacob and Beth Ann?"

The youth stared wide-eyed. "You forget, Nathanael," Jesus smiled, "that I'm a Nazarene. Beth Ann is my kinswoman. We can just make the wedding."

She came beaming to the celebration, eager and early, not alone in the hope of seeing her son, whom she fully expected to appear, but because she loved weddings. So childlike in the simplicity of love, and yet so mysterious in their swimming depths, they are the one celebration where all the streams of life run together into the human ocean. Bereft of ecstatic bridal couples, nuptial bliss, and happy families, who could endure life?

Never did she fail to delight in the eager longing and innocent passion melting the faces of a young bride and groom—she smiled at the thought of how young they always seemed now. Then there were the feasting children who were a feast to behold, and the anticipation of the children life promised.

Each youth and girl pledging their troth made the years fall away to her own bridal day and birthing, and lit the walls of her imagination with the stored lantern slides of all the happiest families she had ever known. The whole experience always set her heart throbbing with desire for the best, which faith in God assured her was yet to come.

The bride's family lived close by the groom's, in the same housing compound—dwellings of one room, joined wall-to-wall, forming a fully enclosed courtyard into which all windows and doors opened. As she and her nephew James approached, the blind fieldstone rectangle gave the appearance of a poor man's fortress. In unwalled towns such as this, friends and neighbors conjoined their living quarters for protection against marauding robber bands. When they entered the compound by the single stout gate, the scene was warmer, with playing children, ovens and grindstones and hanging wash, open doors and the bustling about of those making preparations within.

Affectionately she greeted her relatives and acquaintances, with a tender kiss and whispered word for her young kinswoman, Beth Ann, the radiant bride-to-be.

One of the rooms had been stripped of its meagre furnishings and appointed with tables. These the women were loading with plates of salted fish, bowls of baked beans and lentils, and trays of various home-made cheeses. Baskets of locally grown olives, dates and figs were added, together with nuts from the Jordan Valley and rich, honeyed cakes from their own ovens. Baskets were piled high with bread, and hampers in reserve stood under the tables. Men and boys were attending the spitted lambs over the open fires in the courtyard, and the sweet aroma permeated the compound. Other fires were laid, in anticipation of the fresh fish which relatives from the Sea of Galilee had promised. She turned to the mother of the bride.

"Sarah, you have enough to feed an army, if the flies don't get it first." The children squealed with delight. Waving cypress branches to ward off the invading swarms, they were eyeing with watering mouths the forbidden delicacies.

"Mary, did you say your son is coming?" Sarah asked distractedly, gazing helplessly at the many preparations under way. "I hope the neighbors take down that unsightly wash. Beth Ann feels so close to him, I'd hate to see her disappointed on her wedding day."

"He'll come if it's at all possible. You know he's begun the life of a rabbi, so he couldn't promise. He said he had to gather disciples. 'How many?' I asked. 'The traditional five,' he answered, so I said, 'Bring them along rather than miss the wedding.' "

"Oh, they're welcome enough. The whole village will be here anyway. I only hope he comes."

"The work's about done here, Sarah. The room's lovely." She waved her hand at the scene. The walls were decorated with seven-branch stems of the sage plant, called the Moriah in Hebrew, and more popularly known as the Menorah Plant. Citrons hung by the dozens from the ceiling, proclaiming abundance and fertility. Blossoming myrtles sprang from pots in the corners, conveying high hopes of prosperity. The people knew and loved these symbols of the sacred and the secular. "What can I do to help you?"

"You're so good at overseeing things. Just walk around and see what's needed."

She stepped outside, saw that the sun was falling low, and felt the first chill of a November evening in the air. By the gate the elder Jacob was completing the huppah, the booth for his son's wedding ceremony and the bridal couple's first night.

"Fill in those chinks, Jake!" a burly fellow cried. "Remember your first night and you'll paste them in good!" The men laughed uproariously.

"Well, actually," Jacob protested, "I'm the Essene type. You, know, celibate—no women allowed! But I must confess —a sense of obligation led to doing my duty the very first occasion." They laughed the louder, and Mary smiled as she entered the huppah. It was adorned with an iridescent tapestry depicting Adam and Eve in Eden, Abraham and Sarah with the boy Isaac, and Tobit and his bride kneeling in prayer on their wedding night. Displayed on the table were the mattan, the customary gifts of groom to bride.

Behind the free-hanging tapestry she found and counted the reserve skins of wine, and felt her first concern. They wouldn't last the week, unless further gifts swelled the supply. Perhaps the village merchant—well, for the present she'd not trouble Sarah.

"Hello, Aunt Mary!" a troupe of girls chanted.

"Clare and Rachel, Jeannie and Miriam! How you've grown!" She hugged each in turn. "Come, let's inspect the water of ritual purification." The little girls tripped beside her to the six waist-high stone jars. They were full and fresh, and the well was close. Purification should pose no problem.

"And now, girls, we'll festoon the huppah with pomegranates and olive branches and Solomon's Crowns, and lilies of the valley."

Excitedly, the girls ran to the storeroom.

In the tent nearby, the groom was completing his bath, assisted by attendants. "Have you ever seen such a bride?" he enthused. "More bath oil. I want to smell like the forests of Lebanon!"

"Jacob, what if she doesn't please you?" a friend pestered.

"I'll never divorce my sweetheart!" he bragged. "But in that case I may take two or three more wives."

"Not in Galilee you won't!"

"In broadminded Judea then! It's not infrequent there."

"Even there the Essenes fulminate—and how'd you like a personal visit from the Baptizer, quoting from Genesis,

74

'The two become one flesh'—not three or four."

"Oh, let's hope it doesn't come to that. And don't speak of this to my darling or I'll have your heads!"

The voice of his sister Dinah pierced the tent. "Hurry, Jacob, or you'll be married in your bath! The sun's setting fast!"

"What? The towel! My clothes!"

In minutes he emerged in his splendid wedding apparel and, accompanied by his attendants, rushed out of the gate and turned east to avoid the bridal party which would soon be approaching. Until sunset he would parade about town, awaiting the golden moment.

Their pipes in hand, shepherd boys posted by the gate kept a sharp eye on the setting sun. When it touched the horizon, they sounded a clarion call. Up from the west, wearing the setting sun like a golden orb suspended above her silver crown, came the bride, the waves of her shoulder-length hair cascading as she glided nearer. Her lovely face shone joyously through the diaphanous veil. The snow-white bridal dress glowed like flame in the sunset. Its bodice was chaste and simple, but from the waist the dress flowed in a delicately worked brocade. Ten bridesmaids with lighted lamps attended her, the first two supporting the train of her garment.

At some little distance from the gate the procession paused, and waited in silence as the sun fell below the western mountains, below the Great Sea. When the orb had vanished and swift darkness was setting in, the bride came on in her train, the lamp in the hand of each maiden hanging like a star. Again the shepherds sounded their pipes, and the singers began to chant.

She comes, the bride, fair sister of the Dawn,
She flutters near, sweet winsome mating dove.
Her sweep and glide teach grace to woodland fawn.
Oh come and let your charm teach us, teach love!

Where bides the man that won your favor sweet,
Your bridegroom strong, your lord, your only one?
O come, arrive unto this meeting meet,
Bring love as dower for your lonely one!

The procession neared, the song died, the bride gazed imploringly and asked her plaintive question. "Have you seen him whom my heart loves?" No answer came.

6

Given a lamp, the bride stood repeating her plaint. "Have you seen him whom my heart loves?" Still no answer. Then, afar off, a flute sounded. The bride circled before the gate, lamp in hand, and broke into song.

> Has any seen the lover of my heart?
> For now we can no longer live apart.
> This night I left my solitary bed
> My love to find, my love this night to wed.

> The city streets I roam and search alone.
> Ah! To the watchmen let me make my moan.
> But see! No help at all they prove to be!
> O lover come and make your claim on me!

Again the bride fell silent, but soon she repeated her song, continuing her solitary procession. A third time she sang the words. From far away, down the street of the westered sun, there came at last an answering refrain.

> Now hark! The dearest sound the earth can hear
> Tells true my friend, my love, my bride is near.
> Reach out, my arms, be still, my wild heart's beat,
> Now fly, my feet, until our two hearts meet!

Bobbing torches appeared, a cymbal clashed, flutes sounded, and all the people chanted.

> The bridegroom comes, the bridegroom comes, he's near!
> O run to ravish her, she's close, she's here!
> Now see, they've met, he holds her heart to heart.
> O hold him then, nor never let him part!

76

At the symbol's clash, some instinct led Mary to turn, not to the west, but to the east. Up by the Sea of Galilee road came a band of men, her son in the lead. Quietly they joined the gathering as the bridegroom sped to embrace his bride.

Her son slipped over and kissed her wordlessly. They turned to the bridal pair. Welling up in her came a favorite verse from Isaiah, "Now your Maker, he will be your husband, his name the Lord of hosts."

The priest escorted the couple to the bridal hut. They entered to a burst of cheering, and turned to face the rest. The priest began the benedictions.

"May he who is supremely mighty, great, and praised, bless this bridegroom and bride."

The groom drank from a blessed goblet of wine given him by his father, the bride from one given her by her mother.

The bridegroom waited for the cheering to fall away and addressed his bride.

"You have freely entered my home, and are thereby consecrated to me by the Law of Moses and of Israel."

"Now to the banquet!" announced the elder Jacob.

When they had crowded the banquet hall and its approaches, the priest intoned the seven benedictions.

"Blessed art thou . . . who created all things to your glory . . . Creator of man . . . fashioning him in your image . . . making Zion joyful with children. Make these lovers and companions rejoice greatly . . . even as in Eden's garden."

"And now for the feast!" shouted the groom's father.

The bride glided over to Jesus, her face soft and melting like the molten wax swelling from the warm region of lighted wicks. He kissed her cheek, and she brushed her lips against his ear.

"In vain," she whispered, "I waited for my handsome kinsman to lead me into his huppah. Another has claimed me. I love Jacob."

"Be faithful and you will be happy. None awaits me in vain, and I am not lost to you. Return to your husband." At these enigmatic words she gazed wide-eyed, then did as he bade.

The festivities continued late into the night. The next morning, Thursday, the guests presented their gifts. Merriment continued, food vanished in heroic quantities, and wine flowed freely in and out of the voluminous goblets. Girls danced their spirited folk dances to the roisterous applause of the young bucks.

"No wonder the popular word for wedding is *mestitha*," hissed a straitlaced relative of the groom, pointing to the rabbi doing a spirited dance before the laughing bride. "A carouse indeed! Her kinsman, isn't he ?"

"Had the groom provided a mattan to equal this feast set out by the bride's family," snapped a female relative of Beth Ann, "the marriage would be off to a better start! I suppose the groom's traditional payment to his father-in-law was a little mean too!"

"Her father doesn't think so!" the groom's brother shouted. "What do you know?" He drained his goblet angrily and went off to join the youths engaged in contests of strength and skill. He hated these busybodies. Marriage settlements were hard enough to arrange at best.

On Friday, Mary found the wine was all but depleted. She sped a waiter to the local merchant.

"He's sick," the man reported, "and his supply's exhausted. What now?" The encroaching Sabbath forbad the trip to a neighboring village for more. They would have to await the Sabbath's end. Or. . .

She made her way to her son.

"They have no wine."

"Woman, what does that have to do with me?"

"The merchant's out of stock, and the Sabbath's on us."

"My hour has not yet come—has it?"

How she felt the weight and thickness of that question! All these years of his prudent reserve and planning, and slow and subtle manner of self-disclosure—and she was asking this!

Was she right? Had she after all grasped correctly what his father had promised for the final times, the symbolic meaning of overrunning vines, and vats overflowing with the red fruit of the vine? Yes, there had to be joy and laughter and high celebration! The final wedding was beginning for the race. Even at prodigious cost, the feast must commence!

The decision was his, of course, but the request hers. She would not withdraw it.

78

"I can't answer that. It's between you and your Father. But this I know—the very mountains shall drip sweet wine on the day awaited. Joel foretold it, and the Father bids us badger him until it comes."

He nodded. She summoned the waiters. "Whatever he tells you, do it." They stood at attention.

"Fill the ablution jars with water."

They stared in surprize. The jars contained water enough for days. The man named Lucius shrugged and made for the well, and the others followed. Soon they returned. "Rabbi, the jars are full."

"Draw some and take it to the head waiter." This order was too much for a waiter named Ladan. Jaw set, feet splayed, he glared rebelliously. Lucius seized his arm and dragged him off. When they were alone, he placated him.

"Maybe he's a fanatic. Maybe the water of purification has to taste pure."

They went, and with an ironic look, handed a pitcher-full to Adam, the head waiter. "We were told to bring you this."

They watched him pour a little into a fresh-washed goblet, sip, roll the liquid around in his mouth, look pleasantly surprized, swallow, pour a full goblet, sip and drain.

"Call the bridegroom!"

Even as the youth approached, Adam called out.

"The wine you just sent me deserves the highest compliments. Superb bouquet. Is it from Beersheba? But allow me to protest! Why keep the best until tastes are jaded?"

The bridegroom was mystified. "I didn't send you any wine."

"What? These waiters—they brought it for my approval." He turned to them. "Where did it come from?"

Lucius gulped. "You won't believe it when we tell you."

Another waiter ran up. "I hate to bother you, sir," he apologized to the groom, "but I went to the storeroom for wine. It's run out." He had not been involved in the filling of the jars.

The bridegroom looked at them impatiently. "What's going on?"

"Maybe Mary discovered that," Lucius suggested.

"Will someone start making sense?" Jacob bellowed.

79

"I'll explain, sir"—and Lucius did, concluding with, "And that's what Adam tasted."

"He tasted water?" Jacob asked incredulously, speeding for the ablution jars. "A dipper!" He stretched out his hand imperiously, and Lucius obliged. He drew, sipped, and smacked his lips. "It's wine all right. Where did the Rabbi get such a quantity?"

Lucius groaned. "I just told you."

Word of the prodigy flew round the compound and spread to the village. People stared at the Rabbi, but no one mentioned the matter to him. Conversation died when he joined others.

Jesus gathered his disciples. "We're leaving."

"Master, come to Capernaum," Peter urged. "To my place."

When Mary heard she said, "The Sabbath will be on us before we reach another town."

"We'll sleep in the fields."

"We'd best take your cousins too."

"Yes. I'll bid goodbye to our hosts."

At the farewells Beth Ann drew him aside. "Thank you for my wedding wine. But who are you—or what are you?"

"Only my Father can tell you. Pray to know." He kissed her and took his leave. The rose in her hand she pressed to her cheek, and stood wondering.

The party set out. Mary saw how little his disciples understood, how they were both thrilled and frightened by the prodigy. Perhaps a word of hers would help them adjust to this son of thirty years, and make his task a little easier.

What ever lay in store for him, and for them all?

Part Three

SHEEP AND GOATS

1

The trek to Capernaum—even to the overnight in the fields—was a foretaste of the life these men were fated to know with their new Master. Distances were never great—Israel is some 150 miles from Dan to Beersheba—and he rarely crossed its borders, or went farther south than Jerusalem. It was, in the main, to the hundreds of towns and villages in Galilee and Judea that he would carry his message, and always on foot—more than once would his disciples eye with envy a poor man astride an ass.

On that first journey they trudged east across the highlands of Galilee until they stood on the bluff of the Jordan rift. Far below lay the sky-blue waters of the Sea of Galilee, silvered along the far shore where light cascaded down from a luminous cloud. Beyond, the mountains rose in an ascending series of ridges, their purple ranks fading into the distant haze.

Orchards of fruit and nut trees blanketed the slopes far below. The plain fronting the lake was tilled and planted wherever no house or town stood. Near them a brown chameleon slithered down a tree and crossed their path, scouting them with its left eye, while its right examined the path ahead. Donning the hue of the verdant grasses, it disappeared among the windswept tufts. A breeze wafted to their nostrils the pungent fragrance of the ripening oranges peeping through the thick green foliage. When they reached the grove, the Rabbi selected a full, ripe fruit, and the others followed suit.

"The crop"—Peter's voice was thick from the wedge of

fruit in his cavernous mouth—"looks ripe. I hope they have enough field hands to bring it in."

Jesus looked thoughtful. "The crop is ripe —it'll spoil soon. Pray for many laborers."

"No, Rabbi . . ." Peter broke off when the Master dropped the fruit he held, took his mother's hand, and strode rapidly down the hillside, sending a flock of birds fanning into the air. "Oranges last a long time on the trees," Peter growled to himself, "but he knows that. What did he mean?"

As they descended, the smell and feel of the moist air greeted Peter like an old friend after the dry air of the uplands. How good the lake looked. From above it seemed smooth as glass but here it rippled the way living water should—teased by the breezes into crinkled patches, and breaking in splashing waves against the rocks offshore. How was the fishing? he wondered. He missed the feel of the soggy net and the gleam of the struggling fish—and the sweet aroma as they browned in the fire. People living far from water didn't know how fish could taste. Well, it wouldn't be long now. They had to eat. He wondered how his mother-in-law, Hannah, was faring by herself.

Two hours later that Sunday afternoon, they entered the bustling town of Capernaum and received a gracious welcome from Hannah. Knowing her homey ways, Peter was surprised at the deference she showed the Master—even before she heard what had happened at Cana. She was one of the first to sense his holiness, believe his message, and love him.

"Did you hear," Hannah asked the next morning, "that the Baptizer has left Bethany-beyond-Jordan? He's baptizing at Aenon."

"It's time for us to go," was the Master's reaction. "Hannah, put up a little food for our journey." He kissed his mother goodbye, and traveled south on the road flanking the lake and the river. Three days later they tramped into Jericho, bought food, and crossed to Bethany-beyond-Jordan. There they encamped. He began to announce the kingdom of God, and crowds gathered. His disciples did the baptizing.

A day came when the Master said, "The Passover's fast approaching. We leave for the Holy City."

In Jericho, the little band joined a pilgrim caravan going

84

up to Jerusalem for the high holy days. On the ascent of the mountain road, the spring warmth of the Jordan rift—some thousand feet below sea level—yielded to the chill air of the heights. Here the early spring flowers which had already blossomed and faded along the flanks of the river were only beginning to bud.

Not far into their journey the Master said, "Peter, we'll mix with the sheep to learn their needs." Accelerating their pace, they passed among the pilgrims. More than the usual number had caged pigeons suspended on their backs. The Master went up to one such man walking beside his wife.

"Why carry pigeons all this way?"

The man beamed. "My wife's given me a child. They're for her purification." He took her hand proudly.

"Why not buy when you arrive?"

The man's countenance fell. "You haven't heard of the prices? The truth is, it's two years since my wife delivered. The first time we went up, we planned to buy birds in the Royal Portico. We thought that birds bought on Temple grounds would be specially worthy of sacrifice."

"And weren't they?"

"No doubt—but they cost a week's wages. We didn't have it. We shopped around. Got two for under two days' wages—still more than twice what we'd ever paid. The priest found them blemished—my wife couldn't be purified. She's cried a lot since."

"And these birds?"

"A day's wages—and guaranteed unblemished."

"I so want to be fit for the feast this year, sir." The woman looked at him pleadingly, touched by something in his expression. "Only pray that I may."

"Believe me, woman, you will." The conviction in his voice made her stare at him in wonder as he strode on.

"Peter, you look troubled. What are your thoughts?"

"The rumor is the high priests own the shops which drove up the prices—though some say they only rent out the booths and take a commission. Anyhow, since the booths opened about ten years ago, the other sellers around the city have also raised their prices. The only consolation is that so

85

far they've sold only birds on the Temple grounds."

"You fear that will change?"

"That's the rumor. When the booths first opened, the people were scandalized, but they've since gotten used to it. Now I hear that a few lambs will soon be on sale—for the benefit, it's said, of important pilgrims who arrive for the feast at the last minute."

"The Pharisees are strict—aren't they opposed to the practice?"

Peter looked puzzled. "I suppose so—but they're slow to blame the high priests responsible."

"Is there any other reason why the price of sacrificial birds has gone up?"

"Why yes—now that you ask. The scribal theologians of the Pharisees are so strict they've ruled that even a woman who miscarries must offer the sacrifice for purification. The increased demand for doves increased the price. So the poorer women live on in their uncleanness—cut off from the feast."

"How do you think the people should react?"

"I know how they do react—they despise the Sadducean high priests as greedy, power-hungry hangers on Rome. Still, they pay them respect, knowing God's power's at work in their office. And they pity the rank-and-file priests."

"They see them as victims too?"

"They see them go hungry—the high priests sometimes lay hold of the portions of the sacrificial animals due them—and even send the Temple police to take by force the hides belonging to them. The people gossip about these things all the time."

"We'll go among the people again."

Coming up to a group of men in animated conversation, they fell in behind them.

"Just think—the Messiah could come marching into the Temple right during this feast." The tall, thin man raised his arms and clapped his hands together explosively. "Just like that!"

"Right, Daniel—and free us all," the square-shouldered man at his side enthused, "the very eve of the Passover—when we were freed from the Egyptians."

"Who says so besides you, Michael?" challenged a man with a gravelly voice. "I'm a realist."

"Some rabbis," Michael rejoined lamely.

"A lot of rabbis," confirmed Daniel. "And they say he'll work miracles like Moses."

"Why not?" Michael was taking new heart. "The prophet Micah promised it—the Lord'll work marvels for us just as he did long ago."

"Wouldn't it be a sight," Daniel rushed on, "to see the Roman soldiers gaping at the Messiah's miracles from the heights of the Antonia—throwing down their arms—and coming out of their fortress to pray in the Court of the Gentiles?"

"Maybe that's what Isaiah foresaw"—Michael's enthusiasm was mounting—"where he says, 'I will bring foreigners to my holy mountain and give them joy in my house of prayer.'"

"If I had a fowler's net," the self-proclaimed realist broke in with his gravel voice, "I'd bag the both of you before you take right off. In the blink of an eye you've done away with Rome. How? By a couple of enemy soldiers seeing a miracle that hasn't happened. And if it did, would Caesar worship too—even if he couldn't see the miracle from Rome?"

"The Messiah'd have other powers to deal with Caesar," Daniel parried, "the way Moses dealt with Pharaoh."

"Come closer to home," gravel voice drove on. "You worry about Rome—I worry about the high priests. If the Messiah ever works his miracles, the Romans might kneel—but will Annas and Caiphas?"

"And why not?" challenged Daniel.

"Because I'm not sure they even believe in miracles. They don't believe in prophets, you know. They don't accept the great Isaiah—or any of the prophets."

"The Messiah will know how to . . ." Michael began, but gravel voice broke in.

"Say, tell me, why so sure of the Messiah this year? Why's the whole country seething with expectation like yeasty dough in the sun?"

"You haven't heard?" Daniel was incredulous. "Just months ago the Baptizer pointed out a man he called his 'successor' or something like that. He disappeared, but ever since the Baptizer's been worked up like a storm cloud. Something mysterious is going on—and if anybody knows what, it's the Baptizer."

"Right!" Michael interjected. "He reminds me of Elijah. Only he never works any miracles."

"Well, when the high priests start coming around," gravel voice said, "I'll know there really is something going on."

"Tobias," Michael said, "I recognize only one high priest. Why use the plural?"

"I too recognize only one reigning high priest—but how do you discount the non-reigning ones?"

"There shouldn't be any. The office is for life—by the Law."

"Tell that to the Romans—who don't respect the Law, and keep deposing our high priests. Since I have more respect for them than the Romans, I let them keep their titles. Besides, the chief priests of the Temple are sometimes called high priests—the captain and the three overseers and the three treasurers."

"Well," sighed Michael, "when the Messiah comes, he'll have to straighten out that problem too."

"One more problem won't matter to him." Daniel brushed his hand lightly through the air. "Not with the power he'll have."

The Master laid a restraining hand on Peter's arm, and they fell back, and rejoined the disciples.

The next day, for the first and last time, the disciples saw their Rabbi threatening physical violence.

2

Jerusalem—the city God has called in its time beautiful, loathesome, holy, whorish—crowns an undulate mountain peak of Judea. As the crow flies, it lies some thirty miles from the Mediterranean Sea to the west, and fifteen from the Jordan River to the east. Half a mile high, it is hedged in by other peaks—one of which conceals Bethlehem, a two hour walk away. To the east, the Mount of Olives rises, obstructing the panorama of naked desert and Dead Sea.

The city is a natural citadel. It is guarded on the east by the gorge known as the Kidron Valley, and on the west and south by the Valley of Hinnom. Not content with this, its rulers have erected a massive wall around the city, and built the towering Antonia Fortress in the northeast quadrant.

The Temple with its clustered courts rises from the vast esplanade south of the Antonia, on the high ground known as Mount Zion. That name was formerly reserved to the mountain spur now called the Ophel Ridge, which runs southeast from the Temple. Upon its towering ten cramped acres once stood the original city, which David took from the Jebusites. Solomon moved the name and city center to the more northern peak, and built the Temple there.

West of the Temple Mount, the city slides down into the Tyropoeon Valley, then rises to the region known as the Upper City—which surges higher than the Temple esplanade.

It was in the Upper City that King Herod built his fort of three towers, and his opulent palace. These structures have since been commandeered by the Roman occupation forces. Pontius Pilate, the Roman governor, is quartered in the palace when he travels to the city from his residence in Caesarea-on-the-sea.

A short distance from the palace, outside the western wall, looms a skull-like rock where the Romans crucify.

It was early afternoon when the pilgrim cavalcade reached the eastern slope of the Mount of Olives. It continued by the road, which wound along its skirts. When at last the city comes into view along this route, the traveler finds he stands too low to have a panoramic view.

The Master parted from the cavalcade. He led his five disciples up the steep path to the summit of the Mount of Olives. Lining their path were vast groves of dark glossy-leaved olive trees, and verdant grasses dressed with wild flowers. Rain had been plentiful this spring.

On topping the rise the six men paused. Across the steep declivity of the valley, preternaturally close in the pellucid air, rose Mount Zion and its sacred precincts. The eye was drawn to the Temple's gleaming alabaster, marble, and golden crown—a materialization of human vision considered a wonder of the world. Beyond, in lambent amber stone, ranged the city's edifices.

Four porticoes of noble height and beauty framed the perimeter of the esplanade. The most regal was the Royal Portico to the south. It reared a hundred feet, a vast elongated cathedral stretching from east to west.

North of the esplanade Roman soldiers manned the battlements of the Antonia. Alien eyes, uncomprehending and hostile, scanned the worshippers. Ugly hovels and disintegrating shops lined the Ophel Ridge to the south.

The Master intoned a psalm and, chanting, the six descended to the valley and turned south, threading through the swarm of pilgrims, traders, and loaded donkeys. Pilgrim attire afforded a survey of the dress of the nations, for Israelites were gathering from the diaspora.

Peter examined the immense grey ashlars of the retaining wall, which shot up a hundred feet from bedrock to the Temple esplanade far above. Four feet tall and forty long, the blocks were finely polished and bevelled at the joints. He marvelled—they must weigh fifty tons—and thought of his own home of ugly, shapeless field stones.

"Look, Teacher"—he pointed—"one stone is longer than my house. Teacher, is it true that the Temple stands on Mount Moriah where Abraham offered sacrifice?"

"Peter, it's time to be gathering our thoughts to enter the holy ground. What have you to say about that?"

"A pilgrim should leave his traveling bag and walking stick outside—and remove his sandals. But not all do it."

"But we will do it." The Master took the lead in silence. The little band kept to the valley road until they reached the Fountain Gate. Entering, they skirted the Pool of Siloam, mounted the Ophel Ridge, and passed through the old City of David with its hovels and its stench. At the top of the great staircases leading to the Huldah Gates they deposited their few possessions and entered.

They were blinded by the sudden darkness. Torches guttered feebly in their sockets on the blackened walls. Up through the tunnel and underground staircase they traveled, ascending to the Temple esplanade.

The sunlight at the exit to the Court of the Gentiles blinded them once again. Towering and shining stood the great Temple. Clustered low around it were the structures and courts dedicated to ritual purposes. Surrounding the complex stood a five-foot balustrade hung with signs in Aramaic, Greek and Latin, forbidding Gentiles entrance on pain of death. Temple guards stood by the gates.

One fleeting instant the Master gave his full attention to the radiant edifices—then wheeled to face the lowing oxen and baaing sheep. The gentle animal sounds were overridden by the human babble emanating from the Royal Portico— the cajoling of hucksters and the cry of money changers and the ring of coins.

The Master seized a fistful of the ropes at hand. He struck them resoundingly against a wooden table. Heads turned—ears attuned to his voice ringing above the din.

"Out! Out—with all these things!" Whip swinging, he tore away the sheepgate—sent the sheep scurrying down the western staircase, and the oxen trotting after.

He wheeled toward the hucksters standing mouths agape. "Leave these holy grounds. No more turn my Father's house into a business house!" Violently he sent a money changer's table spinning through the air. The coins of the nations flew. He raised his whip. "I said go!"

The hucksters sidled toward the staircase—his whip whistling over the laggards' heads. Trumpets blared from the watchposts. Levitical guards came running. Roman soldiers, small in the distance, raced along the ramparts of the Antonia. The guards trotted up to the Master, espied his flaming countenance, halted and circled him uneasily.

"Make way!" The thunderous cry descended from the inner courts above. High priests, elders, Pharisees and theologians came bustling down. Even as they approached, Roman soldiers clattered up.

"Centurion Longinus," roared a mitred high priest, "the disturbance is quelled. I, Annas, am in command. You are not needed."

"That, your Excellency," the centurion returned haughtily, "is for me to judge." He eyed the situation cooly, cast a curious glance at the prisoner, then snapped an order and

91

moved off with his detachment.

Annas turned to the guards. "Explain this uproar."

"That man"—a guard pointed—"drove out the animals, and forbade any trading here."

Annas glared at the Master, face florid, nose pinched and white. The gaze returned was as unyielding as his own. Icily Annas spoke. "Identify yourself. What accounts for this mad conduct?"

"My conduct," the retort came, "condemns the outrage of making my Father's house a market place." He pointed to his and the high priest's bare feet. "You yourself bear witness to the reverence due this place."

"What constitutes that reverence," Annas boomed, "is pronounced by the teachers in Israel."

"Who teach that not a coin of Caesar shall be seen here."

"You presume to teach Israel's tradition to me, the high priest?"

"The Lord himself teaches you—this shall be a house of prayer for all people. And you reduce the Gentile's Court to a market place."

"Identify yourself!"

"Jesus is my name."

"Home town?"

"Nazareth."

"Age?"

"About thirty."

"Trained under a recognized rabbinic master?"

"No."

"And you presume to teach me?"

"Young Joseph's wisdom saved his brothers—who despised it. Youthful Daniel preserved a woman from the warped judgment of the elders. Let the truth be recognized where the Spirit breathes."

"I condemn your action! I forbid its repetition."

"I condemn the huckstering profanation and the rapine of prices charged. Do not, warns Jeremiah, make God's Temple a den of thieves. Know this, warns my Father through the selfsame prophet, that it is like destroying the Temple with your own hands—for destroyed it will be in punishment. Examine Shiloh's ruins—see what is stored up for this

92

wickedness."

"You interpret Scripture like an authority! And act like you have authority!" Annas was shouting. "Yet you lack age, and training and—a mountain man!—the natural authority which birth and culture bestow on our patricians! You're devoid of every fount of authority. I demand to know—by what authority do you presume to override the highest authority in Israel?"

"I too have a question. Answer, and I answer you. Is the Baptizer's baptism from God or man?"

With cold disdain Annas surveyed the crowd. They stood with mouths agape. All would have heard of the prophet. Most would believe in him. To his theologian he growled low, "What's to be said in the circumstances?" He nodded at the crowd.

"Accept John's baptism," the Sadducee purred, "and crown a Messiah—he's clearly preparing the way for one. But if we reject it in the hearing of these religious fanatics..."

Annas glared at Jesus. "We don't know."

"If you can't read the source of John's authority, I will not tell you mine."

"My authority's unquestionable," Annas snarled, "but yours? What sign certifies the prophetic authority you pretend?"

"Destroy this Temple and I raise it up in three days."

"Forty six years it's under construction—and still not finished. You'd do it in three days?" With mocking laugh he looked at the people invitingly, but none joined in.

Eyeing Jesus, he clipped out through closed teeth, "You'll hear further. I advise you—do nothing to precipitate my action. Dismissed." He turned on his heel and left. His party followed. The guards began to disperse the crowd.

Jesus turned to his disciples and saw the look of mingled pride, confusion, and fear which tightened their faces. He sighed deeply. "We'll enter and pray. Then we'll buy the yearling lamb which must die on our behalf—this year."

In your Temple—where consolation should be the portion
—the hostile forces struck. Yet soon in hostile Samaria—
where my disciples trembled to follow—a gushing virgin
spring of faith burst forth to console us all.

In the one place, I raised a hand in threat. In the other,
I showed only kindness—and the crop sprang tall, ready for
the harvesting hand.

The Temple leaders—blind to the sign of cleansing, and
blinding themselves to the sign of John—demanded signs.
The sign of signs—by Isaiah foretold—sprang to my lips.
The high priest mocked—but I marveled—and marvel still.
So meek your plan, so innocent of all violence. Never shall
I lift my hand in threat again.

The Samaritan woman heard me and put forth the flower
of faith—and rushed to share her blossom with others.

Some in the Temple believed. Yet their faith—smaller than
a mustard seed—provided no foundation to build on.

The next day Rabbi Nicodemus skulked in to me and I
scrutinized him to weigh what he could receive. A wispy
old man, dry and cold, rigid of bone and thought, neither
loving warmly nor hating bitterly, cowardly in his fear
of danger and suspicious of what he did not already know—
yet known as an upright man. Satisfied there was hope, I
went to the heart of the matter—"Unless begotten from
above, none can enter God's reign."

The thin face grew thinner, the eyes wary. "The human
race knows of one birth, and the Israelite of circumcision."

"And you—a teacher in Israel—know no more? Flesh
begets but flesh. Does not the spiritual man know that only
Spirit begets spirit? None but those begotten of water and
Spirit shall enter God's kingdom."

We talked further but it was like patching an old garment
with new cloth—he feared tearing. He went, struggling to
have faith but not having it, too imprisoned by the useful
to stretch out to the noble—too grasping of mortal life to
believe that the Father's Son shares out his life.

Reared in a legalistic system, he has grown too small of
soul to make incisive penetration of truth, but cuts only

half way through the skin, and few there are who cut even to the flesh, except the Baptizer, who cuts to the bone. The others reduce to meanness even what is great, but John sees greatness even in those who are small—calling each man to give his extra cloak, half of what he has. The rest, though they discourse on the world, reveal no more than an atom, while he, in dealing with each human atom, reveals the whole world by disclosing love.

For the moment I could accomplish nothing more in Jerusalem. We descended to the Jordan, where the people flocked to us and were baptized. The Baptizer heard and understood that his mission was ending. I rejoiced that he had read the signs so well. Now if I could bring the Pharisees to realize they must turn their eyes to me! To this purpose John spoke out and said, "You know I'm not the Messiah but his forerunner. Isn't it evident that the bride goes to the bridegroom? Doesn't the bridegroom's friend delight to hear the bridegroom's voice and know he's taking charge? He becomes manifest; I fade away."

Thus it was, Father, that I pondered, to whom go next? To my relatives and townspeople? They were not ready. To the Sea of Galilee, ringed with towns of rustic people, sheep without a shepherd, flocks without pasture? Yes, to them.

"We must return to Galilee now," I announced to my disciples' joy. We crossed the Jordan to Jericho, and travelled the Jordan Valley, but as we went, I remembered, Father, how you said to Abraham at Shechem, "On your descendants I will bestow this land." I knew that I must pass through Samaria to make my claim. So when we came to the fork in the road which led there, on it I embarked.

"Rabbi," Simon Peter stayed me, "it would be better to travel by the Jordan, where we will have abundant water. At the Bethshan Gap, we can turn to any part of Galilee that pleases you."

"No, Simon Peter, we must pass on to drink at Jacob's well. But tell me, why do you wish to avoid Samaria?"

"Rabbi, you know it's dangerous! Jewish pilgrims have been slaughtered there even when travelling with a large caravan, and we are few."

"My disciples, this breach between Jew and Samaritan

needs healing. How shall we work to heal it?" The men were silent for a moment—until John burst out: "Rabbi, you may have to call down the power of God!"

"We shall see what is to be done."

Mount Gerizim was to our left behind, and Mount Ebal towered before our eyes when Jacob's well came into view, in the valley between the mountains. The valley was golden with ripening wheat, the prospect marred only by an overgrown patch of mounds and pits which marked Shechem's ruins. Off to the east lay the town of Sychar, not twenty minutes away. When we reached the well, I dropped exhausted onto its stone lip, right in the burning sun.

Simon Peter examined the rope and pulley. The bucket was missing. He peered into the well. "It's all of a hundred feet deep," he reported, his voice reverberating from the depths. "Master, stay and rest. We'll go into town for food and a bucket."

They grew small in the distance as I surveyed the ruins of Shechem. To it had come so long ago Father Abraham, raising an altar there, and later, Jacob, buying a little land and hoping to settle in the town—until his daughter Dinah was raped, his revengeful sons murdered the townsmen, and they took flight.

An age passed before Joshua came to Mount Gerizim, and there proclaimed the blessing of keeping the Law, and beyond at Mount Ebal the curses to fall on those who sundered it.

I waited for her who was to come and she came—a woman from Sychar town. Gracefully she approached, bucket in hand, with a pitcher poised upon her head. She neither spoke nor looked openly at me, but went about her business of fastening her bucket to the rope, and lowering it with the winch. She was a woman of middle-age, whose face and figure still bore remembrances of her youthful beauty, and the tragic marks of love gone wrong.

I gazed at her, mind flooded with knowledge of her life and sorrows; gazed at those eyes and that face whose hunger and thirst brought forgetfulness of my own. The strayed sheep had limped to the freshet to drink, and the shepherd must not frighten her—must lay aside all else to tend her with gentle care.

"Why come this long way for water," I began, "with a well to hand at Sychar?" Eyes widening, she turned to me. Winch spinning free, her bucket scuttled down the well.

"Our forefather Jacob's water is good for my health," she returned and, with an upward tilt of the head, added, "And you, a Jewish man—do you speak to strange women, and of trifles at that?"

"I speak to whom I choose."

"I understand your teachers say, 'To wife and woman-kind speak little. Garrulous talk brings evil—and leads to hell.' "

"Draw water and quench my thirst." Her eyes grew large.

"I hear one of your theologians has coined a new saying— 'Bread from a Samaritan? Better to eat swine's flesh.' "

"Have you heard the old saying, 'All's clean to the clean'?"

"I've heard," she persisted, cranking the winch, "another says"—here she averted her gaze—"that Samaritan females begin menstruating at birth."

"You think sorry thoughts from sorry men."

"I think that a Jew shuns anything in common with a Samaritan—as unclean."

"Extremists only. The rest will share a meal with them, and count them equally in determining which form of prayer to use."

Her pleased smile began to turn ironic as another thought came. "But only men need be numbered, because even Jewish females don't count." She brought up the bucket, rinsed the cup, and filled it to the brim. She hesitated, then proceeded to set it on the lip of the well, so I need not touch her. Quickly, I took it from her hand and drank.

I handed the cup back. "If you knew God's offered gift! If you knew who asked you drink, of him you'd ask living water."

With graceful slowness, she sat on the lip opposite me. A tinge of fear quivering her lip, but the curiosity in her eye prevailing, she stared at me for signs of frivolity or irony. What she saw, she reflected in a deeper, more serious gaze. "You've no bucket, and it's deep." She nodded toward the well. "Some with ear laid to the stones say they hear water running below. Is that why they call it Jacob's Fountain? Do you think it spouted up in his day? But even he'd need a bucket now—and you have none. Surely, you don't pretend to be greater than he?"

"Drink this water and thirst again. Drink the water I shall give, and thirst no more—find a spring of eternal life welling up within."

Into her face old thirsts sprang, and into her eyes many hungers—like the tale of her onerous history. "Sir, give me some. Never to get thirsty, never to have to carry water home—" She could neither fully fathom my meaning, nor adequately express her own, but her trembling lip told me she was reaching deeper than her words could say. She was understanding not my words but me.

"Go, call your husband, then return."

Grief and hope collided in her fluid features. "I don't have one."

"True. You've five behind you, but him you live with is none."

My sorrow was contagious. The grief came first, and she sat blinking back the tears. Then the realization seeped through, and wonder opened wide her eyes—"I see you're a prophet, lord. Our forefathers worshipped on these heights." She pointed to Mount Gerizim. "But you Jews think we're heretics to offer sacrifice outside Jerusalem." Shrinking into herself, she bent low, as if to expose her back to blows.

"Believe me, woman," I returned gently, "an hour's coming when you won't worship the Father on this mountain"—I swung toward Gerizim, and saw my returning disciples staring—"or in Jerusalem."

"I don't understand," she grieved.

"You worship the Father—but don't yet understand. We do—salvation is from the Jews."

"Help me understand."

"The Father is Spirit. The hour comes when true worshippers will worship him in spirit and truth."

Her eyes lightened. "Yes, the hour comes—the Messiah, the Christ, is going to come from God. He'll straighten it all out."

"The hour is here."

Wonder flushed her. "He's come? You know where he is?"

Crisis. Careful I had to be—not to stampede my people. But this poor soul—one chance—was I to risk it? If it spread from this little way place, would it cause harm—or be taken as mere Samaritan superstition and exaggeration?

"I am he," I said softly—not for the ears of my approaching disciples.

She, who had been immersing herself in my face and my presence, rose and bowed. Leaving jar and bucket, she hurried toward Sychar.

My disciples came up with shock on their faces and food in their hands. Saying nothing, they set out the repast, and hungrily devoured it. I took none.

"Master, eat," John urged.

"I have food unknown to you."

They looked at me strangely. "You not only talked, but ate with her?" was the word in their distressed eyes.

"My food," I said, "is doing the will and completing the work of him who sent me. When farmers plant, the proverb says, 'Four months to harvest time.' But look up—see fields already white with harvest."

They looked. People were streaming out of the town, white headgear bright in the afternoon sun. They trooped toward us on the road through the golden grain.

" 'Behold, days are on their way,' " I quoted Amos, " 'when reapers will still be reaping last year's abundant crop, and it will be time for the plowman to plow for the coming year.' Many have sowed through the ages. Now reap this harvest you have not sowed."

The people listened that hour. They pleaded with me to stay on, and we abided there two days. The townsmen said to the woman, "We believed you when you witnessed that he told you all you ever did. Now we've heard him, and have come to know he really is the Savior of the world."

These despised Samaritans had received the witness of a woman and accepted my word without ever themselves seeing one sign. How many of my own people would show such faith?

On the second day of our stay, I was instructing the people on a flower-carpeted hillock outside the town when John, who had gone for food, came back running. "Master, Herod's arrested the Baptizer! If only he had stayed out of his territory, especially since he was thundering against him for marrying his brother's wife."

"At last report," interposed Simon Peter, "he was at Aenon near Salim, in the territory of the League of Ten Cities. It's not under Herod's jurisdiction—the Baptizer's too shrewd to walk into Herod's net. My guess is that an illegal raiding party seized him."

"We must go at once," I announced.

"Where to?" Peter asked, eyes anxious. "We could run for Bethshan, ford the Jordan, and make our way up the eastern shore of the Sea of Galilee into the pagan settlements of Prince Philip's jurisdiction. The people would cross over to us there—and we'd be safe from Herod, Pilate, and the Sadducees."

"The Baptizer has prepared the way. We go north to Galilee."

4

With the earnest folk of Shechem waving poignant farewell, the little band set out, signaling fondly in return until a sweep of the road cut them off.

The road skirts the western flank of Mount Ebal, slopes to southern Galilee, crosses the Plain of Esdraelon, and ascends into the mountainous region of Nazareth. It winds on through Cana and off to the east, curving through the radiantly wild Pass of the Pigeons, and down to the floor of the Jordan rift at Magdala—a town lapped by the Sea of Galilee's sparkling water.

The Sea of Galilee has other names. Called of old the Sea of Chinneroth, it came to be known as the Lake of Gennesaret, and—since Herod Antipas founded the city of Tiberius— the Sea of Tiberius. Is the persisting name of Sea—though its crystalline water is pure and sweet—due to its impressive magnitude, or to some dim ancestral memory of a time when its waters were salty? To this day trickles of salt water flow in from lakeside springs.

The heart-shaped lake, nestling deep between the shoulders of surrounding mountains, is sunk eight hundred feet below sea level in the mighty Jordan rift—creature of some ancient cataclysm. The rift begins not far to the north, at Mount Hermon's feet, and extends south along the Jordan Valley to the great Dead Sea and far beyond to Africa.

Such is the Sea of Galilee's length—half again its amplest breadth—that a traveler may spend two days circumnavigating its pulsing shores. The sky-blue waters, two hundred feet in depth, are fed by springs, and by the Jordan's flow, which originates from the icy outpourings of towering Hermon's melted snows. Having lent its stream to the lake's upper expanse, the Jordan departs from its nether regions, wanders down the deepening valley, and surrenders its flow to the vast lifeless body of the Dead Sea.

At times high winds, sweeping down into the cratered bowl and seeming to gather fury in the fall, lash the lake to a frenzy, terrorizing fisher folk trapped on the heaving bosom.

Warmed by the bowels of the earth, and lying open only to the azure sky, the region enjoys a sub-tropical climate unique in Galilee. In this garden spot, almost every tree will flourish, every crop grow. In the limpid waters, fish teem.

These advantages were not lost on the people of an arid land. Small towns and villages ring the lake, and some ten cities boasting a population in excess of fifteen thousand.

It was toward this region that the little band traveled. In the course of the journey, a time came when the Master took the lead to pray alone. Hardly was he out of earshot when there burst from Philip words he could no longer contain.

"Those Samaritans think our Rabbi is the Messiah!"

"We heard that for ourselves," Andrew returned.

"What do you make of it?" Philip asked. "Is he?"

"If the Baptizer wouldn't or couldn't say," John snapped, "are you going to let ignorant Samaritans tell you?"

"Naomi said he told her himself," Peter interposed.

"No doubt she interpreted him that way," John agreed, "but would he tell her and not us?"

101

Peter threw up his hands.

"Why do you think she was so certain?" Philip persisted.

"I'm best qualified to answer that," Nathanael put in. "I had an experience like hers. She said the Rabbi told her her life's story the first time he laid eyes on her. How could she help but be impressed? It staggered me to hear him describe my thoughts the moment we met."

"It's impressive to meet a prophet," Philip admitted, "but not every prophet's the Messiah."

"Exactly," Nathanael concurred. "I overreacted on first meeting him. I'm still searching for his meaning."

"So are we all," exclaimed Peter. "So are we all."

At Nazareth, the Master's mother joined them for the short trip to Cana. There they sheltered for several days with Beth Ann and Jacob. The morning of their planned departure for Capernaum, a knocking sounded at the outer gate. Jacob went, and returned with an imposing figure robed as a magistrate. His craggy face appeared to be assembled of granite slabs. The severe look contrasted with the gentle manner and the words he addressed to the Master. They came low, like a subdued rumble from some fissure in the earth.

"Sir, come and heal my dying son."

"How do you know me?"

"I was told about the wedding wine on my arrival. I'm a Capernaumite—Simon knows me." Distractedly, he gestured toward Peter, who nodded.

"He is Jehu ben Eliseus, a judge in our city—a kind man."

"My son's dying. The doctors can do nothing, nothing. Come with me, please."

"You people always need signs and wonders."

The magistrate was too distraught to catch the implications of this charge.

"Sir, come before he dies."

The Master scrutinized him. Most telling were the eyes. The glassy look hinted of a dark experience within, as of an unending duel with resident devils plaguing him to loose some primeval urge to subjugate and buffet others. At last he seemed satisfied.

"Return home. Your son will live." The brusque words— they had the ring of an order—shocked the magistrate out of his intense preoccupation. He scrutinized the Master as the Master had scrutinized him. Relief suffused that craggy countenance.

"My thanks, sir. I will." He bowed and left.

The next day Mary returned to Nazareth, and the little band descended the Pass of the Pigeons and headed north toward Capernaum. At the suburb of Seven Springs, a contingent of Roman cavalry with an officer in the lead galloped past.

"That's Mark the Centurion," Peter remarked to the Master. "He's a good man, and loves our people. He made heavy contributions toward our new synagogue. I think he's going to become a convert."

"Good he may be," Nathanael said, "but he'll need luck to escape with his life in this region. Look at the workmen."

The artisans along the roadside had stopped their activities, and were glaring at the cavalrymen.

"You probably know," John confided, "that this region is a hot-bed of the Zealots." The Zealot party, a focal point of the people's hatred for the Roman occupation forces, fielded guerrillas who employed terrorist tactics.

"Mark's an embarrassment to the Zealots," added Andrew. "They claim every Roman is arrogant, vicious, and hostile, but if they were as good as Mark they'd have to change their tactics."

The little band passed the dye factories, tanneries, and potteries located in Seven Springs. These water-employing industries are located here to take advantage of the many artesian wells—the most abundant in Galilee.

They had almost reached the city when a lone horseman charged up, leaped from his mount, and without a word fell on his knees before the Master. It was the imposing magistrate they had met that morning. The Master took his hand, raised him up, and spoke.

"Your son is well."

"Before ever I got home. My servants met me on the way with the news. I asked them when he mended."

"Was that necessary?"

"Not for myself. I'm a man who knows authority. I recognized. yours. The question was for the sake of my

103

household. When I told them the boy recovered the hour you promised it, they all believed. My friend, Mark the Centurion, saw you approaching and informed me. Will I see you, hear you teaching?"

"I will be at the house of Simon the fisherman. You will hear." The magistrate bowed, mounted, and galloped away.

The city smelled of fish, for it boasts of a prosperous fishing trade and a fish-salting industry. It is as well a trading center, strategically placed at the upper reaches of the lake, near the borders of Trachonitis and Syro-Phoenicia, on the imperial highway which ascends to those regions. The city consists of a narrow half-mile strip of homes and shops lapped by the azure waters of the lake. Peter's house lies near the west end of the city, not far from the docks. The men found a warm welcome there.

On the first Sabbath of his stay, the Master attended the morning service at the synagogue, which lies on an elevation a stone's throw north of Peter's house. That Sabbath morning the synagogue was crammed, for word had spread that a rabbi credited with curing a local boy from a distance had taken shelter at Simon the fisherman's house.

The president of the synagogue knew of these reports, and after the reading from the prophets he said, "We have with us a visiting rabbi from Nazareth. Rabbi Jesus, would you address the assembly?" The people craned their necks to see the tall man in white who rose and ascended the aisle. In the silence— broken only by the inevitable coughing—his sandals slapped gently. At the pulpit, he wrapped the tallith around his shoulders, prayed with eyes closed and face composed, and began.

"The prophets have warned you that the awesome and terrible day of the Lord is coming!" He spread his arms wide, as though to embrace it. His strong, clear voice easily reached the overflow crowd at the doors. "Ezechiel warned that your doom comes, the day approaches. Daniel wrote his words of vision and sealed his book in preparation for the end time nearing. Zephaniah proclaimed that it was hastening fast.

"This day I bring Good News to God's poor—the day of the Lord is come! Today, this hour, this moment, his light shines out with healing in its rays! From now on oppressors hasten to their doom. Turn back, or be counted with them. Turn back to God! Turn back to faith. Believe the Good News I bring from the Father! Like a wave surging out of the Sea of Chinneroth to Capernaum's shore, the kingly reign of God sweeps upon you.

"I have much to say to you about the Good News of the reign of God, the end of the reign of evil spirits . . ." Blood-curdling shrieks cut across his words. All eyes turned to the giant reeling down the aisle raving and throwing his arms—then abruptly clear of speech.

"Do you think we want dealings with you, Nazarene Jesus? What have we in common? You've come to wipe us out! I know your identity—God's Holy One!" His words were torn and battered by a wild frenzy of emotion that brought answering fear to all faces. A fleeting moment of silence. Then a little child, who had been wandering happily about the room, began to bawl loudly. As if it were a signal, the people leaped to their feet to turn and gape at the wild man, who resumed his incoherent ravings, and with convulsive jerks tore shreds from his mantle and hurled them about. The voice of the Master rang out over his.

"I tax you to muzzle your mouth and come out of the man!" A terrible spasm contorted the bulky figure, a disembodied scream rent the air, and the man stood motionless. His face relaxed, he looked around at the gasping faces, saw his torn clothing, and said in a puzzled voice, "What happened?" Even as he spoke, the Master reached the weeping child, took him up, and comforted him.

"Saul, you're going to be all right," said the man next to him. "Here, let me help you remove those tatters. It was that unclean spirit again, but this time the rabbi drove him out. Let's go home." These last words loosed every tongue in the room.

"Who ever saw the like?"

"Who is he?"

"Or think he is?"

"Think! He commanded an evil spirit as a lord commands slaves!"

"What other rabbi has that kind of authority? They do no more than quote the traditions."

"I believe in him."

"I too. He talks like a prophet!"

"Aren't the days of the prophets over? The Pharisees claim their office."

"Over? I knew they weren't over when I heard the Baptizer."

"John doesn't speak like this man! Did even the prophets?"

"The unclean spirit called him 'the holy one of God.' "

"Blasphemy! God is the only Holy One."

"Aaron is 'the holy one of God' according to the Psalmist."

"Are you implying this rabbi's as holy as Aaron?"

"Of course not. Do you think I believe unclean spirits?"

The worshippers spilled out into the sunshine, where the more adventurous souls gathered around the Master. One introduced himself.

"Rabbi, I'm Judas Thaddaeus, son of James. Jude for short."

"Why that's a coincidence," the man beside Jude smiled. "Rabbi, I'm Judas, son of Simon of Carioth-Hesron. Known as Judas Iscariot. A trader by profession. I'd like to hear more of your teaching."

The Master scanned the two faces. The trader was attired like a nobleman, and had a nobleman's face, refined of feature, pale, composed, dignified. Handsome—except that the eyes lacked sparkle. There was an opacity about them, as though they were sculptured of stone.

Jude projected the image of a typical robust fisherman— which he was—of medium stature and stocky build. His distinguishing features were a massive chest and lucid brown eyes aglow with such childlike innocence, simplicity, and honesty that it was disarming to peer into them.

"Come," the Master invited, "Take a meal with us at Peter's house."

106

5

Peter led the way from the synagogue past an attractive multiple dwelling to a second structure—older and poorer—which stands nearer the wharves. With his memory of the noble edifices of Jerusalem still fresh, and the distinguished Judas along, he felt ashamed of his house. Built of black, dingy fieldstones, it was thrown together with a number of similar houses to form an enclosed courtyard shared by all the tenants. Except for the one stout gate to the compound, no doors or windows looked out—they would have afforded an entryway to thieves and robbers.

He tried to cheer himself up by attending to nature's efforts to relieve the drabness. A carpet of grass sporting wild flowers ran up to the walls, leafy vines climbed them, and a line of dark, towering cypress trees stood like sentinels beside them. In the distance, the lake sparkled invitingly.

"Welcome back to our royal quarters, Teacher," he exclaimed, flinging open the gate with a flourish.

The irregular courtyard reflected the haphazard size and shape of the individual dwellings. Hard-packed clay lay underfoot, except where a few blades of grass survived near the walls. Playing children swarmed over the bake ovens and grindstones—which were everywhere—and raced up and down the steps to the roofs. The dwellings were generally of one room—none as much as twenty feet long or ten wide. Each featured a single doorway, and one or two windows opening into the enclosure.

"Rabbi, Rabbi, you're back!" cried one little girl. In company with other small children she raced to him and clutched him about the legs.

"Ask us another riddle!" a clear-eyed little boy cried.

"Tell us a story about God," begged another.

"The Rabbi's busy now," pronounced Peter, pulling the children from his arms and legs like burrs from a cloak.

"I am busy—with the children," the Master retorted. "Let us be, Simon Peter." A child in his arms, he sat on a millstone and the others clustered around.

"Rabbi," Judas protested, "I thought I was going to—we were going to—hear more of your doctrine." He turned to

Jude for support, only to find him seated on a nearby oven, his foolish grin showing his contentment only too well. Judas turned stiffly to Peter. "Simon, are you going to show me your house?" Without waiting, he proceeded into the compound, and Peter followed reluctantly.

The Master watched Judas go, then turned to the children. "What," he asked, "goes up and up and never comes down again?"

"Birds!" one little tyke screamed.

"No silly," his older sister scolded. "Eliab, you know they always come down again."

"We give up," came a chorus of voices.

"The stature of little children—until they're as tall as grown-ups." The children laughed happily.

"Ask us another!"

"You ask one."

"Why did the chicken cross the road?" shouted Eliab.

"To get to the other side," his sister replied in a bored voice.

"And now for a serious story," the Master said, "about a father who had two sons."

"Tell us! Tell us!"

"They were named John and Jacob. 'Boys,' said their father, 'I go off on business early tomorrow. Take your nets to the lake bright and early, so we'll have fresh fish for dinner.' 'I won't,' bristled John."

"Oh, a bad boy," interjected the little girl in his arms, clasping and unclasping her hands. The Master laid a comforting hand on her head, and went on.

"Jacob said, 'Sure, Abba, I'll go.' But at dawn Jacob stayed in bed, while John, feeling bad about saying no, went fishing. Now I have a question—which of the two obeyed?"

"Master, Master," interposed Peter, running up. "My mother-in-law is pretty sick. A burning fever."

"One moment, Peter. The answer, children?"

"John! John obeyed!" they chorused.

"Now a harder question. Whom should you imitate?"

"John!" shouted the clear-eyed little boy.

"Wouldn't it be better to imitate Jacob in saying yes, and John in doing it?"

"O sure!" The boy gave his forehead a resounding slap. "Now we'll go to Hannah." The children trailed them as they threaded between two houses and came to Peter's door. The Master entered. The flickering oil lamp little helped the dim light coming into the room, so he walked to the far side of her mat, allowing the light from the door to fall on her.

Her face was flushed with fever, her eyes aglint—but as she recognized him, he saw another light shine out.

He took her by the hand, and drew her up without a word. She understood at once, and struggled to rise—she was a big, heavy woman. In moments she was on her feet, talking matter-of-factly.

"You men must be hungry. I've lain down on the job long enough, haven't I?"

Peter's mouth fell open. He stared at her, approached her, and laid the palm of his big hand on her forehead. "Why, the fever's gone. How do you feel?"

"Right good."

"Master"—Peter spun toward him—"you cured her!"

The children at the door took up the cry. "He cured her!" They flew in all directions screaming the phrase.

"If you men," Hannah said, "will get ready for our Sabbath meal, I'll bring the prepared food out to the courtyard."

Before Hannah could follow through, a neighbor woman popped in. "The children said you're feeling better."

"I'm well, Leah."

"How did it happen?"

"He took my hand, helped me up, and the fever's gone."

"That's what the children said."

"Would you help me serve?"

"Be glad to. Where is Simon's wife?"

"Her sister Rebecca is sick. Mary had to go to her."

All that day friends and acquaintances "just happened by," but in moments were asking about her cure. The Master had gone down to the lake.

At sunset, when the end of the Sabbath lifted the ban on carrying burdens, a man appeared at the gate with a sick little girl in his arms. He announced that he wanted to see the rabbi from Nazareth who was curing people. When the

109

Master saw the child with her pus-filled eyes, his lips parted in lines of grief. He took her into his arms and gazed at her father.

"Do you believe I can help her?"

"Please help her—she's been suffering so long." Tears trickled down his face. Using his index finger, the Master touched her eyes, first the one and then the other.

"Abba, Abba, I can see clear! It don't hurt no more neither!" The child reached for her father. He took her, turned to the Master, gave him an eloquent look of gratitude, and reverently touched the hand which had touched his daughter's eyes. Hugging the child close, he went out the door. Peter entered with two men carrying a third on a cot.

The prone man, tied hand and foot, was foaming at the mouth. Low, incoherent sounds were coming from him, but the moment his glazed eyes focused on the Master he shouted lucidly, "I know who you . . ."

"I forbid speech"—the Master cut him off—"Go out of the man at once—soundless!" The man writhed, his face cleared, and he relaxed. "Untie him," Jesus directed. The men untied him.

"Where are we?" the prone man asked.

"In Simon and Andrew's house," a stretcher-bearer explained.

"And so is the rest of the city," added Simon Peter happily. "Master, the yard's full of them."

"Rabbi Jesus," continued the stretcher-bearer, "drove out the unclean spirit."

Peter and the other disciples were hard-pressed to keep order among the people forcing their way into the courtyard. Judas and Jude did what they could to help. Nathanael was absent. He had remained in Cana to visit relatives, and was due to return in a day or two.

One after the other, the sick were brought to the Master, and he healed many. It was well after midnight before they stopped coming. Simon Peter thrust the last hangers-on through the outer gate. "Go home now! We're exhausted. It's enough for one day." When everyone had gone, including Jude and Judas, Hannah went to bed, and the five men sat together in silence for a while, sorting out their thoughts.

110

It was difficult for the disciples to grasp what had happened. After the first few healings, a kind of routine had set in, though deep down a current of excitement continued to agitate them. Now, as they reflected on the whole day, the wonder of it began to register anew. But as they sat in repose, fatigue also made its full claim.

"Rabbi," Peter said at length, "I'm all in, so if you'll excuse me, I'm going to take a little walk in the woods, and then go to bed. Hannah has laid out our mats."

Simon Peter awoke just after sunrise, to the sound of children's voices, and the morning round of little Barak's loud bawling. As usual, his father was commanding him to be quiet in the emotionally explosive voice that upset him the more. Peter discovered that the Master was already gone from his mat. He awakened the others, and when they had dressed, he called to Hannah in the women's quarters behind the curtain.

"It's safe for you to come out now, Hannah."

"I've been waiting to get your breakfast," she called back. "Good morning Rabbi! Good morning everyone!"

"The Rabbi's not here," Peter said. "I didn't expect him to awaken early after that workout. Has anyone seen him?"

"I stirred awake sometime before dawn," Andrew answered, "and he was gone."

When breakfast was ready, the Master had still not appeared, and people already crowded around the gate to see him, Jude and Judas among them. "Men," Peter announced, "we'll just have to go out and find him. Hannah, hold breakfast."

When they had explained to the crowd that Jesus was gone but they would fetch him, Peter asked the others, "Where do you think he is?"

"If he went out to pray undisturbed," John reasoned, "he wouldn't go south toward the tradesmen's area, or down to the docks where he'd meet the returning fishermen. He'd take the road north, and head up one of the first paths leading into the hills." Some distance along the second path they found him—atop a hillock, obscured by the tall grass and the underbrush, kneeling in prayer.

"Shalom! Shalom!" he greeted them, rising as they

111

approached. "Boker tov—Good morning. Are you rested?"

"Rabbi, everybody's looking for you," Simon announced.

"My disciples, we depart to announce the Good News to the little market towns round about. That's why I have been sent."

"Teacher, I'm coming with you," Judas declared.

"Judas Iscariot, to faith I call you, but not to discipleship. I have chosen my five. That will suffice for now."

"But Rabbi, I've seen only four. I thought I'd make the fifth." He looked unconsciously at Jude.

"The fifth—Nathanael—is visiting his family. Do you come often to Capernaum?"

"Monthly."

"When you return, inquire at the house. Then we shall see. Jude, since you reside here, come to me on our return."

"I was hoping—thank you, Master," Jude replied.

"Come and eat now, Rabbi," Peter urged.

"No, Peter, we leave at once."

"Hannah has breakfast!"

"Judas, tell Hannah we went on. She will understand."

They took the road north, up the high bluff overhanging the lake in the region of the town of Corozain. After some little distance, the Master looked back. Judas was stalking into town; Jude was standing dejectedly in the middle of the road, looking after them forlornly.

"Shalom!" the Master called. "We shall return!"

6

We made our ascent to the bluff overlooking the Sea of Galilee, and gazed down on the whole region. On all sides the centers of human habitation—towns on mountain slopes, towns on hill tops, towns in shaded valleys. Each separate, yet all sharing one life through the unseen pulse of social relationship and commerce. How like each individual inhabitant—pridefully distinct, yet intertwined with family, friend and citizen. But, O Father, when blight spreads down the joining tendrils! Then vines and shoots are all one inseparable tangle of sickness.

How much sickness I see—how ungodly their clinging to food and shelter. The dread of losing these sends their souls' roots into the plot that feeds them and the stones that house them. A threat to these prompts terror, and separation spills the heart's blood. Of earth and one another they have fashioned chains, for he who puts you second is in bonds.

On I went to the towns and the people. They made bold to come to me, but how soon they found their tethers reining them in. Desiring to join me but fearing to break their chains. Longing to sport in the sea of freedom my word disclosed, yet fearing to lose their security. Listening with shining eyes—calculating with divided hearts. Watching me battle their oppressions—fearing to join the fray. What would friends think? What scorn from business associates? What resistance be mounted by relatives? What deadly adders be loosed among their human intertwinings?

They came for their bodies' healing, but how many came for truth and freedom—which breeds terror. Yet plant I did the seeds—only at harvest will the measure of the crop be taken.

To the untrained eye, my efforts succeeded—but already I grieved at what forevision made too plain. Was I toiling for nothing, uselessly spending my strength to free Israel to free the nations? More powerful works must be set in motion.

If grief seeped into me, pity seeped in as well—from the common pulse of our shared humanity. And this too had to be kept from undoing me. I too must struggle—was I not struggling?—to free myself of false claims and the tendrils of conformity. Shall I go counter to my Father's will?

The people had to be resisted. My mission is to obey you, Father, and theirs to follow—by whatever path the Spirit leads. On that path lies my good and theirs.

By becoming one of them I have entered into these human intertwinings blighted by sin, for to that purpose was I sent— to learn compassion and love, to struggle up out of the morass, to conquer and ascend—and, in my flesh and bone man was contained and would be saved.

113

Even that morning, on leaving Judas, I was postponing a problem. I wanted Judas, wanted to appoint and favor him, but he was a man divided. He desired to follow me—and to follow only himself. How hard for the most gifted to give self!

The next day a simple-minded messenger boy caught up with us. "Nathanael's mother is sick. He said he's not coming."

"Is that his only message?" I prompted.

"His mother's sick," the boy repeated, and was capable of telling no more.

From town to village we went in Galilee, and did our work. Two and three days we would stay, and then move on, reluctant to leave, touched by the longing in an old man's face, the yearning soul in a woman's eyes, the youths eager to learn more, the children clinging to my hand.

When our travels carried us to the vicinity of my home town, it was time to announce the Kingdom there. You know, my Father, how I had longed for the hour, and how I had dreaded it. In my affection for friends and dearest countrymen, I longed to give them first what I had come to offer all. But there was cause to fear they would believe nothing, accept nothing—use me to condemn themselves. That was the reason for the delay—to give them time to receive and digest good report of me.

I found it was all of no use. Had I not grown up with them? The news that the moment the carpenter left them he had begun doing what he had never done before was too much for them. They viewed me with open scepticism.

On the Sabbath we went to my synagogue. The official acknowledged my presence only in passing. "We welcome home our fellow townsman, Jesus, son of Joseph the carpenter whom we elders remember, and of Mary daughter of Jacob.

"Today we have the privilege of having with us a distinguished guest from Jerusalem, Rabbi Zechariah, son of Zechariah. He will address us."

At the reading from the prophets, Rabbi Zechariah began the fifty-third chapter of Isaiah. In accord with the custom, he read a few verses in the ancient Hebrew—unintelligible to the people—and rendered a free translation.

"This passage," the rabbi explained, "is about a servant of the Lord who is a sensitive man; in fact, too sensitive, like many of our people, who moan about being crushed by the burden of the Law. This servant goes so far as to imagine that his fidelity costs him his life, that he is slaughtered like a sacrificial lamb. But then he comes to himself and perceives reality—that he had exaggerated his burdens, and that the Lord is in fact giving him a pleasant old age, in the comfort of his home, with his children around him. And so he is a figure of us all. We must not call the Lord's way too hard, or turn a blind eye to our blessings."

My anger rose at this blind and fanciful rendering of the passage, but I waited until the study period to set things right. When the service was over, and the women had gone, the men began the study of the Law, and then I spoke.

"Rabbi Zechariah, your Aramaic rendering of the reading from Isaiah the prophet sounded strange in my ears, since I am quite familiar with the passage."

"You challenge me, young man? Who are you?"

"Surely," I replied, "having heard me welcomed an hour ago you know."

"And how do you understand this passage?" At the question my fellow townsmen fell quiet.

"The chapter," I replied, "describes clearly the faithful servant of the Lord. Like many prophets before him, he is despised, rejected, wounded, and slain. But about him Isaiah says new things. He is a lamb of sacrifice who atones for the sins of the many. And he rises from the dead."

"That is exactly the unlettered understanding of the text I wanted to ward off," the rabbi cried. "We Sadducees challenge anyone to show us anywhere in the Torah a clear teaching that there is such a thing as resurrection. And what is in the prophets must be interpreted according to the Torah because it is unacceptable if it goes beyond!" He had shouted the last sentence, and when he recovered himself he added condescendingly: "But I mustn't be too hard on a rude young man earnest to understand but lacking the rabbinic training of the Jerusalem masters—you do lack the advantage I enjoy, do you not? But for the sake of argument, let us not demand a comprehensive grasp of the Torah. Let us return to the

Isaian text. If I put in your hands the passage I translated, will you point out the word 'resurrection' or the statement, 'He rose from the dead'?"

"I will point out that if you see a man dead, and then see him alive again, you don't need to see the word 'resurrection'!" The earthy men present guffawed at this interchange, and the Rabbi frowned darkly.

"Demagoguery in lieu of scholarship," he shouted. "We have had more than enough insolence for one day. I will now expound the Torah and I want no interruptions."

"And I," I retorted, "want no more withholding of the word of God under the pretence of conveying it." I strode from the synagogue, and my disciples followed.

It was evident that the four could be of no use to me there. I sent them home to await my call.

During the following week I spoke to the healthy and prayed over the sick, but found so little faith that few cures were worked and few seeds planted.

I had delayed visiting my Uncle Yeshua because of the difficulty he presented. He had always been irreligious—a worldly man. A shrewd businessman and a wealthy farmer, he lived in a sumptuous house outside the town. An old man, a widower, childless, he was now bedridden by a stroke. Before I went to him he sent a messenger bidding me come.

I looked at his withered face, with the lips twisted by a stroke, and felt pity in my bones. I had always liked him despite his crusty ways. Now the baggy eyelids sagged half shut, and the skin hung in folds from his jaw, only half obscured by his patchy beard. His work-gnarled old hands were victims of paralysis.

"Shalom, shalom, Uncle Yeshua," I greeted him. He waved a calloused hand as though to dismiss irrelevancies.

"Yeshua the carpenter! I heard you were in town, and I heard of your goings-on. But," he added peremptorily, "I didn't summon you for that."

"What then, Uncle?"

"I have a business proposition to help you get your head back on straight. Like your father Joseph."

"I have all the business I can attend to, Uncle."

"You no doubt saw my inadequate barns as you

116

approached," he went on, ignoring my remark. "Three big ones, all crammed with produce, and the last of the harvest still piled under the sky, with the rainy season not far off. I need more barns. Roll up your sleeves, go back to your carpentering—forget the other stuff—and I'll pay you fair wages and give you a little bonus for speed. I've heard you've got followers. Employ them too. What do you say?"

"I heard," I replied, "that you bought your nephew as a slave—only for the six years which the Law allows you to buy a fellow Jew, of course."

"Oh that—just another mutually beneficial business deal. He enslaved himself to his spend-thrift wife, and will no doubt have to sell himself again when the six years are up."

"Uncle, who promises you six more years? Aren't you concerned about God's judgment?" How I grieved for him and pitied him. "Wouldn't you like me to pray over you?"

"Enough of that stuff!" His outcry was wild, the words warped by the twisted lip. "Leave it to the priests who aren't welcome here! You're of the kingly tribe of Juda—with affairs of the world to conduct!"

"Uncle, have you no faith? Don't you know I'm called by God to what I do?"

"If you're asking whether I've heard the folktales surrounding your childhood—doesn't every Jewish family have its private religious fables? Why, the nation's creeping with expectation of a Messiah! It entangles itself in our affairs like mud in wheels. Forget it and get on with life. Now what about my proposal?"

"I have an alternate proposal."

"All right. Out with it!"

"You're an old man with no dependents, unwell, alone in your wealthy home. Your barns are crammed. Within miles people go hungry and look in vain for work—your relatives among them. Call them, give them what they need and hire them to take the rest to market. From the proceeds be generous with the poor. Your light will shine in Nazareth, and at your judgment your good deed will be counted in your favor."

His eyes bulged with outrage.

"Have you gone mad? Servant!" he screamed to his

117

nephew, "Bring your stick and get rid of this man!"

"You grieve me with your choice," I said. "Goodbye, Uncle Yeshua."

The next I heard—weeks later—he was dead.

My mother invited relatives and friends to a reunion. About half came. The rest were busy. Most I never saw again. At the reunion, when I spoke of the Kingdom, the subject was changed each time I paused for breath. I could do nothing. The worst of Nazareth was stored up for the next Sabbath.

7

Haunting is the chilling memory of that night my townsmen herded me up the windswept cliff to lynch me. Up we went through the pines and over the scrubby ground, higher and higher, past the blighted shrubs and few blades of grass until there was only the treacherous, stone-littered rock, and the whine of the wind, and the ominous black clouds scudding across the full moon, and the thunder and smell of rain.

One last effort had taken me to the synagogue on the following Sabbath when twilight descended and the ram's horn sounded. Yearning for their well-being had driven me to be ready—to dare it—to make an open secret of my mission.

The little room was crowded.

"Since the distinguished Rabbi Zechariah has departed," the head of the synagogue intoned, "I will invite our hometown boy, Jesus, to read from the prophets and address a word to us. Some deem him a rabble-rouser, and I'm a man of peace, so I trust he'll not abuse the privilege."

Unrolling the scroll of the prophet Isaiah, I read the Hebrew, and rendered it in the vernacular: "The Spirit of the Lord rests on me, anointing me to announce good news to the poor, bandage up broken hearts, proclaim

118

liberty to captives, freedom to prisoners—the year of the Lord's favor, with recovery of sight for the blind, and liberty for the oppressed."

All eyes were on me, and the faces, none strange to me, had their say even before I spoke—eyes narrowed in judgment, mouths sour with displeasure, cheeks stony and indecipherable. I rolled up the scroll, and the scraping of the papyrus was the only sound as I began.

"Brethren, my Father is a God of power. He created the starry world. He breathed his likeness into men and women, and began the human family. He lifted Noah above the corruption which he washed away with the waters. He gave wandering Abraham faith in an unbelieving world, and power to see his future homeland and children countless as raindrops. The fratricidal plot of the sons of Jacob against their brother Joseph he wrested to their own salvation. He made sport of Pharaoh's power, swerving it to his own undoing.

"He raised lowly Moses to mastery over men and nature. He is an ever-present help. He made Samuel the power of his word, David the power of his arm, Solomon the power of his wisdom, and Isaiah the power of his goodness. He purged his people of superstition and unfolded his fatherly plan to give them rebirth as his sons—to make them gods, as the Psalmist says. His prophets announced your glory— not to conquer peoples as the pagans lust to do, but to send forth the light of a Savior to free every man.

"The Baptizer called you to prepare the way of the Lord's Anointed by beginning the works of mercy upon which he will set his stamp. And now I am with you."

At this last, sound burst as from a swarm of angry bees.

"Pretty words! Where did he get them, this carpenter?"

"His father worked for us. Does he teach us?"

"He planed my sticking door—his words stick in my craw!"

"Capernaum talks big of him—but what have we seen?"

How mindless and how tragic was this blind refusal to believe the words, the witnesses, the presence, the word in their ears. Summoning them to silence, I spoke yet once.

"Kith and kin to me, friends and people among whom I plied my trade—you know me. What, then? Learn the scriptural warning. Joseph foresaw his glory and his jealous kin rose up like Cain. Moses was appointed leader and the people all but stoned him. Jeremiah was sent with warnings and they brought him near to death.

"Do you take offence at my origins? Abraham was a nobody, Moses a foundling, David a shepherd boy."

This time silence prevailed, but jaws were set in defiance and eyes stared into the distance.

"I do not reach you. Is it that I have never despised being one of you? Have you never heard the proverb: 'A prophet goes not unhonored except in his own neighborhood, among relatives and those of his house?' Does your silence say, 'Do here the mighty works Capernaum reports and we will believe you'? No farmer seeds stony and unyielding soil. In the famine Elijah was sent to no widow in Israel with the food of God—only to the Gentile widow of Zarephath. Elisha cleansed no leper of Israel, only Naaman the Syrian who came with faith to be cured. And I—what faith have I found here?"

"Throw him out!" a carpenter bellowed, leaping to his feet, and they surged toward me.

"Whip him with forty less one!" roared Jason the smith, our neighbor.

"Off the cliff with him!" became the mad cry.

The mob seized me unresisting, with shouting and raving, dragged me close by my mother, and into the darkness. It was far to that precipice, and as it neared, they fell into an ominous silence. On its stone brow there was only the moaning of the wind—as when Joseph stood there long ago to disclose my origins. My voice broke the chilling silence.

"How is the plough working now, Jacob?" The man with the iron grip on my arm looked confused, looked in surprize at the massive hand encircling my wrist, and removed it.

"Is the crib still serving your family's latest arrival, Samson?" The self-appointed warder on my right pulled back his hand as from a fire, and rubbed it as though all feeling was gone. Turning from the abyss, I strode toward those blocking my way. They parted in soundless waves, and soon there lay beneath my feet the road to the Sea of Galilee.

Hold not their sin against my townsmen, Father! Are they

that different from others—from the family that received me next morning when I knocked at their door? They saw a man chilled by the night and lit a fire. The woman of the house boiled eggs, and laid out bread and cheese and jam and fresh fruit and a steaming herbal cup. My townsmen would have done the like, had I come a stranger—and listened as eagerly as did that farmer. Anxious I was, yet never doubting I was safe in your hands, Father, for my work was not yet done, my hour had not yet come.

As that day was memorable for its infamy, that night was memorable for its struggle. I climbed another mountain where storm clouds surged, where the light of heaven was blotted out.The sheets of rain slashed down, the cold of the night fell upon me, the winds roared, but I sought no shelter except your arms, and no nourishment except your will.

I knelt through the night of storm, reviewing my rejection, praying for your guidance. The difficulty of my way had never been plainer.

"Father," I lamented, "when your people hear I'm the Messiah, who will believe? When told to embrace the Gentiles, will they not rage? When I proclaim the Law's fulfillment and surpassing, will I not be cast out? When they hear they must be resurrected through feeding on me, shall I not be called madman? On hearing that I AM, will they not stone me?"

Yet that night my spirit was restored. Nothing can withstand your will, nothing resist your purpose. Your Son and servant must stand ready to march on—even through the doors of death—confident that beyond every trial and every defeat lies victory. I would make Capernaum my base. Its people had been responsive.

Yet from Nazareth, I knew, that hard disease of the soul would come creeping, and other towns roundabout would feel it coiling around their hearts. Then so be it. Have I been sent to Saints? Or to reach out to sinners, and shine on them the light of salvation?

Part Four

THE REMNANT

1

The Master strode down the imperial highway flanking the inland sea and entered Seven Springs. He was eager to regather the five and resume his mission. How wonderful his relationship with them. How mysterious his Father's workings. Dormant in their souls had lain the seeds of expectation, those seeds cultured through the ages by covenant and prophet, and nurtured by saints. Now they had germinated at heaven's touch.

Unconscious of what awaited them, these men had pursued no distinctive ways. To the eye they were like other fishermen —yet fish out of their element, plants seeking their sun, sons in search of their patrimony. Sprouting they had been in body and soul, yet in spirit drowsing, awaiting unnamed forces to stir the sleeping life. Grown men or near-grown, yet somehow like children among men of the world—or men of God among sense-bound children. Living day by day, yet feeling deep down that they had yet to begin life. Waiting for meaning to come—waiting for that something to show itself which would explain the music of the minstrel song of their longing. Their winter had awaited some springtime unknown except by ancestral intimations inherited with their bones.

Then he had arrived and recognized and chosen them. In his presence they had germinated and put forth roots to his stream and turned the flower of their bloom toward his sunlight, as had been planned from of old.

How they consoled him. In the face of Simon Peter he had recognized at first meeting the register of the Spirit, and chosen him—and had gained not only a born leader, but more important, a man grasped in his depths by the Father. John of the farseeing eyes was a soaring eagle whose mind penetrated more deeply into his mystery than any other. Andrew was sound and solid, an admirable man. Philip was no genius, but he possessed a devoted heart and the gift of prudence. Nathanael—he had failed to return and must yield to a replacement. Soon the choice must be made.

Who would it be? Jude? Judas? Certainly not Judas, until the man found himself. Besides, he would like to meet John's brother, James, who had been away. If anything like John, he would be the one. It was time to summon others as well—in a provisional way, without the unique bond reserved for the five. Here is where Jude and Judas would fit in.

Up ahead, the millers were busy at their tasks, their harnessed donkeys circling the millstones they rotated. Flour dust hung in the air, raucous voices and the grating of millstones sounded, and over against them the burning lake cast up the rays of the morning sun rising above the mountains across the lake. The vats of the dyers stood hard by the beach, where a purple effluvium discolored the water. Nearby the potters were at work, their pots, jugs, and vases set out to dry. Black smoke issued from a kiln.

"Look, the rabbi from Nazareth!" a laborer shouted, but the Master did not slacken his pace. Several of the workmen hastened after him, among them the man he had cured of lameness, and the demoniac he had exorcized in Peter's synagogue. The stir attracted the attention of the little boys playing along the shore.

"It's the rabbi who asks riddles!" one screeched. Some came running, while others went flying ahead into town shouting, "The rabbi's back! The rabbi's back!"

The Master scoured the mile-long stretch of shoreline between suburb and town. At length he espied Peter and Andrew busy over their nets at water's edge, their boat moored beside them. A few hundred feet away, John sat in a boat alongside another youth with features resembling his own, intent on mending nets. Nets tore frequently on the jagged bottom stones whenever the fishermen had to resort

126

to fishing close to shore. Commercial fishermen employed nets, and did their fishing during the night, but there was no sign of a catch. Use of handlines and baited hooks was a last resort, and this morning several men stood with handlines in the water.

Peter, looking up, saw the Master, dropped his net and came running, with Andrew behind. "Rabbi, it's good to see you! How did it go in your home town?"

"From now on, Peter, this is my home town. Where I have been welcomed, there I make my home." Peter looked both distraught and happy.

"Is there anything we can do, Rabbi?" he asked. At this point John sped up with his companion.

"Master, this is my brother James." Jesus examined him, a youth of medium stature, with a face chiseled into bronze lines reminiscent of lightning bolts. The look of his face and the rhythmic movements of his powerful body gave the impression of sheer untamed energy transiently quiescent, poised to flame out unpredictably.

"Shalom, James, shalom. I want you to follow me." At these words the bronze lines of James's face radiated fiery joy.

"Done!" His voice caged the same fierce energies as the rest of him.

"Over there," said John, "is our father Zebedee with his hired men." He pointed, and the family resemblance was evident.

"Look, Rabbi." Peter nodded toward the road. People streamed from the town, and others descended from the fields. The first to arrive crowded in close, some boldly fingering his garments; the late arrivals, at least those of short stature, could not even catch a glimpse of him.

"We want to see him too!" a woman on the fringes lamented. The Master surveyed the situation.

"Today," he said to Peter, "we will put your boat to good use." He set out for the water's edge, the crowd reluctantly making way, and climbed into the boat.

"Watch out for the fish hooks!" Peter cautioned.

"Don't go, Rabbi!" a girl cried. The others looked on sadly.

"Launch the boat, Peter!" the Master directed. Peter and Andrew hastily retrieved their net, threw it into the boat, and with the sons of Zebedee launched the boat and leaped in. The people stood in disappointment at water's edge.

"That's far enough, Peter." With the vessel just offshore, the Master rose from his seat and faced the people, who saw with relief that he was not abandoning them.

"You long for me because you long for the kingdom of heaven." Saying this, he pointed to the net thrown across the seat. "The kingdom of heaven is like that net. Simon throws it, drags it, and fills it with fish." He looked at Peter and added whimsically, "Except last night!" The people smiled knowingly. Peter didn't like coming home empty-handed. He considered himself a peerless fisherman.

"The net fills with fish of every kind," the Master continued, "which he and Andrew bring ashore and sort, keeping the good ones, and throwing away the bad. You've seen them many times." The people nodded.

"It will be like that at the end-time, with the angels for fishermen. The evil men they will sort from the righteous, and throw into the fiery furnace where there will be weeping and teeth-gnashing. Do you understand?" Heads in the crowd nodded—among them the solemn faces of little children, and those of Philip, Jude and Judas, and near them a man wearing the tax collector's badge. He looked afraid.

There were housewives in the crowd, and more just arriving. Jesus waited for them to join the throng. "We'll all be hungry before long, and when we sit down to eat we'll find our food the more enjoyable if the women have baked fresh bread for us. We've all seen a woman making bread. The kingdom of heaven is like breadmaking. She takes the amount of flour she intends to use—a good heap of it—hides a little yeast in it, and mixes it well. She shapes it into unimpressive little loaves and puts them in a warm place. And when she returns, lo, they've grown into big, healthy loaves ready for baking. Yes, the kingdom of heaven is like breadmaking. The word of God works in your hearts like the yeast in the dough. Do you understand?"

"Yes, rabbi!" cried one woman, "but when will the kingdom of heaven arrive?"

"Pray for it to come, and come swiftly," the Master replied. "But pray rightly. Don't imitate the hypocrites—praying where their piety can be seen and admired. I tell you, admiration is the only answer their prayer is going to get. When you pray, pray in secret to your Father whose very existence is secret. And your Father who sees your secret prayer will reward you.

"Don't keep repeating your prayer in the superstitious belief that he will answer a prayer said forty times, but not one said four times. Don't imitate superstitious people. After all, your Father already knows your needs. Did not David say, 'Even before a word gets to my tongue, lo, Father, you know it exactly'?"

"Lord!" a man's voice cried, "teach us to pray!"

In the midst of the crowd Judas whispered in Jude's ear. "He *is* teaching them. He's breaking the monopoly of the pious and the learned. He's giving prayer to all. He's liberating religion itself!"

"What do you mean?"

"Why, the rabbis hardly dare let holy men call God *Father*. Our Teacher is inviting the grubbiest sinner to it. He's out to close the gap that separates the masses from God. Rabbis hardly expect saints to be heard. He's saying even sinners are!"

"Quiet!" a stranger admonished. The Master was speaking again.

"If you understand what I've said, you'll pray like this: Our Father in heaven, holy be your name. Your kingdom come. Your will be done on earth as in heaven. Give us this day our true bread. Forgive us our sins as we forgive those who sin against us. Lead us not into temptation, but deliver us from the Evil One. Amen.

"Call God your Father, and live as his child. Treat all as brothers and sisters, children of the same Father. You've heard you must love your neighbor, but can hate your enemy. I say to you, love your enemies! I say, pray for your persecutors— even the tax collectors!"—here the Master gazed at the official with the tax collector's badge and smiled. The latter looked disconcerted. A man about thirty, named Matthew, he had an intellectual face gone to flab, and haunted eyes.

129

"Don't you see," the Master went on, "that only then will you be God's true son or daughter? Doesn't he send that needed rain on the field of the just as well as the unjust farmer? Doesn't he send fish into the nets of the dishonest fisherman as well as the honest one—I'm not discussing you, Simon Peter!" The people laughed delightedly.

"You'll have to lower your prices, Peter!" a fish vender who bought from Peter shouted.

"If you love only those who love back do you deserve anything for that? Don't tax collectors do as much?" He smiled broadly at the tax collector, who managed to smile back. "You've heard it was written: 'An eye for an eye, and a tooth for a tooth.' But I'm here to teach you to be as kind as your heavenly Father. If someone strikes you on one cheek, turn to him the other also. If he forces you to go one mile, go two. If he sues you and is awarded your tunic, give him your cloak as well. Give to one who begs, and loan to one who asks to borrow. In short, become perfect as your heavenly Father is perfect."

"This shocks me!" To Jude, Judas' hoarse whisper sounded outraged as well. "It's one thing to call virtuous men like ourselves to such aspirations, but how realistic is it to exact them of common folk? Who is he, to dare demand so much more than Moses?"

The Master sat, and Peter leaned over to him confidentially. "Teacher, just look at the thoughtful faces of those folk." He nodded toward the shore with a jerk of his head. "You sure have the knack of touching hearts. And I admire your healing touch too. Did you heal many in Nazareth?"

"No." The Master stared hard at Peter. "No faith."

"You mentioned our next meal," Peter went on musingly. "Unfortunately, your healing touch won't put food on the table. We're out of fish."

"Then, Simon Peter, call the others aboard and put out for a catch."

Peter only fidgeted. Jesus stared at him, and he finally opened his mouth.

"Teacher, you know how I respect you as a teacher and healer." His tone was patronizing. "But fishing is a different matter. You ought to leave it to the experts. We commercial fishermen fish nights."

"You fished last night."

"Yes, we lowered the nets—and got nothing all night. The fish just aren't forming schools. That's why night fishing is bad—and when night fishing is bad, day fishing's useless." Emboldened by his explanation, he added, "So we might as well forget fishing for the present." He settled back comfortably.

"Simon Peter, you don't understand. We go fishing." The tone of voice sent a shiver through Peter, and he leaped involuntarily to his feet.

"You, James and John," the Master continued in the same tone, "borrow your father's boat and follow." Lithely, the two leaped overboard and made for their father. The Master turned to the shoreline and scanned the crowd.

"Philip! Judas! Jude! Come here!"

The moment the trio approached, Peter jumped into the water. "Too many jagged rocks here. Help me launch her into deeper water!" He lay his own back to the task.

The onshore figures had shrunken to the size of ants when Peter rested at his oars. Without turning to face the Master who was in the prow, he called, "Rabbi, where do you want to fish?"

"Wherever you decide."

"Anywhere will do. Andrew, show those landlubbers how to handle the net." With the clumsy help of the neophytes, Andrew heaved the net overboard, and returned to his oars. Almost at once the prow dipped and the boat slowed.

"The net's fouled!" Peter groaned. "Andrew, up with it! See what the bad luck is." His brother heaved mightily. Silver bodies gleamed in a spray of water.

"Full to breaking! Never anything like it!" Andrew's cry was taut. "Philip, Jude, Judas, Rabbi! Give a hand!" He hardly knew what he was saying.

"You Zebedees!" Peter bellowed across the water, "Help!" By the time the others rowed alongside, the big fisherman's boat was so loaded with fish that the gunnels were riding dangerously low. James and John drew the net, still gorged with fish, into their boat.

Peter looked around like a man awaking from a deep sleep.

131

For the first time he realized what was happening in his life. He had pegged the Master as a healer, but had soon gotten used to the healing routine. The whole tally of healings together didn't fire him up like this catch of fish. Only now had the Rabbi invaded the domain where he, Peter, was master, and knew what could and what couldn't be done—and made it evident who was Master even here. Peter cast aside his oars and clambered toward him over the leaping fish, rocking the overloaded boat dangerously—paying no attention to the water rushing in.

"Peter!" Andrew barked, "you're sinking us!" Peter never heard him. He fell to his knees before the Master, the fish squirming and leaping out from under.

"Lord!"—he didn't use the word often; he reserved it for judges, kings and God—"Lord, keep away from me! I'm a sinful man!"

"From now on, fisherman," Jesus declared in a ringing voice, "you will be catching men!"

They made at once for shore. When they reached it, Jesus stepped out of the boat and strode off. Zebedee came running with his hired men and gaped at the catch. The seven left the boats and followed Jesus. Zebedee shouted after his sons, but they never even heard him.

2

Those mounds of dead fish staring at me with sightless eyes —like all who've seen my signs and not seen me. The throbbing problem of signs—how weak their power to reveal me.

It was good to rejoin my disciples, and yet troubling to see how their faith eroded during my absence. They— tempted to size me up as simply another healer—were using my cures to conceal my identity! To fish Peter in, how necessary that catch of fish. Time will blur its memory, tempting some to dismiss it as a stroke of fortune—but never Peter.

The problem of signs. Becoming one of them, I came to live as all men may, but they resist my doing it—refuse to know me unless I live as no other can.

My signs—insoluble problem. How wrong, those demanders of signs—imagining they solve all problems. Thinking that by signs they shall come wholly to know me—when I, Son of Man, cannot fully comprehend myself—your Son, the I Am, born before the daystar.

How carry men with me on this journey to myself? My Father, you who alone comprehend your Son reveal to me the way to make myself known. Through power, hisses temptation, but you whisper, "No, through weakness." A shiver runs down my spine. My flesh cringes, but I listen with open ear.

The religious authorities coil around me to squeeze out always one more sign—as if it would settle anything! Eyes will never take me in until the heart does. To the heart I address my signs most earnestly—and with the fish, reached Peter's.

The religious authorities, jealous of their prerogatives and weighed down by their responsibilities, demand signs made to prescription—empty signs not told to the human heart. Consideration they deserve, and I show it—but the sick throng me with their needs and pleading that break the heart. Can I, in cold detachment, work my signs? In pity I heal—and what? It hinders my task! They desire their bodies healed—forgetting their sick souls. Passion to postpone their dying deafens them to my call to life.

Healings reveal me, but how many attend to that? Had I not taken to Peter's boat, I'd have been pressured for cures, not words—not word of the true way to life.

The night of the catch, I pondered these things. The next morning, when the leper came begging, I saw the chance of a kindness that would be a guarded sign to the priests—and them alone.

"Simon Peter," I announced that morning, "we continue our tour of Galilee."

"Teacher, do you want to begin with Corozain? I have friends there to put us up." He pointed to the bluff above the lake, and I nodded.

133

As we were leaving, Nathanael came hurrying into the compound. "Rabbi, I'm back!"

"Shalom, shalom. Your messenger cast doubts on your returning."

"My mother was sick—I came as soon as I could. Travelled most of the night."

"The work of the kingdom had to go on. James has filled your place." His bright face saddened in the pre-dawn darkness. "You may trail along with Jude and Judas."

"Sorry I failed you, Master. I'd come along as porter."

We kissed Hannah goodbye, and toiled up into the highlands fronting the northern extreme of the lake. How fair to look down as dawn broke—to see the lake cloaked in the fires of the rising sun, and the boats of the night fishermen still carving their ephemeral paths through the calm waters.

The short walk to Corozain—the man rummaging in the garbage dump, some castaway in hand. He taking the road toward us—head depressed, not seeing us. White spots and patches on his face, quick raw flesh and suppurating wounds, bleached patches of hair and spreading scab. A leper. My heart melting with pity—for his body and his lonely burden of avoiding all but fellow exiles.

John, alarmed by his unlawful approach, seizing my arm— "Rabbi!" The leper—spearing up his head—running off the road. Raising his garment across his mouth—shouting, "Unclean, unclean!" Yet staring, staring—suddenly crouching, gaping, shouting, "I know you—Jesus of Nazareth!" Forgetting injunction—running toward us. "Lord! If you want, you can cleanse me!"

My followers rushing to ward him off. Peter thundering— "Keep your distance!"—with threatening gestures.

"If you want to . . ." His voice trailed off.

Snorting, battered by feelings—reflections of the night whirling around me—My God and Father, to heal every one—why else have I come? To restore bodies to Adams and Eves—and more! But heal one man and generate another obstacle to redemption of the many? If healed—could he be silent?

The Law—priests must examine healed lepers, or outcasts they remain. Could he be relied on to obey? To make the sign serve him and all—by addressing none but them—to allow the authorities a quiet judgment that I seek no glory? In his face, ill promise of it.

All this in an instant—his words still trailing off—I crying, "Of course I want to!" A step closing the gap—reaching hands laid on each cheek—feeling the running flesh. "Of course I want to"—more gently—"Be healed." The flesh growing dry and firm. Face taking on comeliness. He leaping up, fingering cheeks and face and hair.

"You've healed me!"—a shout to inform the town.

"Be quiet! I order you—say nothing to none at all! Go straight to the priest. Report as the Law requires. Witness to the priests, and to them alone." Severe—to that face feverish with desire for glory.

If he'd obeyed! If the priests had received private testimony of leprosy—that symbol of sin—wiped out, would they have realized the Awaited One had come?

Did he do my will? Rather his own! Trumpeting his healing far and wide.

The result? To walk into a town was to be mobbed by searchers after better bodies—not better lives—not resurrection life. I slipping in at night like a thief—or not at all—keeping company with owls and lizards. They had their nests, their shelters—I had no place to lay my head.

People kept coming out to us. The wilderness breathed its calm into them. I managed to speak my heart—and I healed hearts. Here was happiness—but not for long.

3

Joseph Caiaphas, reigning high priest, slammed the gate of his palace courtyard and hurried north down the street that would carry him past the Upper Market to Annas' palace. It didn't pay to keep his father-in-law Annas waiting.

Caiaphas-the-high-priest was the creation of the powerful Annas, and knew it. Once high priest himself, Annas had

135

been deposed by the Roman governor over ten years ago. His successor was ejected after a year, and thereupon Annas had engineered the appointment of his son Eleazer to the post. He too lasted but a year. The then-incumbent governor of Judea was hard to please. Annas had other sons, but they were not yet adequately groomed for the role, so Annas maneuvered the governor into appointing him. Caiaphas.

Caiaphas smiled. He was a skillful politician, and Annas had recognized his talent. He was also a political chameleon, and considered it a virtue. Adaptation meant survival, and he had survived—for ten years, by taking his cues from Annas. He and Annas made a great team. Annas was a powerful personality who could arouse dread even in the hearts of Roman governors. He was also a brilliant political analyst capable of engineering the shrewdest possible compromises, though that was a wasted talent during his own reign. Annas personally could not yield to governors or emperors, being himself the stuff of both. Now Annas briefed him on the proper course in every crisis and provided the political steerage with skill and pleasure.

Caiaphas was jarred out of his reflections—thrown to the ground by a hulking giant side-swiping him with a cruelly overloaded little donkey.

"You simpleton!" he shouted. "Don't you have the good sense to give way before the reigning high priest?" He brushed off his vesture while the giant apologized profusely, but he haughtily ignored him and strode on. No doubt the collision was deliberate, and the giant's apology pretense. He would not have dared to come crashing into Annas that way, but Caiaphas lacked Annas' imposing stature and intimidating features, chiseled like a Greek statue.

The collision was symptomatic of the friction between high priest and people. Israelites revered the common priesthood, but despised the high priests as political appointees subservient to the occupation forces.

The high priesthood—once the honor of Israel. Appointment by succession—in the Zadokite line of Aaron. Possible in the old days—it was a cultic office. But when king and kingdom went, secular power gravitated to the high priest—and foreign overlords took interest. That Antiochus IV

136

Epiphanes—he high handedly deposed Onias II. Seated his brother Jason.

Two centuries ago that was—and the Romans played the same game still. High priest—political appointee. The people scandalized. The Essenes scorning him—shunning his Temple worship as illegitimate. Awaiting the priest-Messiah who would restore everything.

Caiaphas sighed. Sometimes in his own mind he played out the role of the Scriptural high priest: sacred, set aside for God, perpetual meditator on the Law, bridge between God and man like Aaron, participator in the highest holiness accessible to mankind. But for him it was only a dream. How long would he remain seated if he attempted to live his dream? At the moment, he'd settle for walking the streets invested in his official Temple vestments gleaming with gold and royal purple. No scum of the streets would dare collide with him then! At any rate, he should have had his slave precede him in the customary way, thumping with his staff loiterers slow to clear a path. But he had decided that this unexpected summons by Annas showed the marks of an affair best kept as secret as possible, so he wanted no superfluous ears along.

Annas' palace lay on high ground near the center of the city. As he approached it, the Temple rose into the sky radiant and stately, high up on the Temple mount near the eastern wall of the city. The highest slopes of the Mount of Olives were visible beyond, vestured in orchard after orchard of dark-leafed olive trees.

A slave gave him hurried entry and conducted him into Annas' chamber. Imperiously, Annas waved him into the spacious room. It was dark after the brilliance of the morning sun, though the palace, in the Roman style, was comparatively well-lighted by windows. Wavering spears of flame rose from the numerous ornately-carved gold lamps hanging from silver chains.

"I came as soon as I got your summons, Hananiah." Caiaphas liked to use the Hebrew form of Annas' name when it could be slipped in without ostentation, for Annas occasionally emitted subtle signals that it pleased him, at least in circumstances which excluded Romans.

Annas peremptorily waved him to a seat, and he settled into one of the sumptuous chairs appreciatively. He might as well try to relax. Annas was beginning to make him nervous. He was seated in his hard, high-backed chair that had more than a hint of royalty about it, despite its austere style. The man hated soft things, and besides he was cursed with a bad back. He was by nature a stately man, and the rigid carriage his disability necessitated only added to his austere dignity. He was lean and hard, and despite his age had no intention of running to sloppy fat.

Annas launched his dissecting gaze at Caiaphas—a handsome man, in a soft kind of way. Large, wide-set eyes, full mouth, shapely nose and ears, and trim black beard. He radiated a desire to please that was generally ingratiating. Annas could have liked him greatly except for his weakness. Annas hated weakness.

Without preliminaries he began. "We are going to have to deal with the self-appointed rabbi from Nazareth. He's gaining a large following in Galilee."

Caiaphas looked relieved. "Oh?" he exclaimed, as if to say, "Is that all you wanted?" Then he added, "I think you're making a mistake taking him all that seriously. I've . . ."

"In such matters I never make a mistake! I assure you, you'll live to see that in this case. I foresaw the problem when he had the temerity to confront me in the Temple."

Caiaphas wanted to bite off his tongue. It was stupid of him. In these matters Annas never did make a mistake. "Mine was a thoughtless remark," he confessed. "But you said Galilee. Can't they handle him locally?"

"Who? Who is going to handle him?"

"I was thinking of the area governor, Prince Herod Antipas." His answer was without conviction.

"Him? It will take more than that jackal. He was unmanned two decades ago when the Romans deposed his brother Archelaus—and crucified two thousand of our people in the process."

"No doubt you're right," Caiaphas agreed, but hedged his admission—"I was surprised at his recent show of courage in seizing and imprisoning John the Baptizer. He braved the danger of a popular uprising over that coup."

138

Annas snorted. "He was driven to it by his consort Herodias. And she was driven by the Baptizer's denunciations—afraid Herod might in the end become convinced he shouldn't be married to his brother Philip's wife."

"But," Caiaphas pushed, "he was worried about John for political reasons—as we're worried about the Nazarene."

"Worried, yes—but paralyzed by fear."

"Do you think," Caiaphas suggested, "that we can wait for the Nazarene to repeat the baptizer's denunciation? Then Herodias will plague the prince to arrest him too."

"I suspect that's what Herod feared," laughed Annas. "And to ward it off he acted—in his jackal's way. Sent his undercover boys—feigning concern—to advise the Nazarene he'd better skip out before big bad Herod strikes. He reportedly replied, 'Go back and tell that fox I'll leave when the time is ripe.'"

"But he'll have to denounce Herod. He's John's heir."

"He's nothing of the kind." Annas was scornful. "The prestigious Baptizer considers himself this man's servant. He'll not denounce the marriage because he's after bigger stakes—whatever they are."

"Then what's the problem?" Caiaphas expressed as much impatience as he dared. "Why not simply apply our usual technique? Order the religious leaders there to catch him up on his speech, arrest him, and put him out of circulation."

"The problem," Annas clipped out, "is that he possesses the verbal skill to slice those provincials to pieces and make it appear in court—if they ever get that far—that he was administering a beauty treatment. No amateur will trap him."

"You're intimating I must take some action that will not be popular with the people. Yet our political situation is not favorable at present, Hananiah."

"Precisely! That's why we must act—to ward off further erosion. Galilee—a tinderbox since David's time—is so hot for a Messiah to throw off the Roman yoke it's ready to fabricate him out of thin air. If the Nazarene continues stirring the people, he'll have an uprising on his hands even he doesn't intend. Are you content to wring your hands while a schism like Jeroboam's forms? It took a Solomon to

139

delay it, and the Maccabees' forced conversions to reverse it. Joseph, face up to the issue!"

"Hananiah, you know I rely on your genius for guidance. I'm only reminding you that our base of popular support is dreadfully weak. We high priests and our Sadducean party are everybody's whipping boys in these unsettled times."

"Am I ignorant of that? The Zealots hate us for not backing their mad plans to attack Rome with a sling shot. The lay aristocracy blame us for coddling the Zealots. The Pharisees anathematize us for not believing in a coming Davidic Messiah. The rank-and-file priests view us as rapacious with self-interest. The common people despise us for our wealth and worldliness. And the Romans accuse us of inflexible Jewish nationalism."

Caiaphas managed to laugh weakly, but it only made him sound like a man in pain. "You make our position seem worse than even I had realized. But getting back to the Galilean rabbi, let me ask you one question." He hesitated so long that Annas looked at him with suspicion.

"Is there anything to this Jesus? Anything authentic, I mean? I've heard he works miracles."

Annas scrutinized Caiaphas' face with clinical detachment. Fear—he detected fear, and a certain religious awe, and even a kind of lift of the cheeks and the eyes and a parting of the lips that registered hope.

"Miracles?" Annas lifted his eyebrows. "Have you ever seen a miracle of his? Have you ever"—and here the pitch of his baritone voice rose uncharacteristically, strained by its weight of cynicism and scorn—"have you ever seen *any* miracle?"

Caiaphas recoiled. It came as a surprize to him to hear his tight voice persisting—"I've heard there's a former leper running around Corozain claiming Jesus healed him, and eager to give the whole world a blow-by-blow description of the cure. Have you checked the story?"

"That would dignify a delusion with plausibility."

Caiaphas crumpled. "What do you propose?"

"We must muster the support of the Pharisees and raise the issue in the high court."

"And our tactics?" Anxiety gripped Caiaphas' face. He

was usually more inscrutable. This matter was getting to him. That Jesus was indeed a power to be reckoned with.

"We must use whatever means are necessary. It may prove possible to discredit him and enhance our own prestige in the process. We have some shrewd theological spokesmen. We'll propose dispatching a team comprised of experts from all parties, but under our control, to investigate, harass, and expose him, and if necessary impose censures. We may not have to go further than that. We will see."

Caiaphas looked relieved. "It sounds reasonably harmless. It could even be for his own good. But will the Pharisees cooperate? His doctrine seems to fall along Pharasaic lines; he speaks about angels, spirits, and resurrection."

"They'll cooperate. They fear nationalist fanaticism more than we. Their party is far more susceptible to it. Besides that, they're losing unfluence. The Nazarene's usurping their teaching authority, not ours. It's unthinkable he should ever usurp our high priesthood. By now they probably smell heresy as well. Challenge their authority and they smell it right off. They'll cooperate all right."

"That's it then?"

"Yes. Work out a plan of action and submit it for my scrutiny. And one more thing."

"Yes, Hananiah?"

"Joseph, the Pharisees are wrong in claiming man lives on after death and undergoes judgment. He doesn't. And if you persist in thinking they may be right, I submit that you will provoke an earlier judgment—Pilate's—that for some unfathomable reason you're no longer capable of functioning as high priest."

Caiaphas looked startled. "I'll draw up a good, firm plan of action, Hananiah."

"O, Joseph, one more thing about this Nazarene—be careful. You might become a believer."

Caiaphas laughed a hollow laugh. Annas did not laugh at all.

Restlessly she stared out at the bustling little town. Sadfaced donkeys plodded by sagging under bales and boxes, familiar people hurried in and out of the shops, and at the end of the lane traffic was backed up at the tax collector's post.

The town owes its flourishing trade to its strategic location. Flanked on the east by the navigable blue waters of the inland sea, it is delineated on the west by the Imperial Highway. Beyond, Mount Arbel soars, pocked with caves the Maccabees immortalized in their wars of liberation. Its north rim falls off sharply into the flower-decked Pass of the Pigeons, which alone breaches the high cliffs in the region, providing easy access to the uplands of Galilee.

Her mood was out of harmony with the peaceful scene. It found more kinship with the eternal stink of fish blowing on the wind. Boatloads harvested in the night are heaved to the docks each morning. Scaled, gutted, salted and packed, they are sent to market over the lake, the Pass, and the road. That is, they are sent after the snarling exchanges between the fishermen and the local tax collectors exacting tribute for the puppet prince, Herod, and the occupying power.

She stared and thought of her life gone wrong. She was a practitioner of woman's oldest profession. Not that she had begun that way. She had been a respectable married woman, wife of a tanner, who should have been proud of her. The beauty of her face was often remarked on, and the glances of men made any remarks about her figure superfluous. Yet she had been forced to dress in rags like her husband, who was a miser.

His rags by day and his body by night reeked of the foul odors of the tannery and of the dung used in tanning—dung which he personally collected from the farms because he was too stingy to employ a middleman.

She could have endured it all for love, but her workaholic husband rarely used the night for any purpose but to quench his exhaustion.

Her parents had arranged the match, possessed by the conviction that their daughter was a girl in love with love, in need of a mate more practical than herself. Still, she entered his home sure of her powers, sure she could fire him with love. Love meant everything to her—and so her shocked disbelief when she discovered she was powerless to awaken him. He was awakening her hate instead, and at times a wild desire for revenge shot out of nowhere, frightening her.

If she woke no passion in him, she did in other men, and that sped her undoing. She was living in a stormy climate of raging rebellion against life—it had betrayed her—when she met a certain Roman adventurer. An officer in Herod's forces, the young man was sleek and lithe as a panther, dashingly uniformed, intriguing in his foreign culture, and urbanely skillful in enumerating her charms and expressing pity for her plight.

Allured from her bog of depression, restless and reckless with desire for the joys of love, she awaited the day they would run off together. She still believed too much in herself to recognize that he was only dallying with her. Well aware that it was easier to prospect for gold than for a woman of her people to find grounds for divorce, he pleaded the impossibility of going further unless she obtained one.

Ironically, she learned that a dung collector's wife who found the reek of her husband intolerable could obtain a divorce, and she got one. Off they went to Sebaste, and for a time she was fascinated by their induction into the social circle of the prince, though only as hangers-on who intrigued the dissolute man, at least for a time. Pressing her panther to marry, she discovered he had no such intentions, and indeed had a wife and family in his foreign home. Burning with shame and anger, she returned to her own town. There she met with scorn and rejection. It was this and her fury which led her to become a streetwalker. Flying in the face of her instinctive shrewdness, she drank her clients' wine to drunkenness, and endangered her life by ransacking their money belts. It seemed she was paying life back in full by taunting it to destroy her.

In one thing she remained clever. She saved her money. When she had enough, she set up shop, dressed with allure, and attracted some of the leading men of the town, and wealthy traders passing through. Even so, she remained surly and miserable. She liked to think of herself as a woman worshipping at love's shrine, but love had gone wrong—she knew little of love after all.

Later that day the local shepherd slipped in. He was one of her favorites, sturdy of body and ardent of nature. Contrary to his usual good humor, he too looked down at the mouth.

"I'm glad you're available," he murmured. She poured a cherry liqueur into two delicate Sidonian goblets and passed him one.

Preoccupied, he sipped through tight lips, and glanced around the little room. It radiated intimacy and warmth, even passion, so had she made it reflect herself. A profusion of flowers sprang from pots and vases, delicate brocades traced the contours of the couch in silver and gold, and the flaming red and royal purple of the intricate rug rose like vapors.

"Aren't you lonely living by yourself?"

She tossed her head indignantly, resenting the prying yet understanding only too well. When you're down as low as he, loneliness is unendurable.

"I've more company than I can manage. You were just lucky."

"I mean family."

"My parents want me back." Why discuss what he really meant—a family of her own. "They squeeze the passion out of life and keep the pressings. They'd do the same to me. I want to be free, free to find love, wherever it is." Her tone was bitter.

"You must want to raise a family." His stubborn persistence would have been intolerable if it weren't laced with a kindness that touched her, and made her decide to laugh it off.

"Are you proposing then?"

"You know I have a wife and kids."

"If I could wipe out the past, I'd find the right man and start all over again."

"Even God can't change the past."

"Can't he?" Her challenge was angry. If he had to drag God in, why not say, "He's forgiving—makes the past count for nothing. Start over again." But maybe he didn't want her to—she was too convenient to have around! Who really cared about her happiness?

He reached for her hand, and she drew it away. "I'm not ready. I have a new song." He showed no interest. "I've kept it for you," she lied. Picking up her ten-stringed lyre, she plucked out notes and then began.

Come love and whirl through our hearts
With raging fires and fiery darts
That carry us on flames ascending
To fleeting joy with taste unending.

To love we turn with song of fire
And to him give our full desire
To make this passion's day and hour
When love flew on us to devour.

Then once love's full delight we've tasted
We'll know our lives have not been wasted
And so we'll laugh at death and age
And call us each the wisest sage.

He stirred restlessly. He enjoyed her singing, but not that song. It made him uncomfortable, even a little frightened, especially when he saw the color coming into her cheeks and the melting of her face, as though she were already making love. The making of love belonged to the body, not to words. Passion stirred by words was a hot fire without light, a flying arrow without direction, a love without joy. People dependent on words must be looking for some disembodied kind of love. Still, he couldn't fault her past performance, except when he displeased her—he never quite knew why— and she sulked or flew into one of her rages. Then he always wished he had stayed in the hills tending his sheep.

She repeated the words, and he tried to escape them— why did she have to mention death? He tried to block out the words by concentrating on her face. Across the sensitive and delicate features a kind of heat lightning played. The passionate and determined set of the lips gave the distinct impression that, like some goddess, she was set on creating for herself the supreme experience of love which fate had denied her.

He became even more uneasy. In this charged atmosphere

145

he was bound to fail her unreal expectations, and then she would grow shrewish. Or turn into a pillar of ice.

She liked him, but could never accept him for what he was—far too simple to match her complex moods. And worse, he was moody himself today because of the trouble in his flock. He'd come to be cheered up.

Seeing he wasn't responding, she thrust the instrument aside. Without his usual happy playfulness, he was like a broken pitcher that can't be filled.

"What's wrong?"

"Do you remember Eva?"

"Certainly. Your favorite ewe." Any woman would be proud to have him describe her the way he described Eva— her quick intelligence, her high spirits, her beauty—the most comely of all his flock. She secretly enjoyed it when he called her his Eva in the course of their lovemaking.

He sat dumbly, so she prompted him. "What about Eva?"

"She's dead."

"Oh! Was it a leopard then?"

"I slaughtered her myself."

"You didn't!"

"I told you how wayward she was—creeping under my fences, abandoning my rich pastures for the wretched grasses on the dangerous slopes outside."

"You always loved her for her high spirits!"

"I kept neglecting my flock to bring her back. I was patient until she began leading the others astray as well." He threw his hands high in despair, his youthful nut-brown face crinkling in anguish.

"But surely you know how to train a ewe!"

"Yesterday while I was shearing a ram, she escaped with her lamb and two other ewes and climbed Mount Arbel. When I found her grazing by herself, I also found the others— dashed to pieces at the foot of the cliff."

"So their stupidity is her fault?"

"I couldn't let her destroy the whole flock!"

She engaged him with passion because she was drawn, but her heart was hostile to him for what he had done to Eva. When he slept, she found five small silver coins in his money belt. He had them counted, no doubt, but she could deal with that. For one she substituted a brass coin rubbed with pigment to look like silver at a glance—a trick learned from the merchants.

That didn't satisfy her resentment, so she slit the belt and took all his coins. She'd never stolen from him before. When he was leaving, and reached into his belt, he looked at her in dismay. "I lost my money. I can't pay you today."

"Ha! How that threadbare excuse bores me!" Strange how real her feigned anger felt. "Why not tell me your clever Eva stole it along with your precious lambs?"

His eyes opened wide, but he only said, "If you like." Then he added, "Funny how the sewing's given out."

"What! Have I taken to sleeping with paupers?"

"I'll pay you next time—beforehand."

"Your little Eva may not exist for you next time—a stupid wretch who slaughters his best sheep!"

"Had to be done. Soon I'd have no flock."

"Soon you'll have no paramour."

When she said that, he looked so sad she relented a little. "Don't come back without a money belt that serves its purpose." Sullenly she eluded his embrace, and he went away with head bent low.

The next day the depressing recollection buzzed in her head like a swarm of gnats. Why let a wayward ewe interfere with her lovemaking and her living?

To distract herself, she strolled through the town and beyond. The dirty embers of a dying campfire caused her pain, and she resisted the irrational impulse to build it up again. Sighing, she turned for home.

From out of the clay at the approach to the town rose the decaying post inscribed with its name. The sight brought a surge of grief—a woman of her gifts swallowed up by a trifling village whose name few have ever heard, stifled by endless sorrows none would pity.

Suddenly inspired, she began to stare at the inscription. She had once explained to a foreigner that the name meant "tower." Now that name comforted her. It proclaimed that the little town went on occupying the region in proud self-possession—as undaunted by the world's inattention as the

147

mountain towering opposite it. That must be her attitude too.

It was, after all, a pretty town—and a pretty name, Migdol. She perked up. From now on she would ally herself with that name. She would call herself Mary of Migdol. But wait. The Greek form of the name, which was coming into fashion, had a softer sound. Yes, henceforth, she was Mary of Magdala.

That afternoon she waited impatiently for her slave, Naomi, to return and fix her hair. The girl, who had gone shopping, came bursting in breathless.

"Kish the cured leper's in town. He's telling all about the wonder-worker who cured him."

Her heart leaped, and this confused her. What explained it? Certainly not faith! She'd heard of the holy man but her professional experience, which had confirmed her prowess over men—despite her dud of a husband—taught her not to believe in any man. Why, then, this stir of the heart? Deep down, did a spark of hope still burn? Perhaps.

"Oh?"

"He described his cure. It made me feel I was there!" She dramatized the ex-leper's report, like him extending her hands over an imaginary supplicant.

"Did he take up a collection for his trouble?"

"He said he needed it to go on with his work."

"I thought as much." Iron laced her tone.

"He says the prophet never does."

"I'll bet."

"He said the prophet and his followers do accept free-will offerings since they're full time into spreading God's kingdom. They sleep under shelter if it's offered, and in the open if not. They depend on people's kindness for food."

"So his cure taught him all about his miracle worker?"

"Since his cure three weeks ago, he's stood in the crowds round him many times and listened."

"And learned how to sell his product at a profit?"

Feeling the struggle in her mistress' heart, the girl ignored her cynicism. "He admits it's not easy to live the prophet's teaching, but says he's trying. The prophet talks a lot about the only thing which makes giving and taking one."

"And now, folks, the answer to that riddle is—?"

148

"Love." She stared expectantly, while her mistress hesitated.

"Love has many meanings. I give love and take money. That's not the exchange your wonder-worker is talking about. It would be interesting to hear him say what is."

"Oh! Then you're going tomorrow? May I come?"

"He'll be here?" Her heart surged with hope and fear.

"You haven't heard? That's why Kish the leper came."

"Sent by the prophet?"

"No, on his own. He learns his plans and rushes ahead."

"Sounds like a scheme to me. How else would he know?"

"The Master's taken to sending a pair of his disciples ahead."

"Well, tomorrow we'll talk about whether to go."

The next day her slave, pottering about nervously, burst out with her concern: "Mistress, it's time. Are we going?"

"You go on, Naomi dear, I'll be a little late." She was ashamed that she planned to dress for business. If the famous man became her client, so much for hope. If not, perhaps she'd become his. She laughed bitterly, but hurried her preparation.

In the Pass of the Pigeons a grimy little girl with a tangled mop of hair stared at her and, when she smiled, grinned from ear to ear, awakening nostalgic memories of her lost innocence.

She stationed herself at the gate—poised for a quick exit should it prove a bore—and surveyed the crowd. Her clients avoided her, but stared nonetheless. She was provocatively dressed. She had opened the most expensive gift she had ever received, an alabaster flask of perfumed oil from India, equal to its fame. Even for this epic conquest she had restricted herself to a touch of it.

She was yawning from tedium—or was it her subconscious effort to escape the mob excitement?—when a cluster of little boys came sailing down the road screaming, "He's coming! He's coming!" Sound ceased as though a great door had closed, and a distant stir became audible. She felt the electricity in the air, felt her composure rocking like a boat.

Then he was standing in the courtyard gate robed in white. He affected her as though his coming were wholly unexpected. It seemed like the morning of the world. She craned her neck, looking over his shoulder for a glimpse of Eve.

He gazed straight at her with a tender, joyous smile touched with sorrow. In that instant she knew she was Eve—the sordid Eve, still mucking up the world. Blinded by sudden hot tears, she rushed past him out the gate.

It seemed an age before her slave returned. Straining for nonchalance, she found her question escaping before the girl had closed the door. "Well, what was your impression of your miracle worker?"

"Oh! He's wonderful! Indescribable! And his teaching!"

"Which was?"

"Didn't you hear? I saw you come in."

"I left early. Tell me."

"Right at the beginning he was baited by the Pharisees, and lit into them. He said they make a big to-do about little things like washing hands, and neglect big things like faith and love. He said they accused him of keeping bad company because he didn't shun the sinners who needed him most."

"What did he say about sinners?"

Naomi's face fell. "We didn't fare too well either. When we hear the bad news that we have to repent, we don't shed a tear. And when we hear the good news of God's kingdom, we don't rejoice. The great king calls us to the marriage banquet, but we're too busy to go, and send our excuses instead. The marriage banquet seemed to be a symbol of our weekly holy day. At least," she added with an apologetic little bow, "that's the meaning I took."

"Is he staying or leaving?" Mary choked on the question. Bitterness loomed down the tunnel of her mind. Had she let her golden chance pass?

"He took the road out of town, but whether he's camping there or going on I don't know."

"Naomi dear, please hurry and find out."

"I'll do my best." She was happy her mistress had said "please." Her commands were not always gracious.

When the girl left, Mary did what she hadn't done for years. She prayed.

When the door burst open, the happy cry came, "He's staying!" She breathed deeply, and a few silent tears ran down her cheeks. She was grateful the light was dim.

150

"Naomi, see if the lamp needs oil."

"After the bright sunlight, I can barely see the flame. Why look, it's all right. Don't you want to hear where he's staying?"

"Where is your wonder-worker staying?"

"With Simon the Pharisee. You know, his head chef comes here sometimes!" she cried triumphantly. "He's holding a banquet for the Rabbi tonight."

"A Pharisee is honoring him after the critical things he said about them?"

Naomi's smile vanished. "I did hear a rumor that the banquet is not really to honor the Master at all. A team of Pharisees and Sadducees and their theological experts will be there, and it's whispered that the Supreme Council sent them to investigate him."

"Did you hear anything else?"

"One of Simon's slaves said the head chef has been instructed to serve a frugal meal, and to skip the customary anointing of heads. I'm so empty-headed I dismissed it as mere servant gossip."

Mary made a sudden decision. "I want you to slip the head chef a note. While I'm writing it, prepare my bath and lay out a change of clothes."

"You're bathing again so soon?" Then her eyes widened. She put her hand to her mouth, and looked as though she were about to cry. "You're not going to try . . ."

"No, Naomi, I'm not. Lay out the beige dress and veil I wear on visits to my father."

The girl ran to embrace her. "I'm glad. I always knew you were better than people say. I mean . . ."

"I know what you mean, Naomi."

When Mary arrived at Simon's, the kitchen help let her slip in unmolested. She had written the head chef that she was coming for religious reasons, and would not compromise him. Her plan was to honor the wonder-worker by providing the anointing his host so pointedly planned to omit. She would pour a little of her expensive ointment on his head. Passing through the kitchen, she stood in the shadow of the entrance to the banquet hall and examined it. It was like a feast of light. Not only was the wick in every lamp burning, but there were so many! Simon must have borrowed all

151

he could get hold of. At the center of the bath of light was Jesus. Then she realized that the guests were staring at him like hawks. He was on the couch to Simon's right. The upper class had long since adopted the Roman style of reclining at banquets.

Dinner, already being served, was so frugal as to be insulting. Missing too were the flow of conversation and good humor normal to a banquet. Nor did the heads of the guests show anointing. Mary recognized the unique headgear of the Jerusalem rabbis worn by some of the guests. Naomi's whole report appeared to be accurate.

She directed her attention to the wonder-worker, and almost at once he saw her and nodded in recognition. The play of light revealed a face calm and noble—and expressing something more which she could not explain, but which alone explains what she did next. As in a dream she crossed the room, silent tears streaming down her face, clutching her gift to her heart, unaware of the staring waiters, passing the other guests, coming to the foot of his couch, falling on her knees. All plans were completely gone from her head. Bowing over his feet, her tears falling, she took those feet in her hands and kissed them. Undoing her veil, letting her tresses cascade down with her tears she began to towel his feet with her hair. He reached out and without a word laid his hand on her head. A new shower of tears fell. With each tear she felt freer and cleaner, like the time she had run through the rain on the plain of Esdraelon as a little girl.

When there were no more tears but still great sobs—the only sound in the room—she remembered her jar, opened it, and poured the whole of it on his feet, filling the room with its rich scent. She rubbed the ointment on his feet, removing the excess with her tresses, passionately kissing the feet that were bringing her such happiness.

When she looked up, Simon was gazing at the Master in horror, as if to say, "If you were a prophet, you'd know it's no honor for a man of God to be touched by *her*." A heart-rending groan escaped her. What had she done? Had her desire to honor this good man only brought him disgrace? Could she do nothing right with her seven devils?

He was looking at her, reading her thoughts, and he too

groaned in pain. Then he spoke in a voice that reechoed from the rows of marble columns and rang in the overhead arches. "Simon, I want to say something to you."

"Go ahead and say it."

"There was once a man who had a large sum due from one of his debtors, and a small sum from another. Neither could pay him, so he cancelled both debts. Which of the two came to love him more?"

"I expect," Simon mumbled, "it'd be the one with the bigger debt."

"Good. Now compare your conduct to this woman's." He sat up and looked at her. "You omitted the usual courtesy of a footbath, while she provided it with her tears, and the towel was her hair. You omitted the traditional kiss of greeting, but she never stopped kissing my feet until your look froze her. You didn't anoint my head, while she poured costly ointment on my feet, and sweetened your whole house with it. Simon, her sins are many but they are forgiven, for she has loved and loved. There are people with little to be forgiven who have shown as little love." The guests stirred restlessly. Jesus stood up, bent over the kneeling woman, and lifted her up. He looked long into her eyes, then spoke: "Your sins are gone and forgiven."

Loud buzzings and grumblings broke out, and then a voice: "Who does he think he is, pronouncing the forgiveness of sins? No prophet—not even Moses—dared do it!" Ignoring the words, Jesus spoke to her again.

"Your faith has saved you. Go in peace."

She bowed low to him, her face melting. She turned and left, resisting the impulse to run and dance, feeling as if she had just climbed naked from some river in Eden which had birthed her anew. The wonder-worker had done with her past what had never been done. Others had stared at the dirty embers and seen only the sordid, the unmentionable, the irredeemable. He had stirred them and uncovered to all the hidden fire of love. By the new light shed, he had reinterpreted her life. For all practical purposes he had done what her shepherd denied even God had the power to do—he had changed her past.

She felt captivated, enslaved, yet never freer, never more

153

able to do all her heart desired. She laughed for joy at the paradox, while her mind raced. From the first sight of him, her heart kept telling her something she didn't understand. *Who was this man?*

She rushed home to share her joy. Wouldn't Naomi thrill to the announcement that, in his honor, she planned to free her from her bond of slavery?

5

Did ever impetuous devotion rise in fuller flood? A torrent sweeping that room full of shriveled hearts—of religious savants doubting and spying, come not to know but to deny me. Decisively you shamed their scheme to dishonor me through that reverence done me—new and fresh in the human story—lavish gift of a sinful woman.

Your will—which they circled in mincing pretense of doing—she did. Giving it full entry—disclosing, to the seeing eye, that in me which my signs do not disclose as ably.

Her mind fails to know me—even now—but her bruised heart found me out. It believed—was healed—put forth its love. Without signs you conducted her to faith—that gift, fairer in action than a leaping fawn—while so many have not seen me even in my signs that I do not count heavily on my signs.

How you tutor me to see the powerlessness of my powers unless the Spirit draw—and how he draws with the Son of Man!

To clear my path I work signs—and believers weave them into wild hopes that entangle me. Ease they'd have me substitute for effort—a dole to the able-bodied. Shall I rob man of his good?—of the labors that sweat out his sins? Of finding joy in the commonplace—in children and home and marketplace and laughter? Of the evening meal after his work, speaking thoughts laden with time and eternity? Of the joy of man and wife loving in the night, and giving birth to tomorrow's children? No! With these things I shall not tamper.

Selfishness and sin—these are the spoilers—these I would change.

Bodies sicken in a wicked and adulterous society—and my heart breaks to cry out, Bodies, be healed! I do it—they flame with passion to cast off the human—to receive all, to give nothing, do nothing, making empty what you made and what they can make.

If I manifest the Glory too brightly, can they do otherwise? The sight of it makes all else seem but crabbed weeds.

Worse still—show them my power and they will cry for revolution, smashed heads and rivers of their oppressors' blood. How make them see what was promised?—that I am Savior of oppressors too.

The authorities rightly fear that lust for rebellion—fear false prophets. Rightly do they scan my ways—in search of messianic signs. And they'd see them—if they weren't so blind.

So I prayed at Magdala, as we went by the dark road to Capernaum, and slept the night through before word that I was at home got round. Crowds came jamming Peter's house like the full fishnets of his dreams—braving the cold, rainy fall day, standing in the courtyard, and huddling round the door.

Within, those Jerusalem Pharisees and their theologians peering at me from their stools—respectfully allotted them by the people settled on the mats—listening with narrowed lids. Then the scrapings and rendings—the falling clay and wattle distracting every eye. The big fisherman gaping with open mouth.

"Peter"—I smiled—"you didn't mention you were roofing your house in the rain." Laughter—but not Peter's. He leaping up.

"Out of my way! Somebody's wrecking my house!"

"Peter, stay put. You must see this."

The sound of tearing planks—falling clay and rain—daylight pouring in.

Peter shouting—"What's going on up there?"

A shadow falling across the opening—something descend-

155

ing—a cot let down with care. Scrambling to make room—for a young man soaking wet.

A cry—"Kenan the paraplegic!"

Pitying—the Spirit leading—I spoke and measured not the cost—"My child, your sins are forgiven."

On his face, relief—and on the savants', outrage. A Pharisee leaping up.

"Dare any creature be so presumptuous?" His frantic gestures sending a lampstand flying—the clay shattering against the stones.

"Watch it!"—Hannah crying—"Put out the wick before someone's toasted!"

"Who forgives sin but the One?"—the Pharisee ranting unabated. I rising.

"False accusations? Do you say any madman can spout words of forgiveness? Do I lean on words? If I say, 'Get up and walk,' what then? Will you believe the Son of Man has authority to forgive?" To the youth—"Rise, take your cot, go home." He rising, threading through the door, cot scraping noisily on the lintel.

The ensuing hubbub—noises from the roof again—an ancient, scowling face peering down, with screeching—"No peace in our homes! No room in our courtyard! Take your services to the synagogue!"

"Enough for the day"—Peter chiming in—"I have to fix the roof."

I to Hannah—"Dear one, arrange for the repairs."

She—"Then you must go?"

"We leave at once."

The road north—with the five, plus Jude and Judas, and the women—Susanna, Joanna, and Mary Magdalene.

By the little custom house adjacent the Roman military post, the tax collector—he who raptly listened by the seashore.

To Peter—"His name?"

"Levi, son of Alphaeus—also called Matthew. He's under Lot—that officer in the booth—concessionaire for Roman taxes."

So. Matthew—Mattanyah—Gift of God.

He—preoccupied with records and shekels—didn't look up.

156

Features—youthful—not so harmonious as to be handsome. Habitually wistful face—grey eyes—searching look—as for something lost and half forgotten. Sensually full lips—set in a declining curve of sadness. In the face—traces of the classic delicateness of the perpetual scholar—submerging in the rising puffiness of a too-fond feaster. Cheeks pale beside my robust disciples—but strength in the shaven jaw. The tousled hair of Roman cut fully exposing the giant ears so finely carved.

"Levi." He looking up. "Follow me."

Silent communion between us—his expression flashing across fleet changes—disbelief, wonder, discovery, gratitude, devotion—resting in joy and triumph. He on his feet.

"Lot! I'm resigning."

"You can't do that!"

"It's done."

"I'll give you a raise."

"I've been raised."

Walking on—Matthew at my side. Peter running up, gripping my arm.

"You can't make him your disciple! He's a sinner!"

John challenging Peter—"Have you forgotten? You professed to be one too!"

"That was different!"—the others laughing, he earnestly persisting—"I may be a bigger sinner—but he's one of the career tax collectors. Called by the people Rome's blood suckers. Condemned by the Pharisees as hopelessly corrupt—having endless chances to cheat the ignorant."

"I don't cheat."

"That doesn't matter! Who's ever made one a disciple? Master, you'll make unnecessary enemies—bucking the unwritten laws."

Matthew's shining face darkening like an eclipsed moon—"He's right, Master. I'd bring you trouble. I'm a loser."

I laying my hand on Matthew's shoulder—"Peter, what does the title rabbi mean?"

"My master, my lord, my teacher."

"Be taught."

Yet I knew—the weight of Peter's objection would bear down on me too soon.

6

Walking beside Jesus round the curve in the precipitous road with weary step and stomach growling for food, Matthew peered through red eyes at the welcome sight. His home was just coming into view far below, where Capernaum nestled in the lowlands lapped by the upper reaches of the lake. For weeks on end his head had never lain twice in the same place, and they had at times gone hungry—his leaner face showed it. Besides, he'd picked up a cold. Not his kind of life—yet he'd never been happier. Still, thoughts of his own full larder prompted a word.

"Rabbi, may I whip up one of my old-time banquets for you, giving my friends and confreres a chance to meet you?"

The Master gestured toward his trailing disciples. "Can you feed them all?"

"Gladly. You'll come then."

It was a happy feast, Peter mused, eyeing his sparkling Sidonian goblet full of the best wine, which he sipped appreciatively, and he had to admit Levi's friends were jolly. At the tap on his shoulder he turned to the waiter who bent to speak in his ear above the revelry. "Three messengers from John the Baptizer, asking for you." His pulse quickening, he seized John's wrist and beckoned him to follow. Jude saw them leave and trailed behind.

Peter recognized the dust-laden trio, staffs in hand, and noted their distress, especially the shortest, who appeared beside himself.

"Greetings, brothers! What's wrong, Baruch?"

"Just what we'd like to know!" the bulky little man growled fiercely. "It's what Solomon and I came to find out!" He jerked his head toward the tall, ascetic figure beside him.

"What do you mean?" Peter began, then—"But it can wait. Come, first refresh yourselves at the feast."

"No, *that* can wait, with the Baptizer in Herod's hands—a killer when he has the courage! Besides, I don't party with the Romans' blood suckers."

"Did the Baptizer send you?" John asked.

"Yes and no," Solomon hedged.

"He didn't send me," volunteered the third man, whom John recognized as Simon the Zealot, won away from the party of assassins by the Baptizer. "I tagged along to meet the Nazarene."

"What do you mean, yes and no?" Peter demanded of Solomon.

"Why doesn't your Rabbi denounce Herod and demand John's release?" Baruch interrupted. "We asked our master and he didn't know. We reported that your Rabbi was selling some vague kingdom that evaporates when you try to sink your teeth in it!" He gnashed his massive jaws with loud clicks. "He's not coming to grips with political realities! We asked John if he didn't make a mistake—if your Rabbi's really the one he was to point out."

"What did he say?"

"He shouted," Solomon grimaced, "that he'd given his witness and, if we weren't satisfied, to go, ask him."

"So you've come," Peter temporized. Why disturb the Master at his rare relaxation, his first full meal in weeks?

"Answer our questions!" Baruch blurted. "Is your Master afraid?"

"Never!" bellowed John.

"Then why no thunder?"

"Maybe it'd be futile; maybe he's awaiting the moment; maybe it would hinder something more important."

"More important?" Baruch screamed. "That from you? More important than John? What's more important than his life?"

"Eternal life. Our Rabbi came to bring it."

"Your Rabbi's a dreamer! Ours teaches with social clout!" Baruch was a charging bull. "No bribing, no cheating for tax collectors, no arrogance for soldiers—strip down to one coat and give the rest away. And yours? He teaches love, and his love has no teeth!"

"What are you talking about?" Peter shouted, to conceal his own confusion.

"I heard him with my own ears," Baruch roared on. "'When struck on one cheek, turn the other.' The Romans love that doctrine!"

"He works wonders. He heals and casts out demons."

159

"He heals a handful out of an ocean! Meantime, the rich get richer, and the poor poorer and sicker—faster than he can heal, if he does!"

"Taxes skyrocket," Solomon added, "while the Romans grow more arrogant, and the only hope on the horizon is in jail. Yet your Rabbi only says to love and give each his due—even the Roman Emperor."

"That sounds fair," Peter ventured.

"Fair!" Baruch raged. "Nothing's due the Emperor—let him say it!—and cast out the Roman devils and I'll follow too! If he can't do that by his so-called powers, let him be forgotten!"

"You'd mock your own mother," Jude deplored. "We all know rage and rebellion by heart—we don't need to be taught. Give our Master a chance with his new doctrine. It's made some give up their sins and turn over their wealth to the poor."

"You're all missing the mark!" John barked. "There's only one question—is the Master from God? If so, obey. If not, don't. God's our only hope, and his will the only way."

"Right, John," Peter agreed. "Teach the poor to deserve God's blessing and they'll get it."

"I say," countered Baruch, "God helps us help ourselves. Moses led the people to freedom."

"How?" John demanded. "By murderous guerrilla wars? No, by signs and wonders. Besides, how do you know Jesus wasn't sent with a better way?"

"Is Jesus greater than Moses now?" Baruch's eyes popped. "So we shouldn't lift a finger against our enslavers?"

"We should—against our sin and selfishness." John glared at him. "Don't they enslave us?"

"It's all too vague," Baruch growled. "I'll tell my leader what I think of it all."

"Yes, report what you think—not what you see and hear," John retorted.

James saw his brother leave, but shrugged and stayed. If needed, he'd hear. "Andrew, have you noticed the Master enjoying himself?" he asked. "I've never seen him relish so many courses before."

"I never stowed away so much myself," Andrew returned.

160

"I was starving. You're doing yourself credit too."

"I know. Blame Matthew—or his cook!" He turned to catch a glimpse of their host, who was conversing with the Master in high good humor.

A little later, sounds of shouting penetrated James's consciousness and, though he couldn't make out the words, now and then he recognized his brother's voice, or Peter's, and smiled. Those two could handle themselves. He saw the Master cock his ear, gaze toward the door, then give his full attention to his host, and he heard their laughter ring out. Mary Magdalen spoke to Matthew, who raised the silver bell at his elbow and sent its peals cascading until the merriment subsided.

"I have a pleasant surprize. The Magdalene has offered to lighten our hearts with some happy little number."

Mary rose, wearing the now-familiar simple tunic which became her just as well as the expensive wardrobe she had given to the poor. Her new bloom of serenity and joy made her more lovely than ever. "Levi's party is such a fine affair," she began, "that I've made it the theme of my song." James listened contentedly. Her voice reminded him of the sparkling Sea of Galilee. "And maybe I'll dance a little too," Mary went on. "So here is my song."

> We eat, my friends, we talk and laugh,
> And Levi's drink we raise and quaff.
> Unheard this joy of losers, sinners.
> Shall I acclaim us as late winners?
>
> Some new thing is taking place
> Among the sons of Adam's race.
> The good, the bad, sit side by side
> Without a wound to either's pride.
>
> How does this marvel come to be?
> I think that now I've come to see.
> When Jesus came, pride scurried out,
> So let's acclaim him with a shout.

Even as Mary concluded and bowed gracefully, Matthew was on his feet clapping and cheering. When the applause faded, he turned to the Master. "Rabbi, I have a final course

161

for you alone." He rang his silver bell, and while all watched attentively, a waiter approached with a silver tray bearing a bulging sack. "That money bag," Matthew announced, "holds the proceeds from the sale of my house. It will go to the poor. My one regret, Master," he concluded, "is that now I'll no longer be able to hold feasts for you."

"Son of Alphaeus, you have provided me with a perpetual feast." The Master turned to the guests. "Friends, feasting with you has been a joy. May it be only the beginning." He rose and made his way to the exit.

Baruch and Solomon had turned to leave when Peter saw the Master coming. "Baruch! Solomon!" he shouted, "Here's our Rabbi. Ask him your questions!"

"We have a question to ask him too!" a harsh voice broke in, and Peter spun around. Several theologians of the Pharisees stood there. "What we want to know is this," one orated, timing his words to catch the Master's ear. "Why does he eat with tax collectors and others of ill repute?" All eyes turned to the Master.

"I shall answer for myself. The reason is simple. The sick need the doctor. The healthy do not. I came to call sinners, not the self-righteous."

"Will you identify these 'self-righteous' for us?" his interlocutor inquired, head tilted back, eyes slitted.

"I will tell you a parable. A Pharisee and a tax collector went up to the Temple to pray."

"You mean separately, don't you, Rabbi?" Jude asked, and the disciples smiled.

"Within himself," Jesus went on, "the Pharisee said, 'I thank you, God, that I'm not like others—extortionists, adulterers, thieves—or even like this tax collector who at least prays. I fast twice weekly, and give ten percent of my income.' The tax collector, who had stopped just inside the entrance with eyes to the ground, struck his breast whispering,'God, show this sinner mercy!' I'll tell you which of the two went home enjoying God's favor—the tax collector."

"Rabbi," Baruch spoke up. "John the Baptizer taught us to fast. The Pharisees fast too. Yet when I came up, I heard you at a rowdy feast in there." He pointed accusingly at Matthew's house from which the sound of partying still

162

cascaded. "I never hear of you fasting or making your disciples fast," he added.

"Yes," Jesus agreed, "John came fasting, and his critics said, 'He's possessed!' The Son of Man came feasting, and his critics said, 'Look at the glutton and the drunkard!'" Jesus gazed searchingly at Baruch. "Son, I have a question— do wedding guests fast when the bridegroom arrives?"

"Of course not!" Baruch was indignant. "That's the time for feasting. It's a religious duty!"

"So it is now with my disciples. The day will come when the bridegroom is taken away, and they will fast." Baruch stared wide-eyed. "And there is also this—do my disciples live like John or the Pharisees?"

"No, Rabbi, they travel all over. We had trouble catching up with you."

Jesus turned to Peter. "Simon Peter, did you eat yesterday?"

"Once, Rabbi. And once the day before—and not a square meal at that!"

"Were we fasting?"

"We couldn't get food on the journey."

"So you see, son," Jesus said to Baruch, "the new is different from the old. You don't put new wine into old wineskins— you know that. They're hard and brittle and would burst, and you'd lose both wine and skin. New wine, new skins." Baruch nodded.

"Rabbi," Peter reported, "they came from the Baptizer to ask whether you're the awaited one or not. They say you bring not liberation but promises." The Master groaned loudly and in the stillness that followed a gecko scampered across the road.

"My mission is to give life—in abundance." He turned to Baruch. "Find the answer to your question with the eyes and ears God gave you and report it to John—the blind get sight, the lame healthy limbs, the lepers cleanness, the deaf hearing, and the penniless have the good news preached to them. And blessed is he who doesn't stumble over me."

"We'll tell John," Baruch promised. He set out with Solomon but the Zealot stood where he was. "Are you coming?" Baruch called.

"No." He turned to the Master. "Rabbi, I'm not stumbling

163

any longer." He gazed at Jesus expectantly. He was still a youth and his youthfulness would have been enhanced by his hair, cropped short in the Roman style, except that both hair and beard were milk white—as though drained of color by some great sorrow, yet too young to succumb fully to the graying of age. The pale cheeks, brooding eyes, and lined brow further encroached on his youthfulness. Somehow, rather than old or young, he looked timeless.

Descended from the Maccabean warriors, he liked to express his deepest feelings by frequently recounting the story of his paternal grandfather, a great freedom fighter who despised cowards. When the old man, on his deathbed, showed no signs of life, the doctor said, "I'll feel his feet. No one ever died with warm ones." "Perhaps," came the old man's sepulchral voice for the last time, "but some live with them—for a lifetime." Those were his last words.

Jesus eyed the Zealot searchingly. The latter, shaken by that look despite himself, found his right hand reaching down to his side, groping mindlessly for the weapon he had determined no longer to bear. Shocked by such habitual instinct to violence even before this holy man, he raised his hand smartly and laid it across his chest.

"You will now follow me," the Master said at last. Simon nodded slightly, his brooding eyes lighting with a pulse of joy.

In the course of these interchanges the host and his guests had drifted out. "Levi," Jesus said, "it was a good feast, but now we go." He took the road north with his followers, Simon the freedom fighter walking proudly among them.

The theologians peered after them. "Well! He's incriminated himself this time," gloated the one who had queried him.

"He did and he didn't," another brooded. "He seemed to say he was the Messiah—but analyze his express words and you'll find it's all innuendo, rather than the kind of hard evidence needed in a court of law."

"We musn't discuss it," the first man barked, "lest we invalidate our individual testimonies. I for one shall delate him to the High Court. Judgment is theirs."

"Can we at least agree," a third member of the group asked, "that the Romans must hear nothing of this?—or we will all pay for it."

The others nodded.

7

Joseph Caiaphas, summoned to discuss affairs of church and state, was seated in the council chamber of the Roman, Pontius Pilate. Pilate was governor of Judea. He had an arrogant style of leadership that brought Annas to mind, though Pilate suffered from the comparison. He projected a similar forcefulness, but lacked Annas' charismatic appeal. He was too evidently a selfish man, and marked beside by a streak of vindictive brutality that made even his friends wary.

The meeting had gone well, but Caiaphas remained nervous. Who knew when the man would take up his predecessors' sport of toppling high priests?

"So much for current affairs," concluded Pilate, waving dismissal in that humiliating fashion habitual with him. Caiaphas rose.

"Oh, one more thing." The off-hand remark put Caiaphas on guard instantly. It was the governor's habitual technique, meant to be disarming, for introducing the most explosive item on the agenda. "You recall that fracas in the temple months ago, provoked by some Galilean? What was his name?—Jesus. Jesus of Nazareth. I indicated a follow-up was in order, to assess the need of further action." The high priest began to sweat. There was no doubt now—his intelligence service was keeping him posted on the mushrooming of the Nazarene's following in Galilee. Still, he had best bluff it out.

"Yes, we're keeping tabs on the itinerant preacher in question," he said casually. "If it proves necessary, we'll act."

"If it proves *necessary*?" Pilate repeated in lilting tones. "I see. Of course, one man's necessity is not another's. I've

165

heard that this preacher has set to boiling the pot of Jewish messianic expectations."

"You've heard that?" His contrived surprize masked his uncontrived alarm. "Well, you know how mystical my people are."

"What bothers me," Pilate retorted, "is that their mysticism is hooked into down-to-earth expectations. Brief me on this messianic notion."

"I assure you, Governor, it's all very ambiguous," Caiaphas deprecated, "like our murky Jewish history. No doubt you're familiar with our revered King David of a millenium ago, anointed to office by a prophet while his predecessor Saul still claimed the title. Since the anointing was purportedly at God's bidding, it constituted David the Anointed King— that is, the Messianic King. Our word Messiah is the Hebrew for *the anointed one.*"

"I know of the prophet Samuel and the crisis he provoked." That was a signal he'd better put the facts on the table. "And of course, I know that the Greek word for Messiah is *the Christ.* Now update me."

"David supposedly received the revelation that his reign would go on forever in his descendents. In point of fact, his grandson Rehoboam lost the bulk of the kingdom to the dissident upstart, Jeroboam. This triggered the notion that a scion of David would one day restore the kingdom. He would be the Messiah."

"A dangerous doctrine for Rome, is it not?"

"Oh, the notion's been watered down and spiritualized since," Caiaphas gushed. "The prophet Isaiah gave the messianic doctrine a very other-worldly turn. You know, all people were to become one happy family, the wolf would lie down with the lamb, and so on." Pilate riffled through documents on his desk, picked up a scrap of parchment, screwed up his right eye, and read.

"The Lord himself will give you a sign. See, a virgin shall conceive and bear a son, and shall call his name Immanuel—that is, God-with-us." Pilate looked up. "That's from Isaiah, too."

"Yes."

"No doubt he's the God-Hero mentioned by Isaiah in another text—and the Son of God mentioned elsewhere in

166

your Scriptures. It seems your prophets expect God's Son to come in human guise."

"Oh, if you'll pardon me, that's"—the high priest sniffed, enjoying his superiority—"That's an interpretation possible only to those reared in the light of Gentile mythology. Israelite belief has been guided to an utterly transcendent notion of God the One. He has, and can have, no son." Before his words were out, Caiaphas regretted his brazen statement, but the governor seemed preoccupied.

"Reports persist that the Nazarene is working prodigies." The words sounded bored—but did Pilate's hand tremble on the parchment as he spoke them? The high priest studied him—how tackle this one?

"Pardon me for asking," Caiaphas brazened it out, "but have you witnessed one of these miracles? Have you ever witnessed *any* miracle?" He enjoyed borrowing from Annas anonymously. "None of our top-ranking Jewish intellectuals takes the notion of miracles seriously," he exaggerated. Pilate lifted and tinkled a silver bell. An orderly appeared.

"Refreshments for my guest." A slave entered with a tray, and set before each a silver chalice filled with a golden liquid. "*Ad multos annos*," Pilate toasted, and sipped the liquid appreciatively. Caiaphas tasted his. It was a banana liqueur from Jericho. Not bad, but his suppliers did better. He filed a mental note—how to ingratiate himself when next a gift was in order.

"You may continue."

"As I was saying, the notion has been spiritualized."

"So that's what explains the fever of expectation among the common people?" Pilate sneered, "that they no longer expect some strong man—or something more—to come and throw the Romans to the wolves?"

"Well, of course," Caiaphas crumpled, "the ignorant masses always romanticize religion."

"Yes," Pilate sneered, "the way the Galileans romanticized it two decades ago, shedding buckets of blood in the camp of their would-be Messiah, Judas the Galilean. The way the Zealot party he inspired romanticize their wanton murders. Very romantic! And now forego the fancy footwork and stick with the facts."

167

"I only meant to be helpful. I'll boil down the complications. To begin with, we of the Sadducean party—both high priests and lay aristocracy—don't believe in a kingly Messiah. Some of us do await a priestly Messiah. That is, of course, a less damaging idea to Rome." He couldn't help editorializing when it offered a chance to placate.

"That's true," Pilate counterattacked, "only if one forgets that as far back as Aristobulus the First, the high priests began to claim the Davidic title of *king*. Isn't that what drove various lay groups to rebel against the priests? Isn't it what spawned the Essene sect who reject your priesthood? Isn't it why the lay people formed the party of the Pharisees to guard the rights of the dynasty of David and await the expected Davidic Messiah?"

"Partly, no doubt," Caiaphas admitted without grace. "But it's very complicated, as I warned you." He threw in the word "warned" in anger. The governor had a good mentor, whoever the turncoat was.

"Go on." Pilate's voice was edged with steel. "Bear in mind that I'm merely checking my sources."

"Briefly, it's this way," Caiaphas said tonelessly. "Long before David, Moses promised a prophet like himself. Many still await him, but few take him for the promised Messiah. Later, the prophet Elijah was taken up to heaven alive, and his return is expected. Some think he will prove to be the one Moses promised. If so, he will be a forerunner of the Messiah."

"A man like John the Baptist, perhaps," Pilate prompted. The high priest looked as shocked as he felt. Did this Gentile know everything?

"Yes, but none of the official parties agree that John's the one. To go on—later came the prophecies about the Davidic king-messiah. Finally, enemies overthrew our kings and invested subsidiary political authority in our high priest. This escalated the importance of the office and led to new insight into an ancient promise, found in the Book of Deuteronomy. It seems to say that the mantle of political authority would ultimately fall on the shoulders of the priestly tribe of Levi, because of its fidelity at Massah and Meriba."

"It's as usual with double-tongued prophecies," Pilate

168

observed caustically. "Each interprets according to his own vested interests. Or," he added as an after thought, "is there some party which holds that the mantles of priest, prophet and king will fall on the shoulders of one person— like that God-Hero of Isaiah?"

"No. I've told you where the Sadducees stand. As for the Essene sect, they expect all three—a prophet, a priest-Messiah, and a king-Messiah. They have their secrets though, and we've never learned whether they believe the prophet-to-come has already arrived in the person of their founder. As for the Pharisees, some expect a Davidic Messiah who will at once usher in the world-to-come, ending all this world's kingdoms without ever raising a sword. So he's not a political figure in the ordinary sense. He will rule, in their mind, over everyone, since the Pharisees believe in resurrection and eternal reward or punishment for all."

Pilate sprang up and paced nervously. At length he returned, picked up his scrap of parchment, and studied it. *"Ha-melekh ha mashi'ah*, the Anointed King," he read slowly, "is to come in the power of God to smash the heads of pagans and sinners, restore the kingdom of Israel, and enlarge it to contain all who have yearned for righteousness. This kingdom will never more be shaken, nor have an end." Pilate replaced the scrap carefully on the table. "Does my source tally with yours?"

"That's one interpretation."

"Then the crux of the problem, from a political perspective, comes to this—is the new kingdom to be presented in the wink of an eye, or must the Messiah's adherents use the sword?" Completely trapped, Caiaphas said nothing until Pilate's impatient, "Well?"

"I thought you weren't interested in my personal opinion," he temporized. Pilate glared and he went on: "Some of the Pharisees believe the one thing, and some the other. But Sadducees and Pharisees both agree it would be suicide to resist the might of Rome. Therefore, by definition, we label as a false Messiah anyone who counsels war. The Essenes are more of an enigma, but they're so withdrawn from society and politics that their esoteric doctrine enjoys limited popular appeal. From Rome's point of view, they're

169

impotent." At last Pilate seemed satisfied.

"May I consider this session terminated?" Caiaphas snapped, feeling tattered, but slightly redeemed by this final piece of insolence. Pilate did not deign to answer. He paced back and forth, his face screwed up in unwontedly deep reflection.

"One more question. Who is 'the Son of Man'?"

"On that, your sources may be better than mine," Caiaphas breezed, but under the governor's hard stare he yielded. "The term is used by the prophets in different ways, and I'm no theologian. If it's hard to tie down the notion of Messiah, it's wading in quicksand to get at 'Son of Man.' "

"Start wading."

"In some texts it seems to mean simply a man. In others it appears to mean the chosen people." Caiaphas used that provocative phrase deliberately, disdaining the more neutral 'the Israelites.' He let it sink in, then added, "The Pharisees have a carefully guarded arcane interpretation. It's been leaked to me. They claim the Son of Man is a mysterious personage destined to descend from the heavens on mission from God himself—as one who's been abiding at God's right hand without traceable source or lineage, awaiting assignment. Some think he will be the Messiah." It was imprudent, but how he enjoyed letting the whole truth come out—and seeing Pilate's eyes dilate with fear.

"I understand," Pilate purred, recovering himself quickly, and now studying him in turn, "that the Nazarene is using the phrase in such a way that it could be taken of him." An unexpected thrust! Caiaphas felt disemboweled.

"We are concerned about that too."

"Concerned!" Pilate shouted. Caiaphas remained obstinately silent. "Herod was wise to arrest John—though of course for the wrong reason," he smirked. "Let John cool off his camel's hair in a dungeon until his feverish disciples disperse. They always do at forced inaction." Caiaphas still said nothing. "John is dangerous, but John's not a Galilean. Every Galilean is a potential Judas the Galilean—wild, wild-eyed and rebellious."

To be contrary, Caiaphas thought, "Or insuppressible, faith-filled and patriotic," but he said nothing.

"Jesus," Pilate went on, "is a Galilean. He's gathering the

170

rabble. What are you doing about him?"

Caiaphas longed to retort, "Galilee's none of your business!" But unfortunately, he was Pilate's business, and the man knew perfectly well that his influence reached to all Israel. "The High Council has met on the matter," he confessed. "We've sent a team of experts to investigate and report."

"Is the team properly weighted—in our favor?"

"The only one likely to withhold condemnation is Nicodemus the Pharisee. We maneuvered him onto the team precisely because, while his integrity is unquestioned, he's congenitally incapable of deciding in favor of the man with so much at issue."

"Good!" Pilate looked pleased at last. "Put a damper on the fever pitch up there. Mind you, I'm not the least bit interested in your Messiahs. My concern is with disturbers of the peace who provoke political uprisings. They're a nuisance for us and death traps for the rabble."

"And perhaps for your political ambitions," Caiaphas thought insolently. As if reading his mind, the governor added, "An uprising could cost me my appointment. If I go, you can be sure my successor will clean house, from the high priest down." He waved dismissal in that infuriating manner he himself used only with lackeys. He turned and left, seething with such resentment that he thought only distractedly of the problem. He would have to take action. That itinerant preacher! That troublemaker in Galilee!

8

Rabbi Bela stalked the study room of Peter's synagogue, breathing the stale air in distasteful gasps, impatiently awaiting the others. He was well into middle age, and his ponderous figure, already paunchy in youth, was swollen with fat, which further neutralized his unimpressive features.

The door swung open, and Nicodemus entered in his mousy way, piping out his weak-voiced greeting. Strange,

171

Bela thought, how the substance of this man and his voice had evaporated with age, while he himself grew more flourishing in both.

"Rabbi Nicodemus—here at last!" His voice rang out with that majesty which had made more than one auditor gape in surprize to find it issuing from that undistinguished face. The resonant power of it was such that even his peers listened with unwonted attention to his most trivial utterances—though he was not often trivial. A keen mind hid behind the beady black eyes. The voice and the mind had elevated him to prestige even in the High Council.

"Why, am I late?" Nicodemus inquired in his fragile voice, knowing he was not.

"Are you cold?" Bela returned, watching him wringing his hands, which he ceased doing at once.

Rabbi Shimron and Lord Jonah arrived together. Shimron, about forty, was a flaming-cheeked man indistinguishable from the fishermen he served in Capernaum, except for his unfastidious scholar's garb—a typical provincial.

Lord Jonah effected considerable distinction by virtue of his expensive dress, hawk's nose, and neatly trimmed beard. The washboard cheeks broadcast notice of his advanced age. Though the man attempted an ingratiating style, it simply irritated his peers. It was a veneer which peeled easily, exposing the underlayers of irritability and vindictiveness as crude as his corrugated cheeks.

Bela called the meeting to order. "Revered colleagues, you know the purpose of our meeting."

"I respectfully suggest," said Nicodemus, "that here at the outset you formally specify our agenda." He had wasted many an hour at meetings which floundered in high seas of ambiguity. Besides, in this matter conscience was at stake, and he intended to clarify his stand at every step.

"We have assembled here today," Rabbi Bela intoned, "to consider the case of Jesus the Nazarene. We're meeting apart from the investigatory commission to which Rabbi Nicodemus and I were appointed by the High Council, to consider, as Pharisees, any evidence of wrongdoing. We will then determine whether to take preliminary steps against him on our own authority." Nicodemus half rose in protest, and then sank back. The notion of taking punitive action on their own—he hadn't envisioned it, but he had to admit it couldn't be ruled out.

"Rabbi Nicodemus and I," Bela continued "agreed to invite two distinguished Galilean members of our Pharisee party, chosen at my discretion, to broaden our perspective on the issue in hand. I chose Rabbi Shimron because, as a resident of Capernaum, he has observed the activities of the Nazarene. I chose Lord Shallum as a leading Capernaumite—a person in contact with the political implications of our subject. Further, as a Herodian he represents another political dimension of the issue."

Nicodemus climbed to his feet. "With all due respect I protest your choice of Lord Shallum—not as a person, you understand, but as a Herodian, a member of the political arm of Prince Herod. The prince has the same attitude toward ascending religious stars as his father—the king who slaughtered infants because of some seer's prophecy that a future king was among them. Already he has incarcerated John the Baptizer."

"Rabbi Nicodemus!" Bela exclaimed. "No one is asking you to agree with the Lord Shallum's political views. Would you deny us the advantage of having represented here the divergencies within our party?"

Nicodemus sat down. He would indeed like to rule out such immoral representation, especially since this meeting had just been decreed not a consultative but a deliberative assembly. But he was no controversialist, and knew his protest would be in vain.

"If, then, there are no further objections? Good! Let us proceed in the form of a question—what has been observed in the teaching, activity, and manner of life of one Jesus of Nazareth which has raised the questions the High Council is asking concerning his authenticity and orthodoxy? Lord Jonah?"

"Respected rabbis, I'm no scribal theologian. I do not enjoy the privilege—nay the duty—of those such as you, who share ordination, not to the priesthood, but to sacred scholarship—the duty, I say, of making official judgments and decisions regarding religious matters, regarding the

173

very meanings of the Sacred Writings themselves. As a Pharisee, I am aware that our ordained scholars create the tradition that binds and looses us all—that is equal to and in some matters is recognized to surpass the authority of the Torah itself!" He said this with a breathless reverence that struck Nicodemus as slightly exaggerated, although, he admitted complacently as he tapped one set of fingertips against the other, the man knew his doctrine well enough.

"Before you, then," Jonah went on, "I place what troubles me deeply. Deeply, I say, and I say it troubles me as a Pharisee, a man of faith, an Israelite, and a leader of a flammable people. It troubles me as a patriot, a member of a chosen people, a chosen nation. It troubles me as a father and head of a family. Let me begin there. The family is the building block of every community, of every nation, of all human intercourse. And yet this Rabbi Jesus—who is not an ordained scholar—I stress it, he is not. He does not enjoy the recognized authority of your reverences to pass formal judgments in religious matters. He is a carpenter! He has not studied under a recognized rabbi, nor has he reached his fortieth year, the age to be attained before study of the Law and the traditions can be crowned with the mark of official acceptance."

"Lord Jonah, be less prolix," Bela exclaimed.

"I see," Jonah gushed, "that I am repeating what you already know. Forgive me, but see how this appals us laymen! To get to the point, then—this youth of some thirty years, this self-styled rabbi, has neglected the duty of marrying, and has induced married men to neglect their families to follow him. He has drawn them to leave the wives of their bosom and the children of their loins to wander heaven-knows-where. Each of us respects the sacred tradition of our party of faith which lays the heavy duty upon a man to propagate his species, to neglect it for no cause. Family life is being called into jeopardy, your reverences."

"How many has he called to leave their families?" asked Bela.

"I have heard of as many as five, four of them married."

"That does not yet sound the death knell of family life," Nicodemus snapped. How few people, he thought acidly, know how to make their point with scholars. "There is a tradition that Moses himself withdrew from his wife after his calling, and on occasion a rabbi has wed himself to the study of the Law as his only bride. It has been proposed that he who comes to keep that Law perfectly is led to perfect chastity. My colleagues, the God who called man to propagate man also called him to put the Creator before man, and that could be the case here."

"Your reverences," Jonah said tartly, "I see I must proceed in more sparing fashion. I have observed that the rabbi in question has abandoned gainful occupation, and induced his five immediate disciples to do likewise. I leave it to you to contrast this with the tradition of the Pharisees. Even priests, entitled to be supported from the altar, practice a secular occupation to augment their income! I do want to insist that as a leader of the people this kind of a precedent troubles me."

"What else, Lord Shallum?" Bela prompted.

"He preaches a doctrine that to me—to me, I say—sounds irresponsible. He urges such trust in divine providence as to imply that all should leave their gainful occupations as has he, and rely solely on God—though how anyone will eat if no one works, I do not know."

"But did you actually hear him say that?"

"No, I confess I did not actually *hear* it, but I did hear him say, 'Love your enemies.' Now I fear, gentlemen, that such a doctrine could destroy us. How shall we maintain law and order? How guard our homes? How have a police force or an army?"

"Other charges?"

"The truth is," Jonah cried, "I think he foments a revolution which could have no effect except to dash us to pieces against the rock of Rome. Mind you"—he raised voice and hand as Nicodemus sought to interrupt—"I realize I appear to contradict what I just said about his promotion of absolute pacifism, but let me explain. Whatever his intentions, he charms a swarm of followers by preaching about a coming kingdom of God. Now it is the history of such movements that frustrated and ambitious followers take them into their own hands and twist them their own way. I know our flammable people. They want a kingdom now. They want Rome out now! And who can say this Jesus will not himself abandon his idealism when, lifted up by his growing power, he learns that it leads nowhere because of the impotency of his vaporous teachings? No, Herod is worried for the *peace*, your reverences, and I am worried."

"Now you are speaking good sense, Lord Jonah!" Rabbi Shimron interposed. "This is what worries us leaders in Galilee. False prophets and false messiahs have shed enough blood."

"Rabbi Shimron," protested Bela, "what we seek is evidence that this man *is* a false prophet."

"Then let me proceed. First, he presumes to teach the Law without having mastered it. Not only does he not study under a recognized master, but he does not take time to study at all. Worse, he lifts himself up as a rabbi and a holy man, yet cultivates the company of lawless rabble and the dregs of society—people I wouldn't trust with the key to my storeroom! A man is known by the company he keeps."

"I have heard," Nicodemus said dryly, "that he acquitted himself well when that charge was lodged against him!"

"What of this?" Rabbi Shimron flung out. "He had the gall to claim to forgive sins, and without even calling on the Name! Who in the history of the world displayed such arrogance? Certainly, not Moses!"

"Who does he claim to be?" Bela peered with narrowed eyes.

"Why, now that you mention it, his identity was challenged when he forgave this sinner—a paralyzed man in one Simon Peter's house. He responded by saying something like, 'I'll show you that the Son of man does have power on earth to forgive sin.' "

"He claims to be the Son of man?" Bela asked. "This is a charge with substance. You're sure?"

"He said it clear as a bell. Plenty of witnesses."

"Slow, Rabbi Bela," cautioned Nicodemus. "What are you concluding?"

"You of all people are surely familiar with our arcane Pharisaic knowledge concerning the meaning of the phrase!"

"But is Rabbi Jesus? You know how closely we guard the

176

secret of this truth, so subtle, so easily corrupted, and so capable of inflaming the imagination of the unstable. Even the Sadducees are not privy to our interpretation. The phrase can mean as little as 'a man.' Isn't that the meaning given it by the prophet Ezechiel? I also seem to remember that the Galilean dialect has a usage in the matter that injects further ambiguity." He looked at the two Galileans, who nodded. "But Rabbi Shimron," Nicodemus went on, "you mentioned a proof of his power to forgive sin which Rabbi Jesus offered to give. Did he give it?"

"To the paralyzed man in question, he said, 'Get up, take up your bed, and make for home.' And he did. There is no doubt he has the healing touch. I know the young man in question."

"Yes, he seems to have some strange power," Bela mused.

Nicodemus fleetingly recalled that sense of awe he felt in his clandestine meeting with Jesus those long months ago. "Then surely, we must proceed with reverence in dealing with this man!"

"Reverence, yes," Bela snapped. "Paralysis, no! Rabbi, you know as well as I that such signs—if genuine—are accepted by us as proof of a man's *holiness*. That is all. They constitute no mandate to teach and interpret the Law. Since prophecy has ceased, we Pharisees explain the Scriptures in accord with tradition and the learned reasoning of official theologians such as ourselves. We accord no interpretative office to holy men."

"Rabbi Bela, the people disfavor that stand, and it troubles me as well. It throttles the prophetic tradition. Now permit me to ask—don't all of us here await the Messiah? Don't we expect him to end the burden of the Law?"

"I certainly hope so."

"Yet if we're not prepared to accept signs of power as witness to the Messiah's identity, how shall we know him, or accept his announcement that now we go beyond the Law to its fulfillment?"

Bela looked startled, then brushed the objection away with a wave of the hand. "I anticipate more apocalyptic signs than a few inconsequential healings. The Messiah will just have to do better than that." Nicodemus slumped in his chair. "Now

177

as to this Galilean's signs and wonders, I ask you to recall how Egypt's diabolical magicians aped Moses' signs of power. We must be cautious."

"How true! How true!" Jonah purred.

"And now let me confide to you what most perturbs me about this man from the hills of Galilee." Rabbi Bela's intimate tone induced his auditors to bend closer. "It is his attacks on us Pharisees. We—the ones who have labored through the darkest hours of our history building up the authority to preserve the divine message. We—entrusted with the shreds of the prophetic mantle until the Promised One comes. And now this untutored Galilean criticizes us freely —and there is nothing that so undermines authority."

"But we must be fair," Nicodemus cautioned. "Perhaps there is substance to his criticisms. Some of our number have such a fixation on exact observance they forget that the purpose of observance is faithfulness. They have lost the doctrine that difficult circumstances *can* excuse one from certain Sabbath observances—and certain other traditions as well."

"You," Bela retorted, "are famous for seeing both sides of a question. But go on," he added resignedly.

"It just seems to me that the prestige syndrome has reached epidemic proportions among us—so much so that at times one wonders about the question at issue, whether it is a truth of revelation or a matter of whose prestige must be kept intact." Rabbi Bela had risen and was peering out the window.

"The sun is dropping rapidly," he announced. "Sabbath will arrive within the hour. We will conclude this present meeting with our final remarks. Firstly, as to your last comment, Rabbi Nicodemus, I say that no organization is perfect, but we can do our housecleaning without the untutored help of an outsider."

"But what if he *is* from God?" Nicodemus anguished. "Isn't that the issue?"

"Rabbi Nicodemus"—Bela's tone was testy—"I don't think you give weight enough to the issue of the authority of the Pharisaic rabbinate! Since the time of the Maccabees we've banded together to safeguard the revelation in the teeth of encroaching secularization, paganization and the atheistic Grecizing of our high priesthood and power elite. Are we to stand by—" A barrage of knocks rattled the door. "Come in!" Bela thundered, and a man sidled through the half-opened door.

"Rabbi Bela, I came fast to report that the Nazarene and his followers are on the way back, less than an hour behind me, coming into town by the headland road!"

"You have done well, Tobit. Await us outside." When the door closed, he went on: "My colleagues, I adjourn this meeting at once in favor of a field trip. Let us meet the returning rabbi, observe his followers, and perhaps discourse with him. Ponder what has transpired here, and return prepared to finalize our decision. The matter is urgent. We meet tomorrow eve at Sabbath's close. Agreed?"

"Agreed."

"Then let us observe this preacher from Nazareth."

9

Lord Jonah and the three rabbis made their way north out of town, guided by the courier. On the steep grade Nicodemus, breathing heavily, paused to catch his breath, and glanced idly about him. He gasped at the beauty of the silvered lake and the verdant fields. At home he cultivated a little flower garden, but here the whole hillside was strewn with blossoms. Delicate windflowers were everywhere, the blue more numerous, the orange-gold drawing the eye. A sudden breeze set the flaming red poppies swaying like miniature lanterns in the last light of the setting sun. Sprouting at his feet was a cluster of the tiny cyclamen called Solomon's crown. He plucked a blossom and absent-mindedly examined the delicate amethyst petals rising from the tiny, deep-purple crown at the base. The throat of the crown was dabbed with scarlet, as from a fallen drop of blood.

An exclamation burst from their guide, and he pointed to

179

the travellers coming into view far above, where the road wound down from the head of the bluff overlooking the lake. "The Nazarene!" In the vanguard strode a tall, bearded young man in a white tunic. They watched the caravan approach as the sun dropped below the western rim of the valley, and sudden twilight drenched the landscape.

"Look at that horde of camp-followers." Bela's voice was toneless. "We scholars exhaust our lives in study and pursuit of the Law and the wisdom of our fathers, and this rabbiless Rabbi—too young to know the Law—is mobbed by supposed seekers after knowledge. There is a danger descending upon us." Silence settled around his words like falling snow, for no one had anything to add.

The descending caravan disappeared behind an intervening hill, and they awaited its reappearance. As it came into view on the road winding down from the near side of the hill, there floated up from Capernaum the clear peals of the ram's horn announcing the onset of the Sabbath.

"They're not coming by the road!" The guide pointed. The Master was making for town by cutting across a field of barley, his followers close behind. The five men rushed to intercept them.

"Look! Look what they're doing!" screamed Lord Jonah, pointing a delicate finger. Nicodemus strained his eyes in the twilight, and at last made it out. The Nazarene's followers were plucking the heads of barley, rolling them in their hands, and tossing the freed kernels into their mouths. His first reaction was surprize. Not for weeks would the barley in Judea be ripe. But of course, this was the plain of Genesaret, nestled in the warmth of this low-slung valley, fabled for its fertility. Then with a shock it registered—they were plucking grain on the Sabbath!

"Why, I don't believe it!" Bela exclaimed. "They're profaning the Sabbath under our noses!"

"Oh, we're not surprised," Shimron returned. "When you become conversant with his high and mighty ways, you don't know what he'll do next. But I must admit," he conceded grudgingly, "that the country people—and even their rabbis —are not as strict in interpretation and observance as you Jerusalem savants."

180

Bela was already running. Nicodemus, following less rapidly, mumbled, "They're doing it behind his back, in the dark. Perhaps he doesn't know."

"Look!" Bela fumed, "your followers are plucking grain, and it's now blessed Sabbath!" The Master did not respond, but nodded to acknowledge he had heard. The four men rushed up and blocked his path.

"We're shocked!" Lord Shallum's tone was scandalized. "In your very presence they do it!"

"Surely," added Shimron in his most professorial tone, "you are acquainted with the thirty-nine classes of work unlawful on the Sabbath? Why, Exodus itself clearly forbids reaping!"

The Master's burning gaze searched them one by one, and they fell silent. He breathed deeply, and sighed. "Haven't you read what David did when he was hungry—he and his men? Into the house of God he went, and ate the bread of the Presence, unlawful except for priests—and fed his companions."

"But surely," Jonah puffed, "you don't claim his authority?"

Rabbi Bela impatiently waved Jonah to silence. "David was in mortal danger. Your tagalongs do it yards from town— and food! I, Rabbi Bela of the Supreme Council, demand to know why."

"Sabbath has begun. We cannot buy food."

"You could have—should have—anticipated this common need. Such irresponsibility cannot be condoned." The followers of Jesus were gathering around, and Bela projected his outraged tones to reach them.

"You must know," said the Master, "that for hours we traversed sparsely settled highland places where the crops were unripe. In this valley alone is the standing grain edible."

"The ordained rabbis and theologians," Bela retorted, "have considered—and rejected—such thin excuses. As do I!"

The Master stared at him, then spoke with a ring of finality. "The Sabbath was made for man, not man for the Sabbath. Therefore the Son of Man is Lord even of the Sabbath." With that he strode on. His chosen five followed him into town. The rest sought a campsite.

He reached the synagogue near Peter's house and entered, Bela and his three companions trailing after. The official acknowledged the two distinguished Jerusalem rabbis, and invited Rabbi Bela to do the reading and address the congregation. Rabbi Bela hesitated, looking around searchingly. "As to the honor of reading, transfer it to this man." He pointed to a well-dressed man with his right hand cradled in his lap—curled, shrunken, useless. "And as to the honor of the pulpit, offer it to this rabbi." He pointed to the Master.

When he ascended the pulpit, the Master wrapped the tallith about him, said the accustomed prayer, and began. "Rabbi Bela has called to our attention a man of affliction." He pointed to the first reader, the man with the paralyzed hand. "Sir, come here!" Hesitantly he came forward, and stood by the pulpit.

"We of Israel," the Master went on, "have hundreds of laws. When they conflict, the unwritten law in our hearts determines which must hold sway. The substance of all the laws is contained in two—love the Lord your God with all your heart, and all your soul, and all your might; love your neighbor as yourself. Tonight the law of Sabbath bids us rest, while the law of love looks on the need of our disabled brother. I ask, then—is it the law to do good or to do harm, to save or to neglect? We have learned rabbis here. Rabbi Bela? Rabbi Nicodemus? Rabbi Shimron?"

No response came. Color mounted in the Master's face. His chiseled face turned back and forth across the room. "Will none speak?" Anger flamed in his voice. He turned to the man with the disabled limb, and his features softened. "Stretch out your hand!"

The man struggled to raise his arm. It trembled violently. With his other hand he gripped it, lifted it. It hung there, shriveled, ugly.

Gasps broke out. It was taking on flesh and bone. The afflicted man gaped at it with bulging orbs. It was normal. He flexed the digits, felt their strength. "I'm cured! I'm cured!" His voice pealed an unearthly excitement. He spun around, revolving the hand at the wrist, flexing the fingers. The people clustered around him, buzzing in wonder. The Master strode out the door. His disciples pushed through the crowd

182

in pursuit.

Rabbi Bela called the meeting to order. "We've now observed the conduct of Jesus of Nazareth. Our respect for the Sabbath rest has allowed us time to reflect. The issue is this—can we await the ponderous investigation of the Supreme Council, or does conscience demand that we use our authority?"

"How can we wait?" Lord Jonah asked rhetorically.

"We witnessed his scandalous, his obstinate disregard of Sabbath!" barked Shimron.

"Brethren, let's not be swept away!" implored Nicodemus. "His conduct is not that clearly scandalous. In the healing of the hand, he did not lift a finger. Of what *work* can we accuse him?"

"And I suppose his camp-followers didn't lift a finger to gather the grain?" Bela's voice dripped sarcasm.

"Remember," Nicodemus pleaded, "that he cited a necessity for that. Need I remind such an august meeting of the accepted rabbinical saying, 'The Sabbath is delivered unto you, and not you to the Sabbath?'"

"Yes—delivered to be obeyed!" Shimron snapped.

"No, no!" The cry was desperate. "I invoke Isaiah's teaching that the Sabbath is to be a joy, not a burden! We cultivate the tradition of meeting the Sabbath with gladness, as bridegroom meets bride."

"Yes—but with due observance," Bela retorted, "just as marriage has its laws."

"But he cited a genuine necessity!"

"Necessity? He cited an irresponsible life style!" Bela was shouting now.

"But he claims to be a man with an urgent mission! Was David's case so different?"

"David!" Bela thundered. "Don't compare *him* to David! David was a prophet! His life in danger!"

"Can you swear this man is not a prophet? And as to danger—I sense lives at issue here!"

"And now you're playing the prophet?"

"No, no," Nicodemus demurred.

"Rabbi, you are proverbial for your indecision," Bela

asserted. "The rest of us know our minds."

Nicodemus stared in unbelief. His jaw began to tremble. "But we haven't so much as mentioned the miracle. What of the miracle?"

"Miracle? What miracle?" Bela was cool now. "I saw a prodigy, but hardly a *religious* prodigy. It flew in the face of the Sabbath—put me in mind of Pharoah's diabolical magicians—compelled me to view this man as a possible, if unwitting, tool of Beelzebub."

"My sentiments exactly," purred Jonah.

Nicodemus sat stunned.

"Since there are no more objections, I call for our decision," Bela announced. "Do we take action against this deranged teacher?"

"We must!" snapped Jonah.

"I agree," purred Shimron.

The three stared at Nicodemus. All confusion, all indecision was gone. With stately bearing, he rose, and spoke in solemn tones. "I sever my connection with this council and all its works and pomps." Without a pause he turned and exited. For one moment, Bela was shaken, but before the door had closed he went on.

"Now, we do not wish to be, or appear to be, vindictive. We have one goal—to stop this preacher and disperse his camp followers lest he endanger the rule of the authentic teachers in Israel."

"If we accomplish that—irreversibly—I will indeed be satisfied," Jonah announced. A hard note had crept into his usually wheedling tone. Shimron nodded uncomfortably.

"Two procedures have proved effective in these cases," Bela resumed. "The first is to use our authority to enlist the support of relatives. A discreet letter to his mother and kin will advise them of his condition—beside himself, carried away by strange influences, in danger of formal condemnation."

"A good beginning," Jonah conceded.

"Secondly, we must warn his hangers-on that we discern in him powers from the realm of evil, and that a time may come when he and they will be cast out of the synagogue."

"It sounds . . . moderate." Jonah's tone conveyed dis-

184

appointment, and a hint of rebellion. To make himself even clearer, he murmured, "Perhaps too moderate."

"An acceptable plan," Shimron announced.

"Then we draw up our letter, sign it, and send it."

Rabbi Bela's messenger handed him the missive. "You mean his mother sent a written reply?" Bela asked. "Who wrote it?"

"She herself."

"Unusual for a mountain woman." He broke the wax seal on the small cutting of papyrus and read:

Your Reverences:
I have considered with care your counsel. Permit me, however, to remind you that my son is no stranger to me. Thirty years he lived at my side. Time and again I have been faced with searching decisions concerning him. Once other had need of my counsel. "Do whatever he tells you," I said. It is what I have always done, and continue to find good cause to do.

Your respectful servant, Mary
His Mother

Angrily, Bela twisted the papyrus scrap into bits. "This carpenter," he murmured between clenched teeth, "proves harder to be rid of than I supposed. For once, that fool Jonah was right."

He strode to the window and threw the bits out. A gust took them and blew them to the four winds.

10

How beautiful the greening I saw in Galilee, and how short-lived. Spiritual buds were bursting, hearts opening, lives flowering. Then swept in the chilling winds of innuendo, propelled by secret schemes and underhanded orders. The blood of the people chilled, and the winter of hearts returned.

The shrunken hand swelling to fullness, I striding out,

185

hopes shrinking. High but necessary was the cost of that healing. It is the Kingdom on the way.

Rabbi Bela's intrigue multiplying the synagogues which close their doors—a stone wall in my face.

Hysteric desire for cures barring my way to use of the towns—rabbis forbidding the pulpit—Jerusalem dangerous —my home town rejecting me. My plans sweeping out to sea on raving tides of hostility.

The next morning, in the fields, the throng around me shared our bread and olives—friend and foe alike. Eating slowly, I cast my eye over the diverse assembly. I had to ward off the troubles I foresaw—the sudden enthusiasms of the mercurial Galileans, the raillery of the Judean savants, the wildness of the Idumean bedouins, the dubious loyalty of the Arabian ethnics from Transjordan, and the ready religious frenzies of the superstitious Sidonians.

South we went to the seashore—provision for swift escape by water. As we walked, Peter pointing and exclaiming— "Rabbi, look at that set of millstones—bigger than I am."

I—smiling—"Peter, do you feel them turning already?"

He—startled—alert to the danger from the crowd, concern on his face.

Leaders and people were grinding me, Father, determined to mill out of me what I shall never give.

So glaring the sickness of souls. Priests offering animal sacrifices no longer seen as merely symbolic. Lay leaders thinking only of restoring a worldly kingdom. Sadducees intent on their secular goals and adopted culture. Pharisees making legalism their hope. All in the name of the God of Israel!

Self-interest blinding vision. Sadducees blocking the march of saving history at the Pentateuch—rejecting the prophets who curtail their pretensions and condemn their corruption. Pharisees piously hemming in your Law, Father, with an added thicket of their own—and soon preferring their laws to yours. Bruising and crushing the tendrils of continuing revelation. Professing belief in the promised Messiah, then choking off the paths by which I come. Sealing themselves into their cocoon and suffocating. How ever deem their authority greater than yours? Good Jeremiah—scourging the theologians for praising the Law while turning it into a lie.

Of John I once asked, "Why do the Pharisees impose so many laws of ritual purity on the people?"

"I suppose," he replied, "to honor them by making them imitate the holy lives of the priests."

"Is the ritual purity of the priests holiness, or an outward sign to the people that they must cultivate purity of heart?"

He was thoughtful. "A sign."

"And whom did Moses appoint to give the sign?"

"The priests."

"What happens now that the sign is imposed on the people as well?"

"Many don't observe it. They complain that they can't without neglecting their jobs, families and friends."

"John, sort the true from the false."

John must learn that holiness is not humanly-imposed ritual, but the purity of selfless love sending forth its flood of energies to complete, Father, your creation.

Simon Peter crying happily—"Look, Lord, our boats." We gliding through the green grass and the gold-hearted daisies to the water's edge. I turning to that mass of people, that sea of faces.

What currents of hope, what eddies and whirlpools of desire coursing through the hearts swathed in those farmers' dirt-stained tunics and housewives' homespun and the fine, many-hued garments of the aristocrats and educators.

What say to them, how proceed? The rabbis benumb the people with case upon case of legal precedent that leaves their hearts empty. The teachers of the Gentiles build castles of knowledge neither accessible to the common people nor a font of salvation to the learned.

So little time—none for esoteric doctrine. The people had to learn at once! The Kingdom had to grow under their feet, steal into their hearts, grip their minds, flame before their eyes, reveal the Messiah and King.

And so I taught as always.

"Last winter, a sower planted that field," I began, pointing to the grain-covered hillside, and they turned to look at the ripening barley. "See the promise of a rich harvest.

Yet how anxious the sower was! He saw birds gobbling up the seed which fell on the paths. Some fell on those rock outcroppings, and he knew that if it germinated at all in their sprinklings of soil, the young plants would shrivel when the sun burnt down.

"Observe those patches of weeds—he was aware that thistle seed too was lurking. It sprang up swiftly and choked to death the nearby grain. But mostly there was rich soil— look at that heartening crop. It promises to yield thirty and sixty and a hundredfold. If you have ears to hear, make them work for you!

"Since the kingdom of God can be understood by such stories, hear another. A man scatters seed on the ground, wearies, and goes off to bed. He sleeps and wakes during the cycle of the seasons, and the seed sprouts and grows without his understanding how. Up from the earth comes a blade, an ear, and the grain swelling out in the ear. Then the planter returns sickle in hand to harvest it. The kingdom of God resembles this."

"Master," a lame man bellowed, "heal me!"—unaware of the healing in the word of my planting. In pity I healed him and healed many that day, and expelled evil spirits. I was nearly trampled, but in the end we didn't need the boats. That day I had once again the grief that none but the evil spirits proclaimed, "You are the son of God!" And them I silenced.

The failure of the people to recognize that I AM troubled me little, for how many can reach so deep? But is it not stunning that not one of my own people had publicly confessed me the Christ? They asked the Baptist if he was the Christ, and bandits you never sent were hailed as the Christ, but they had not hailed me—not one of my people.

The day was spent when we climbed the mountain opposite. High on a level spot we camped, and sitting took our food as we gazed on the azure lake crinkling in the evening breeze, purpling in the setting sun. Darkness was shrouding the land when I summoned Peter and James and John. Through the heavy brush we clambered a hundred feet to the summit. There they slept, and there I wrestled with the enemy, and hewed new paths through the thickets of prayer the whole night long.

Grievous and somber was my crisis as I looked up to the flaring and fading stars pursuing their slow march across the heavens. Blood red one bright star on the horizon flashed, fled across a flaming sequence of orange, amber, and turquoise, poised fleetingly in purple majesty, and assumed once again its robe of milky white. My self-manifestation to draw Israel to my heart had failed—for now. Henceforth I must gather the remnant. To help me, shepherds were needed. Yes, twelve there would be, after the twelve tribes of Israel. It was the hour of choosing.

By the time of the morning star I had done it. At dawn Simon Peter descended to the camp to summon those whom I desired, and they came. The Twelve stood solemnly before me as the orb of the sun gleamed across the mountains of Gaulanitis and ignited the lake with its flame. The morning light lit the faces anxious to learn my will.

At Simon, son of John, I gazed, recalling Jacob's last words to Reuben the firstborn: "You . . . are unstable as water." In solemn tone I announced, "Simon, you are to be ever with me for my sake and the Gospel's, but I charge you to remember always that of Simon I have made *Peter, Rock.*"

Hard then I stared at James and John, a team of brothers, fierce sons of Zebedee, the word of Jacob ringing in my soul —"Simeon and Levi, brothers—weapons of violence are theirs." The only violence I would permit this pair was the roar of their voices sounding around the world. "James and John," I prophesied, "you shall be my sons of thunder!"

Thus proceeding, I spoke a special word to each by name —Andrew and Philip and Bartholomew, and Matthew the tax collector, and Thomas, and James the son of Alphaeus, and Thaddeus known as Jude, and Simon the Zealot.

Hammering in my mind came the words of Jacob, "Judah is a lion's whelp; from the prey, my son, you have ascended." How my heart beat with longing and dread as I fixed my eyes on Judas of Kerioth. His present struggle and show of good will were winning him his chance. Swiftly he had to decide —or disappear into the quicksand of his own ambition. "Be quick," I exhorted, "in doing what must be done, Judas!" How dreadful to know what his decision would be.

To them as one I spoke then. "Above all others have I chosen you to share my fellowship. Before all others, to my mission I have appointed you. To preach the Gospel and cast out demons I send you. Now we go down to the sheep waiting to be pastured, and proclaim the kingdom of heaven."

11

The Twelve—strong young men—sanguine, great-hearted, hopeful. Eager to join company for great causes and inspired deeds. What expectations, what scorning of danger! Yet how unstable—eager for honors, easily offended, crushed by defeat. Strong, but apt to violence. Not grasping that the Kingdom cannot be forced, and its treasures cannot be stolen. Disposed to follow me, but hopeful of riches—not recognizing that poverty is a gift received.

Only days before I named them the Twelve, their voices rose in loud debate with critics who contended that even I failed to live the doctrine I taught. Poorly they answered—almost apologizing for my way of life—not seeing that my life is my teaching—the pattern for living my words.

Arguing among themselves about fine points of my ordering of values—failing to grasp my truth—that into the world had descended the Gift that eclipses all other values, and to it human values must kneel.

Ready to lift the sword in a flash to bring the Kingdom I preach—failing to comprehend that I extend permission *not* to confront the violent with violence. The Kingdom gallops toward the end-time—delayed by a justice that employs violence—speeded by the disregard of all that does not accelerate its journey.

Tides of mercy flooding the world, drowning the pretensions of men, breaking down the wall between saint and sinner—all called alike—salvation a gift to all who accept it. Sand castles of human pride and prejudice washing away in the rising tide of mercy—love the solvent. Cheek turned to

190

the striker speeding the Time—the lifting of swords retarding it.

So long with me, and still their blinders led them to hold they were to love only good men—not registering my call to love what can grow to goodness. How often had I spoken of the fertile earth—nurturing the seed until it yields fruit? How often have they seen the married couple who first love —and from their love, children? And the artist—from his love, the lovely. Love—the warm moist earth awakening the seeds in every heart.

Love—the bursting sunlight above, eliciting the teeming shoots of goodness.

My mission—not to reward the good, but to beget them.

I had now prepared to say these things.

We went to where the people were just stirring from sleep—the Twelve beaming with pride and joy. My heart going out to them in love and pity—little they knew of the Kingdom whose overseers they were. Judas gliding in high elation, his feet spurning the earth.

Joining the folk in the sunrise—sitting and breaking bread, even as new pilgrims labored up the mountainside. All satisfying their appetite, then gathering around me and falling silent. I studying them pensively. Some had followed for weeks, hunger in their eyes. Others had been cured, and now would not leave me—sensing greater things to come. Most clothed coarsely—not a few in tatters—shivering in the dawn chill. The Twelve in the vanguard, clothes as poor as most—faces cheerful as the morning. My heart surging within me—my voice rising to send echoes into the hills.

"Blessedly happy you poor who lean on the Lord. You are the heart of the kingdom of God. Blessedly happy you who hunger for what is right. You shall be sated. Blessedly happy you who weep now. You shall laugh! Blessedly happy the non-violent. They shall inherit the world. Blessedly happy the merciful. They shall obtain mercy. Blessedly happy the pure of heart. They shall see God. Blessedly happy the peacemakers. They shall be called sons and daughters of God."

"But Rabbi"—a plaintive voice from the crowd—"in our poverty we're trodden down, and for our coming to you, mocked." Swift my reply.

"Blessedly happy are you when men hate you, avoid and revile you, and use your name as a password for evil because of your faith in the Son of Man. Skip about like lambs, rejoicing in the greatness of your heavenly reward. Remember— their fathers used to treat the prophets just that way!"

Like the rising sun setting ablaze each wave on the Sea of Galilee, understanding lit the sea of faces before me—but not all. Here and there, like lamps extinguished, were faces dark, accusing, sneering. Dour Rabbi Bela murmured into the ear of Lord Jonah, who glared at me blackly. Their fine clothes and those of their companions stood out in the gathering, marked with the insignia of their office. One of them bent to the ears of the others and spoke, eliciting a mocking laugh, whereupon the people nearby lost joy and, turning, looked at them in confusion. At this, I raised my voice again.

"You wealthy ones face ruinous trouble, for you have gotten your consolation! Ruinous trouble for you sated ones— hunger is stored up for you! Ruinous trouble for you recipients of perpetual praise, for in that identical way their fathers praised the false prophets!"

Long and full were the teachings of that day. Before the shadows fell, I urged them to make for home, and that seemed the hardest teaching of all.

We went to Peter's house, where for days such crowds descended that we missed many a meal. Critics carried their accusations abroad, and rumors flew. Peter hurried up to me one day, full of concern. "Rabbi, lying reports have been buzzed to your relatives and townsmen—that you're out of your mind, gripped by delusions of grandeur, running about neglecting to eat, looking like a skeleton. They're on the way to see for themselves."

"When the blind lead the blind, both fall into the ditch."

"I feel sorry for your mother!"

"Have I not told you—blessedly happy those weeping now. They will laugh!"

Even this brief interchange was not managed without a disturbance. Some burly fellows came up tightly gripping a possessed man. At once I freed him.

"No denying he casts out demons!" came an angry voice behind me. "He is mad—possessed by Beelzebub himself!

And by that prince of demons he casts out demons!" Arguing broke out. I called for an end of it.

"Who makes the accusation?"

A tall, thin man, his pinched face white, shouldered his way through the crowd with several of his confreres. I recognized him as a scribal theologian recently arrived from Jerusalem. "We all do!" he screeched, turning his head this way and that to the crowd. "We all do!" The contagion of fear marked many faces. The authority of these men was formidable. A little child began wailing, a few individuals slunk away. The rest awaited my response.

"Tell me how Satan can cast out Satan? If Satan be divided against Satan, his kingdom is breaking up. He is finished."

"It's a trick, a deceit! Haven't I heard you call Satan a deceiver? Then he is a trickster."

"Examine this man I freed. Is it a trick, or is he free? You've seen others freed and healed. Are they healed or not?"

"I say you do it by Satan!"

"Then by whom do your own exorcists cast out demons?" The man held to a sullen silence, trapped in his own net, and I went on. "Then let your own exorcists be your judges. For if by the Spirit of God I cast out demons, the kingdom of God has advanced upon you.

"You accuse me of being in the grip of an unclean spirit. Can you call the tree bad and the fruit good, or the tree good and the fruit bad? No, the worth of a tree is measured by the quality of its fruit.

"Listen when I tell you that all sins and blasphemies will be forgiven except one—the sin of the man who speaks evil of the Holy Spirit. He will never be forgiven his eternal sin."

If they treated the Master thus, how would they treat his servants? How clear it was that my followers would be like the works of an unrecognized master artist—assessed at a pittance by a world which could not honor them enough did it heap all its adulation at their feet. But how happy their bitter tears, and what beatitude their eternal laughter!

12

Mary stumbled and almost fell into the mire. When her nephew James leaped to her side with a steadying hand, her great, luminous eyes gave him a look of gratitude which momentarily transformed her pale, grief-stricken face. Nephews Joseph and Jude paused, but the rest of the party kept up its harried pace.

"Mother, rest a little," James urged, his eyes glistening. "You look so tired."

She pressed his hand. "No. It's not the journey."

She was middle-aged, but the weariness was in her heart, not her mountain-country legs. Her dear, dear son! How fared he? The stories, the charges! She sighed deeply. If only Joseph were here!

Still her thoughts turned to Joseph, and her heart beat more quickly. Such a love! They had shared things no children of Adam ever had shared—and had done without much and endured much as well. Hard it was, but it only nourished their tenderness for one another. And for their son.

How sublime to see him grow like a yearling lamb at their side! What joy to watch him gamboling and tumbling with the other children, chock-full of life and its childhood joys. But then, as he matured, a certain reserve set in. He grew more silent, took to thinking and praying much, and walking the hills alone. Yet never had his warmth abated, or his filial devotion dimmed.

So understanding had her husband been, and so faithful, that she felt no need to ask, "Do you have any regret of the pact we made?" Yet at times she grieved for him. Daily she had said in wordless ways that her son was his, yet it must have been different for him. Their people had a saying that a man without children is a kindled brand that throws no light.

Her son—so truthful and good!—how doubt him? But doubt their leaders did, and now these ugly rumors he was demented or possessed—or both! Yet never had she known a clearer head. Still, the strain upon him was so great . . . she shivered and pressed hand to forehead. Lord and Father of my son, abandon him not, for send him you did, and care for him you must, though all others care not!

The letter from Rabbi Bela was the cruellest of all. She felt pain in her heart at the thought of it. Before it came, rumors had begun to circulate that anyone attaching himself to her son was in danger of expulsion from the synagogue, and his letter contained a veiled hint that just such a fate might befall her, should she not abjure his teaching. She a heretic! O heavenly Father, I will not doubt—I have no cause to doubt! Never has he given me cause to doubt, though full understanding I never have! And never have I sought or done ought but thy will—or desire ought else now!

She gazed at the grim party bespattering themselves with mud as they stomped along determinedly before her. They badly lacked understanding concerning her son, but doubts they lacked not at all. It was her neighbors, along with his cousins Joseph and Jude, who had organized this party—they too had received communications from Rabbi Bela and his colleagues. She had tried to deter their going, but go they would, with or without her—so she went too.

Her neighbor Jason was splashing and sloughing along in the lead, with a wild look about him. "Your son's nothing but a laborer—like me," he growled to her on setting out.

"Each is what God appointed him," she returned calmly.

" 'A thread is always hanging on a tailor.' Does he think to teach learned rabbis? He plays with danger playing the prophet! Someone has to pound sense into him—save him from himself!" The look she gave him then made him add lamely, "We only want to help him. He is our fellow townsman."

Such help—yet could they be right? Satan, liar, go! Father, I've recognized and believed the truth that he is your Son—my Son—though I understand so little.

Tears began to fall, and sobs rent her. Gazing into her face with pity, James laid his great arm around her frail shoulders, and she felt the throbbing of his body, and saw his tears falling beside her own.

Only a laborer! Another laborer might see no more, but learned rabbis? Did they not know that when a man has learned what human knowledge cannot teach, he need not be taught but listened to, as one taught by God?

"It will not be long now," James consoled her. "You'll see

it is not so bad. My cousin knows what he's about—your son! I'd have followed him myself, if not asked to remain behind to care for—things."

When they arrived at Peter's house and saw the press around the door, the Nazarenes ploughed forward aggressively, identifying themselves in loud voices. Someone called to Jesus, "Your mother, kin and neighbors just arrived."

A heavy silence fell. Rising to his feet, Jesus studied the Twelve, and then the other disciples. At length he spoke in solemn tones. "Who are my mother and my brothers?" He pointed to his followers one by one, intense devotion in his eyes. "Here are my mother and my brothers. The doer of God's will is brother and sister and mother to me."

"We've got to see you!" Jason bellowed.

"Now go for a little while," Jesus said, but when the Twelve began to leave too, he motioned them to remain.

Burly Jason barged in first. "We've come to take charge of you," he bawled. "We've been told you're no longer"—at the sight of Jesus' eyes his words faltered, and trailed to a feeble conclusion—"no longer able to care for yourself." He shuffled back.

"Which of you," Jesus demanded, "does this man speak for?" None answered. "You have heard many things about me. Now you see me. Do you see what you heard?" Still none opened his mouth. "What are your plans?"

They eyed Peter's bulk, surveyed the fiery sons of Zebedee, took note of the look on the faces of the rest—and one by one, began to sidle through the door.

"Now, if you are finished," his mother said to those who dallied, "I would like to see my son—alone." The rest crept out, and the Twelve, receiving Jesus' nod, followed. He embraced her tenderly and kissed her. "You look thin," she said. "I knew that much would be true."

"The Good News must be preached in season and out."

"A number of women are following you about."

"Yes. You saw them here. Their money buys our food; their hands prepare it."

"Evil rumors circulate. I will join them."

"Rumors are not reason enough. Rumors cannot be stopped."

196

"There are other reasons. Then it is settled."

The way he looked at her then made the floodgate of her tears break down and sweep away in a torrent. With utmost gentleness he embraced her and kissed her. "The doer of my Father's will," he said gently, "is my brother, sister, mother."

After that, she traveled about with him.

During the evening meal he said, "In the morning we leave for the feast in Jerusalem." He turned to the man from Kerioth. "Judas, I have need of your talents."

"Speak, Rabbi."

"Remain behind. Find camping places near the towns and villages we have yet to visit roundabout. Search out the food we must beg or buy. Learn which synagogues will receive us. I will return two weeks after the feast of the spring harvest."

"And the Good News?"

"Preach in the time you have to spare, but do not neglect the preparation. Jude, you will go along, that they may have two witnesses." He turned to them all. "You have seen what happened here today. Be prepared for persecution in the Holy City."

In the morning they set out.

Part Five

THE CHRIST

1

The late rains were over and gone, and June clothed the shores of the sky-blue lake in its fair summer vesture of green woodland and emerald meadow sprinkled with parti-colored blossoms. Two months since, reapers had put their stone sickles to the standing barley, and later the golden wheat. Birds chirped melodiously in the stubbled fields, yellow bees buzzed ponderously among the flowering shrubs, and glistening brown-skinned boys laughed in the waters of the bay.

Two weeks had passed since Judas and Jude Thaddeus—mission completed—had returned to Capernaum. They were in time to join in celebrating the Festival of Weeks, praising God for the grain harvest and enjoying the feasting. Today was the day appointed for the Master's return.

"Come, Judas-not-from-Kerioth," his companion bubbled, "let's take our supplies and head south to speed this blessed reunion." Jude strapped on the back pack. They departed Peter's house, and as they walked along the lake shore, Judas threw his arm jauntily over his friend's shoulder.

"You're unusually light-hearted today," Jude Thaddeus observed.

"And you are your usual cheerful self. Thaddeus, your parents hit the nail on the head when they gave you a name meaning chesty and hearty. It describes you body and soul. As to my exuberance—why not? Our Rabbi returns today."

"I hope their work prospered."

"If their undertaking fared as well as ours," Judas exulted, "they'll return in triumph!"

Jude stirred uncomfortably. What had they achieved to justify that brag? He decided to change the subject. "An abundant harvest this year." He nodded toward the golden stubble gleaming in the morning sun.

"Yes, the reapers made the best of the planters' labor—as will the Master of ours."

"The birds are getting their share." Jude pointed to the sparrows flitting among the stubble. "I'm minded of the parable of the sower. The birds eating the seed symbolized the devil."

"Oh, I'm sure that wasn't to be taken literally. The enlightened leaders of the day would doubtless give that a Midrashic interpretation."

"No doubt the enlightened leaders are the ones who agree with you." Jude's effort at humor fell flat, so he added soberly, "The Master's not one of them. He's plain enough—Satan's his enemy."

"Sometimes he does puzzle me," Judas reflected, then added airily, "though I'm sure you'll see I'm right in time. He has to adapt his message to his hearers—simple people like yourself. That's the best technique. Surely, among Jerusalem's elite, he taught differently. I should've been there—but he did require my expertise here."

"Speaking of that, you worried me by making it sound as though the people's troubles would end the day he comes. You know they look on the occupation forces as our biggest trouble."

"You need more faith, Jude—and more understanding." Judas exuded confidence. "You haven't grasped yet what's about to happen. In fact"—he paused, drawing a great breath and staring at Jude with his impenetrable eyes—"I don't think the rest of the Twelve have either."

"I can't say," Jude hedged, suppressing his irritation, "but your preaching's not like the Rabbi's. You sound like a salesman, not a prophet." Long he had wanted to say this, but the man had been in one of his sour periods, and couldn't handle criticism.

"A little diplomatic skill in preparing for the Master is never amiss. And please notice that I was chosen over all the rest for this assignment, Judas-not-from-Kerioth."

"Yes, but the assignment was to pre-arrange food and shelter and a welcome, not to preach." He really felt it was necessary to burst Judas' bubble for his own sake. When he saw that he was not getting through, he plunged on desperately. "The Master didn't pick you for his right-hand man. He picked Simeon Peter"—he used the Hebrew form of Simon's name to enhance his dignity—"and please don't call me Judas-not-from-Kerioth. Call me Judas, son of James, or just call me Jude." It annoyed him that Judas always saw everything in reference to himself.

"Jude, you have a big chest, but you think small!" Judas bent down and selected a pebble which he fingered as they walked. "You're a minimalist, and you're irritating me. Has it occurred to you that the tribe of Simeon was absorbed by Judah long ago? When the Rabbi fully appreciates my talents, history is likely to repeat itself. Now we'll drop the subject."

Jude shifted the back-pack and said nothing. The pack contained food for the returning men, since they rarely had enough when traveling. It was he who finally broke the long silence.

"Look at the bee eater!" He pointed to a bird whose two central tail feathers projected farther than the rest, as if the others had been chewed off. "Funny habit, eating bees."

"The strong aren't satisfied with a cream-and-cookie diet, young man."

"Whatever that's meant to imply. It reminds me of the time you confided to me your criticism of the Master's teaching on the beatitudes. I wanted to challenge you then, but didn't feel equipped."

"You felt reality, Jude. I've analyzed our Rabbi's weak and strong points beyond your competence."

"What weak points?"

"He asks too much of mortal man—of flesh and blood."

"He asks nothing he doesn't do."

"His doings and men's are not to be equated. You haven't seen that yet, have you?"

"Judas, you steer our discussions into quicksand where I can't walk. Let's get on firm ground. I think we can do what he asks."

"You mean play the child, meek and mild? Speak for

yourself."

"I knew a sea captain. What a leader! He put me in mind of the stories about Alexander the Macedonian. He didn't believe in God, so he played god. He didn't believe in anything but himself. Then he was shipwrecked. Alone on a plank for weeks. Helpless as a child. He said he began shouting to God like a child to his father. He was rescued. After that he was a changed man—humble, kind, gentle."

"Was it a change for the *better*?" Judas demanded with raised eyebrows. "Did it make him more of a *man*?" His friend stared at him but made no answer, and he went on. "It's not easy to be a man. The Greeks have done a lot of thinking along those lines. Yet what did it avail them? Even at their peak, they were only a race of beautiful youths playing lofty games of the mind. But we Jews are a race of seasoned men who grimly throw our lives behind our realistic convictions."

"Judas, don't get offended if I say that your thinking reminds me of a Greek."

"What do you mean by that?" The sharpness with which the question was put made him pick his way so warily through his jelling thoughts that he got nothing out before Judas barked, "Well?"

"It's just that the rest of us follow the Master with a simple devotion—"

"That's painfully evident!"

"We follow him the same every day, while you—I know this is crazy . . ."

"That's all right, Jude. Every man has his own streak of craziness. Let's have it."

"You seem to follow him differently every day."

Judas stopped in his tracks, eyes widening. "Go on."

"It's as though you follow not him, but an idea of him, and that idea's always changing—you're always thinking, so your way of following is always changing. And not only your way of following, but whether to follow. You worry a lot."

"You can't understand that, can you?"

"No."

"Well, you see, a person with my gift of understanding takes such a large view of things, and sees such a forest of

204

possible interpretations, that it's impossible to make the flash judgments of simple folk. And as to their tumble-right-out emotional loyalties, why it's unthinkable for me so to narrow my life and possibilities."

"Just a little while ago you were telling me with cocksureness to expect great things. Now it sounds as if you're not sure of anything."

"Jude, we're in a different perspective now. You know how my mind reaches out to the whole sweep of history at the same time it's dealing with our current national situation. Our situation makes that of the Greek thinkers child's play. They narrowed their horizons to man's because they modeled even their gods on men. But for us, the mystery of the God of otherness, and his plans and purposes, guide our every decision. Possibilities are unlimited—and I at least am aware of that. And so, for me to commit myself to our Rabbi as unthinkingly and simplistically as the rest of you would be *immoral!*"

"Well, I admit you have such a great brain that you worry more in one day than we do in a year."

"That's it, Jude! Mock what you can't grasp—and in the name of religion, no doubt! 'An ignorant man bedecked with piety is like an ass encrusted with jewels.' "

"Easy Judas! I was only joking."

"Jude, you're enamored of heroes. Do play one by battling your urge to humor."

"All right, now I'm serious. Don't we *have* to believe in our Master, after what we've seen him do, the way our people believed in Moses after the wonders of the Exodus?"

"Believe *what*? Jude, I just explained the problem to you!"

"Believe he's from God—a prophet, and maybe the Messiah."

"*Which* Messiah? The one the Pharisees believe in? The one the Essenes believe in? The one the Zealots believe in?"

"The one he says he is."

"Can you be so stupid as to claim he *has* said? Has any of us confessed him the Messiah?" Judas was shouting now. "Jude, the only hope of an ignorant man like you is to put his hand over his mouth and listen to the wise."

"I'm listening."

"No, you're fishing. You're persuading—except that you persuade me of nothing!"

"Well, how can you ask if he's the Zealot's Messiah? They're assassins, and he opposes violence. It's as if you don't know him!"

"Enough of your insolence! Enough of your words!"

After that, they walked in silence. Late in the morning they reached a point where the lake shore swept out in an arc, and the road followed its contours. "A shortcut—a path of my own." Judas turned up a by-way rising sharply into the hills. A conifer woods soon engulfed them, and thorns and burrs tore at their legs. The silence was pierced only by the sweet trilling of a trumpeter bullfinch. Jude peered around but saw only a goldfinch feeding in the bracken.

"My wife and I have a caged goldfinch like that," he observed. "It's a lovely singer."

"Jude, it's cruel to cage a bird like that."

"I suppose you're right. I never really thought about it. My wife says she feels like our caged bird because she can't follow the Master too. We have a child."

"I'm glad I'm free—except here." Judas laid his hand on his chest. "My only chains are what the authorities have the temerity to call truth. Especially when they begin canting about the advantage of embracing sufferings and sorrows!"

"To follow the leader we follow," Jude burst out, "I find any suffering a cheap price—because in him I find things become worthwhile. I find myself worthwhile."

"The difference between us is that I don't need anyone to find myself worthwhile."

Jude had no response to that. "Did you notice what the goldfinch is eating?" he asked. "Thorns and thistles. A strange diet. I avoid them when I can." He rubbed his scratched shins. "Brave little creatures."

Judas hurled his pebble. The goldfinch spun into the air, fell, and lay still except for a feather stirring in the wind.

"Why did you ever do that?" Jude's voice was plaintive.

"I never thought I'd hit him. I guess I was annoyed by his trilling—as though all of life were cookies and cream."

"That wasn't him singing. It was a trumpeter bullfinch."

206

"Well, what does it matter? He was just a bird—and they steal seeds, remember?" He kicked the body into the bracken. They walked on in silence. The singing finch had fled.

Some way along, a hovel stood by the footpath, and propped against the frame of the open door was an old man. His gray hair hung in strings, his clothes were patched and dirty, his great sunken eyes shiny, and his gray-spotted beard spiny as a porcupine. He hobbled up to meet the travelers.

"D'ya have something to give an old timer?"

"Didn't you beg from me before, old man?" Judas demanded.

"Can't say, sir. Me memory's become a forgettery."

"Are you hungry?" Judas peered though the door. "Why, you've got plenty of bread!"

"Won't last long."

"We don't have enough to help lay up stores, old man."

"If ye can't give, talk a little."

"You had a wife. Where is she?"

"Died 'bout a year ago. Been terrible lonely. Don't have no one to ignore me no more." The old man sidled up to Judas, and with grimy fingers felt his clothes. Judas thrust him away.

" 'Spensive clothes. Much nicer than your friend's. Sure you can't afford nothin'?" Haughtily Judas strode away. Jude had only a few pennies—Judas kept the funds. He slipped them furtively into the extended hand, signalled for silence, and sped after his companion.

"Jude," Judas clipped out, "apparently you don't agree with my way of disbursing funds."

"I leave that to you."

"I saw you sneak him money."

"That wasn't a criticism of you. Just my soft heart."

"Exactly—and soft head. You probably feel good about it, but think about this—you've cheated someone of greater need whom we'll be unable to help at some future date." Jude said nothing. Giving wasn't a matter of logic, but who could explain?

They had walked a long ways in silence when suddenly Judas began running. His startled companion peered into the distance and, in a little stir of dust, saw a knot of men approaching. Knowing the eagle eyesight of his friend, he sped after him.

Judas ran up to the Master with outspread arms, embraced him, and kissed him fervently. "So good to see you, Rabbi. I accomplished my mission. The people are excitedly awaiting you!"

"Then you have done well, Judas. And you, Jude," he said as the latter came up to greet him.

"Rabbi, I thought to bring you food." Judas pointed to the back pack Jude was unfastening.

The Master surveyed the terrain. A patch of lush, waist-high grasses sprinkled with golden flowers lay between the road and the shore. On a nearby stretch of beach, an out-cropping of rock caught his eye. "Peter, we'll eat there. Prepare while I pray." He seated himself on a boulder projecting above the tall grass.

"Did anything special happen in Jerusalem?" Judas asked.

"Anything special!" Peter exclaimed. "Can you guess? Both the Roman authorities and our own watched our Rabbi like hawks. Word was out—which I couldn't confirm but believe—that they're hunting for an excuse to stone him."

"Your worries are pointless!" announced Judas with an assurance that made Peter stare in amazement. "Obviously, you haven't grasped the implications of what he's done—of who he is!"

"Judas, your cocksureness would have blown away like chaff if you'd been there."

"Drop the theatrics and give us the facts." Judas' words dripped acid. "What happened, if anything?" Peter stared at him without a word. It was John who spoke.

"You're familiar with the pool of Bethesda near the Sheepgate, where the sick look for a cure when the waters stir?"

"Certainly. The Pharisees hate the place. Pagan superstition, they say. The waters are stirred not by an angel but by a natural pulsation having to do with pressures in the earth—of the kind that produce artesian wells. The waters of Siloam show the same pulsing at their underground source outside the city. Of course, by the time the water reaches the Pool of Siloam through Hezekiah's Tunnel, the pulse is dissipated, so the people aren't aware of it."

"The Sadducees hate the place worse than the Pharisees," Jude added, "because they don't so much as believe in angels to begin with." He looked at Judas. "And no one has explained why people really are cured if it's only an artesian well."

"We were at Bethesda," John resumed, "and the plight of a paralyzed man named Tertius touched Jesus. He had a hopeless look about him. He didn't have a friend to cast him into the pool when the waters pulsed. Jesus cured him."

Judas groaned. "Did the rest of the sick mob the Master?"

"No, he worked the cure in private, and wasn't recognized even by Tertius, whom he told to keep the matter quiet. When the Pharisees asked Tertius who cured him, he didn't know."

"So he did blab?" Jude asked.

"The cure was on a Sabbath, and the Pharisees caught Tertius carrying his bed-roll home, so he had to explain why. He didn't know Jesus' name, but later he saw him again and rushed to inform the Pharisees."

Judas scowled. "Of all places, he picked the pool at Bethesda to work a cure! What an irritant to the religious authorities!"

"What irritated them most," John reported, "is that he cured on the Sabbath, but did it without lifting a finger, so they were frustrated when they wanted to charge him with breaking the Sabbath."

"Some tried anyway," Peter interjected. "He only answered, 'The Father works right up to now, and I work.' "

"He said that!" Judas thrilled. "What else did he say?"

"His words to the sophisticated Jerusalemites were deeper than his teachings around Galilee—and seemed just for their benefit. He said a lot that I wasn't able to follow."

"Once," John chimed in, "he declared, 'The hour is coming when the dead in their graves will hear the Son of Man's voice. Up to the resurrection life will come those who have done good, and to the judgement those who have done evil.' "

"I knew it!" Judas was elated. "You've nothing to fear. Wait until the Master really begins revealing himself!"

"You're very mysterious," John observed, peering at him

with interest.

"All I know," Peter concluded, "is that I was happy to walk away a free man—and happy our Rabbi walked away at all. And now I'll call him to eat. He knows from experience that man can't live without food in his stomach."

Thus Peter dismissed the issue with an external show of command, but like a lion's jaws the question cleaved to his mind—who was this Master of theirs? "Our Father in heaven," he groaned, "you sent us your servant Jesus. Who did you send? What is he? A wonder worker? A prophet? The Christ?—or more than the Christ, as Judas claims? How shall we learn? When shall we know?"

2

Peter was in his element. The Master had resumed headquarters in his house, and in preaching made use of his boat. His boat! He was mildly amazed that even the Master could draw him away from that magnet. It was in his boat that his great bulk sat the tallest, the twinkle in his brown eyes was the brightest, and the upturn of the ends of his mouth most pronounced. When he was on the water with his crew, his boat became a world of its own, where he was captain and king—at ease, at home, in complete control, a master of his trade and his men, one with the water and the ship and all who were in it. In his boat—he might as well admit it—even the Rabbi was his subject, dependent on his mastery and content to let him take command.

He thought much about the Master, and when he thought about him now, he decided it was no surprise at all that he was a greater magnet than his own boat. Devotion and dedication to such and so great a leader gave him a sense of finding and spiritually joining the ideal of his manhood. For his people, the hero was not the man of war, but the man who mastered his passions, triumphed over pagan ignorance, and battled the forces that warred against the Lord. Even

210

David, the great king, was remembered less for his exploits of war than for his prowess in living the life of the chosen people and singing the songs of God. And as he thought of it now, he knew it was only pretence to see the Master as his subject in his boat. What nonsense. If he really thought that, he'd not leave the boat to follow him, not for an hour.

A couple of days ago, the Master had led them out of town, up into the adjacent highlands to the southwest, because of the unbearable heat. In honor of the profound discourse given there some weeks ago, the place had been dubbed the Mount of the Beatitudes. For the moment at least, the Jerusalem scholars who harassed him were absent, probably home enjoying the summer coolness of the Holy City. Their welcome absence, the lovely pastoral setting, and the breath-taking view from the Mount were lulling Simon Peter back into the sense of ordinariness he enjoyed. This respite only increased the shock of the unearthly event about to ripple and tear across the fabric of his life.

Ordinarily the Mount was cool, but presently it was a cauldron. The dreaded khamsin was blowing, driving in like a movable hell the fiery heat of Arabia. Dust from far-away desert sands hung high in the sky, blanketing the air in a mantle of gray, darkening the noonday sun to a smear of light in the haze, and extinguishing the stars.

This morning the heat remained, but the eastern horizon had cleared slightly. Burnished by the risen sun, the lake was a pool of molten silver against the basin of Gaulanitis' misty hills. The firs exuded their tang in the hot air, and the flowers in the grassy fields and the fruits and nuts ripening in the orchards rendered the body languid with the pleasure of their scents.

Feeling the heat surging up from below, Peter decided that if he had to be away from the lake, this was the time for it. In fact, he was happy to be here when he recalled that anything he touched down in the valley would feel hotter than his body. After washing up, he joined the Master for breakfast.

"This morning," Jesus announced when they had eaten, "we descend to the lake."

Peter lifted his bushy eyebrows, made sure Jesus ob-

211

served him wiping the sweat from his forehead—actually, it was carried off by the hot, dry wind before the beads could form—and spoke. "It's going to be a hot one even up here, Rabbi." There was protest in his tone. "People down there will bake like a fish." He waited expectantly.

"We leave at once." The Master made for the steep descent, and the others followed. At the shore, he turned and surveyed the great throng. "Launch the boats. Have them standing by." He leaped onto a great ebony boulder lapped by the waves, seated himself facing the people, and when they settled down he began.

"You've heard me announce the arrival of the kingdom of heaven. What is it? Can we illustrate it by something familiar?" He looked around, as though searching. Along the shore, fishermen were casting their nets. Above the road a farmer was weeding his field. Two sparrows darted past, landed in a shrub, and began to chirp. "Ah, listen to those sparrows! They're happy to find a perch in the mustard tree. The kingdom of heaven is like the seed from which it grew. Once the tiniest on earth, it grows and becomes the greatest of shrubs. Look at those generous branches inviting the birds of the air to come and nest in the shade."

One after another, Jesus told his parables. Some the Twelve had heard before, but others were new. The people, responding with more than the usual cheering and clapping, at times interrupted him with wild outbursts of enthusiasm. As the day wore on, it became evident that they threatened to go out of control. Growing edgy, Peter motioned John to join him, circulated through the crowd to get the feel of the situation, and hurried back to Jesus. "Rabbi," he whispered hoarsely, "Zealots who've seen your miracles are suggesting you're capable of more than talk about the Kingdom. They're inciting the people to acclaim you leader—to rise up against Rome. Officials in the crowd are wild with concern."

"Order the Twelve into the boats."

"The wind's gusting and the sky's lowering. We're in for a storm." Peter pointed to the scudding clouds.

"At once."

Peter barked: "John. James. You Twelve! Over here!" He herded them into the boats. Jesus turned to the people.

212

"Elemental forces threaten us all. Return to your homes now. Ponder the mystery of the Kingdom." He waded into the water and leaped into Peter's craft. "Make for the other side." With a sigh of weariness, he settled on the floorboards, laid his head on a weather-beaten old cushion propped against the seat, and closed his eyes.

Peter observed Jude eyeing the Master speculatively from his station at the other end of the boat, and saw a question coming. For all his simplicity, Jude was no fool. The Master censured stupid questions, and if this proved to be one, the circumstances, adverse to holding a conversation, would prove advantageous.

"Rabbi," Jude called, "why always teach in parables?"

Wearily, his eyes opened. "So that, with the Kingdom before their eyes, they may be blind to it, and with it sounding in their ears, they may be deaf to it. Why? Lest they repent and be forgiven. But to you I give the secret of the Kingdom—I explain my parables." His eyes closed.

Peter and John were manning the oars in front of him. Peter watched him until he was sure he had fallen asleep, then turned to John, his left eye screwed up in puzzlement. "What'd he mean by that?"

"He was quoting Isaiah," Jude put in from behind him.

"That may be," Peter growled over his shoulder, "but his answer puzzled me more than the question."

"Me, too," Jude admitted. "It's rough water, Peter." He was staring at the heaving surface and his tone was worried.

Judas, beside Jude, spoke in his most formal teaching style: "You have to bear in mind that the Creator won't force salvation upon us. It's offered, but if we don't want it we won't have the intelligence to recognize it."

"Judas, you have something there," John observed, "but I'd put it differently. Jesus once said that his Father reveals his truths only to the little ones. So he does the same. His parables speak in the simple way they understand. We have to bow our intelligence down in faith to what he has to say to us—not to what we think he should say—if we want to enter into it."

"Then he uses parables to protect people from them-

213

selves!" Peter exclaimed. "Once when the rabbis were contradicting every word, he murmured to himself—or to me— 'If I hadn't come, they'd have no sin. Now they have no excuse for their sin.' "

"No intelligent person," Judas bawled, "would deny the clear truth!" This seemed to Peter to contradict what Judas had just said, but it was certainly more in keeping with his usual view.

The boat crashed violently into a wall of water. Every timber creaked, and spray lashed the occupants.

"Peter, the wind's getting bad," Jude wailed.

"That's obvious. Just keep rowing. We've got to keep her headed into the wind or we'll go down!" The boat rocked wildly in an onrush of broken waves, raced down a deep trough, lifted sluggishly to an oncoming breaker, and took a great sheet of water from stem to stern. Peter stared in alarm at the water they were shipping.

"John. Grab a bucket and bail. I'll man both oars." John vacated the seat, and Peter slipped to the middle. He twisted his head and shot a glance toward the prow. Judas and Jude, manning the forward oars, looked like scared wet rabbits. "Can't you keep that prow to windward?" he bellowed. The water was coming in faster than John could bail. The gunwales were riding alarmingly close to water level. They were in danger of swamping.

A blast of wind struck them from the west, and water burst in from all sides. Peter shipped the oars, laid one hand on each gunwale to steady himself, and lifted his face to examine the heavens. There was no rain, as it was not the rainy season—but a few dark clouds were swirling in from the Mount of Beatitudes and tearing to shreds overhead. Coastal winds were sweeping in from the Mediterranean and doing battle with the khamsin. They were in a whirlwind.

The boat spun out of control. A bloody patch of sky marked the sun. He'd forgotten about the sun. It was like twilight.

"Peter," Jude bellowed, "wake the Master!"

Peter stared in amazement. The Master was before his eyes, and he hadn't given him a thought. The lower half of his body was submerged in water, rolling with every wave, yet

214

he slept on. Peter jumped up, lurched toward him, almost fell on top of him. He grabbed him by both shoulders, shook him roughly, and shouted in his ear: "Teacher! Doesn't it mean anything to you that we're done for?"

He opened his eyes, saw the storm, the condition of the boat, the frightened faces, rose to his feet, and lifted his face to the roaring winds. "Be silent!" The winds ceased. He cast his eyes on the raging waters. "Be stilled!" The waves subsided. The surface lay quiet from shore to shore.

Peter gaped. Trancelike, he stared at the others. John's sensitive face showed mingled awe and fear; Jude's, terror; Judas radiated an ecstatic glow of vindication and triumph. This upset Peter the more. The Master spoke first.

"Why so cowardly?" They fixed their eyes on him with mouths open. He sat down, and the familiar action galvanized the stunned Peter.

"Man the oars! John, take up your bailing." He seized his own oars and rowed vigorously, hardly knowing what he was doing. Who is this man? he marveled, commander of sea and sky. Judas—what does he know we don't? A smart man, I have to admit—but so's John, and his judgment's better.

They landed on the eastern shore of the lake, near Kursi. Jesus disembarked, found a suitable place on the beach, and lay down.

"What do you think of that?" Judas was still exultant.

"Who is this man?" Peter whispered. "Judas?"

"What I've been hinting," Judas exulted. "No 'man' at all."

"What're you talking about, man! Explain yourself!"

"Listen for a change, and I will. Recall the visit of the three men to Abraham. They *looked* like men—"

"You're not saying he's an angel!"

"—but none were," Judas went on evenly. "Two were angels—no doubt supernatural apparitions, since it's unlikely angels exist. The third 'man' was in reality *the Lord himself.*"

"You're not saying . . ." Peter's voice trailed off.

"I concluded some time back, after toying with other possibilities, that he's not a man. *He* has come as he did to Abraham."

"Judas, get a hold of yourself!" Peter was wild-eyed,

215

his voice thick with fear.

"Peter my friend"—Judas was patronizing—"I must inform you of the Lord's promise to come in person one day to care for his sheep. You'll find it in Ezekiel."

"He's a man!" Peter's words came like the charge of a bull. "He eats, sleeps, wears clothes, and"—he hesitated—"and takes a walk in the fields when it's necessary. His body's flesh and blood like ours—didn't you see me shaking him just now?"

"My dear Peter, so-called angels in human guise imitate all human qualities. But consider his sleep. What *man* can sleep in a storm like that? He drops these little hints for the alert. And tell me, what prophet, what angel, ever did what he just did?"

"He's a man!" Peter was shouting. "He preached and preached and was exhausted. Once I fished day and night and they had to pummel me to wake me in a storm. What do you think, John?"

"Judas is making us all think." John was pensive. "I haven't pieced it together yet, but we've lived many months with him, and I agree with you, Peter, that whatever else, he's a man. Furthermore, he calls God his father. How does that make sense in your interpretation, Judas?"

"So you think"—Judas was caustic, his eyes narrowed to slits—"that a man gets up and orders heaven and earth about without so much as asking God's leave?"

"Don't take offence. You have a point. I said I don't have it worked out. Look, the other boats are arriving."

Matthew catapulted from his craft as it beached and trotted up. "Did you see how that storm subsided? I didn't expect to hail another sunrise. Peter, you've been on the lake so many years you've seen all her moods. Did you ever see anything like this?"

"No. We were discussing it. We'll fill you in later. Right now, we're hungry, and we came away without food. Let's find some. There must be fish stranded on the beach after that storm." Peter walked down the beach by himself. He hoped he sounded in control again, but it wasn't food he wanted; he wanted to get away from his fear. He felt his blood curdling in his veins—as though the Master had only moved the storm from outside to inside. How long could he take this? He was a man used to being in command.

He did not calm down until he remembered to pray, when it came to him that, sooner or later, he would find the answer. Until then, he could endure. He was a man. Only, he must never stop listening, thinking, searching, praying— or following.

3

Out from human consciousness goes a flickering ray, feebly beating back the night. Winds of doubt arise, the torch flickers, and smoking darkness closes in with ghostly clutchings. But fed the oil of faith, the light flares afar—filling the heart with gladness at the sight of its Father's house. So goes the fragile life of earth's children, to whom you sent me to be the new Torch.

In amber glory where forever you dwell, dwell I the inseparable Child of your heart—and I dwell on earth as the man in which I became flesh. And in that peril on the lake, mortal consciousness and eternal I AM together summoned the storm to nothingness. And the man I became tasted, through that glorious deed of power, what I bring—tasted, in yet another way, through the medium of the storm, MYSELF. Oh, the homesickness since.

And now this flesh of men's flesh cries up in longing to you for that experience always—for me and for them. Father, the Son of Man yearns to come home to himself and to you, with the children of men in his train.

Yet my labors go on. Little is a man his own master when love masters him and presses him to labor. Behold your Son, the servant of men—exhausted and harried. My difficulties counsel concealment—and on the lake your storm made it urgent that I choose to do what could only astound and mystify.

Later that same day pity moved me to free the possessed

Gerasene running naked among the dead, wild and self-destructive. Would not your Son have wanted that mercy shown him, were he in such straits—whatever the cost to the doer? Next, my pity complied with the plea of the demons—"Don't send us out of the land. Send us there into the swine!" Concerned I was about confusing my followers. Yet how shall they learn of love but by seeing your Son want even for demons the boon he would crave in their place? And did not the pigs plunging crazed into the lake serve to convey the horror of evil spirits—that even pigs chose death to their dominion?

The next day—as if cautioning your Son against mincing prudence—you pressed me into service as healer, not of one but of two. First came Jairus—when we had crossed back to Seven Springs. How long he had remained uncommitted, despite all he had seen and heard as head of the synagogue. Running he came, shouting to the crowd to make way—the command, the suffering in his voice opening a path for him—and he plunged to his knees. "Teacher, come. You've got to come—my little daughter's dying." He saw my hesitation—was I to exercise a power that would drive that ungovernable crowd to frenzy?

Leaping to his feet, that distraught father seized my hand and tugged me, crying, "I've been a fool. Blind. You can heal her—I've seen you. You must come!"

How embarrassed his friends—unbelief signalled in the very shuffling of their feet. Tears—streaming down his seamed face, dripping from his beard. His daughter I knew and loved.

Father, how could I not go with that father? Through the press we hurried—bumped and clung to—forcing our way.

Then I felt the healing power go from me—never had it happened. Always before you had left its use to my counsel. At once I yearned to instruct the others by the faith that had won your heart.

"Who touched my cloak?" At the question, what horror contorted the faces of the Twelve—it asked if my reason had given way. Wild with alarm, Peter seized my arm to take charge.

"Rabbi," he whispered, "they're jostling you on every

218

side." Then she justified me.

"Here I am," cried a woman's voice, and I wheeled. Her triumphant countenance distinguished itself in that sea of faces the way, in a dark storeroom of lamps unlit, one stands burning. "It was I who touched you," she sang out, "because I knew it would heal me. And now my blood has stopped flowing after twelve long years!"

"My daughter"—I resisted Jairus' tugging—"your faith has healed you. Go in peace. Be cured of your disease."

"I only touched your cloak and I'm well," she babbled. "I went to all the doctors and got worse, and they touched me for all I had." The people laughed, but Jairus pulled me urgently.

"Please, Teacher," he begged. And now another group of Jairus' friends approached and blocked our way. Their spokesman addressed him loudly.

"Sorry to have to tell you, Jairus. Your daughter died."

"No use for the teacher now," another said, glancing at me.

"Why harass the exorcist further?"—this from the friend who had watched with distaste as Jairus appealed to me.

Jairus' face blanched and his barrel chest slumped. He staggered, collapsed onto a nearby rock and stared off into the distance, the hue of the skin of his face leaden as the Sea of Tiberias before a squall. In this manner did his friends support that distraught father to whom had been given healing faith as surely as to the woman.

The signs were clear—you were at work in him. He had to be helped though it scatter my plans like straw in a whirlwind. Turning from the doubters, I laid my hands on his shoulders. "Jairus, don't let despair grip you. Only believe." The cured woman squeezed to my side.

"Yes, only believe as I did, and I'm well. Do it for your daughter!" By the hand I drew him on as he had first drawn me.

"You people, trouble this father no further," I admonished.

"Return to your homes. Peter, James and John, follow me." We hurried on while the Twelve worked to disperse the crowd and deter pursuers. As we approached Jairus' courtyard the air bore to us the pagan cries of shrieking women and hired minstrels wailing songs of despair. Jairus' relatives and servants stood tearing their hair and their garments and raining dust on their heads.

"Be silent!" My shouted command cut off the hubbub like a lopped branch and they gaped at me in amazement. "Why churn up a tumult of weeping? The little one's not dead. She has fallen asleep." Anger hammered out my words. Despite your works, promises, and prophets, there rose those pagan ululations denying that the innocent child had simply passed into life. My rebuke served a second purpose—it would enlist their unbelief to my purpose.

"Look who's talking, and he hasn't seen her," a huge woman with the tears still wet on her cheeks cried with brazen scorn.

"We don't know what death is," an old man mocked.

"Ha! We're weeping to entertain ourselves," someone rasped.

"Listen to his words of wisdom. Dead is dead, I say— and I'm the doctor who just closed her eyes!" They laughed mockingly.

"Peter, put them out."

He herded them through the gate and locked it. With weeping mother and grieving father we entered their daughter's chamber. The twelve-year-old lay on her bed unmoving, her face white as snow, her raven hair fanning out on the pillow, the delicate lashes of her closed eyes embroidering the marble cheeks. Her breast neither rose nor fell. Her mother sobbed aloud—wanting to throw herself on her child —her father restraining her.

The delicate hand was ice-cold in mine.

"Arise, little lamb."

Around my words fell the silence of forest depths. Roses blossomed in those pale cheeks, a cherry red stole into the lips, the delicate lashes lifted, and she looked up at me in surprize. "Rabbi, thanks for coming to visit me. I feel so much better."

Even as her voice splashed into the room, she sat up and bussed my cheek with unutterable sweetness, and I embraced her tenderly.

"Evie!" The cry of wonder, the spring to her side, the maternal caresses, the father's wild joy, the stunned look of the Three, dictated what I must say to them—but first, the girl . . .

"You must give your little lamb something to eat," I told her mother. "Evie, are you hungry?"

"Hungry enough to eat a whole boatload of Simon Peter's fish!" She gazed fondly at Peter. "We miss the fresh ones he used to sell us"—she turned to me—"It's all right, though. He's doing something more important." She leaped from her bed and danced around the room. "I feel so well again."

"And now you must listen to me." The seriousness of my address registered in their quiet attention. "Say no word about what happened here."

Evie's eyes widened in innocent wonder. "Did you heal me, Rabbi?"

"You too are to say nothing, little lamb."

"But Lord," Peter objected, "how can we keep it quiet— keep people from knowing?"

"Describe nothing. What they know will be left to them." Those who had refused to find any sense in which she was not dead would now find no sense in which she was ever dead. And their cynicism would serve me—would bank the wild enthusiasm of those who believed.

Under the unblinking stars that night I weighed the faith of the Twelve. How limited it was—how shaky. Much they had seen, and the Three more still—yet my works stunned them that day. What can ever teach them that he who received the power into his human hand and he who gave it are one and the same—your eternal Son become Man?

Yet would it not be less of a mystery did they search more their own mystery—of flesh and spirit fused?

Still, I will not obscure the uniqueness of your Son, addressing creation from out of his human awareness, yet communing with his eternal Self.

On the day Peter asks how this can be, what a joy to turn the question on him—ask of those human experiences wherein knowledge and impulse spring from that secret inner core of himself which man fails to understand.

"But," Peter will persist in his honest way, "what if you

who became one of us wants one thing, and you who were before us wants another—doesn't that make two persons?"

"And you," I will ask, "have had—have you not—the desire to follow me faithfully, together with the impulse to run in fear? Was that impulse at your beck and call?"

"You know it wasn't," he will say with a grievance in his eye.

"Then it has a kind of will and center of its own that is still you."

"But, Lord," he will blurt out, "how can God and man be one you?"

"Think, Peter, of that mystery in which man and wife are one. If human love fashions such union, what can divine love not do?"

Peter is far from such questions, but closest to realizing I am the Christ. Yet John has probed more deeply—your Spirit illuminating his mind even as he inflames the Magdalene's heart. He cannot express the mystery he touches—yet bravely he opens his heart to receive love's fire.

Judas—troubled Judas. Colliding with the outer fringes of my mystery, and shrinking back into his own inadequate resources to fathom it. A parade of endless guesses marching through his head, he seizes on one after another. He sees me not as the Sent One to be followed, but as a puzzle to be solved.

Father, your Son calls every child of Adam out of his loneliness to share this union which he has brought. Only through experiencing it will they ever understand. Hasten the day. Speed the events that will bring the many to the knowledge that I AM.

4

The streaming sunlight caresses the earth and crops spring up, and these blessings inspire people to give thanks—but not all. Some complain that summer came late, and others grumble of its burdensome heat. Even nature is not of one mind. The shining draws moisture to the skies and clouds form and clash and thunder and storm the earth, destroying crops and human habitations.

Like the bright sun's rays, the Master's presence raised storm clouds—in men's hearts. This the Twelve witnessed. On the rounds of the Galilean villages they were saddened by the rising currents of resistance. Towns formerly wild with enthusiasm now showed formidable reserve or open hostility. That the Master was a wonder-working exorcist could hardly be denied, but it was equally clear that he was embattled. Few were willing to expose themselves to the dangerous winds of controversy.

Contributions had slipped and shelter was chancy. The little band was footsore, ragged, and thin from travel and hunger. Judas, treasurer and provisioner, had grown sullen.

Jesus was presently teaching in the marketplace of a small village near Sepphoris. The weather had turned unseasonably cold, there was a lowering sky, and a few large raindrops pattered down. The Master raised his face to examine the cloud formation, the drops spattering against his brow, shiny little globules clinging to hair and beard.

"You can see"—his tone was humorous—"that the Father makes his rain fall on the just and the unjust alike. So, too, he makes the sun come up on both good and bad. Be like him. Love even your enemy. Pray for him. Prove you are sons and daughters of your heavenly Father."

Only a handful of people had turned out from the village. His disciples outnumbered them. A hostile collection of Pharisees, Sadducees, Herodian sympathizers and members of such splinter parties as the Zealots still trailed them, or pressed around to argue and heckle.

Jesus concluded his teaching, sent the people to their homes, and summoned the Twelve to take council apart. "What changes have you noticed taking place of late?"

"Everywhere we go," Peter replied, "the hostility worsens. Even some of the simple people are turning against us."

"You're no longer welcome in most synagogues," John observed, "because the leaders are unfriendly, the people who want healings provoke public disorder, and the Zealots

223

who foment revolution cry out for rebellion. For the same reason you rarely enter the large cities. We are reaching fewer and fewer people. And before long the religious authorities may outlaw us all together." Judas' face was working furiously as John spoke, and he could hardly wait to begin.

"Rabbi,"—his tone was accusatory—"you are choosing smaller and smaller villages. I don't mention how that conflicts with the urgency of the Good News, I only stress the difficulty it injects into my role as provisioner. We number more people than we attract, making it impossible to beg or buy sufficient food. We men can't live like *angels!*" He stared at Jesus.

"Anything else?"

"Perhaps I should mention, too," Judas answered, "that our money is all but gone. The few affluent and generous women in our entourage are growing as poor as the rest of us."

"Rabbi," Jude lamented, "when the crowds were large, we Twelve could minister to distressed individuals, but now we have nothing to do."

"I love the country," Philip began, "but we have to find a way to preach to the city folk once again."

"Despite the hostility aroused by your detractors," James added, "most of the people who come do so with good will."

When they had finished, the Master spoke. "You see the hunger of the people," he said sorrowfully, "like sheep unshepherded and unpastured. It is time for you to go to them—even to the cities."

"Us, Lord?" Thomas asked in surprise. "What shall we say?"

"For many months you've heard my parables—revealing that the time is fulfilled, the kingdom of God is arriving, summoning all to repentance and to faith in the Good News."

"But Lord," Peter objected, "you not only preach the Kingdom—you make it come with healings and exorcisms and other works of power. Who will believe *us?*"

"Here and now"—the words were solemn—"I give you authority over unclean spirits, and charge you to anoint the sick with oil and heal them."

"When shall we go?" youthful Thomas asked eagerly, flexing his long legs in anticipation.

"Am I," Judas asked, "expected to acquire supplies for twelve separate itinerants?"

"You will go in pairs. James and John, set out in the morning for the territory of Dan. The others I shall mission in the course of our circle of the villages. Live as you have seen me live. Take no bread, and"—he looked at Judas—"don't have even a penny in your money belt. The laborer is worth his support."

"May we at least wear two tunics?" Judas asked with raised eyebrows.

"No, but you may carry a walking stick."

"Shall we do without sandals too?" Peter enthused.

"Sandals you may wear."

"Where shall we stay?" Jude enquired, looking at Judas out of the corner of his eye. On the journey the two had taken, Judas had arranged elaborate accommodations, offending the poor in the process.

"Under the roof of the man, rich or poor, who with a good heart offers you shelter. Stay there until you move on."

"What if they won't listen?" John asked.

"Shake off the dust of that town from your feet and go elsewhere. We will meet at Peter's house four weeks from today. Peace!"

The weeks had passed, and the return of the Twelve was imminent. The Master was teaching at Capernaum when Joanna, a long-time disciple, came running. She was the wife of Chuza, King Herod's business manager. "Teacher, I have terrible news. My husband sends word by fast horse that Herod has murdered the Baptizer. Cut off his head. Salome instigated it—collecting on the king's crazy promise to do anything she asked because she had danced practically naked. Her mother Herodias put her up to it. Afraid he might heed John and end their illegitimate marriage. You're in danger too. My husband fears all who follow you are."

The Master took her hand. "These scandals must come, but woe to those who cause them! The Twelve will return

225

tomorrow, and I'll decide what's to be done."

Judas slapped Jude on the back as they trudged along. "Well, Judas-not-from-Kerioth, it will be good to return to our leader and report our exploits." Jude sighed. He had given up telling Judas not to call him that. He studied Judas and thought of another matter he had often pondered. It might be good to broach it while the man was on one of his highs.

"Judas, do you mind my asking you a personal question about our Rabbi?"

"My friend," came the expansive reply, "you know I'm generous in sharing my insights with you. Ask away."

"Well," Jude dragged the word out, still pussyfooting, "do you remember your opinion after the storm on the lake that the Master is no man at all because he's . . ."

"I remember," Judas said sharply. "What about it?"

"Do you still believe that?"

"I never actually *believed* it. You have to understand that I'm an intellectual, always theorizing. What you are referring to was simply a provisional hypothesis. I always meant it to yield to a more solid conclusion which was bound to come when we had more evidence."

"Then you've dropped it?"

"Dropped it!" Judas bellowed. "How can I simply drop it when we haven't yet solved the mystery of our rabbi's identity? No, I've not *dropped* it! I've *modified* it to suit the accumulating data. I've scaled it way down, you might say."

"Who do you think he is now? One of the prophets?"

"I'm not ready to come right out and say without more evidence. But I'll hint this much. He's far more mysterious than that. And I'll put you on to the central thread of the evidence. Haven't you noted the impossible sacrifices he demands, as though not quite aware what it means to be a man? Let that suffice for now, my friend."

Jude was troubled but knew better than to pursue a conversation Judas had terminated. More and more conversations were ending this way. He had tried to raise the matter of following the Master's instructions more faithfully, but Judas had impatiently and airily exclaimed, "My dear Jude, don't get picayune. Instructions have to be maturely interpreted!"

Jude saw off in the distance a spacious mansion of tawny massive stones cut and polished in the Roman manner. Cypresses towered over the patio and lined the open courtyard where workmen were grinding meal at a millstone worked by a donkey. A groomsman was leading a handsome silver-gray stallion to the water trough. Even the barn was a more desirable shelter than the hovels that had housed them on the journey. Judas had repeatedly tried to carry the Good News to the wealthy first, but none had listened.

"Look at that lovely place!" Jude exclaimed in admiration. "People in homes like that don't often listen to us, do they?"

Judas began by tapping his money belt. "Never you mind, Jude. When our Rabbi comes into the Kingdom that he keeps promising, we won't be begging lodgings. And when I sit as his administrator, never hesitate to ask me whatever you want. Count on my liberality."

Jude looked up in mild surprise. "Is that what you think he's promising? The Kingdom he talks about sounds different. I don't think things are going to turn out the way you imagine."

Judas spun sideways and glared. "I've learned the hard way that the old saying is true—when a sage is fool enough to converse with a fool, two fools are conversing!"

The Twelve returned in pairs, and the Master listened attentively to their reports. The next morning he said, "Peter, send everyone away. The Twelve must come with me to the wilderness for a rest."

"Rabbi, may I make a suggestion?" Philip asked. "Let's head for that uninhabited region near Gergesa with the springs and meadows."

"It's not far from your Bethsaida with the olive orchards you love," Judas observed unsmiling.

"That's why I know about it," Philip said defensively.

"We'll leave at once for that very place," the Master decided. "Get one boat ready, Peter."

Peter tramped down to the shore of the lake. When he

passed under the branches of a stand of towering pines, it was like entering a sanctuary with soft light and stillness, and for incense the pungent exhalation of the trees which the dampness of the season enhanced. Peter breathed deeply, inhaling earth and plant smells, and the scent of pine fresh as the promise of tomorrow. And tomorrow held promise indeed, for the thought of going off to rest with the Master and the Twelve lifted his heart. His troubles were falling from his shoulders the way the myriads of pine needles had fallen from the trees and cushioned the ground so pleasantly, making him walk with a spring.

To his ears came the piercingly beautiful song of a bird hidden in the branches, and Peter thought, "My temple has its choir, too." But as he approached it, the bird hurtled from its perch in alarm and swept so close to his head that he heard distinctly the pulse of its little wings. The bird reminded Peter of himself. His heart sang an achingly beautiful song whenever he thought of the Master, a man so like himself with his unaffected love for humankind and the people of Israel in particular, and all God's creatures. And he taught a simple, selfless way of life that brought everyone closer to nature and to his brother, and above all to the Lord. But just when Peter was most off guard, he would manifest a totally mysterious self and Peter's heart would pulse in terror like the bird's wings and speed away to hide in some sanctuary of its own.

They squeezed into their biggest boat and set out. The day was bright and sunny, but chilly. It was the rainy season, and the meadows near the shore looked fresh and green. "What a view!" Jude exulted. "From here you can see the whole lake. Notice that man near Bethsaida. He's pointing to us—at least, that's what it looks like." No one responded. The boat slapped its way through the gentle waves, and they were content to be silent, letting their tiredness ooze to the surface, coaxed by the hypnotic song of the waves. Jude yawned cavernously, and settled back contentedly.

"Do you smell fish?" Peter cried, leaping to his feet and wheeling about, gazing sharply at the surface.

"Peter, that's an old wives' tale," Thomas, a callow landlubber, said disparagingly, "thinking you can smell approach-

228

ing fish still under water!" Even as he spoke a school of fish broke the water to windward, flashed their silver bellies mockingly, and disappeared below the surface. "I see," Thomas conceded.

"Let's fish a bit, Master," Peter coaxed. "We need food."

"You're just itching to do what you do best," Judas snapped acidly.

"Brother, the boat's too full to ply our nets," Andrew gently reminded, and Peter sat down.

Two hours later, they made for the distant shoreline of their destination. John shaded his eyes and peered. "Your uninhabited place, Philip," he announced, "is featuring a welcoming committee." Thomas turned and squinted.

"There are hundreds," he groaned, "and more coming!"

"So much for your good idea, Philip." Judas' voice had the quality of curdled milk.

"How could I know they'd spot us in the boat and pass the word? Must be what happened—and you didn't foresee it, either. Look, they're running up from all directions."

"Rabbi," Peter suggested, "let's make for another location."

"What does the shepherd do, Peter, when he sees his sheep coming to him hungry, and the hirelings nowhere in sight?"

"He pastures them."

"Beach the boat."

The Master taught the people at great length, and when he rested the Twelve prayed over the sick, or took individuals off by themselves for counsel. As the afternoon wore on, Judas grew more and more restless. When the sun was sinking below the Horns of Hattim, bathing Mount Arbel in gold and purple, he marched up to Jesus. "Rabbi, dismiss this crowd or they'll be in trouble." His tone was uncompromising. "It's late, and they haven't eaten all day."

"Judas is right, Teacher," Peter joined in. There must be five thousand people here in the wilderness."

"Your usual exaggeration," Judas disagreed, "but enough to get us in trouble. Why, they've dragged the halt and the blind to this godforsaken place."

"Send them to nearby farms and villages," James suggested, "before folks go to bed. They can buy what they need."

"You give them something to eat," the Master directed.

"How?" Judas demanded.

"Philip, where can we buy bread?"

"Around here? No place I know of." He looked at the people spilling down from hill-top to shore. "Anyway, six month's wages wouldn't buy half enough."

"When the blind and lame start dropping from hunger we'll be blamed!" Judas blurted out, face dark.

"How many loaves are available?" the Master asked. "Go and find out."

"I have," Andrew revealed. "I was concerned, so I checked around. These people came in a rush from work in the fields with no more than their basket lunches—long since eaten. One lad here has five barley loaves and two smoked fish, so I brought him in tow—but what good is that?" He indicated a ruddy-cheeked boy toting a basket of bread and two fish wrapped in green leaves. Peter examined them.

"Two little perch! And I've caught dozens, hundreds, in an hour! I've caught boatloads!"

"You're a prodigious fisherman!" Judas snarled. "They're waiting to be renamed the Peter Fish in your honor! And are we five thousand to starve while you boast?"

"You denied there were five thousand," Peter rejoined.

"Tell the people to sit down," the Master said. "Give the bread and fish to me."

"I'll arrange the people in an orderly fashion to make the distribution possible," Judas decreed, glaring at him. "Jude, come along." When the others were out of earshot, he added, "I don't know what the Rabbi would do without us."

Jude thought, "He means, without him." Aloud he asked, "What are you referring to?"

"Why, he has no feeling for handling human affairs. Look what he's up to now! My theory's that he's an angel sent on some mission, and now he thinks he can make us all live like angels! You noticed that on our missionary journey I laid in a few supplies contrary to his unreal instructions."

"Yes. I felt guilty about it."

Sullenly, Judas pushed and pulled the people into the arrangement he had conceived, and returned to the others. Jesus was entertaining a flock of children nearby. "Now

230

that he's going to feed this swarm of hungry locusts with five loaves," he growled, "I've divided them into groups of fifty and a hundred, so we can give each contingent a fragment to portion out. That way each can get a crumb— if he has to have his symbolic angel's bread. A far cry from the feasts of the final times the prophets raved about!"

"You know what?" Jude asked.

"No riddles, please!" Judas snapped.

"Peter was right! There are about five thousand." Peter smiled, and Judas glared, and seeing the glint in his eye, Jude added soothingly, "Your idea to divide them up that way was brilliant."

When Jesus joined them, Judas announced, "They're settled on the green grass, waiting to be fed. He turned and admired the geometrical divisions he had engineered. "Now we can readily keep track of what we distribute."

The Master had broken the loaves into pieces and arranged a heap of fragments in the bottom of the twelve empty baskets they had scouted up. He broke the smoked fish into morsels and laid them on the leaves. Now, with a basket of bread in his right hand and the fish in his left, he strode to the top of the hill, looked up to heaven and in a clear, ringing voice prayed: "Blessed are you, O Father, King of the world. You bring forth bread." He gave a basket to each of the Twelve, and in dismay they went off through the crowd. The Master passed among the people, handing out the fish.

When the Twelve reassembled, there were still a few pieces in the baskets and some morsels of fish on the paten. "I don't know what happened," Peter grunted, "but they don't seem to want any more."

"Now we can eat," the Master said. Afterward, he directed, "Take your baskets and collect the fragments."

"The fragments!" Judas exploded. "To feed some ant?"

"Do as I say." The Twelve returned with baskets overflowing. The people closest, who had seen and heard everything, began to pass swift, confused explanations through the crowd.

"Manna in the desert!" someone shouted.

"Another Elisha!" acclaimed a man with a beard to his waist.

"The prophet we've been awaiting!" a great voice bellowed. One group, among whom Peter spotted some known Zealots, began shouting, "It's the promised king! He has come at last!" They drew their swords and waved them wildly. Jesus spun around and faced the Twelve.

"Run for the boat!"

"Lord, don't you see?" Judas cried, wild-eyed. "This kind of backing is power!"

"Into the boat!" The Master thrust Peter forward. The Twelve ran pell-mell for the shore, but Judas delayed long enough to seize one of the full baskets. Jesus wheeled toward the uproarious crowd.

"Return to your homes!"

"Our King! Our King!" The bellowing mob swarmed him. The Zealots struggled to hoist him to their shoulders. Jesus broke away and raced toward the heights beyond.

The dark, overcast night hid him when at last, far away, he fell to the ground, panting and praying, a solitary figure on a mountain top.

5

Behind sounded the turmoil of the hysterical crowd as fleet-footed John fled down the beach into the water—the spray reminded him of the day he ran through the Jordan to the Master—and he was torn by indecision. Why flee the event longed for since childhood, the assembly wildly acclaiming the leader from God? Had they not come to escape the enmity of Herod, and now were they running from friends? Had the Master at last proclaimed himself the prophet like Moses by Moses promised, like him feeding a multitude in the desert? Then why run? Yet had even Moses stilled a storm? No, but he had parted the Red Sea. Who could sort it all? Not even the leaders of Israel! His strong limbs drove through the water, but his mind was entangled, drowning in a sea of weeds.

232

Flashing into his thoughts came the sight of the Master commanding this flight, and he abandoned his guilty protest. Never before such magnetic force in those bottomless eyes, never such a look of command on human face!

In a rush they launched their craft into deeper water, leaped aboard, and rowed vigorously against the rising wind into the misty twilight. No one spoke.

Preoccupied, he watched Judas draw fragments of bread and fish from the basket he had salvaged, and devour them ravenously. Why, when they'd just eaten? The puzzle dissolved his train of thought, and he frowned.

"What an opportunity missed!" Judas exclaimed between mouthfuls. "That army of supporters could make our leaders change their tune." He stared on-shore. "What stirred their sudden enthusiasm?"

John couldn't believe his ears, but before he could speak Peter barged in—"Are you still hungry?"

"Starved. Those contemptible crumbs—I ate nothing. Where did those leftovers come from? Aren't you hungry?"

"Why, no"—Peter was embarrassed—"The food was in front of us, and I kept picking until I was satisfied."

"Then you don't know what happened—either of you?" John marveled.

"Those crumbs," Judas spit out, "had some mystical significance for those country bumpkins. It overcame their greed, so they dug into their satchels and shared their private hoards."

"Look in the basket." John's voice was taut. "What do you find?" Judas shook it in exasperation.

"What you'd expect. Bits of bread and fish."

"What kind of bread?"

"Barley of course. You're annoying me."

"Any wheat?"

"None that I notice, but it's getting dark. I said you're annoying me. What're you driving at?"

"If those leftovers were from their private supplies, wouldn't there have to be some wheat bread—and other grains as well?"

"Possibly." Judas rummaged again. "Ah, here's some wheat."

"Let me see it."

"No, on closer inspection, it's barley. I said the light's poor. But of course, wheat's preferred. They'd eat it first."

"Is there anything but smoked perch? You know the varieties of fish from the lake, and most people don't smoke fish, they broil it. And if wheat bread's the favorite, so is perch."

Judas fumbled again. All the fish was smoked perch.

"What are you hinting? You're annoying me."

"I'm asking you to remember that with twenty barley loaves Elisha fed a hundred hungry men, and Moses the whole people with no bread that man had made."

"Are you suggesting . . ."

"I'm asserting it! And why not?"

"For lack of evidence! I say the people are still hungry."

"Still hungry, and they turned in those leftovers? What about us?"—John shouted over the wind—"Anyone hungry? Plenty of food." No one was. "No, Judas, that crowd wasn't as virtuous as you—or as hung up by what they imagined. The food kept coming, and they ate until they had enough— and realized what had happened."

"Peter, this wind's getting bad," Judas bawled. "Head for shore." Startled, Peter looked around.

"You two had me so caught up I neglected navigation. There's nothing we can do but keep facing into the wind. Making for shore would swamp us."

"A great helmsman," Judas snapped. "I say, land her."

"We'll land where we can, when we can. Now take up that bailer and bail. You others, lay into those oars harder." Peter stared at the breakers. A gusty northwester was battering them and throwing them off course, but there was no great danger.

"By the way"—Thomas wanted to rekindle the discussion— "I saw Greeks and Romans in the crowd. Were they spies, or genuine seekers?"

"Oh, genuine, I think," Peter volunteered. "That is the Greek territory of the Ten Cities."

"How," Thomas asked, "would you describe the difference between the Greek religion and ours?"

"The Greeks," Judas shouted above the wind, "made their

234

gods in man's image. The true God has revealed to us that he made man in his."

"And the result?"

"We have to bend every effort to learn about him and his will for us—and do it. The Greeks know and serve their gods by knowing and serving their own impulses."

"They think we Jews are too other-worldly," Thomas said, "concerned not with this world, but with the Messiah and the world to come."

"That's untrue, of course," Judas pointed out. "God appointed man an ongoing task in the world—to beget children, fill the world, and take dominion over it."

"Then why," Thomas asked, "do we seem so much less preoccupied with this present world than the Greeks? Think of the teachings of our Master, like the Beatitudes." Judas hesitated, and John leaped in.

"It's because, having made their gods in their own image, they consider man the measure of all things. They make their own judgments and decisions about right conduct. We obey God's revelation."

"And also," Judas added, "the Greeks set limits according to man. God lifts us beyond our limits."

"Yes," John agreed. "We crossed the Red Sea with dry shoes. The Egyptians tried it, and died. The Egyptians, the Greeks and the Romans have their myths but we have our history of wonders."

"Then," summarized Thomas, "the Greeks decree for themselves what is good and evil, possible and impossible, but God tells us. And that, I suppose, is why we know our bodies will come bounding out of the grave, and they have no hope."

"The result," John added, "is that the true Israelite goes about his task in keeping with the Law and that makes him look inept for this world even to the unfaithful Jew."

"And at times not without reason!" Judas exploded. "Some twist and turn God's word into such an ascetic view of man that it robs the pleasure from his palate and the flesh from his bones, and even tears the sex from his bowels! They neglect gaining righteous control of government, and prate about the afterlife!" This sudden change of Judas'

235

mood extinguished the conversation.

The hours passed, but the boat progressed hardly a mile. Gusting winds broke the cloud cover, and streaming starlight turned to ghosts the tattered shrouds of mist which flitted by. The silver moon scudded through the luminous clouds like a tipsy skiff. Thomas the landlubber stared at the alarming waves and pictured the hundred and fifty feet of water beneath. "Are we to be here all night?" he blurted out. "I'm tired."

"And I'm cold and hungry," Peter retorted. "There's no help for it but to wait out the wind. Judas, pass me that bread and fish."

"What time is it?" Bartholomew asked, stifling a yawn.

"About three in the morning," Andrew said.

"Look! What's that?" Thomas exploded. "Something floating!" They stared at the object to which Thomas pointed—and began shouting in voices too strained to be recognizable.

"It looks like a man—on the water—walking."

"It can't be."

"It is!"

"It's a ghost!"

"It's coming our way!"

"Veer to port!"

"It's passing by!"

"My guts are churning!" Then, from the direction of the figure cloaked in the tattered shreds of fog came a familiar voice, rising and falling on the gusting wind.

"I AM. Stop being afraid."

"It's Jesus!" John exclaimed.

"Lord, if it's you"—Peter's stentorian tones cut across the wind—"order me to come to you over the water!"

"Come." Peter bounded from the boat and ran. He had almost reached the figure when a strong gust of wind threw him off balance. He began to sink beneath the waves, crying out in terror. "Lord, save me!"

Jesus ran forward and grasped him.

"You little-faith. What made you doubt?"

They climbed into the boat. The wind sighed and ceased. They made for shore southwest of Capernaum. A man spotted them and ran to spread the news. When they landed, Jesus went off by himself to pray. "We'll be overrun with people soon," Peter predicted. "Before that happens, let's talk."

"Once again I tell you," Judas blurted out, "he's an angel, not a man!"

"The last time you told us who he was," Peter reminded him, "he wasn't a mere angel."

"I was more optimistic then." Judas made it sound like ages ago. "Besides, more evidence is in."

"I tell you, I know men, and he's a man."

"I know men, and he's no man." Judas retorted.

"I know men," John joined in as spiritedly as the others, "and he's a man—but that doesn't explain him either."

"Who ever heard," Judas hissed, "of a man walking on water?"

"I'm a man," Peter proclaimed, thumping his wet chest, "and I walked on water."

"Walked?" Judas was incredulous. "You sank!"

"What?" Peter bellowed, but caught himself as he saw Jesus at prayer, and rumbled, "Didn't I walk *before* I sank? I didn't sink until I began thinking the way you do." He turned to the others. "You saw me, didn't you? I must have gone twenty feet."

"And nearly as many down," Judas mocked.

"Peter"—Jude was apologetic—"we were all so exhausted, so afraid and confused we don't know what we saw."

"Jude, speak for yourself," Matthew said calmly. "I was sitting next to you, Peter, and I saw you jump out of the boat. I saw you running up and down those waves like hills. I saw you almost fall, and then you lost your nerve, and I saw you drowning, until . . ."

"Thank you, Matthew," Peter interrupted. "I never liked tax collectors, but that's all changed."

"There goes our high-level discussion, degenerating into trivia," said Judas sourly.

"I said he's a man, and more," John persisted. "He's like Daniel's son of man, who comes on the clouds of heaven, as though he's been waiting in the wings of eternity. I've heard the rabbis speculate about his timelessness."

"Do you think I haven't made the connection with Daniel's son of man, my young friend?" Judas demanded. "In fact, I *explain* him instead of having him waiting around in eternity. Instead of an angel, he may be an ethereal human being compounded of some star-like material superior to our flesh. That would explain his walking on water, and a lot of other things."

"What other things?" John asked.

"Around Bethlehem rumors circulate that he had no father. And I've seen him at night faintly shimmering like a distant star. Haven't you noticed?"

"But we all know Mary his mother!" exclaimed Peter. "That makes him a man. And of course we've seen his faint glow at prayer. But that's been seen before among holy men. I saw it once myself—one of the Essenes at Qumran."

"He doesn't eat enough," Judas went on, "to keep a flea alive."

"He eats as much as the Baptizer," John retorted.

"In prayer," Judas said confidingly, "he puts forth fragrances like some garden among the stars."

"Judas," Peter said, "that *happens* to some who pray. It even happened to me once. Do you remember?"

"Oh yes," Judas sneered, "you explained your smell by saying your wife spilled perfume on your tunic. Did you lie then or now?"

"Neither. She did, but I washed it out, so that wasn't what you smelled. Judas, I'm desperate to make the point that for these things to happen, a man doesn't have to be stardust—unless we're all stardust."

"I agree," John cried. "When I said he may be more than a man, I wasn't denying he's as human as we are. I think Daniel's son of man is. That's what the phrase *emphasized*—he's of human stock. But Daniel's saying, 'Don't stop there. You have more to learn.' "

"I think you're wrong, young man," Judas rejoined. "But why don't you ask our Leader?"

"Why don't you ask him about your angel—or star-like material?" John shot back. Judas had no answer, but Peter spoke thoughtfully.

"I can point and say, 'That's a stone,' or 'You are Judas,'

but when it comes to our Master, names fail me because he's something I know less about. He's gradually letting us know who he is by what he's doing. It's the only way we can find out."

"When I was a tax collector," Matthew injected, "Prince Herod was under Emperor Tiberius, and I under both. Taxpayers expected me to prove I was authorized to charge what I did."

"So your cheating wasn't as easy as we thought," Jude jested, and Peter choked off a laugh.

"The result," Matthew went on patiently, "is that I used to plaster their decrees up all over the place."

"What's the point?" Judas demanded.

"Just this—that Moses and the prophets claimed to speak for God, and the rabbis quote the venerable fathers chapter and verse, but the Master does neither. He lays down his own word as if it were God's, says we have to build on him, and works his signs without calling on God. It confuses me. There's no precedent. But one thing I can't doubt. He's a man."

"If he's a man," Judas hissed, "why this circus act tonight? It doesn't feed the hungry or heal the sick."

"That's strange," Jude said. "Did you smell sulphur? There are no sulphur springs in this region."

"Jude, you simpleton, don't interrupt," Judas exclaimed.

"To answer your question, Judas," John said, "maybe he's giving us another kind of food. Peter, do you recall how he spoke last year at the Feast of Tabernacles? When the authorities tried to squeeze his identity out of him like juice from a grape, he told them, 'When you have lifted up the Son of Man, you'll come to know that I AM.' His expression made me think of the timelessness of Daniel's son of man."

"To tell you the truth," Peter admitted, "whenever he exchanged words with those highbrows, I was lost."

"If I don't know what's going on," Judas snarled, "it's because when you go to Jerusalem I'm sent off to slave in Galilee!"

"Judas, you're needed to plan our journeys," John placated. "We're not equipped for it."

"Possibly," Judas admitted. "But one thing I know—

the authorities are losing patience. Our Rabbi has to declare himself openly soon, or they'll repress him and disband us. It would be a pity. We were hoping for so much."

"*Were*?" John asked incredulously. "You say that after what has happened in the last twenty-four hours?"

"And just what has happened?"

"To our unspoken question, *Who are you*? he has answered with two acts of power which shout at us from the top of their lungs. And you learn nothing—you even criticize him for not toeing the line of the little code of conduct you've set down for him!"

"Now that your over-active brain's had its say, my young John," Judas said icily, "here are the *facts*. We've experienced one ambiguous event concerning a few dollars worth of barley bread, and one fantastic event concerning water. I'm not impressed."

"What can I say?" John asked with rising inflection.

"I'm not finished," Judas hammered on. "My goal is the redemption of Israel, and nothing less by a jot. Our Roman overlords won't lose sleep over the trick he worked tonight, since there was no mob to mesmerize. It didn't break our chains. It didn't bring us freedom."

"Judas, the freedom Jesus offers us is freedom from ourselves!"

"What are you implying?"

"Think about it."

"And you, young man, think about this—if this Rabbi of ours rouses mob hysteria by his fantastic actions, it'll provoke a hopeless uprising that'll end in the senseless slaughter of our people. His followers can't permit that."

Dumbfounded, John watched him stalk off, too worried to think clearly. Was that a veiled threat? It couldn't be — after all, he was one of the Twelve. But the man was growing more erratic—wanting something of Jesus, and not knowing precisely what, but knowing he wasn't getting it. His hardening opposition and confused thinking were clouding the faith of the Twelve. His caustic comments during the miraculous feeding had blinded them to what was happening —to what the people saw readily.

That wasn't the worst of it. Judas was on a collision course with the Master, and if his last words were more than a fit of anger, he posed a threat—though he no doubt simply meant that they had to influence the Master's decisions more.

Yet his criticism couldn't be mindlessly ignored. Why had the Master walked on water? No answer came.

6

There in the morning light by the shore those little ones sat, still wet from the waters of the night. Trying to peck their way through the shell of their blindness into the kingdom of light. Failing to understand the bread on the hillside and the body on the sea. Not yet knowing that they were being introduced to the bread, the body, and the high priest of immortality.

Oh, to hear their feeble efforts resisted by that devil of blindness kicking up his heel against me!

I prayed for him. Prayed against him. Prayed for them to shatter the blind shell of history—to join Abram the wandering Aramean ascending up from the valley of death, up into the land of the rising sun. I was besieging the ramparts of time, on fire for my hour of the Cana of God. Incendiary with desire to beget them—use my flesh to father the world. Enough of the signs! Enough of the symbols! The ramparts of time had fallen, and now to the work that would open the door of God. Give I would the gift I alone can give, give myself as none other is able—and at last, Father, make them realize your love.

Yes, Judas would fulfill the prophecy, sit a traitor at my table—how I had tried to protect him! Into Galilee I had missioned him while in the Holy City I spoke words which would have exploded in his fervid brain. I loved him, chose him, knew he could be a great apostle if he so willed, yet each day saw his face turn more away. My heart grieving for him, I wrestled with your will, and gave you mine. He was free to make his choice. Heaviness weighed me down. If the

241

Twelve, so long with me, stumbled darkly, how was I ever to lift all peoples to the heights? I sorrowed, but I also knew what my parables taught. Though the soil was as hard and rocky as that of my beloved land—harder had I labored to cast in the seed, and when the time was ripe, the crop would appear. The farmer who loves even the stones can coax a crop from any soil. I knew what their hearts could bring forth—was not my heart the heart of the Son of Man? Had I not laid hold of their lot, set out on pilgrimage to their cave of death so that they might wing their way upward with me to life, to the torrents of your pleasure?

The shore that morning was crimsoned by the orb of the sun rising to light up the morning, and the birds were throbbing with their own song of life. The waves lapped the shore melodiously, and the tall reeds swayed in the undulant breeze, graceful as dancing maidens at a wedding. Above in the farmland, the golden wheat was drooping its heavy heads of grain—sprouted from rocky soil.

On the water, I saw boats arriving from across the lake, making for Capernaum. "We go into town now," I told the Twelve. "Peter, hurry ahead to Jairus. Tell him I will teach in the synagogue."

People were clustered around the door when we arrived. Beside Peter stood Jairus with his wife and sprightly young daughter, who ran up and kissed me. As I entered the synagogue, the boats were beaching nearby. Going forward, I took my stand before the carved stone ark, replica of the wilderness ark bearing the stone tablets and manna.

The doors burst open, and people flooded in—the same whom I had fed. They gaped at me. "Rabbi, how did you get here? We didn't see you in any of the boats."

"Why ask?" I challenged. "Signs don't interest you—only free bread. Don't work for bread that turns moldy! Work for eternal-life bread which the Son of Man will give. He's sealed with the Father's stamp."

"What work does God want of us?" interposed Rabbi Bela. His feared and respected voice chilled the room.

"This—work to have faith—faith in his Sent One." I turned my glance to Judas' face, and met a mask.

"What sign do you perform?" Bela shot back. "What work

do you do? When Moses demanded faith, he showed convincing signs—not doubtful ones! He fed a whole generation with manna. As it's written, 'He gave them bread to eat from heaven.' "

"Believe me—that bread wasn't heaven's. My Father above gives heaven's true bread—him descending to give the world life."

"Lord, give it!" The elated cry came from Judas, who glared around in triumph. A cadence of voices echoed him.

"I," I returned, "am the bread of life. Come to me, and never hunger. Believe in me, and never thirst."

What a range of expressions greeted those words! Joy, longing, love—and raw doubt, sour distaste, stony rejection.

"We don't believe you!" came a bellow from out the silence.

"Haven't I said so? But the ones the Father sends me will come, and them I'll cherish. I've come down from heaven to do my sender's will."

"What is your sender's will?" The words—Rabbi Bela's—were chill with cynicism.

"Not to lose one of the ones he sends me. To resurrect each on the last day." My words were met with a chorus of scorn.

"What's this? I wasn't sent by anybody!"

"His mother was sent recently—thought he'd gone off center, didn't she?"

"Listen!" At my command, the hubbub died. "Stop murmuring!"

"They murmured at Moses too!" John thundered. I waved him to silence.

"You can't come to me for resurrection, except by the Father's sending. 'All shall be taught by God,' the prophets wrote."

"His father's dead!"

"Shut up!" Bela screamed, raising an imperious hand. With arms raised, he turned on me like a swooping hawk. "Who do you claim to be?" Judas' eyes narrowed, and he leaned forward.

"The bread of life. Not the manna your fathers ate in the desert, and died. This"—I laid my hand on my chest—"this

243

bread came down from heaven so that the eater may not die."

The people looked confused. Bela pursed his lips, drummed his fingers together. "How does one eat this bread?"

"The bread I'll give for the world's life is my flesh."

A tumult broke out—arguing, shouting, demands I be cast out. But interspersed among the outraged faces were faces full of wonder and, here and there, a face calm with belief, and on Judas' face, shock. Jairus, who had been standing nearby, whispered, "Give it to my family." Then he hammered on the pulpit, and the clamor died. Frightened little children sobbed, and one I picked up and comforted. With him in my arms, I turned to the people.

"You must believe me. You have no life in you unless you eat the flesh of the Son of man and drink his blood . . ."

The congregation exploded.

"He's gone mad!"

"They said he was possessed!"

Bela leaped up wildly, shouted for silence, then turned on me with a calculating look. "Surely, Rabbi Yeshua," he began, his voice unnaturally calm, "you're aware that our Law—not just our traditions, mind you, but Scripture— forbids drinking even *animal* blood. Life's in the blood, and life's under the direct dominion of God. Further, the Law abominates human sacrifice. Abraham was tested, but not permitted to *murder* his son—heaven forbid! Pagan dogs do such things! They do say the Baptizer of sacred memory called you the 'lamb of God.' I refused to believe it—but, now, tell me, are you some human sacrifice and sacrificial meal? Surely, you can't mean that? Make yourself clear—at once!"

"He can't make it all plain at once," Peter shouted. "We learn little by little. Sometimes words don't help, but only what he does and what he is."

Rabbi Bela was clearly annoyed by Peter's intervention. "But surely you can say more," he rasped. And I did.

"The one eating my flesh and drinking my blood has everlasting life. I'll resurrect him on the last day. My flesh really is bread, my blood; drink. The one chewing my flesh and

244

drinking my blood lives on in me, and I in him. The Father who sent me is my life, and I the life of him who chews and eats me. This is the bread coming down from heaven—not that which your dead fathers ate."

"I can't even digest his words," a follower mocked, and others guffawed sourly. Distaste and shock were on the faces of other disciples.

"Does this scandalize you?" I put the question calmly. "Then what would you make of it to see the Son of Man ascending to where he was to begin with? Don't misunderstand me—the flesh of itself leads to a dead end. What I'm offering is spirit and life—but only the Father makes it possible for you to come to me." So saying, I strode out alone, out of town and up through the crops and the thickets to the Mount of Beatitudes, and there I prayed.

Father—I grieved—the world is sin-laden, suspicious, and blind to the obvious. How can it understand? Only by first believing can it ever understand. And yet, why can they not understand? Have they not experienced the twining of the bands of Adam, the cords of love?

O Love, what are you but spirit and life? Do they not know you then? Father, my tide of love rises despite misunderstanding—their blindness is not strong as love!

When the Twelve found me, dark-countenanced Judas attacked. "Rabbi, they're deserting in droves!"

"And you? Do you want to go away?"

"Go to whom?"—Peter looked to be sinking once again into a night sea—"You have the words of everlasting life!" The others nodded dumbly, but Judas, back to me, stared down at the town.

"Haven't I myself chosen you?" The words rolled heavy as thunder across the heavens, so that Judas looked over his shoulder to stare at me. "Yet one of you is a devil!"

That day marked the turning point in my mission. Plainly I had told them what I came to bring, and hinted that the sign of my identity was life handed over. For my Twelve, I'd done more—made bread accomplish what no baker's product can, made flesh walk paths beyond its pale, so that when at length I say, "Take and eat," they will accept the might of love.

245

People who cut and dry and measure religion by mere external observance had begun to abhor me—the worldlings to drift away, the Zealots to look elsewhere. So be it.

Greater than my grief was my joy. The seed of my sign was sowed, and first shoots of the harvest illumined the eyes of the Twelve—except one. And in Peter were clear signs of an early yield, for which I had not much longer to wait.

7

Peter bent down, picked up a pebble, and fingered it reflectively. He hardly recognized himself in the quiet, thoughtful mood welling up so frequently now. How it contrasted with his old spontaneity! Why, that day he first heard of the Master he had barged right up to him to learn for himself who the man really was. That was almost two years ago, and still he hadn't decided. His old brash, impetuous manner was a memory, overlaid with layers of endless thought. Even his big, open, outgoing face was taking on a new look. He just wasn't his old self.

Since that Bread-of-Life teaching several months ago, he felt more at sea than ever. And yet that wasn't quite the case either. That day something had happened to him, but he still couldn't put his finger on it. Almost, it seemed, there was a place deep down inside him where the answer to the riddle of the Master stirred that day—only he wasn't brave enough to go down and look it in the face. Yes, that was it. The only reason he didn't know now was that he was in dread of knowing. He didn't need more information—he needed more courage!

That idea came as a shock to Peter. He—afraid? He, leader of men, hanging back? What was happening to him? Sweat formed on his brow, though it was a cold day. By nature he was a man of action, not reflection, a snorting warhorse eager to charge wildly into battle—and led instead into bogs and quicksands that made the terror show in his flashing eyes.

Indeed, bogs and quicksands were child's play compared with the terrain into which his Master was driving him—into the unknown, into mystery, into faith. Then that is where he would go. Soon, he'd make that interior descent, face up to what was hidden there. With a thrust, he wiped the sweat from his brow.

"Are you hot, Peter?" Jude asked. "I was wishing the summer hadn't gone so fast." He got no reply. "Peter, you're a million miles away—but not for long. Look at the people coming."

For the past several months the crippled, the blind, and the helpless had been harvested from ever-widening circles, clinging to Jesus and obstructing his efforts to teach with their clamor for healing. Even worse, his enemies infiltrated the crowds, casting their nets of trickery, thrusting their gaffs of mockery, ever intent on discrediting him. Self-seekers and enemies and sheep to be tended were wearing them out.

Very early that morning, they had trod the muddy road into the market place of this small Galilean town. Now, as the crowd collected, the Master began to teach. His first words were still in the air when a disturbance arose. He paused and waited. A group of Jerusalem theologians shouldered their way forward.

"Rabbi Yeshua," their spokesman said, clipping his words like scissors cutting paper, "enroute here, we saw some of your close followers plucking produce from the fields and eating unwashed. Why"—his voice rose—"why do they offend thus?"

"Where in the word of God is what they do forbidden?"

"Surely you, a teacher in Israel, know I'm referring to the traditions of our ancestors."

"About you hypocrites," Jesus retorted, "Isaiah prophesied with pinpoint accuracy—'This people draws near me with lip service, but how far away their hearts! They worship me in vain because they teach doctrines made by men.' You do just that. You abandon God's commandments to adhere to human customs."

"Hardly," the theologian sneered. "We adhere to both—and you don't teach both!"

"You adhere to both? Then why not obey Moses? He said,

'Honor your father and your mother,' but you teach that a son may inform his parents he has 'dedicated to God' the support they need, and after that give them nothing. You do other like things, cancelling out God's commands in favor of your traditions."

The theologian sputtered. Jesus turned to the crowd. "Listen, and grasp what I say. It's not what goes into a man that defiles him. It's what comes out!"

John whispered into Peter's ear, "That's a thunderbolt. They intended to show him up by burying him in quotes from oral tradition concerning the purification ritual. He cut to the heart of the matter, as always. But this time he shocked me, too. Can we ignore the food laws?"

There was fear in Peter's eyes. "I don't know."

It was nearing midnight before the people dispersed and the disciples fell exhausted to the ground, wrapping their cloaks tight against the cold and remembering no more.

Peter opened his eyes to a heavenful of stars, with the Master's hand on his shoulder. "Peter, get up quietly. Rouse the Twelve and the women. We're leaving."

He led them through the night toward the Mediterranean Sea. The sun was peeping over the mountains behind them when they crossed the border into Phoenicia north of the Carmel range. John said solemnly, "I've never been in this pagan territory before."

They pitched camp on the white sand, and sank into deep sleep, lulled by the lapping of the waves.

Peter woke to the screeching of the gulls. He watched them skimming the water, plunging to the surface, and rising with beating wings, silver fingerlings in their beaks. "They're good fishermen," he said to Andrew, who was sitting beside him already awake. "Come on, let's outdo them." They drew fish lines from their belts, baited their hooks with small fish robbed from scolding gulls feeding on the beach, and cast in their lines.

The rest awoke to the aroma of fish sizzling in a fire. They squatted around the flames and broke their fast. "Above there is where Elijah called down heaven's fire to consume his sacrifice," Judas remarked to Peter, pointing to the jutting cliffs of Mount Carmel. "What a great prophet.

He slaughtered the pagan priests of Baal to the last man. If I'd had the chance to follow him!"

"Oh? I'm satisfied with the Master."

"I suppose you're overjoyed with the way things are going."

Peter was annoyed. He looked around for a distraction, saw the mother of Jesus plucking burrs from her cloak, and pointed. "She needs help." He went to her. "Good morning, mother. Let me do that. After all the fishhooks, these fingers won't even feel the burrs." Mary handed him the cloak.

"Be careful, or you'll tear the cloth."

"Mother, you need a new cloak. I'll tell Judas."

"Not yet, Peter. The Magdalene had a dream last night. Call her." Peter did. He saw that her eyes were sparkling, her features alight with suppressed excitement.

"You had a dream last night," he prompted.

"Yes. There was something different about it—not just what it contained. I can't explain."

"Tell me."

"We were following the Master and it was growing always darker. The earth began to shake and buckle. I was terrified. All at once you cried, 'Look.' The star of David streaked up into the sky and hung there, big as the harvest moon. I heard a voice—I think it was my father's—whispering in my ear, 'It's for your wedding.' My terror dissolved, and I was full of joy, though the darkness and the earthquake continued. Then I awoke."

"What does it mean, Mother?" Peter asked.

The mother of Jesus took them by the hand. "You're blessed, children. You'll see."

That day they traveled north along the coast toward Tyre. About twilight, they camped on the beach south of the city. Peter gazed at the great ships riding at anchor, and watched the sailors bustling about on deck. Like a seagull with spread wings, a vessel in full sail would appear on the horizon and enter the harbor, and the sight filled him with nostalgia.

In the morning they continued north toward Sidon, which lay less than a day's journey ahead. That day, through Matthew's good graces, a Jewish businessman of the town of Zarephath opened his palatial home to them, and promised

249

to keep their identity secret.

The plan failed. That evening, a Gentile woman camping at the door ran up to the Master and plunged to her knees. "My Lord, come and heal my daughter. She's possessed."

It was a busy street. Passersby stared and slowed their gait. A band of urchins came speeding over to gape. The Master sidestepped her and strode on, the Twelve hurrying after. "Thank heaven, he's ignoring her," Philip sighed. "If he gets involved and heals her daughter, hordes of cure-seeking locusts will descend on us."

"A cure would certainly scuttle our plans for a rest," Peter agreed. "And you need one, Philip. You look like you could sleep for a week! You don't look any better, Matthew."

"I could eat for a week—and was hoping to."

"Was?" Philip sounded anxious.

"Yes, *was!*" Matthew bit into the succulent orange garnered from their host's garden. The juice spurted into his beard, and beads hung suspended in its tangle. "Just listen to her."

"Lord, my daughter, my daughter," the woman was bleating as she ran crablike alongside the Master.

"I feel guilty, but I hope he doesn't answer her," Philip confessed. "Encourage a Greek—even with a no—and you're finished!"

"The Greeks say the same of us Semites," Matthew laughed. "And when you used to descend on my office with your olive crop and argue about the tax rate, I was convinced they're right."

"She's no Greek," Judas interjected. "Her features say she's a descendent of the Canaanites who people this region."

"This town's where the persistent widow made Elijah restore her son's life," Simon the Zealot recalled. "And judging by this parrot's hanging on like a burr, she's her direct descendent."

"Heal my daughter. Heal my daughter," she droned. The curious were falling in with the trailing urchins. Judas ran up to the Master.

"Send her away. Her gull's cries are summoning a flock."

"At this rate," Jude said in an aside, "our rest may turn to an *arrest*—for disturbing the peace."

250

The Master stopped, and when he spoke, it seemed he was addressing not Judas, but his own dilemma. "Only to the house of Israel's lost sheep was I sent." The woman perked up, encouraged, as Philip had predicted.

"You've got to help me!" She shouted the words at the top of her lungs. Jesus stared at her, and she stared back, watching him with little, hawklike motions of head and eyes.

"Do you think it's right," he asked in a voice thick with fatigue, "to throw the children's bread to the puppies?"

Consternation invaded her thin face. Her body began to wilt. Then, with a whoop of triumph, she came erect. "No, Lord—but when the kids throw them crumbs, it's not like taking bread out of their mouths!" Jesus looked at her admiringly.

"You've won. On your way now. Your daughter's already freed of the demon."

"Do you mean"—Peter was astonished—"you'd already healed the girl?" The woman burst into tears.

"I'll never forget your kindness. Never, never!" She turned and ran back the way she had come.

"Thomas, return to our host," the Master directed. "Tell him we can't stay. Bring the other disciples. We'll wait north of town." Thomas sprinted off on his long, gangling legs.

"Well, Matthew," Nathanael drawled, poking his friend's shrunken midriff, "there goes a week of succulent fish, steaks and venison, liqueurs and sparkling red wines of ancient vintage, sherbets and the delightful pastries of this decadent region."

"And with it your days in the depths of a soft couch, dreaming sweet dreams of olive orchards high over the Sea of Galilee."

They had not traveled far when a red-cheeked teenager sped up from behind and singled out the Master. "My mother says her daughter's fine, and thanks again."

"Son, how'd you find us?" Peter asked.

"Mother said I'd find a gang of twelve ordinary-looking Jewish men, and a thirteenth with a face like fire. I couldn't miss you." He turned to the Master. "Thanks, Lord, for healing my sister!" With that, he spun round and ran back.

That night they sat hunched beside the pounding surf, munching barley bread and watching the freshly caught fish brown in the flames. The aroma made John's mouth water, and kept tugging his mind away from the question he was formulating.

"Rabbi," he began at last, "before leaving Israel, you said a man's not made unclean by what he eats, but by what he emits. The theologians were scandalized—and I don't understand either." Jesus raised his drooping eyelids and stared at his earnest face, and at each of the others in turn.

"Do not even you Twelve understand?" His voice sounded flattened by some mountain of grief—it made them feel ashamed. "Don't you realize a man can't be defiled by what enters his belly, not his heart, and comes out again, into the latrine?"

"What does make a man unclean?" John persisted. "Even Isaiah confessed he had unclean lips."

"The deep heart's outpourings defile man—sexual immorality, thefts, murders, deceit, arrogance, an earth-bound spirit."

"What about the food laws?" John wanted to shout. "You observe them yourself!" But his courage wilted.

The next morning they set out early. "I don't know how we're ever going to get a rest," Jude yawned. "The Rabbi can't say no anymore." He gazed at Jesus, walking ahead in prayer.

"If you think so, ask for the wrong thing," John laughed.

"Still," Judas interjected, "he's too kind for his own good—not to mention ours."

"His pity alone doesn't explain it." Peter's face was screwed up in concentration. "I keep remembering his teaching that no one can come to him unless the Father sends him, and he'll never turn away anyone who's been sent. That's what explains it. When someone comes—like that woman yesterday—the signs tell him whether the Father sent her. If so, he acts; if not, he doesn't."

"Peter"—John was excited—"you're quoting the bread of life sermon. Shouldn't it tell us something about his identity?"

"Whatever that was, it was only talk!" Judas interjected. "Deeds are what we need."

"Words and promises are as good as deeds," Peter objected, "if we trust him."

"Speak for yourself. God no doubt works through him—at times. But that doesn't make him infallible."

"Judas, don't pretend you don't trust him," Jude chided. "If I didn't know better, I'd think you didn't even like him."

"I *must* like him—he's a man of God. But he still seems like a stranger to me—though, for that matter, I feel as if there's another stranger, inside me, trying to come out. I suppose we all feel that way at times, don't we?"

Peter stared at Judas. The Master was a mystery to him, but never a stranger. No, he, Peter, had a devoted love for him, and no one loved a stranger. And if, nowadays, he found surprizing things emerging from himself—like his new habit of thoughtfulness—he saw good reason for the change. It was growth, to deal with the mystery engulfing him. No, he had no stranger inside trying to come out. "John, I'm with you. That Bread of Life sermon makes me feel as though I know who he is—almost."

"If he gives that bread," Jude enthused, "it'll make him a prophet as great as Moses!" Peter eyed him curiously. "Jude, it'll make him more than a prophet like Moses."

"What are you saying?" Judas demanded.

"What's evident—what he pointed out himself. The bread he promises gives immortality. The manna didn't."

Judas peered at Peter. "Who do you make him out to be?"

"Judas, your eyelids look swollen," Jude interjected.

"Shut up, Jude. I'm having trouble sleeping. Well, Peter?"

"I'm not ready to say."

"If he were anything more than a prophet," Judas rasped, "would he choose such a cast of characters for his intimates?" He swept an arm around scornfully.

"His problem, Judas," Simon the Zealot retorted, "is that he didn't appoint you to pick his associates!"

"Judas makes a point, though," Andrew remarked. "I keep asking myself why—if he's who I think—he's gathered disciples like us. Of course, that excludes Judas." He smiled, the others chuckled, and Judas scowled.

"I feel stupid for not having pinpointed his identity long ago," John confessed, "but it's difficult to come to a decision

253

with the learned rabbis tearing him down, and treating us like dirt. Still, I must be stupid—the Baptizer seemed to have the answer the very day he first pointed him out to us."

"Is that why he later dispatched his minions to ask who he is?" Judas' words dripped acid.

"Maybe he sent them because they wouldn't believe him. Maybe his dungeon—and who knows what else—darkened his mind."

"That's where we are—hanging on a thread of maybe's."

"One thing I'm sure of," John returned: "He's no Judas the Galilean, inciting a guerrilla war against the Romans, and getting himself and his men killed like ants stomped by Roman boots."

"John, you bad-mouth that patriot as if you were an eyewitness of his exploits," Simon the Zealot retorted hotly. "The fact is, you weren't even a gurgling baby at the time!"

"No doubt you fought in his army—at about five."

"No, but my relatives did."

"Our Rabbi's no Barabbas either," James put in. "The report is that he's using hit-and-run tactics."

"We're not hitting," Judas snarled, "but we're running! We can't stay in one place. Swarms of cure-seekers harass us. The poor plague me for handouts. The religious authorities close in. We can't go on like this. Something has to change."

"What would you suggest?" Peter asked.

"First, let's sit down and talk with the Pharisees. Our Teacher lives by their teachings, even if he condemns their trivial emphases. We could compromise with them. Second, stop giving away the pittance we have to live on. Third, the Rabbi must recognize his weak points, and yield to one of us the planning and policy-making. Frankly, I'm losing interest in things as they are. Given the authority, I'd see that we all got more rest—and not let the rabble barge up at any hour. Our religious authorities have office hours."

Jude smiled his innocent, limpid smile. "Can you picture the Master keeping office hours for the sick?" Judas scowled at him and he coughed. That ended the conversation.

A few days later, without explanation, the Master turned back toward Galilee. He set a leisurely, restful pace. He did no public preaching, and they kept to the countryside.

254

Except for his hours of prayer, he spent his time with them. Sometimes he taught them, but mostly he encouraged them to relax, rest, and enjoy the opportunity for closer fellowship, which he shared himself, at times joining in the banter. Even Judas thawed.

When they reached the Sea of Galilee, he headed directly for the boats. To their surprize, he made them cross over to the League of the Ten Cities, which was pagan territory. They went on a preaching tour there, and on that journey he cured a Gentile of deafness and a speech impediment. The pagans had high praise for him. "He does all things well," one of them summed it up. "He even makes the deaf hear and the dumb speak."

One night, John invited Peter for a walk. "You've seen how enthusiastic the pagans are," he said.

"Why shouldn't they be?" Peter replied.

"They're more open than our own people."

"What're you driving at?"

"That the faith of the pagan woman of Zarephath is what led him to visit the pagans of the Ten Cities. That he's broadening his mission because our people are hanging back. That if things go on as they are, our leaders will reject him. Peter, we're facing failure."

"Don't talk like that."

"How should I talk?"

"Like a man who sees the facts."

"What facts?"

"John, the Master was sent by God—that much I know. And sent with powers no man ever had. Whatever he came to accomplish, he will! I'd bet all the fish in the Sea on it!" He picked up a stone and hurled it into the lake.

"Peter, before it's over, you'll bet more than that!"

John lay awake that night thinking of Jesus. He was perpetually longing to have that noble, that extraordinary man for a friend, and perpetually surprised to realize he did—Judas had certainly touched on a mystery when he wondered why he had chosen such as them. The Master's choice of him never failed to draw the most noble sentiments of devotion from his wild nature, as a waiter might draw the finest wine from the ugliest cask. Left to his own urges he'd

255

spew the raw violence of the Zealots, not the meekness of the beatitudes. That was what particularly thrilled and excited him, that this man possessed the same fearless vitality, bravery and patriotism as the Zealots, while at the same time pioneering an exciting new way to exploit such qualities—not now to kill, but as he insisted, in some holy and mysterious fashion, to give life.

One of his strangest and most consoling experiences was the realization that this strong man needed him. The experience sank its roots in the day he took a slow, long look at his face, and found stamped there some quality he couldn't fathom. He deciphered it much later, thanks to the joys and disappointments of his first missionary journey, with its triumphs and rejections. What was stamped there was the seal of grief, the leaden grief which lays like a stone in the deepest heart of one who has experienced unrequited love. It stunned him that this self-possessed man had the same unrelenting need for friendship and love as he—only the Master's case was more hopeless by far, for he sought friendship of every man, and what could be more hopeless than that? Ever since, John felt like a drop of water slaking parched lips. Indeed, the roots of his devotion took nourishment from that unquenchable thirst.

The more he thought, the more he believed he had expressed the awful truth to Peter. Affairs were worsening, and before it was over, they'd have to risk everything to be faithful to him.

"It's true, though"—he objected to himself—"that experience says we shouldn't get too downhearted. Every time the leaders think they've turned the people against the Master, they let up on us—and the crowds return in force. Or he works some new wonder, and nothing can keep them away. It's happened over and over."

Somehow, that reasoning rang hollow. There were recurrent peaks and valleys in the Master's popularity—true enough— but the same pattern held in a trip east across Galilee—and yet you always ended in that great hole in the earth, the Jordan rift. He covered his stone pillow with the edge of his cloak and slept.

8

Fall weather brought chill nights and, when dark rain clouds sailed in and blotted out the sky, even the days were cold. The Master was still preaching in the wilderness that engulfed the pagan towns along the eastern shore of the lake—part of the region of the Ten Cities. So eager was one crowd of about four thousand people, many of them pagans, that the Master remained with them for three days. When their barley bread gave out, their devotion made them ignore their hunger, and he was so moved that he fed them as he had the five thousand.

When he bade a heartfelt farewell, they begged him to remain, and many broke into tears. With deep emotion, he pleaded that he had other sheep to feed, and took his leave. The Apostles filed after him down the path trampled through the spindly blond reeds, and clambered into their craft. Across the cold, black waters the boats speared their way to Dalmanutha. Their passage was spied on—a party of Pharisees bustled up the moment they landed.

"We attempted to trace your genealogy," a rabbi told the Master unceremoniously, "and came up with nothing. The Babylonian captivity fragmented the records."

"So when the scion of David appears," another theologian asserted, "he'll have to identify himself by mighty deeds."

"You must be aware," the first speaker added, "that two decades ago Judas the Galilean made pretentious claims, and presumed to lead the people to freedom, but in fact led them only to slaughter."

"Now you—also a Galilean—come along," the theologian said, "and make certain unspecified claims, bolstered by medicinal cures of the sort that are too ambiguous to be decisive."

"A man'd have to be blind to say that!" Peter exploded. The theologian's pale, ascetic face flamed red, and Peter added hurriedly, "I mean a man who's seen what I've seen."

"Granting that for sake of argument," the theologian snapped, surveying Peter contemptuously, "healers abound in our history, and even Pharoah's magicians displayed magic powers." He turned to Jesus. "So, to protect our people, we demand you certify your right to continue teaching in this region by giving a sign directly from heaven."

Jesus looked at him with a fiery eye, turned, and went back to the boats. Only when the shore had receded did he speak—and his voice was fierce. "What's the reason this generation needs to seek a sign from me? Accept it when I say it'll get no sign!"

Soon, a cold, leaden rain began plummeting down, obscuring the shore of Bethsaida for which they were making. Jesus wiped the water from his face and beard reflectively. "You too, must beware of that leaven which the Pharisees use in common with Herod." At these words, Judas looked up sullenly.

"Peter, I told you to take the time to buy bread!"

"We didn't have the time!"

"What does bread have to do with it?" the Master demanded. "Are your hearts stony, eyes scaly, ears plugged? How many leftovers did you collect from the five loaves for the five thousand?"

"Twelve baskets," said Peter.

"And the seven loaves for the four thousand—how many?"

"Seven."

"Don't you understand yet?"

The boat grated against the pebbly beach at Bethsaida, and they leaped out. Peter sent Judas off for bread, and dispatched the others to gather firewood and forage for edible roots and berries. Jesus went off down the shoreline to pray. Peter collected and crisscrossed the most likely driftwood, and started a blaze. As the others returned, they squatted around the fire. Jude tried to coax a more cheery flame from the smoking wood. "What did the Master mean about the leaven of the Pharisees?" he asked.

"He didn't mean we'd neglected to take bread," James remarked wryly, and they laughed—except Judas, who turned and looked out to sea.

Jude pursued his question. "What is the leaven of Herod and the Pharisees?"

"Ask the Master," Peter suggested.

"You ask him, since you don't know either."

"It might be better," Peter admitted, "to think about it."

258

"I've been thinking," Andrew announced. "I'd say the leaven of the Pharisees is law. They first list God's laws, then make laws to protect the Law, and so on."

"Lately, they're leavening everything with criticism of the Master," Jude observed. "Maybe he sees signs we're doing the same, now that the heat's on." He stole a glance at Judas.

"What do you think, John?" Peter prompted.

"Jesus spoke of the leaven common to Herod and the Pharisees. That narrows the problem. What preoccupies both is politics. We're on that bandwagon, with our concern for national liberation."

"Do you infer," Simon the Zealot bristled, "that our Rabbi's not going to contribute to national liberation?"

"I mean that's not his top priority."

"What does the Master leaven with?" Jude asked. "Faith?"

"With truth," Matthew claimed, "as against the hypocrisy of those who'd rather have it their own way."

"I'd say with love," John disagreed.

"Would you say that, John?" Peter was surprized. "Himself is the foundation of his message. He leavens everything with himself." John turned and stared at him wide-eyed.

They were on the way into town, intent on making for Peter's and Andrew's paternal home, when a band of men bore down on them. Their facial similarities, especially the tilt of their oversized ears, broadcast their kinship. Thrusting forward a man with wide, staring eyes, one of them cried, "Rabbi, our brother Thomas is blind. Make him see!"

"I never believed in you," the sightless man confessed, throwing his face upward so that his blind eyes stared at the sky. "But Abel—my brother—saw you cure a deaf and dumb Gentile. He believed, and wasn't even an Israelite. I felt ashamed."

"Come." The Master took his hand and walked off, calling back, "The rest, go home." His relatives shuffled and fidgeted.

"Want your brother healed?" Peter snapped. "Then go." The men obeyed. In the woodlands outside the town, the Master paused by a stand of willows fronting the marshlands. A brace of heron paddled off, and a flock of geese took wing noisily.

259

He spat on his finger tips, anointed the man's unseeing eyes, and laid his hand on his head. "Thomas, can you see at all?"

"I can see people—but can only distinguish them from the trees because they're moving." He laid on his hands again, and the man sang out, "Master, I can see your face and your eyes and even the hairs of your beard!"

"Go home to your family. Don't enter the village."

"I don't know the way!"

"Give me a lead," Peter prompted, "and I'll direct you."

"We live near Methuselah's grinding mill."

"Cut through the woods by this path." He pointed to a grassy trail which snaked off into a cluster of pine oleanders. "Where it meets the road, go up the hill. You can't miss the mill."

Thomas sped away. Peter turned to the Master. "Rabbi, won't you take us off by ourselves, and open our eyes?" Jesus looked long at Peter before he responded.

"Simon Peter, fetch the disciples awaiting us in Capernaum." He turned and viewed the rain-swollen waters of the Jordan, which originated in the land of Dan, and here raced down to the Sea of Galilee. "Tomorrow we leave for the inheritance of Dan."

The landscape tilted up toward the sky, feasting the eye with vast sweeps of rich pastureland, forested hill, and running stream. Ahead on the horizon loomed the mighty bulk of Mount Hermon. The dying light of the westering sun transmuted the mountain's soaring peak into a rose-and-lavender island floating upon the clouds.

"What a pleasure to tramp through this land!" Andrew stopped and looked about. "Here in upper Galilee I forget the stones, boulders and deserts strewn across most of our country. Why did the Creator make the promised land so stony?"

"Maybe," said James, "to remind his people of stony hearts."

"It's beautiful up on this tableland, but cold," Matthew complained. "Barley bread's not the right food for me up here." He shivered miserably. Peter observed it, but said nothing. He looked at the disciples behind the Twelve, and the little band of women in their midst.

"Lord," he prayed silently, "provide food and shelter in this land of Napthali. We're disciples of your servant, Jesus." A little later he spotted a hunter coming down from the hills with a red deer slung across his shoulders. "Judas, that hunter's had luck. He's got himself a six-point buck. Buy it if you can. Take Jude along." When the two set out, Peter spoke with Jesus, and then called a halt to the march. Judas returned without the deer.

"He wanted twelve days' wages. I wouldn't pay it."

"We need it," Peter said. "Buy it."

"Go yourself!"

"Give me the money."

Judas sullenly counted out twelve denarii. "Twelve days' wages," he snarled, "for shooting an arrow!"

Up against the mouth of a cave they built a fire, roasted the venison, and ate. "You're looking contented again, Matthew," Peter observed, taking a massive bite from his slab of meat.

· "A first-class feast and a warm fire," Matthew purred, "do work wonders for the spirit, not to mention the body."

"Look at Peter," Judas railed, "gorging himself like a ravenous beast. And he imagines himself a man of prayer!"

"Judas," Peter retorted, "when I eat, I eat; when I pray, I pray. I admit you look ascetic, but if you'd worry less about the purse and enjoy the food it provides, you'd be a happier man."

"That's it, mock what you don't understand—asceticism— and prate about worldly pleasure!"

"Judas, let me remind you—pleasure's God's invention, not mine. There's something sacred about it. You find it in heaven, not hell—and I'm looking forward to plenty of it."

"They ate, drank, danced and went down to hell—that's my summary of scriptural warnings, Peter."

"Yes, that's *your* summary. God created wine and women and pleasure. That's my summary. Men created drunkenness and lust. That's sin! And that's the point of Scripture's warning, Judas. As to dancing!"—Peter leaped to his feet— "the way we do it, it's just fun. Thomas, where's your shepherd's pipe? Give me a tune!"

Peter began a jig, Thomas piped, and the others clapped in time to the music. Judas sat alone in sullen silence. The Master beckoned him over, and when he came and sat beside him, he laid a hand gently on his arm. "My friend, hear what Peter has to say. And be assured, when the time is right, he'll fast."

The applause was loud when Peter bowed and sat down. Then Matthew arose. "I've put together a little number to entertain you," he announced. "It's about travel."

"Is it from the time you traveled in comfort and style, Matthew—on my tax money?" Philip asked to the merriment of the rest.

"Listen, and see if it was a good investment, Philip," Matthew replied, and began.

> I've always loved to come and go
> Where David lived and fought the foe,
> Where Abram sought, and seeking found,
> Where prophets spoke, and shrines abound.
>
> I've visited Machpelah's cave,
> And traveled to the Great Sea's wave,
> And gone where Rachel ope'd her womb,
> And wept my tears at Hebron's tomb.
>
> Our promised land's a snatch austere,
> Yet full of all I hold most dear,
> Of loam and stone and burning sand,
> Of sea and stream and mountain land.
>
> I went about to seek and find,
> I sought good fruit and found but rind,
> And never saw what good men see,
> And wondered what was wrong with me.
>
> Continued I to come and go
> Through desert and through mountain snow,
> To see our people's hallowed ground,
> But what I sought I never found.

262

Then stepped our Master up to me
And straightway bid me follow free,
And now with joy I come and go,
For what I found I'm sent to sow.

And so we travel by his plan
On up to Napthali and Dan,
To give our people living there
What we have found and what we share.

O noble land of Galilee,
Of forest green and tallest tree,
You once were last but now are first,
For here a promised Bud has burst.

When Matthew finished his song, there was no applause,
but in the campfire's glow he saw shining eyes, faces melted
with devotion, and cheeks awash with tears. Quietly, he sat
down.

The Magdalene arose and came to the center. In her
richly timbred voice she announced softly, "Friendship's
my theme. Thomas, the melody's from David's 'Song to
Abishag.'" And so she began.

The simple friendships are the best
For days of joy and times of rest,
For helping us to grow and live,
For all that love can ever give.

Now I have known the upper crust,
Where this is 'do' and that is 'must',
And love must bow and bend and slave
And wilt just trying to behave.

So give me simple friendship, friends,
Where love can follow its own ends,
Where smiles and laughs and tender looks
Teach joys of love not taught by books.

So count me in, you band of brothers,
And let us welcome any others
Till one and all have come to know
What we have found in friendship's glow.

The Magdalene was too well received to refuse an encore. When at length she tired, Thomas leaped up and, tall, slender frame swaying gracefully to his music, played in turn melodies joyous, exuberant, sweet, and sad. At times there were lyrics, and the fellowship sang along, filling the night with gladness.

That night they sheltered in the cave warmed with their fire, and the next morning resumed their journey. Their destination was the towns nestling in the valley at the southern talus of Mount Hermon. The Master led the way, solitary in prayer. Coveys of little birds took wing before his advance, and small animals looked up startled, and darted into the underbrush.

"Oh what wild, beautiful country!" Jude reached up, broke a twig from an overhanging branch of a cedar tree, and chewed it reflectively. "All so unspoiled and magnificent, with the freshness of new-born life. It reminds me of the Master's face."

With that bare statement Jude, in his simple way, did the impossible. He made them open their hearts. He precipitated thoughts and sharings about the Master's appearance which they would always remember, and even quote in their later missionary work. But before any now spoke, they probed their own memories of the face, which could project a sternness and grandeur exceeding the Baptizer's, yet be instant to flash a smile. Somehow it conveyed the burden of all the world's sorrows, yet never knew defeat, for how could defeat but glance off the set of that jaw and flee from those bottomless eyes, which projected the intensity of a crouched lion? Yet pluck up courage to gaze straight in, and a lamb gazed back. That mouth, beset by the vital black beard, looked spiritual as a fasting Essene's—until the advent of the cheering grin that split the face from ear to ear.

The whole countenance was instinct with firm self-pos-session, yet had nothing of the hardened mask of immobility some fashion. On the contrary, it was both firm and yet mobile to the degree that it could simultaneously orchestrate the whole range of human emotions, as the sea displays its complex pattern of waves, ripples and crosscurrents. Perhaps that very complexity accounted for the impression, at times, that you were gazing at the face of every child of Adam, even yourself, and when you looked away, memories of particulars eluded you.

The people gazed untiring into that face, gazed into those eyes as into another world, saw him as attentive as a youth to his bride, heartening the most repulsive outcast to dare an approach. Yet one always hesitated at the last, as unworthy to engage him. Even the official theologians, who demand such reverence from all and display it toward none, respond at first sight with a reluctant respect tinged with wariness and awe.

"His face," John took up Jude after a pause, "takes me on a journey into far lands of the spirit where no man has ever gone before. It lifts my thoughts better than climbing the crags of Mount Hermon at sunrise."

"A strong face," Judas demurred, "but too other-worldly."

"The chiseled face of a man's man!" Peter disagreed. "To look at him is to know what a man ought to be!"

The Magdalene, trailing them, had heard and slipped among them. "The day I first looked into his eyes, I learned what no one else had taught me—what it means to be a woman."

"And I learned," Matthew reminisced, "the answers I had found nowhere in Israel."

"I love the out-of-doors," Philip asserted, "and to me a face is a river bed which carries the currents of human thoughts and feelings in a way that reveal the smooth places and the shoals and quicksands of the heart. It has its sunny days when the surface reflects the sunlight, and its stormy days when it's lashed by furious winds. Well, his currents are so deep that it's a wonder if there's any bottom at all, and they're so powerful one thrills with the fear of being swept down rapids and falls that lead no one knows where."

After these utterances there was a period of reflective silence, broken finally by Jude, "I was hoping someone

265

would put my experience into words for me, but I'll have to fumble for them myself. We put on expressions the way Greek actors don masks in a play. His are himself, the way a burning log is fire. He is happiness, or sorrow, and when he's healing someone, he's love."

John's bowed head shot up. "Good going, Jude. Once when he was speaking of the Father I stared at him and thought, 'So that's what God's like!'"

"That's putting it brazenly." Jude's voice was full of respect. "You're describing my kind of experience exactly."

"These pretty imaginings are greatly edifying," Judas said in a stinging tone, "but I'll raise the real issue. Can any face reveal what we need to know about this man?"

"Whether he's the Messiah!" growled the Zealot.

"Exactly!"

"What will identify him?" Jude prompted.

"His works will sweep away every doubt!" Judas dogmatized.

"He'll make God a whirlwind in our lives!" thundered James.

"He'll teach us to serve God in freedom," Andrew proposed, "with a calmness purged of religious fanaticism."

"He'll fulfill all the prophecies," Matthew said.

"He'll show us the way to goodness," Jude sang out.

"He'll join man and God," John declared, "friend to friend, son to Father, bride to bridegroom—as the prophets foretold."

"The Christ," Peter asserted, "will show us what man must do, what he must become!"

"You sound like a Greek!" jeered Judas. "On the contrary, he must put our minds at rest about *God*. Forget about man!"

"And I," roared Simon the Zealot, his prickly beard ready to fire milk-white barbs in all directions as it vibrated with emotion, "will recognize him when he ends enslavement and suffering!"

"Why have we suffered so much?" The question was Jude's.

"Because we've been persecuted so much!" Thomas exclaimed.

"Obviously!—but why?" Simon cried in pain.

"That I'll answer," Judas pontificated. "Change your perspective—put yourselves in the shoes of the nations. How would you treat a race arrogant enough to claim themselves God's chosen people?"

"I don't like your choice of words," Simon bristled.

"All right—insolent enough to make that claim."

"If you mean it took chutzpah to accept God's call, I'll let it pass. The sages claim there'll be chutzpah even in heaven."

"However our suffering got going," Jude interjected, "how will the Messiah end it?"

"That he'll have to work out!" the Zealot bellowed.

"But give us a hint," Jude urged. "Will his solution touch on Rome?" The others laughed. The ex-Zealot had renounced his espousal of guerrilla warfare, not his patriotism.

"I'll tell you how he can end our persecution," Philip said.

"Speak, O wise one," Matthew invited.

"By ending our uniqueness—by calling all men to salvation." There was shocked silence.

"Let him exterminate us while he's at it!" Judas screamed in a sudden rage. "That would do it too!"

"Lots of scriptural passages," Philip persisted, "speak of a universal call to God one day—of universal salvation."

"Our call is unique and irreversible!" the Zealot roared.

"I know, but when the other peoples come in, it'll no longer be unique in the same way, will it?"

Philip's remark streaked across Peter's brain like a meteor, lighting up those words in the Bread of Life sermon, 'The bread I will give for the world's life is my flesh.' For the *world's* life! Up from his inner depths came another light, flames of light, and in the flames he saw the Messiah—and recognized him! His lips parted to shout it out at the top of his lungs—but something restrained him. Instead, he smiled his old, impetuous smile, and slapped Philip on the back. "Friends, we're not far from the kingdom of God!" This sudden burst of optimism disconcerted the rest. They walked on in silence, eyes riveted on the figure in the lead.

"There's the town of Dan, off there." Andrew pointed. "Dan—meaning 'he judged,'" Jude mused. "Strange name." "Not to Rachel it wasn't," Matthew recalled. "After the way Leah despised her for her barrenness, she understandably felt God had judged in her favor when Dan was born."

"The woman cured of the hemorrhage said she lived up this way," Jude recalled. "What was her name—Marosa?"

"Berenice," James answered.

"She lives in nearby Caesarea Philippi," Judas added.

"I'd like to see the pagan temple Herod the Great built there, near the grotto to the god Pan," Andrew said. "What a scandal it must have been! What drove him to it?"

"He was buttering up Caesar Augustus," Matthew answered, "for adding this territory to his dominion. The town was then called Paneas. His son Philip changed the name to Caesarea Philippi—also to butter up Caesar."

Up ahead, half hidden by the trees and tangle of high grasses, a wide chasm loomed. "Lord," Peter called to the Master, "we'll have to find a way around that depression."

"It begins there." John pointed. "We can easily skirt it."

"You Twelve, come with me," the Master said. He began descending into the chasm. Peter called a halt to the march, and led the Twelve down after him.

"What's he up to?" he murmured to John.

"Don't know. What's that faint thunder?"

Peter listened intently. "It sounds like a waterfall." As they snaked down the steep path, the thunder increased—and a sudden twist of the trail disclosed far below a torrential flow leaping along the floor of the valley. "Strange," John mused. "Where does it originate? The valley begins there at the cliff face."

Peter exclaimed, "Look!" and froze like a pointing statue. From the face of the cliff a sea of water leaped, fell wildly, dashed against the boulders below, and raged down the valley.

"A river's birth!" John's awed whisper drowned in the roar. They went down to the Master beside the leaping cascade, bathed and shining wet in its spray. Lifting his powerful voice above the thunder, he spoke.

"Who do people say the Son of Man is?"

John said, "Some say you're John the Baptizer, back from the dead. Rumor has it Herod believes that."

"I heard people saying you're Elijah," Jude reported. "That was after you began censuring the Pharisees."

"Many say you're one of the prophets." James added.

"You—who do you say I am?" There was no answer but the roar of the falls. Then Simon Peter's voice rose over the waters.

"You are *ha mashi ah!*"—the Anointed King, the Messiah, the Christ.

Joy flooded Jesus' face. Looking up to the sky he cried in a mighty voice, "I witness you with thanksgiving, Father, Lord of heaven and earth. What truths you've hidden from the learned and the intellectuals you've disclosed to infants. Yes, Father, that's what it pleased you to do." He turned solemnly to the Twelve. "The Father's entrusted me with everything. None knows the identity of the Son except the Father. None knows the identity of the Father except the Son—and anyone to whom the Son chooses to reveal him." At these words, Peter, too, glowed with joy.

"Thank you, O Christ, for choosing us!"

Jesus turned and gazed long at Peter. At length, with a burning eye that seemed to look through Peter and beyond him through the face of the cliff and the river of time, he spoke, "You're blessed, Jona's son, Simon. No human has disclosed what you've come to know—my Father has done it—he alone! And I disclose this to you—you are Peter, Rock, and on this Rock I'll build my Church, and the Gates of Hell will fall before it. I will entrust to you the keys of the Kingdom. Forbid anything on earth, and it's forbidden in heaven. Allow anything on earth—it's allowed by heaven."

He turned, then, and began the ascent, and they followed. On the way up, he faced them again. "Tell no one I'm the Christ. And now, learn that it's necessary for the Son of Man to suffer, be rejected by the lay leaders, chief priests and scribal theologians, and be killed—and after three days be resurrected."

They stared at him, stunned and mindless. Impulsively, taking him by the arm, Peter drew him aside. "Rabbi, stop talking like that! We've had a hard time. You're overworked, depressed—but this despair's not right!"

Jesus spun around, caught the rest eavesdropping. He spun back to Peter. "Don't lead—follow, Satan! You're thinking with men, not with God!" He pushed past Peter with a face like the stone cliff, and flew up the precipice. Panting, the Twelve clambered after. When they gained the plateau, he was already addressing the disciples.

"Do you want to walk with me? Deny yourself, take up your cross, follow after! Try saving your soul and you'll lose it. Lose it for me and the Gospel, and save it!" He glared at Peter who stared at his feet, and in the silence the faint thunder of the cataract grew louder. "Is there profit in winning the entire world and losing your soul? Can you buy it back? Are any of you ashamed of me before the sin-filled breed of this age? Of them the Son of Man will be ashamed when he returns with the holy angels in his Father's glory."

"When will that be?" Challenge glinted in Judas' words.

"Listen well—some here will not taste death before seeing the Kingdom coming—in power!" He strode away, and they followed in silence—except for a handful who stood, indecisive, and then turned back.

Several times after that he repeated his frightful prophecy to the Twelve alone. It fell on the hard ground of their desire for another kind of Messiah—they pretended it a parable, sought its elusive meaning—and awoke frightened and sweating in the night. Peter, James and John were no exception—all the more six days later, when they saw his glory on a mountain.

9

Slower than camels in a bog did the Twelve come to it—naming me the Christ. How late—the wings of death's angel beat about my head. The leaders rejecting me, finished with me—except to rid themselves of me.

Have I prepared the Twelve for the suffering, the dying, the

270

rising? Peter denies my prophecy—deeming it the creeping decay of hope. Truly, the swamps of despair flood around me. I ford the river of death soon, soon, leaving all to the Twelve—so unready.

Departing Dan, traveling six days through Zebulun's heritage. Racing up Mount Tabor. Far lands imploring salvation—a few seedlings planted—time running out—on the Mount the Evil One hovering and stalking with nets of despair.

In Daberath, on Tabor's slopes, they all rested—except Peter, James and John. They with me, fiercely ascending the Mount of Barak's campaign and Deborah's victory. Passing the evergreen oaks and bitter terebinths and carob trees rattling seeds in the wind. Panting—they falling behind, I reaching the pinnacle—climbing the sky to reach you.

Facing the summit in tumult. Behind the northwest hills, minutes away to the circling hawks, my home town seething with rejection. Mount Hermon towering to the northeast— hidden at its feet the springing waters witnessing Peter's confession—he not dreaming that he addressed Emmanuel. Close by, the Jordan rift and the upper reaches of the Sea of Galilee—scene of many labors and few believers—and the hourglass empty.

South, the village of Nein where I made the youth live for his mother—and soon the burden of death will lie in the arms of mine. Farther south Mount Gilboa, tainted by the sword of despair King Saul drove into his vitals. The Temple— invisible in the far south—smoking with fire, dirtied by self-serving and chilled by legalism. Priests offering carcasses in mounds—I peering in vain for the sacrificial flame of love.

Everywhere the teeming people—extending a glad hand to false prophets and messiahs—thieves and robbers—and not recognizing me.

Why this choking field of weeds? Where the blame? The blindness of my people—the pagans more open. Yet pagans have not guarded the Law through the ages. Nor sinned and cowered under their punishment, asses loaded with guilt. Adding law upon law to guard the Law—burdening themselves beyond bearing, and in despair multiplying sin. Rejecting many a false prophet and false god—and now

271

deeming Emmanuel the threat to fidelity! Father, they know not what they do.

The Egyptians—a cultured people fawning before the stars of heaven. The Greeks—learned worshippers of golden idols. Your ignorant desert band—confessing you so beyond the heavens they mocked those idolators and knew the stars for the candles of their nights, the lamps you hung to their use. Abhorring graven images—and so rejecting me engraved in flesh!

I overriding the Law of Moses, forgiving sins, making no distinction between my word and yours, proving my claims with power—and they reject me. Of what use signs when believers no longer believe? My plans—torn on the sharp edges of their broken faith. As prophesied—"The kings and rulers of the earth set themselves against the Lord and his Anointed."

Necessary now to shepherd them into the kingdom by another way, on a long, hard journey of the ages. I must pass through the scaldings and terrors Isaiah foretold. Through suffering they must learn to accept what they left unclaimed in my hand. Power failing, the way now lies in truth and faith and love—this patrimony I bequeath my Church, the great assembly of the ages.

They must build on me—must know that I AM.

Burdened, falling to the earth, soaring up to you. "The Twelve know me the Christ and know no more. It won't suffice when the blow falls. Enemies circle, treachery nears. How sustain them? Impossible—until they know that in me prophecy is Presence and Law is Person. In so many ways I've told them—in cryptic word and work of power and prophecy fulfilled.

The driving, lashing desire to tell them plainly. "How else can they stand when the storm comes slashing and I am gone? Yet would they believe me, when the journey to the knowledge that I am the Christ exhausted them like a journey to the stars? Can I tell them? Is that not an invitation to mockery? Must not you, Father, do it—acknowledge me plainly? As at my baptism—I leaped for joy and John understood. The rest understood nothing—it was too soon—and my own were not yet present.

"Now my allotted time drains to the dregs like wine from a wineskin. Little time is left—no time, O Timeless One. They must know that before I took the nature of a slave I AM. Else in crisis they will backslide—account me No-Christ. See at best Elijah returned or Moses re-promised.

"Father, to glorify you I came. Yet helpless I stand unless you help me—help them to know your Son. Forward your new creation. Assert your paternity!"

And then it happened.

Fire flamed from my face and I went . . .

And when I returned, Elijah in hairy mantle was kneeling to console me—recounting his cries to heaven when all altars were torn down. "I thought me one man alone," he confessed, "but learned all was not lost." Pulling free his mantle, he struck fire and burned it before me.

Moses came then, and my face lit his. His two tablets he lay at my feet. "Ten times and more," he anguished, "they rebelled against me and once infected me and I sinned. But you—never! Given us was the prophetic hope your suffering will redeem ours. Willingly we perished in the wilderness. But thou, my Lord, I beg thee, run thou to Jerusalem—let Abram's brood destroy thee in sacrifice and be redeemed at last! As Isaac prefigured, as Joseph mimicked, as Isaiah plainly foretold. Do thou hasten. The time is ripe, O Suffering Servant of Yahweh!"

The fire and mighty words woke at last the prayerless three. Daringly they circled, dazed. We pitied them.

"Lord! How good to be here!" babbled Peter. "At dawn, let's start a-building. Three shelters—for you, for Moses, for Elijah." Lifted in exaltation, yet resisting—scheming to keep me there, keep me from my path of suffering.

Your flaming cloud swept in. From the flames the *bath kol* thundered—"This is my Onlybegotten. Listen to him!"

And so it was done.

The Three shriveled to the cold earth even as my heart soared in thanksgiving. And I saw their tomorrows—when they would grasp your paternal witness and understand.

I touched them. They revived and found none but me.

Down we raced. While their eyes still flamed with wonder I commanded, "Tell no man of this vision until the Son of

273

Man's rising from the dead." And I saw my prophecy of death glance futilely off the armor of their exaltation.

"You are the Christ," Peter asserted, "but why do they teach that first Elijah must come?"

"Elijah the preparer does precede, as written," I assured them. "But is it not likewise written that the Son of Man must suffer fiercely and be cast out? Likewise Elijah—he came, and they did to him what they pleased." I raced on ahead, but yet heard their hoarse whispers questioning what 'rising from the dead' could signify.

At Daberath the crowd flew to me with hanging jaws. "Rabbi, what happened to you?" a vacant-eyed man queried. "Your face looks changed, looks—bright!"

"What'd you do to your clothes?" another blurted, fingering my cloak. "I'm a bleacher and never saw such white. Where'd you get this done on Tabor?"

Theologians were contending with the Twelve. "What is troubling you?" I demanded. A farmer in their midst responded.

"Teacher, my son gets seized by a dumb spirit. It hurls him down. He foams, grinds his teeth, freezes up all twisted. I begged your men to cast it out. They tried. They couldn't!"

Thomas stepped forward. "The theologians were clawing at us. They claim we're untrained and unfit to exorcise—and endanger ourselves and the boy."

"We insisted," Andrew exclaimed fiercely, "that we had your orders, and have cast out devils before."

"You people of this age!" I exploded. "You people without faith. How long must I rub shoulders with you? Bring the boy." He came, and the spirit saw me and convulsed him wildly. He fell, rolled in the dirt, foamed at the mouth.

"How long has he had seizures?" I asked.

"Since he was a little tyke. It throws him into fire and water. Oh, if you can, do something for pity's sake!"

"'If you can!' Don't you know everything's possible to the believer?"

"I believe. Help my unbelief!" At the commotion, people came running from all directions.

"Go out, deaf and dumb spirit. Stay out forever. I order it!" It came out with a howl—but not before it convulsed

274

the boy terribly, leaving him like a corpse.

"He's dead!" a theologian screamed triumphantly.

"Stand clear!" They scurried back. I took his hand, lifted him. He got up. I gave him to his father.

"Why couldn't we cast this one out?" the Twelve asked.

"Because," I said, recalling the three drowsing on the mountain, "this kind resists everything but prayer and fasting."

We traveled through Galilee secretly. I devoted my attention to the Twelve, driving prophetic word of my victorious sufferings into heads barricaded by fear.

The worldly set of their values kept asserting itself. I caught snatches of a boisterous argument about who was the most prestigious among them. When I asked, "What were you discussing on the journey?" none answered. "Do you aspire to be first?" I demanded. "Then be last of all and slave of all!" Recalling how one of the Twelve had bragged that on their last mission he had been sent to the most influential people, I plucked up one of the children playing at my feet. Fondly I embraced him, and he encircled my neck with his arms and clung to me. "The person who receives one child like this in my name," I told them, "receives me, and he who receives me receives him who sent me."

"An exorcist was casting out demons in your name," John said. "He wasn't one of us. We ordered him to stop."

"A mistake," I said. "He who is not against us is for us."

"Some who heard us preaching were kind to us," Jude recalled. "They volunteered food and lodging."

"Take it for certain," I said, "that one who gives you even a cup of drinking water because you belong to Christ will never be deprived of his reward." John's eyebrows raised.

"What if someone spreads false doctrine in your name?"

"Anyone who leads into sin one of these little ones who believes in me would be better off thrown into the deep with a millstone around his neck. Do you have a foot that leads you into sin? Cut it off! Better to hop single-footed into life than to be thrown full-bodied into hell, that unquenchable fire."

And so, my Father, I went on teaching them. How fiercely I desired the hour wherein they would eat and drink your will, and so put forward my mission.

The first blossoms were white on the almond tree. The fated time had come, the time to leave Galilee and never return on mortal feet. I set my face like flint against my fears and the thunder of my heart—for what awaited me I knew.

Part Six

THE SLAYING

1

Peter, half-waking to the cawing of a crow in the outer darkness, his body sweetly heavy, seemed immersed in some immemorial ritual, possessed of the eons, whether in himself or in his fusion with ancestors. He wanted nothing but to burrow deeper, fall further into the sleep and the comfort of the eternal pre-dawn of the crow. Then the sweet drowse drained away and he came awake and the crow was gone and he was alone in his solitary self and felt diminished and lonely. They were setting out for Judea this morning, and at the remembrance a dread took hold. He shook himself like a wet dog, and rose. He had to start things moving.

Amid the bustle Judas approached. "The Master has to take a more practical approach in Judea," he said in a low tone.

"What do you mean?"

"As I hinted to Jude, his universal call to holiness is a dream. People aren't up to it."

"I've never met a man who didn't want to be good." The pitch and volume of the exchange were rising, and the others, sensing a verbal duel, pricked up their ears.

"Do you really believe that?"

"Every man wants to be good."

Judas lifted his eyebrows. "Sometimes even I don't."

"Sometimes you don't want to pay the price. None of us does. That's why most never become as they'd like."

Judas eyed him with contempt. "You, a grown man, don't believe in malice?"

"Of course." He waved dismissal. "It's another reason we

279

don't become as we desire."

"I might want to become malicious."

"Only if you fail at what you really want—to be good."

"You're blind to the attraction of evil."

"And you to our humanness." Peter turned on his heel and left the room.

When they were ready, they said their goodbyes. The dear ones remaining behind clung tearfully to the Master when they saw the look on his face. By the time they set out, the morning sun had lifted well above the mountains of Batanaea and Auranitis. Only sporadically did it peer through the dark winter clouds parading across the heavens. Then it blazed on the lake, set the pools of water aglow in the muddy road, and limned the faces of the travelers moving south on the lake shore road. The Master strode along in the lead, the Twelve at his heels, the rest trailing after, and the little cluster of women disciples in their midst.

The journey to Judea was negotiated by traveling through Galilee and Samaria, or by following the Jordan Valley.

The Valley route was favored to avoid the hostile Samaritans, but the Master intended to evangelize that people and had sent missionaries ahead to prepare them. He planned to take the Valley route to Bethshan, and there swing west through the Bethshan Gap and south into Samaria.

The disciples were afraid. "I don't relish seeing those Samaritans," Thomas confessed. "You never know what to expect in Samaria."

"We know only too well what to expect in Jerusalem," lamented Bartholomew.

"Bagels and paschal lamb," Jude enthused, and they laughed. John felt the tension too, but it only intensified his consciousness in a way that made his body overflow with sweet sense impressions, as can happen when one thinks he is seeing his favorite scenes for the last time. The resilient soil lent spring to his step, the chunky clouds looked almost close enough to touch, and the stately date palms appeared like survivors of the Garden of Eden. Along the shore, the myrtle and the willow sported a festive air, and the tall khaki reeds filled him with nostalgia.

The heavy-bodied trunk of a towering oak caught his eye

as he passed—and the sound of a door slamming reverberated in his memory. It was the great oaken door of a massive Roman-style edifice in Jerusalem. He had sold fish carried fresh from the lake to its occupants, and the door had slammed shut behind him with such heavy finality he'd had the distinct impression he would never enter it again, and never had. Now he had the sense that many doors were closing with finality, but they were little doors of rooms grown too small. The day he met the Master—the moment he saw him—a door had opened into a spaciousness where flamed a sacred fire with incense rising, and ever since doors had been opening all round, doors into the hearts and lives of others.

John looked at the Master. Did his tread too show that he felt the bounce in the soil and the nostalgia for loved things left behind? Did the others feel the same? Peter was at his side, and he felt him out.

"Every time we leave the lake," he said, "I feel like I'm parting with an old friend."

"And I feel like my fishing arm is dislocated!" Peter gazed longingly at the fishermen's boats plying the lake.

"Look at it this way, men," Simon the Zealot cried gaily, "you're not losing a lake, you're gaining the Kingdom!" Peter eyed him quizzically.

"You have high hopes."

"Peter, this is it. I'll make a prophecy—the Kingdom will be ours by Passover!"

"Why so sure?"

"Look at it this way. The Master has forbidden us to reveal what we know, but when confronted by the high authorities he'll have to identify himself—and use his power to prove it."

"I wish I were as certain as you, Zealot."

"By all the fish in the sea! How can it be otherwise? He barely escaped Jerusalem alive last time, because he wasn't ready to reveal his identity. Now he has to be."

"Simon, you're very sure of yourself, like the typical man of war"—Peter was grim. "I'm not. I still don't know what will happen."

"Whatever happens," John intervened, "I predict we'll

survive—like that caper." He pointed to a prickly shrub thrusting its way through an outcropping of stone.

After an interval Jude said desultorily, "Weeds are infesting the wheat this year." He pointed to farm hands at work in the field.

"Weeds!" the Zealot snorted, striking his forehead. "That's our big problem? Jude, we're discussing the power and glory of Israel!"

At the gates of Bethshan a crowd milled around a little man by a cart loaded with a barrel. He was richly dressed, with a gold medallion hanging on his chest. "I, Manoah, tell you," he was bellowing, "that my son is no longer mine. No longer mine!" He kept parroting the last phrase.

"Oh, oh," Peter said. "Another wayward son."

"He's married himself a female of the Romans!" Shouting the words, Manoah seized a cudgel, and with awful violence struck the barrel. Staves splintered and flew, and gourds, melons, and carob pods rolled into the gutter. "Let his seed be like this garbage in the gutter—no affair of mine. I've warned you beforehand!" With that, he seized the handle of the cart and rattled down the street. The bystanders laughed raucously and, when Manoah was out of hearing, told raunchy stories about his daughter-in-law.

"Let that teach you, young John," Peter said grandly, "not to marry a Roman wench—indeed, to let your parents choose your bride."

When they reached the market place, Judas declared they needed supplies and went off with Jude. Peter stood alongside the Master idly surveying the farmers selling fruits and vegetables, chickens and eggs, and other produce. The stands of the merchants overflowed with kettles, vases, jugs, bolts of cloth, tunics and cloaks, leather belts and sandals, and the hucksters' pitch was as varied as their wares.

Unemployed day laborers loitered nearby in patched clothing, shivering in the wind, hollow cheek and fevered eye signalling a starvation diet. A gaunt scarecrow ran up waving his arms. "A new tax just fell on our heads—a new Roman tax, administered by Herod, lackey of Caesar!"

"We're already starving," a bystander lamented.

"My little Josie's sick," another complained, "and I can't

282

feed her."

"You can't find work," the scarecrow shouted, "and when you do, the filthy-rich landowners keep demanding more work for a denarius."

"What can we do?" asked a man in a stunned voice.

"I'll tell you," the scarecrow screamed. "Join the Zealots. Listen!" And he began his harangue.

Judas stopped to eye the wares of a pearl merchant, examined the best of the lot, a large, milky white pearl—and noticed Jude staring at him. "Jude, at that first stand we passed, they had some fine dried lentils. Buy a sackful, but take your time haggling." He pressed a coin into Jude's palm. Before he reached the indicated vendor, Jude found fine lentils at a good price and made his purchase. Thus he returned before he was expected, and what he saw shocked him. Judas moved on, and never realized he had been observed.

The scarecrow was still inflaming the mob when the two rejoined the others. "Rabbi," Peter said, "let's head out before there's trouble." The Master was listening intently, but he set out at Peter's urging, and the others followed reluctantly. Their blood was boiling at the outrages the speaker reported, their hearts beating wildly at his vision of freedom.

At the town gate, a troop of Herod's Idumean cavalry came thundering down the road. They made way, and the horsemen flew by. "I'd run to warn those men," Simon the Zealot cried, "but there's not a chance I'd make it." His lips tightened. "They killed my father in such a raid."

Just beyond the gate was the crossroad which led through the Bethshan Gap. "Look, Rabbi," Peter cried, pointing to the six missionaries who, by plan, were to await them in Samaria.

"Master," their spokesman explained, "when the Samaritans heard you planned to go on to the Holy City they flew into a rage. We left in a hail of stones." He rubbed a bruise on his forehead.

John's cheeks flamed. "Master, send James and me to call fire and brimstone down on their heads. We'll do it!"

"Is that what you learned from me?"—Jesus' tone was

283

bitter—"You don't know what spirit is gnawing at you." He turned to Peter. "We go by way of Perea." And so it was that they forded the river, and continued down the Jordan Valley.

Like an ass harnessed to a millstone, Jude's mind rotated around the market place and what had transpired there, and he felt sick. A sudden breeze stirred the Jordan, the sparkling water caught his eye, and in his imagination he saw the pearl once again. He slipped up to Peter's side. "I have to talk to you—alone." Peter took him by the arm, and they went on ahead.

"You look down-at-the-mouth. What is it?"

"I don't know whether to trouble the Master about Judas."

"What happened?"

"He spotted a pearl dealer and took special interest in the best one he had."

"So what? I like to look at pearls too."

"Wait. He sent me for a bag of lentils. I returned before he expected, and saw him interchange something with the pearl dealer, and walk away."

"Maybe he asked him to make change."

"No. Once when he claimed we were out of funds, I saw him with two pearls. Later that day he told Mary Magdalene we couldn't buy food. She gave him the last of her money."

"You're sure?"

"Yes. Today I asked the pearl dealer what happened to his best pearl. He pointed to Judas. 'Your friend bought it.'"

"Tell the Master. Now." Jude repeated his story to Jesus.

"You did well to tell me," he said. "Stay here with me to pray for our friend."

Later, Jude heard Judas confiding to Joanna that funds were low. "Take what I have left," she said.

That night, around campfires ablaze in the wilderness of Perea, they talked of the day's events. "Peter," Mary Magdalene asked, "what did you think of that Manoah's antics?"

"What do you mean?" Peter countered. "You've seen that custom before."

"Was his son so wrong to marry the girl he loved? Should

284

he have thrown her over because of his father's objections?"

"I'm no theologian," Peter hedged, "but the Law says, 'Honor your father.'"

"It also says a man shall leave father and mother for his wife."

"Shouldn't it be a wife who pleases his parents?"

"Shouldn't it first be a wife who pleases *him?*" John interjected. "He has to live with her."

"His parents have to live with concern for him."

"Now that Manoah's son is already married," Mary persisted, "should he divorce his wife to please his father?"

"That's not easy to decide, but I'd say no."

"I'd say *yes,*" Judas put in from the adjoining campfire. "He shouldn't allow her to rob him of family peace. Men get divorces for lesser reasons—and with the approval of the rabbis." Before meeting Jesus, he had been tempted to divorce his wife. She used to nag him about leaving her home alone during his frequent business trips—as if he had any intention of squandering money to take her along.

"Once," recounted Jude, "I heard the great Gamaliel telling of a Jewish rabbi who described to the Emperor how God took a rib from Adam and made him a woman. 'Your God's a thief!' the Emperor mocked. The rabbi was shamed into silence. When the rabbi told his daughter, she said, 'Let me handle this.' In she went to the Emperor crying, 'Justice! Justice!' 'What's the charge?' he asked. 'Thieves,' she explained, 'took my silver pitcher and left a gold one.' 'Ho! Ho!' he chortled, 'I'd welcome such thieves nightly!' 'Well,' said the girl, 'that's how good our God is. A mere rib he took from Adam, and returned him a wife.'"

"It's cold," Judas said. "Jude, build up that fire."

The floor of the Jordan Valley was verdant from the winter rains. Even the mountainous walls sported green grass and winter flowers. As the travelers neared Bethany-beyond-Jordan, they stopped to gaze across at Jericho. The city, located on a fertile plain watered by mountain streams and the Fountain of Elisha, was surrounded by great fruit and nut orchards, fields of barley and sprouting wheat.

Peter breathed a sigh of relief. This was where the Baptizer had headquartered, and he hoped Jesus would too. One felt safe here, insulated by great stretches of desert from the major centers of government. Though under Herod's jurisdiction, it was far from his real ambit of power. He had few troops—the Romans would not trust him with more—and so these outer ramparts were lightly garrisoned.

Jericho was in Judea—Governor Pilate's domain. An inconsequential town in a torrid valley, it lay a day's journey from Jerusalem. Not known for breeding trouble, it was of little interest to Pilate. Pilate resided in Caesarea on the Sea, two days away across a tumbled wilderness.

Jude pointed to the highest mountain in the range ahead, overlooking the glassy dark waters of the Dead Sea. "What a view Moses had from Nebo! I understand you can see all the way to Mount Tabor."

"You can," James confirmed. "I climbed it. I used to gaze down on the Essene Community at Qumran, and wanted to go there, but the Baptizer said no, they didn't have the answers." The Qumran settlement lay on the rim of the Dead Sea, just a few miles down the Valley.

"Isn't this where our people entered the Promised Land?" Jude asked.

"You know it is, Jude," John chided. "You asked the last time we came this way."

"O.K., John, but not everybody has your memory."

"This is where the Baptizer pointed out the Master," John recalled. "Where it all began."

"Where," Judas asked darkly, "will it all end?"

Droves of people flocked to Jesus. Pharisees, Sadducees, and their theologians began arriving from Jerusalem to challenge his doctrine.

"We heard of you inveighing against the stoning of an adulteress," a theologian complained in a voice sharp as a knife. "That puts you against the Law of Moses."

"Moses intended enforcers to keep the Law they enforced."

"Well put, Rabbi," another theologian applauded. "Our sinfulness should teach us compassion. Where do you stand, then, on the compassionate teaching that a husband may divorce a displeasing wife?"

"What was Moses' command to you?" The man turned

286

his face to heaven and raised his hands in a theatrical display.

"Oh come now! You, a teacher in Israel, must know. He permits a man to divorce his wife for *erwat dabar,* some indecency."

"Malachy warns you the Lord rejects your sacrifices for rejecting the wife of your youth."

"Oh, that." The theologians smiled. "A mere exhortation to think twice before divorce. Malachy wouldn't dare contradict Moses."

"Therefore," interjected another theologian, "the question is not whether divorce is permissible, but what the grounds are. What is the meaning of 'some indecency?'"

"Exactly!" chimed in the theatrical theologian. "Does it mean—as the School of Shammai holds so sternly—that the wife must be an adulteress? Or does it mean—as the School of Hillel says so understandingly—anything displeasing in a wife? For instance, she may burn her husband's favorite dish. What do you say?"

"What do you theologians say?"

"We say the interpretations of both schools are divine renderings of the Scriptures, and neither is to be rejected." So the theatrical rabbi spoke—and peered triumphantly at the Master, who turned to John.

"Son of Zebedee, what do you think of this teaching?"

"It's strange to hear. The two schools give contrary interpretations, so that one must be wrong—and then each school agrees that the interpretation of the other is inviolate. They empty Moses' word of meaning to honor their opinions."

The theatrical rabbi turned on John fiercely. "What ordained rabbi has certified your opinion?"

The Master silenced him with a gesture. "You people look for empty honor from one another, and not from the only God." He turned to John again. "Will they recognize the Messiah?"

"No."

"Why?"

"How can they, if one school says 'According to the Scripture it is he,' and the other school says 'According to Scripture it is not he,' and they agree that both opinions are inviolate?"

287

"So, then," cried the theatrical rabbi, "you evade our question—refusing to state your position on divorce."

"Moses permitted divorce," Jesus replied sternly, "because of your stony hearts. But God made them male and female from first creation. A man leaves parents and adheres to wife, and of two one flesh comes. See now not two, but one flesh. Let no man separate them. God has joined them."

"This man is too much!" The words escaped Judas in an undertone, but Jude heard.

In the house, the Twelve came to Jesus, with Peter as spokesman. "Some of us," he reported, "think your teaching on marriage means that divorce *should* be avoided; some think it means that divorce *must* be avoided."

"I say to you that a spouse who divorces commits adultery against his or her partner." He turned to a mother who had slipped through the circle of Apostles and was holding her sad-faced little girl out to him. He took her, bussed her cheek, whispered to her, and teased her until she laughed. He blessed her and returned her. Seeing this, mothers began pressing around with their children. Judas coldly surveyed the situation.

"Look how tired the Rabbi is. And you're bothering him with this!" He started herding mothers and children out of the room. The others began to lend a hand.

"What are you doing?" demanded the Master. "Stop it! I want the children to come. To persons like them the kingdom belongs. Listen! If you don't receive the kingdom as a child, you won't enter at all." He attended the little ones, and his laughter mingled with theirs.

That night Peter, James and John bustled up to him in high excitement. "We were told," Peter whispered "that Jericho's fermenting like yeasty dough in the sun. Big discussions go on about whether you're the Messiah."

"The people," John added, "are amazed at your authority in dealing with the theologians."

"If you continue teaching here"—James's eyes flashed—"they'll soon be hailing you as the Christ!"

"Of course," Peter admitted, "fear is putting a damper on their high spirits. The authorities are watching like hawks, and people say a detachment of Roman cavalry is on the way."

Jesus said nothing. In the morning, he summoned Peter. "We set out for Jerusalem today." Peter turned quickly away. He was ashamed of the fear in his eyes.

"I'll tell the rest at once."

2

The day rose golden with promise and, as though it had strayed into summer's course, the winter sun lent ardent warmth to the Jordan Valley, that deepest of clefts in the earth. The Apostles were under the impression they would make the full ten-hour journey to the Holy City today. Not an hour away across the ford of the Jordan lies Jericho. From there the Jerusalem road runs south-west toward the Dead Sea. Before reaching that body it sweeps west, climbing into the jumble of wild, barren mountains and sterile desert which insulate the Holy City.

Since the Master had instructed Judas to provide a nourishing breakfast, fresh barley bread was distributed with olives, cheese and dates, nuts and goat's milk. There were few hearty appetites. The Master observed the mere picking at food, the tangible fear and anxiety, and caught snatches of whispers sounding the alarm at the prospect of going up to the Holy City.

He arose, and began circulating among the people. Seeing him stirring and passing, the company fell silent, captivated by the magnetism of his presence, straining to hear what might fall from his lips, watching his every gesture. With each to whom he came there was some interchange—an understanding glance, a comforting look, a dazzling smile, a touch of the hand, a quiet word. Grins broke out when he straightened the headgear of Fat Alexander—it was forever askew—and tender looks when he brushed a smudge from the tunic of Micah, a comely youth loved by all. Faces grew lightsome and some laughed joyously when, to thin and willowy young Mark, he said, "See, Judas has kindly thinned his purse to fatten those wilted cheeks. Do his fare justice, so we won't lose you in Alexander's shadow." The youth grinned and obliged.

On returning to the Twelve, he stood beside them and addressed the multitude. "Dismiss your fear, my little flock. It has pleased the Father to give you the Kingdom." He turned to Mary of Magdala, and spoke to her in a clear voice meant for all. "Mary, recall the psalms of ascent, and the happy smile suiting our pilgrimage to the City of our desire." His attention evoked her radiance, and seeing this, he spoke to the people. "Let us feast on what the Father has provided, even as Magdala's woman sings for us a canticle of our ascent to Zion." He nodded to Mary, who rose and lifted her timbred voice in song.

O City of Zion with Temple of gold
Our people have blessed thee with blessing of old,
Have set shepherd David on thy pinnacled mount,
Have pilgrimage made to thy courts beyond count,
Have set in thy shrine our one covenant's ark,
And sung of thee songs like the cry of the lark.

O what tongue can tell of thy portent for all,
O what hymn express thine ineffable call
Which made captives weep in Babylon's day
And brought them all singing of thee on the way
When thralldom had ended and home they did bound
To gather thy stones and thee once again found.

O Zion our true hearts remain wed to thy clay
As off to thy courts we set forth on this day,
Our spirits sustained by our hope and our plea
And vision of him who will set us all free,
The King and true Christ who was promised of old
To gather us all in his arms to his fold.

The responding cries of delight and hands clapping were counterpointed, here and there, by silent tears streaming. Fears forgotten for now, the company did justice to the repast and, when satisfied, raised a cheer for Judas the provider—at this, the Master smiled with pleasure. Then they broke camp.

Hardly had they set forth when three horsemen appeared in the distance and charged toward them. They reined in their mounts sharply, and a young man handsomely garbed in purple cloak and a golden rider's tunic leaped down, tossed the reins of his fiery stallion to his attendant, and ran to meet them. His flashing eyes examined each in turn and settled unerringly on the Master. He bounded up to him, gracefully slipped to his knees, and looked at him out of dark brown eyes set in a no-nonsense face, square of jaw and brow. The habit of command conveyed by his whole bearing had the effect of denying his kneeling posture. When he spoke, it was in a low tone, a whisper, rife with confidentiality.

"I've heard of you. Delayed only too long in coming. So many affairs, so much business—but thank God I caught you."

"What do you want?"

"To consult you. Good teacher, tell me—how must I comport myself to enter my eternal inheritance?"

The Master searched the face which gazed back unflinchingly, expectantly. "Why call me good? None is but God alone."

The nobleman looked about to assure himself of privacy. "The people," he whispered, "say you might be the Christ."

"You know the commandments. No killing, adultery, thievery, false witnessing, fraudulence. Honor your father and mother."

Joy elevated the outer edges of the handsome, wide-set black eyes, and lifted the rosy cheeks. "Observed from my boyhood!"

The Master gave him a look brimming with affection. "There is one thing more." The youth's face turned up expectantly, one ear moving closer. "Go, sell everything. Give the money to the poor, and have secure wealth—in heaven. Then follow me."

"Everything?" The word began on a high pitch, and drifted into oblivion. The Master nodded. The youth fingered his jewel-encrusted gold medallion, his face melting into desolate puddles like sandy soil washed by a storm. Slowly,

291

he struggled to his feet—involuntarily, Peter extended a hand to help—and with the puddles of sadness enlarging, he walked ponderously to his horse. Heavily, he mounted, and slowly rode away.

The Master watched him go, then spun round and looked at his disciples with a fiery face. "For the rich, how hard to enter the Kingdom!" Peter gaped, James stared, John fingered his beard, Andrew put his hand reflectively to his forehead, and Judas looked as though stalled at some point between calculation and outrage. They were remembering the centuries-old sayings of the wise, who considered wealth a sign of God's favor—a pledge of salvation.

Jesus read their thoughts. "Children, it's hard to enter God's Kingdom. Easier for a camel to squeeze through the eye of a needle than for a rich man to squeeze into the Kingdom." At this, Peter bellowed like a wounded steer. "Then who can be saved?"

"With men it *is* impossible, but not with God. All things are possible with God."

"Well, anyway"—Peter registered relief—"we've left everything for you."

"Take it for certain that anyone who, for my sake and the Gospel's, leaves home or wife or brother or sister or mother or father or children or lands—that one will come into a hundred times more in this age—with persecutions—and in the approaching age, life eternal."

They resumed their journey, and soon reached the ford of the Jordan. Swollen with winter rain, the river was over-flowing its banks. Running up to Jesus, Peter laid his hand on his arm to restrain him. "Rabbi, the water's deep and cold. We'll carry you." Jesus shook off the hand, thrust his body into the water, and waded across. On the other side he summoned the Twelve, and spoke grimly.

"Make no mistake about it—we're headed for the Holy City. There, the Son of Man will be handed over to the chief priests, the official theologians, and leading laymen. Death will be the sentence they hang round his neck, and to the Gentiles they'll hand him. They'll mock him, spit on him, scourge him, kill him—and on the third day he will rise." Then he called Matthew, and spoke with him privately.

292

James grabbed his brother by the arm and drew him apart. "John, this is it!" He spoke fiercely, with lightning-like energy playing on his face. "He's about to claim the Kingdom! Let's make our power play before it's too late!"

"I don't know," John scowled. "What was the meaning of that parable he just told us?"

"Why worry about that now? Hesitate, and Peter will move in! If we lose out, our mother will never forgive us. She's made real sacrifices to keep us all eating." Their mother Salome was one of the women who accompanied them. She had complete faith in Jesus, and high hopes of a significant role in the kingdom he was promising, and had urged her sons to be more aggressive in putting themselves forward.

"All right. Come on!"

As soon as the Master finished with Matthew and got the caravan on its way again, they trotted up to him. "Teacher, we want you to give what we ask."

"What do you ask?"

"To sit on your right and your left, in your exaltation."

"You don't have any idea what you're asking. Can you drink my cup, be immersed in my baptism?"

"Yes!" they both shouted, forgetting their scheme to keep the matter quiet. The rest of the Twelve edged in closer, cocking their ears.

"You will indeed share my cup and my baptism." His face was grim. "But the posts you ask, I can't grant. They're allotted."

"You sneaks!" Judas snarled, swollen eyelids wide now, inflamed eyes bulging. At this, the Master stopped once more, and gathered the Twelve. They were angry.

"You've seen Gentile leaders and men of influence lord it over the common people. You shall never be that way."

"But Master," Peter objected, "you promised me your keys of power. Don't you plan to make great men of us?"

"To be great, serve all. And to be first, be slave to all. The Son of Man himself came to serve—not to be served— and to lay down his life as a ransom for many people." He spun round and went on. For a long while they stood watching him. Only when those behind nudged them did they proceed.

They reached the outskirts of Jericho, that city so ancient no man knows when it was founded. Beyond the city looms the tawny precipice which forms the western wall of the Jordan rift. Jagged, unscalable, gashed with the black mouths of caves, bleached with the full brilliance of the morning sun, it seemed an incarnation of the naked desert, hovering over the little settlement like a gigantic bird of prey.

The people, having gotten word that the Master was coming, streamed from the city to meet him. Out through their ranks broke a lone horseman. His mount was a small animal slavering badly, smeared with mud, its eyes turned up in hopeless exhaustion. The rider dismounted and, walking stiffly, approached. Peter recognized him. He was a servant of Lazarus, who lived with his two sisters, Martha and Mary, in the Bethany which is a suburb of Jerusalem. The three were dear friends of the Master, who frequented their house when he had opportunity.

The servant bowed. "Rabbi, I have a message for you from my mistresses. The friend you love is very ill."

"This illness," the Master said cryptically, "is meant, not to bring death to man, but glory to God—so that the Son of God may be glorified by it." He bade the servant join them, and continued toward Jericho.

A man-mountain in rags sat by the roadside begging. His great head and over-sized features were handsome in a sensuous, unkempt way. The lips were full—too full; the nose well-sculptured, but somewhat fleshy; the black, thick locks and beard flowed down so copiously they covered everything—he was awash in hair. That pleased him; it kept him warm. What did it matter that the mighty mane fell half across his eyes? He was blind.

His blackened toes protruded from worn sandals. They itched, and he scratched them. His eyes were closed, his wooden cup in hand. He shook it vigorously, rattling the petty coins. Knowing beyond doubt that God had laid the responsibility for his keep on passersby, he waited impatiently for the plink of a coin. Whenever a few minutes passed without one, he habitually let fly an emotional cry of outrage so shattering of nerves that it bent the will of anyone nearby—

and a coin unfailingly dropped in to mollify him for the moment.

At present, Bartimaeus was rattling his cup preoccupiedly with one hand, and pulling at his beard fast and furiously with the other as he sorted out the discussions—or rather arguments—which he had been overhearing for weeks. The people were in a fever about the prophet across the river. He was the Messiah, some swore; some ridiculed the idea. Some were deeply involved in his message; some were mere gossips. They all agreed on one thing—that at Passover next month the matter would be settled. The true Messiah could not let that historic time of liberation pass without action.

Bartimaeus was too needy to fence-sit, or wait for Passover. He had listened carefully, and thought about it a lot. "It's him!" he decided. But one problem remained. He had nobody to take him to Jesus. He left off thinking and gave his attention to the sounds around him. This morning the traffic was heavy, there was a high pitch of excitement, and people were ignoring him even more than usual. He fought back his periodic outburst, and listened intently, but the voices all ran together. Of a sudden, the noise and excitement surged. His rage flashed into a new channel and erupted in a new demand. "What's going on? Answer me!"

"All right! All right!" came an annoyed voice. "Jesus of Nazareth is coming. He's here now!" Without need to think, Bartimaeus raised his cavernous mouth to the sky.

"Jesus, Son of David, have mercy on me! Jesus, Son of David, have mercy on me!" He roared on and on, his words tumbling about in a wild sea of emotions.

"Who knows if he is the Son of David?" a voice challenged.

"You're blind!" Bartimaeus bellowed. "Son of David, pity, pity!"

"Keep that up and you'll cause him trouble," a passer-by warned.

"Trouble? Nothing is too much trouble to get my sight!"

"Button your lip, you tub of lard!" a voice shouted in his ear. "You're endangering his life. The Romans . . ." But Bartimaeus was beyond control. His barrel chest expanded, his cry spewed out.

The Master heard his voice above the noise of the crowd,

looked around, and saw him. "Bring him," he commanded. Peter ran to him. "Cheer up. He's calling you."

With a wild cry, the beggar rose like a mountain in upheaval, sending his tattered cloak sailing over the people. He thrust out his arm, and was led to the Master, who addressed him gently.

"What is it you want?"

"Lord, I want to see you!"

"Now follow your path. Your faith has saved you."

"I can see! Everything!" The huge bulk gyrated. He turned and fell before the Master. "I can see you, Son of David." His voice was subdued, and he bowed low.

The Master set out again, the beggar falling in behind. The crowd cheered wildly as he came along the tree-flanked street. A girl skipped up and handed him a flower. Overhanging the way like a canopy was the bough of a towering sycamore tree, and something stirring in the foliage caught the Master's eye. Perched on the branch, clinging desperately, gazing down at him, was a little man.

Matthew's laughter rang out. "Master, behold the chief tax collector of Jericho, my dear friend—the man I told you of. Hello, Three-a-day!" Three-a-day habitually bragged that neither he nor his guests ever missed a meal.

The Master smiled up at him. "Zacchaeus, hurry down. I have to stay at your house."

His jaw dropped, his grip loosened, and he slipped. Grabbing frantically, he caught the bough and dangled precariously. Peter and Thomas moved in.

"Let go!" Peter called. "I've pulled in bigger fish than you." He plummeted into their arms, and they set him down.

"Rabbi Yeshua, come on!" Zacchaeus chanted. "My house is yours. This way!" Flitting along, he escorted them to his mansion and led them indoors. "I'll arrange accommodations for all your followers."

Judas was sitting in the courtyard with some of the others. "What do you think?" he prompted.

"About what?" Peter asked.

"Doesn't it bother you that the Master gave us a resounding

exhortation to leave everything, and set out for his sick friend—and now that we've fallen into luxury's lap, both the detachment and the friend seem to be forgotten?"

The others looked thoughtful, but Matthew, indignant. "For your information, Judas, the Master asked me where we could lodge in Jericho before Lazarus' servant arrived—so there's been no change of plans."

"Granting the far-fetched coincidence of the very man you planned to search out literally falling right into our hands," Judas remarked sardonically, "does that explain why he's forgotten his sick friend?"

"I just came back from a walk." Thomas spoke hesitantly, as though reluctant to go on. "The people are scandalized that the Master's staying with . . ."

"The same happened when he stayed with me," Matthew broke in.

"Because," Thomas continued, "Zacchaeus is a thief."

"They called me a thief too!"

"Nobody believed it, but I assure you they're angry with the thievery of this man. They're citing his crookedness chapter and verse."

"Then I'd better see the Master," Peter decided. "Matthew, Thomas, come along."

"What about me?" Judas asked.

"What about you?" Peter turned and left.

The Master insisted that Zacchaeus hear, so in his presence Thomas gave his report.

"Master," Zacchaeus said, "you've honored me beyond telling, and I'll not betray you by denying the charge. Before you leave, please come to the door with me." He led the way through the marble halls. A noisy, hostile crowd filled the street. When they emerged, silence fell.

"I have an important announcement," Zacchaeus squeaked in his weak voice. "From this moment I'm a changed man." The hard, unbelieving looks and the subdued hisses lent no encouragement, but he went on untroubled. "Everyone who's been cheated, come with your accounts to my office this afternoon. What I overcharged I'll return fourfold!" Someone cheered, the joy spread, and a mighty wave of acclamation rose. The little man waved his hands in a call for silence, and the uproar died. "More good news!" he cried enthusiastically. "For all the poor of the city. Spread the word that in the morning I begin distributing half my wealth to the needy. But don't try to fake it—I know who was too poor to be cheated. And if Bartimaeus is here, I'll begin with him." He looked around. The beggar stepped forward.

"No, thanks, Three-a-day, I'm not poor any more. I'm a disciple of the Master." The cheering broke into a frenzy. The Master stepped forward and signalled for silence.

"It's now plain that Zacchaeus too is a son of Abraham, and this day salvation has visited his house. The Son of Man came to hunt out and save the lost."

At the soaring tumult he smiled, waved, and went inside.

The glad faces of the Apostles showed their relief. "But," thought Thomas that night, as he lay sleepless in a luxurious bed after a sumptuous feast, "he's still forgetting his sick friend. Is his stay here that urgent? Couldn't he go and come back?"

3

Rooted in ages of ancestral history, unflappable Jericho is like some stalwart, thick-bodied old olive tree which shrugs off storms that send whole forests into wild gyrations. Yet, in the hurricane whose eye was the Master, Jericho flexed and danced like a young sapling. The transformation wrought in the tax collector and the effects of his bountiful ministrations flashed like a thunderbolt across the city. And those who scoffed were demolished by the restored vision of the beggar.

The Master stayed two days with Zacchaeus, who was becoming a folk hero overnight. In a larger sense, he stayed, not with one man, but with the whole people of the city. From dawn to dusk he taught them, and from dusk to dawn argument raged over him. The Roman overlords, well aware of it, had come thundering into the city with troop reinforcements, flaunting their presence, tempering the enthusiasm, and muting many a conversation.

Jerusalemite priests, theologians, and noblemen had also drifted in, prying into everything touching on the Nazarene, and arguing among themselves.

Though anxious about the authorities, the disciples felt that neither Roman nor Jewish leaders would act so long as the Master did not invade their nest in the Holy City. Thus they gave free reign to their joy in the upturn of their fortunes.

This enthusiasm, at least for some of the Twelve, was dampened by two considerations. Hot bloods like the Zealot could not understand why the Master wasted his time on a no-account town; others were troubled by his neglect of the mortally sick Lazarus. Beyond the Twelve, the Master had no closer friend, and his affection went as deep for the man's two sisters. Martha was a great hostess, and the life of the parties she loved to lavish on her friends. Mary, a maiden beautiful in body and soul, surpassed everyone in the way she lost herself completely in the Master, and her faith was as deep and penetrating as John's.

It was with mixed feelings, then, that the Twelve heard the Master announce on the third day, "Now we leave for Bethany."

"Rabbi, don't go!" Thomas blurted out, to his own surprize. Heretofore convinced of his readiness to tramp boldly up to Bethany, he had been tempted to think the Master lacked the courage. Now he knew the truth, and he tried to justify it. "Their spies haunt us even here. Deadly dangers face us anywhere near Jerusalem."

"He's right," Peter chimed in. "You escaped stoning by a grain of sand last time. We're accomplishing a lot here."

"Have you forgotten our beloved Lazarus?" the Master countered. "He's fallen asleep. I'm going to wake him."

"Sleep's the best medicine!" Peter exclaimed.

"He's dead."

They stared at him in horror, grief, and shame.

"We should've gone sooner," Judas snapped. "I knew it."

Jesus stared at him. "For your sakes I'm glad I wasn't there. Your faith will profit. We start at once." They froze, faces contorted. It was Thomas who responded first.

"All right!" He girded his belt more tightly. "Let's go and die with him!" Peter marveled. He certainly lived up to his name, which means The Twin.

They took their leave, and as they filed up the steep mountain road, Peter looked back. What a huge throng! He could easily distinguish the new followers by their mood, festive as folk trooping to a wedding. The veterans looked like condemned going to their graves. It was a tribute to the Master that they were there at all.

Recalling the new name the Master had given him, he tried to harden his face like flint, with, he guessed, indifferent success. He never knew he had such a vivid imagination. The moment he let it loose, a hail of stones came hurling at them—and he even felt one caving in his big skull.

Where the highway carried them up into the tortuous mountain wilderness, out of sight of the Jordan rift, he took one last look southward, down on the dark, glistening waters of the Dead Sea, grave mark of a corrupt city. Towering over its eastern shore stood Mount Nebo, monument to Moses' grief at never entering the promised land. A cry high above drew his eyes to the kites drifting over the wastelands in search of prey. He sighed and looked ahead. The Holy City lay six hours climb to the southeast.

Farther along, a thudding of hooves sounded behind. They vacated the road for the mounted Roman troops galloping past, scintillating body armor scattering the sun. When they reached the first spring, they drank and rested, and watched the sheep feeding on the grassy slopes, a rear leg of each animal tied to its huge, fat tail to inhibit straying. Fierce-looking shepherds lounged about, leaning on iron-bound cudgels, necessary protection against robber bands and wild beasts. The boars, leopards and lions which roamed the thickets of the Jordan Valley at times wandered into these mountains in search of prey. The sheep dogs barked incessantly, nervous at the sight of the invaders.

They started off again. A great caravan of dromedaries laden with spices and condiments from Mesopotamia could be seen far behind, where the terrain permitted. Traders from many lands were converging on Jerusalem, bringing merchandise to the bazaars soon to be crowded with a hundred thousand pilgrims preparing for Passover. Robbers nesting in the caves which honeycombed the lowering cliffs remained in concealment, waiting to swoop on small, defenseless little bands and the unwise solitary wayfarer.

Bethany nestled on the gentle slope of the lowest ascent of the Mount of Olives, beyond which lay Jerusalem. Martha met them outside the town. She came running, but something in her step only accentuated the lassitude which gripped her.

"My brother's dead," she intoned dully without a greeting. "If you'd come sooner, he wouldn't be." Her habitually ruddy cheeks were pale, her eyelids drooping with weariness and swollen with weeping. The Master embraced her wordlessly, and tenderly kissed her. She began to weep.

"Your brother will rise."

"I know," she sobbed, "on the last day, at the resurrection."

"I am the Resurrection and the Life." Taking her drooping face in his hands, he drew her eyes to him. "Do you believe this?"

"Certainly. You're the Christ." She whispered the words.

Leaving him then, she ran back home, where she found her sister trying bravely to be a good hostess to mourning relatives and friends. She put her lips to her ear. "Sister, he's just outside the town. He wants you."

When the girl reached him, she said mournfully, "If you'd come, my brother wouldn't have died." She burst into tears. Seeing the grief contorting her beautiful face, the mourners who had trailed her began mourning and wailing, scalding tears flooding their faces. Waves of suffering rolled across the Master's face. His eyes looked wounded, and seemed to go out of focus from some inner torment.

A man of Jericho looked at him calculatingly. "Couldn't this wonder-working friend of the dead man," he asked his companion raucously, "have prevented his death? He cured that blind man, didn't he? Something doesn't add up."

Jesus emitted a wild cry, and turned to Mary. "Where did you bury him?"

"Come and see," she murmured through her sobs. Jesus began crying. She took his hand and led him along a path through a wooded area, into a glade. On its far side a naked cliff loomed. She pointed to the large stone disc closing the

301

mouth of a cave.

"Remove the stone!"

A woman gasped and loosed a shrill cry. People stared in horror. Had the Nazarene lost his wits? A neighbor of Lazarus, a big farmer, stared at him with the kind of fear men feel in the presence of madness. "Let's go!" He pulled his wife after him. Others turned away, walking toward town. Martha went to Jesus.

"Lord, he's reeking by now!"

"Didn't I tell you that if you believed you'd see the glory of God?" The farmer stopped in his tracks, turned, and watched. Peter led several disciples to the cliff, which was falling into shadow, for it was late afternoon. They laid their weight against the stone. It grated, and began to turn. As the gaping mouth appeared, some raised hands to noses and clamped nostrils shut. An old woman threw her hands across her eyes. Others froze in grotesque postures, paralyzed by unseen forces. Mary stood with composed features, but when the stone moved she gripped the Master's hand. The odor of death came out on the wind.

The Master raised his face to heaven. "Father, thank you for hearing me. You always hear. It's for their sake I voice my prayer, so they may know you sent me." He fixed his gaze on the black hole. In a mighty voice that sent the startled birds soaring from the branches he shouted, "Lazarus, come forth!"

From the cave sound came. Martha and Mary clasped one another. Rays of the setting sun suddenly sprayed back from the black hole—from the standing figure bound tightly in white.

"Unwrap him."

For a long moment none stirred, and there was no sound but the chirping of the birds which had settled back into the trees. John nudged Peter. They approached the swathed figure, and unbound the head. The familiar face of Lazarus was radiant with a wild joy seared by pain. "Why did he do it?" he asked. His tone was plangent with a strange grief.

"Take it easy." Peter spoke in a daze. "You'll be all right."

"Jesus is here," John added unnecessarily. Clumsily they

unwrapped the bands, and Peter whipped off his cloak and shielded the body while John stripped away the linens. Lazarus donned the cloak.

"Come on, we'll take you home," Peter murmured, but Lazarus ran to Jesus and they embraced.

"Lord, I'm afraid to understand. Why call me back?" His voice was calm. "The last I remember . . ."

"Your sisters will tell you about it." Hearing this quiet interchange, and seeing things taking such a normal turn, the people pressed around. A hubbub ensued.

"Look," shouted Peter, barging in. "This man needs food and warm clothes. Give him a chance." The people made way.

"Come, friend, we'll go home." The Master laid an arm across his shoulder, and they set out. The others followed, but Judas seized Jude's arm and dragged him to the cave.

"Let's have a look around." He entered the cramped space, a small hollow in the cliff, with a damp ledge where the body had lain.

"What are you looking for? What could he have left behind?"

"It's too dark to see much," Judas muttered. "Could anyone be hidden here?" He felt along the wall.

"What are you talking about?" Jude shouted. "Who'd hide in here? I can't stand the stink!"

"Jude, didn't you notice how his sister provoked the Rabbi into trying to resuscitate him?"

"What! What're you saying?"

"Besides being incredible, this whole affair doesn't add up. Didn't you hear a perfect stranger say that moments ago?"

"You're implying trickery, Judas!"

"Calm down. Probably not by the Rabbi. I just don't want anybody using him—deluding him."

"You don't believe he brought him back to life!"

"I didn't say that. But how did he get to the entrance bound? It was so shady, there could have been tricks."

"Judas, you're losing your faith—or your reason!"

"So the simpletons are going to teach the wise."

"I'm leaving."

"Jude, please. Don't go. But just remember how strangely it all began. He delayed unnecessarily for three days . . ."

"*You* thought it unnecessary!"

"Jude, you can't deny he's showing the strain of persecution. More and more he won't listen to advice."

"Judas, we all resent someone who thinks he knows it all—even if he does. The Master has power and a special mission from above. We can't tell him what to do."

"You're being unreasonable. We may as well go. It's too dark to learn anything here one way or the other."

"Judas, don't you place any trust in the Master?"

"You have to understand, Jude, that one must know a person well before fully trusting him. We really don't know him yet."

"We? Speak for yourself. I know him. We've lived with him for months and months. How can you talk that way?"

"Do we understand his way of acting, know his plans, his goals? Is he consistent, coherent? I have to keep revising my assessment of him."

"His plans and goals I don't fully understand, but I see no inconsistency. You're the one who's always changing."

"Jude, there is such a thing as growth, growth in self-knowledge. One who's growing keeps seeing things differently. You're like a simple rock—you don't grow and change, so you don't understand those of us who do. Can anything be really certain to us when our own judgments are so flexible?"

Jude didn't answer. Pity was welling up. He was beginning to understand. It wasn't so much that Judas didn't believe in the Master—he never quite got that far because he didn't believe in his own judgments. He didn't believe in himself! He was lost in some inner storm that obscured all guideposts and markers, and shut out all help. How did a man escape such complete isolation? How could his friends reach him, help him?

John had taken Mary's hand as they trailed after the Master. "I'm glad you have your brother back—and even gladder about how. Do you realize what this means?"

"Yes, John, I do. It means we're more blessed than kings to have Jesus for our friend."

"Mary, I'm talking about what it means for everybody," John rushed on. "He's long robbed the devil of souls, but

304

today he robbed the grave of a body!"

"He robs nature itself of our person."

The youth halted in mid-stride, and the girl paused beside him. "What's the meaning of that?"

"What it says. What Nicodemus reports the Master said to him. John, that dear old man's taken to visiting us since he learned we're intimates of Jesus."

"That's him all right." The words sounded bitter. "He lacks the courage to decide for Jesus in plain sight, so he follows not him but his friends."

"Anyway, he keeps talking about the one time he spoke with the Master. Jesus told him that a person must be born again from above, or he can't enter the kingdom of God. He's still puzzling over that."

"But you're not."

"No. Only over Jesus."

"I, too. He's robed in a mystery deeper than the sea, too deep to fathom. The sole choice is to believe in him—or reject him."

4

Peter's first awareness was of a cock crowing. Then he felt a hand gently shaking him, opened his eyes to the Master bending above, framed by a skyful of stars, and heard his quiet greeting. "Shalom, shalom."

He repeated the greeting, sat up, and stretched. "Rabbi, Bethany'll be overrun today after what you did yesterday."

"Rouse the others. We're going to the Temple."

They climbed the steep path to Bethphage before dawn. "Look, Master," said Nathanael, pointing to a tree by the roadside. "The almond tree hasn't yet bloomed in Jerusalem."

They reached the crest of the Mount of Olives and entered Bethphage, where they turned south and connected with the Jericho-Jerusalem road. On the steep descent into the Kidron Valley, Thomas slipped on the wet stones. Jude grabbed his arm and steadied him. "Watch it," he cautioned. "With

305

those long legs you'd think you were falling from the second story."

After private prayer and the morning sacrifice, they clustered in Solomon's portico, which was least exposed to the blustery west wind. There he began to teach. The news of Lazarus' resurrection had boiled through the city, and immense throngs of people were soon pressing around.

A commotion broke out at the rear of the crowd. "Make way! Make way!" a great voice roared. "The Captain of the Temple Guard!" With ill-concealed resistance, the crowd parted like a mighty pair of jaws opening slightly, and down the crevice came a group of chief priests marching briskly, attended by a dozen Levitical police. They gathered around the Master, but said nothing. When the disturbance subsided, he resumed teaching. At length the Captain of the Guard—a man with a massive head, cheeks as craggy as sheared granite, and a voice to match—cut across his words like a landslide.

"I hear teachings strange to my ears—and you quote no authority to shore up these presumptions."

"If I said anything wrong," Jesus returned in words like hammered iron, "offer evidence, not innuendo."

The Captain of the Guard ignored his demand. "These ignorant people," he barged on, "have no defense against your populist misconceptions of the Messiah. Fanciful rumors of your exploits fly, inducing them to swallow all that pours from your lips—but even if the rumors were true, your teaching would remain untrue! But you at least know full well that a man's holiness cannot guarantee his doctrine. The *halakhah*—sound doctrine—is officially interpreted only by ordained rabbis like myself who know the Scriptures and the tradition."

"Boo!" came cries of raillery. "Hogwash!" "What of the prophets?" "Did Moses have the rabbinical ordination?"

"Silence!" thundered the chief Levitical guard. "It is a chief priest who is speaking!" The sporadic cries continued, always coming from some anonymous person lost in the crowd.

"Obey your rabbis," Jesus commanded. "They 've inherited Moses' authority. But don't live like them." The crowd fell silent.

306

"Once before in Temple precincts," the Captain of the Guard resumed, "your authority was challenged. You had no answer."

"I gave no answer," Jesus corrected, "that pleased you."

"We chief priests—who do, indeed, enjoy Moses' authority—are still interested in any credentials you have to offer."

"Then pay attention to this parable. A man planted a vineyard, set up a thriving winery, signed a lease with tenant farmers, and left the country. He sent an agent when payment was due. They beat him and sent him back empty-handed. He sent another. Him they beat even worse, and made a laughing stock of him besides. The owner sent a third agent. They murdered him. Others he sent, too. They beat them or killed them all."

"A long-suffering man," someone cried. "A weakling!" another shouted. "I wish my landlord were half as patient," a third exclaimed. "Doesn't he know what he has to do?" a shrill voice cried.

"The owner," Jesus went on, "said to himself, 'There's only one thing left to do. I'll send my only son. They'll have to respect him.'" At this there were gasps in the crowd.

"He better not," a voice called ominously. "People don't like landlords—especially absentee landlords."

"So he sent his only son," Jesus went on. "Did they respect him? No—they seized him, killed him, and threw his body outside."

"Unburied?" a woman gasped in horror.

"What do you suppose the owner will do next?" the Master asked, staring hard at the chief priests. They stared back, eyes flashing hatred.

"He'll come himself and wipe them out," a voice shouted, and others joined in. "He'll strangle them one by one." "He'll plant them in a dung heap and burn them alive!"

"Are you not reminded," Jesus cried, "of the Scripture passage which says, 'What stone the builders cast away is now the building's keystone. The Lord has done this, and to us it's marvelous.'" At this the people cheered.

"When the Lord's Chosen One comes," bellowed a voice from the crowd, "just watch what happens to the Romans!"

The Captain of the Guard looked calculatingly at the

307

crowd, and asked in an undertone, "Can we arrest him?"

"Captain," his underling returned hoarsely, "we're in danger in this fractious crowd."

"I've spotted some known Zealots," another guard reported. "They'd go up like tow, and ignite the crowd."

The Captain of the Guard turned back to the Master. "Since you like to beguile the people with fables," he roared, "I'll tell you a story—a true one! Seven brothers in turn married the same woman. Whose wife will she be, in the resurrection you teach?" He was a Sadducee, and Sadducees deny the resurrection.

"Isn't this your problem?" Jesus countered, "that you understand neither the Scriptures nor God's power? What do you think God meant when he said to Moses, 'I am the God of Abraham, Isaac, and Jacob?' No God of the dead is he, but God of the living. How wrong you are to deny the resurrection. But as to the dead who rise, they don't get married. They are like the angels."

"Well put, Rabbi," a theologian of the Pharisees exclaimed. "Perhaps you can answer a question that vexes me. I get lost in the jungle of our six hundred and thirteen laws. Is there one guiding commandment in that jungle?"

"Yes," Jesus answered. "The first is this—'Hear, O Israel! The Lord your God is unique. Love him with all you are, heart and soul, hand and head.' The second is similar—'Your neighbor, love as yourself.'"

"How well and true you speak." The theologian looked meaningfully at the priests. "Such love amounts to more than all animal sacrifices and offerings."

"You," Jesus responded, "are not distant from the Kingdom."

The Captain raised his hand commandingly. "Rabbi, since you're so adept at answering questions, I have one to ask."

"Ask it."

"Even the Romans know that our people lust after one thing from the promised Messiah—freedom from Rome." Cheers and cries of "Hear! Hear!" interrupted him.

"You see?" the Captain said. "The Zealots and their camp-followers hold that since God alone is our Lord, it's

308

blasphemy to pay taxes to a foreign overlord."

At this, the silence was complete—no sound but the restless scraping of feet. Then came the cry, "Would you repeat the question?" and the crowd burst into mocking laughter.

The guard thundered angrily for silence, and the Captain went on. "You see how popular such teaching is with the masses. It's also rebellion against Rome. Since you are neither a revolutionary nor a cheap demagogue, you won't subscribe to it, even if it costs you your popularity. After all, you bravely preach love and peace." He said it with mockery. "Besides, if you foment rebellion, some informer will have the Romans down in a flash to seize you." He pointed to the soldiers at their posts in the Fortress. An oppressive silence descended. "Therefore, my question—which someone was so eager to hear a moment ago—is this: Can we lawfully pay taxes to our Roman overlord or not?"

"Why waste your time trying to trap me? Supply me with a coin." The Captain of the Guard nodded to one of the police, who handed the Master a coin. He examined the engraving. "Whose image is this?"

"Caesar's."

"Then give to Caesar what is his, and to God what is his." Total silence met this response. "And now I have my own question. You know how David, caught up by the Holy Spirit, declared, 'To my Lord the Lord said, Sit at my right hand, and I will put your enemies under your feet.' So we hear David himself calling the Christ his Lord. If that be so, how can the Christ be merely David's son—as you official teachers keep saying?" The chief priests glared at him with open hatred, but had no answer. The theologian of the Pharisees, stroking his beard, also remained silent.

"He's stopped them dead!" a voice jeered, but no one took up his lead. Even the Twelve looked confused.

"Be on your guard against the theologians," Jesus cried to the people. "They enjoy rich dress, honored greetings, prestigious seating arrangements, help widows spend their savings, and manage to look preoccupied with prayer. They'll have a heavy sentence."

Throwing him a last glance of malevolence, the Captain

309

of the Guard signalled his head officer. With an officious cry he opened a path, and the entourage threaded through and departed.

Hours later Jesus announced he would teach no more that day and sat down exhausted. Reluctantly, the crowd drifted away. He watched a woman in rags empty her purse into her hand. The two pennies that fell out she dropped into the offering box. "Did you see that widow?" Jesus asked. "She just gave her last two coins. It was the biggest gift made here today." The Twelve looked at him blankly.

Matthew sat contentedly, gazing around the Temple. Slaves were mopping the iridescent paving stones transported from many nations. He saw for the first time how really beautiful they were—as colorful as the massive star-embroidered curtains hanging from the immense lintel of the Sanctuary vestibule. There were thirteen such curtains in the Temple, and he had heard that two were replaced each year, woven by virgins. Priests pattered by barefoot on the cold, wet stones—no wonder they kept the Temple doctor busy with their complaints. The alabaster facade of the Temple showed radiantly translucent, even in the soft glow of twilight. "Teacher," he murmured, "it's so beautiful here. What a magnificent Temple."

"All these imposing structures," the Master replied, "will be so completely destroyed that not one stone will remain stacked on another."

The Twelve gaped in horror, while Peter, alarmed, spun his head to learn if the remark had been overheard. "It's getting late, Master," he said in a tight voice. "We ought to head for supper at the Galilee." The place he named lay on the rim of the Mount of Olives, just across the Kidron Valley, and was the campsite not of his disciples alone but of most Galilean pilgrims.

They left by the Sheep Gate. The smell of the animals was strong, the noise of haggling loud, and the piteous bleat of a lamb sounded on the night air as it passed to a new owner. They descended into the Kidron Valley, crossed the Wadi Kidron, which was in spate and splashed sonorously beneath them, passed the Garden of Gethsemane and ascended the Mount of Olives. Into Peter's mind flashed

310

the memory of how King David had passed this way a fugitive, weeping because of his traitorous son and his fickle people.

The Master did not turn off on the trail to the Galilee, but followed the road to the place directly opposite the Temple. There he went to the steep overhang which provided such a striking view of the Temple and the city, and sat on a great boulder. It was a favorite spot of his. The others settled in little clusters and began to converse in low tones. Peter got James and John off by themselves.

"My guts are churning. You heard what he said about the Temple. Let's find out more." They squatted around Jesus and looked across the valley. Hard by the north end of the Temple esplanade loomed the Antonia Fortress. The sentries walked its ramparts like ants. He could hear a watch cry distinctly, and it filled him with anger. He turned to Jesus.

"Lord," he said in a grief-stricken voice, "what were you telling us about the Temple? When is it going to happen?"

"When you see the abomination desolating the place where it ought not to be, Judeans must flee into the mountains without so much as entering their houses to retrieve possessions." He spoke with such terrible certitude Peter saw the Roman catapults hurling their frightful missiles, shattering the holy walls, spraying pieces of the Temple abroad, sending the immense ashlars of the retaining walls crashing down into the Kidron Valley. Teams of horses, rearing and neighing, lurched against their harnesses, pulling down what remained.

He came to himself as Jesus was saying, "The sun's light will start failing, the moon's go out, the stars tumble from the skies. Men will stare—and see there the Son of Man coming on clouds, approaching in might and majesty, his agents, the angels, receiving and executing their orders to gather his chosen ones from the terminals of the sky."

"When?" John gasped.

"Every spring," Jesus answered, "you see the fig tree coming to life, the sap rising into the branches, the new leaves sprouting. Your reaction is, 'Summer's on the way.' When you see fulfilled the signs I have foretold, you will know he is near, is at the door."

"How long, Lord, how long?" John asked.

311

"Some now alive will be living still when it happens."

"When which happens—the end of the Temple or the world?"

"No one knows the precise day or hour. Not the angels in heaven, not the Son—only the Father. Watch always and stay awake, because you don't know the appointed time." He said no more. Peter sat in stunned silence, the stars careening around his head, his Messianic hopes churned by a whirlwind, the longed-for time moving off into the distance.

"So here you are!" The melodious voice of the Magdalene shattered Peter's reverie. She was standing beside them, Joanna with her. Each had a basket on her arm.

"How did you find us?"

"A disciple saw you heading this way," Mary answered. "Master, you must be hungry. We've brought food."

They seated themselves in a circle, and the women passed out the bread, cheese, and olives, and the skin of wine. "Mary," John observed, "Matthew's friend, Three-a-day, would be proud of you."

"Never mind Three-a-day," Matthew exclaimed. "I'm proud of her." He began eating with relish. The others picked at their food.

"Peter," Mary said, "you look as though you're on your way to bury a friend."

Peter was tempted to answer, "Yes—Jerusalem!" but said nothing.

"I've been working on a little song," Mary announced. "It's not quite ready, but it's time for it anyway." She gave Thomas the tune, went to the center of the little circle and, swaying gracefully to the accompaniment of Thomas' flute, sang her composition.

> My friends about, let us agree,
> Of all our cares, let us be free.
> With Christ among us here today,
> I've holy cause to laugh and play.
>
> Like birds I sing, like lambs I prance,
> And offer you my little dance.
> And if you clap your hands and laugh,

312

And stamp your feet and thump your staff,
Of this my joy you'll have a share,
And chase away our every care.

With friends about and hope agreed,
Forget your tears, forget your need.
Let's lift our hearts to joy and love,
They lift our souls to things above.

The men clapped enthusiastically. "Mary," Peter exclaimed heartily, "you remind us how blessed we are." He turned to the Master. "Lord, whatever's coming, we're grateful you called us. We believe in you."

By the time they rose to go the silver moon had climbed overhead and so many stars crowded the heavens the sky was a blanket of pale light. The watch cry of the Levites floated across the Valley and the glare of the perpetual fire on the altar of sacrifice flickered in the darkness. "We'll return to Bethany now," Jesus said. "Judas and Jude, accompany the women to the Galilee and then come to us. No side trips."

Nicodemus was pacing the floor when they entered. "Rabbi Yeshua, I must see you at once. Alone."

"Peter, James and John, come with us," Jesus directed. Nicodemus raised his eyebrows, but said nothing. They left the house and walked slowly along the deserted road.

"Rabbi Yeshua," Nicodemus whispered, "you must run for your life. The high priest accuses you of deceiving the people by pretending to raise Lazarus. He wants you killed."

"I can't believe it," Peter cried. "Let him come and talk to Lazarus—or his sisters—or other witnesses."

"You forget," Nicodemus said with stricken face, "that the Sadducees have closed their minds to the *possibility* of resurrection."

"But surely, they'll believe his doctor!"

"They won't believe anyone. To them it *had* to be a trick." He turned to Jesus and added, "Of course, they are trumping up other charges to justify the deed."

"I must be in Jerusalem for the Feast."

"Rabbi, it's weeks away. Leave in order to survive for the

313

Passover. Go, and return."

"If I found a suitable place to further instruct the Twelve . . ."

"Good. I have a lodge a day's journey north."

"Secluded?"

"Yes—near the town of Ephraim. In wild country, almost inaccessible, inhabited by a few mountain people. They won't know you from Adam."

"We'll go."

"Good. I beg you, take Lazarus along. They plan to kill him too—ostensibly for being a party to the alleged ruse, but in truth because he's a damaging witness. You must leave at once—tonight."

"We'll set out, with Lazarus, when Judas and Jude return."

"I'll tell Lazarus," Peter volunteered, "and get some food together." He met Jude returning alone. "Where's Judas?"

"He had an errand. Insisted on it. Told me to come without him."

They waited impatiently until Judas returned. "Where were you?" Peter demanded. "The Master told you to return at once."

"If you must know," he replied cooly, "I went into the city, to a money changer. The petty vendors in this area can't change a denarius. I must have small change for our purchases."

"That's strange. We passed a money changer by the Sheep Gate."

"I didn't want to hold the Master up."

They set off into the night. Gusting winds came in from the Mediterranean, bearing ominous black clouds that blotted out the stars. A cold, blustery rain began falling. It was a desolate journey.

5

The last crocus was dying in the mountain country of Ephraim, the spring flowers were bursting into bloom, and the grain stood high. Nicodemus had promised to send word of any further developments, but weeks had passed with only one message, and it told more about his anxiety than of developments in the Holy City. Out foraging for roots and berries, James and John, on their return, saw the Master striding back and forth at the door of the cabin. Lazarus sat warming himself in the sun.

"No message yet?" John inquired.

"No."

As they entered the cabin, James rumbled, "If he doesn't hear soon, he'll leave anyway."

"No doubt. Passover's only a week away."

Jude entered carrying a huge waterskin, and James, assisting him, asked, "Why is Judas scowling around the place?"

"He asked to go to the city for supplies. He was refused."

The others drifted back in pairs. The Master had ordered them not to wander about alone—perhaps because of the rumor that Barabbas the Zealot was training his freedom fighters in these mountains. When their scanty meal was ready, Peter invited them to eat, but Jude hesitated. "The Master's not back."

"He's praying alone. We're not to wait."

They recited the blessing and began to eat.

"We're wasting time here," Judas rasped from a mouth like a sickle moon turned down. "We'd be better off in Galilee."

"Galilee!" Nathanael intoned the word like a benediction. "Ai! How I miss the warmth and beauty of its springtime."

"Do you still dream of dozing under your olive trees, awaiting the crop?" Peter prodded.

"No more than you dream of nets and fish!"

"Or I of my sheep grazing on Arbel," Thomas moaned. "The grass is never greener than now. My sheep get so fat they waddle. And every lamb gambols for joy."

"The women will be working in the fields," John reminisced.

"I suppose we all miss our wives and children," Thomas

sighed.

"Do you, John?" Judas asked.

"You know I'm not married."

"That's what I mean."

"Of course. It's the hardest of all."

"I thought so. I saw the way you looked at Lazarus' sister."

"Judas, being unmarried doesn't mean I can't appreciate a woman. It means I stop there. Besides, Mary's not available."

"No, she's in love with Jesus."

"You misunderstand. She loves the Christ. Don't we all?"

"Well, anyway, marriages aren't lived in heaven, even if made there," Peter put in. "My neighbor's always taking his staff to his wife, while she takes her rolling pin to him."

"That's not completely accurate," Andrew drawled. "Sometimes they switch."

"John," Matthew injected, "do you know why Adam lived so long?"

"I'm sure you're going to tell me."

"He had no mother-in-law."

"This joshing's all right for you men," said James, "but my mind's on higher things. I've been praying that affluent tradesmen might give more to the poor." He glanced slyly at Judas, waiting for him to bite. He did.

"Country bumpkins imagine merchants can squander their hard-earned capital on loafers! Tell me, has your prayer been answered?"

"Half of it. The poor have agreed to accept."

Matthew laughed. "I'm awaiting the day fishermen will give an honest account of their haul, so tax collectors can live in the manner they're accustomed to."

"And I'm waiting," James retorted, "for tax collectors to set an honest example."

"Three-a-day's made a good start, don't you think?"

"Before you cite your own virtue, Matthew," Thomas broke in, "I'm off to stretch these long legs. Anyone coming?"

"Just in time, Thomas," Matthew rejoined. "You won't have to hear me tell of sheep herders who can't count beyond twenty when giving their tax reports on the size of their flocks."

316

"I'll join you, Thomas"—Peter sprang up—"before I lose my new-found affection for tax collectors."

The two men breathed deeply the fragrance of the lofty stand of cedars as they tramped along. The setting sun crimsoned and purpled the high-flying clouds, and lit the woods with a dramatic sweep of light and shadows. Small animals scampered across their path, and wild flowers dotted the open places with a spray of colors. Peter was the first to break the silence. "Thomas, I've never said how I admired your bravery when we left Jericho—'Let's go and die with him!' I'm not sure you encouraged me with your remark"— he laughed—"but I had to admire it."

Thomas stopped and turned a confused look on him. "Don't admire me, Peter. I'm a divided man. You don't know what desperation lay behind those words."

"What do you mean?"

"You were just recalling our wives and children, and I couldn't stand it. I miss mine more than I can bear."

"I'm sorry—we were just easing the pain, or trying to. But what does that have to do with Jericho?"

"Everything. My wife and child came there to be near me while we were at Bethany-beyond-Jordan. I'd slip over and see them, with the Master's permission, as I did while at Three-a-day's."

"But you were ready and brave to leave when the time came."

"No, not ready and not brave—desperate. Peter, I'm a divided man, torn by impulses, never knowing what I'm going to do next. When the Master announced that trip to Lazarus—so near Jerusalem—I was like those changing clouds up there, red with fear, purple with dread that I'd never see my Deborah again. I feared that I'd abandon the Master on the spot. I tried to stamp out the feelings, and couldn't. In desperation I said what I did—before I lost the battle."

Peter threw an arm across his shoulder. "Now I admire you more. You won a big victory for the Christ."

Thomas' shoulders began to heave. "What about the next time?"

"Friend, we have to live today, and trust to God for

tomorrow. I'm proud you're one of us."

"But can't I do something to help myself?"

"I think you can. At times we all have divided hearts. What can we do?—we can learn to listen to ourselves. Both halves are us. If we try to crush and bury one half, it festers underground, and bursts out like an enemy when we're least prepared."

"I don't understand. Don't we have to crush the feelings we disagree with—that betray us?"

"No, we have to keep an eye on them, learn to live with them, to control them. They always have something to tell us. You don't want to stop loving your wife, do you?"

"Of course not."

"Do you see what I mean?"

"A little—but it sounds dangerous."

"It is, but not as dangerous as denying we have those feelings, and letting them live a life of their own. The good ones—like love of our wives—we have to cultivate. The only way to control them is to love God—and the Christ—more."

"How long does it take to do that?"

"I don't know—a lot of time. I'm still not safe. I can't say . . . Look!" Peter pointed. A lone little child, weeping, was crawling toward them. He ran, took her up in his arms, and muttered, "She's crippled." He pointed to her crooked legs. "She can't walk." The child, about two, was wailing piteously. Peter tried to comfort her. Thomas looked around.

"She can't have come far. See—over there." A small fieldstone cabin stood in a nearby dale.

"Mama, mama," the little one bleated between sobs. The door was open. Peter called out, and entered. A young woman jumped from her cot, startled.

"Who are you?" Her eyes were wide with fear. "I must have dozed."

"Friends. We found your child in the woods."

"The Lord's merciful. She must've pushed the door open."

"Where's your husband?" At Peter's question, her fear returned. She examined the two men.

"Dead. Killed fighting with the Zealots."

"I'm sorry." He nodded toward the child. "How did it happen?"

318

"I ran away with her when I heard. I fell."

"My little girl's about twice her age." Peter's voice was gentle.

"Mine's younger," Thomas murmured.

"Can I brew a herb tea? I don't have much else. My name is Susanna."

"I'd like some. I'm Peter. This is Thomas. Do you have help?"

"Yes. Relatives."

Over the tea, Peter decided. "We have a friend nearby, a holy rabbi, a healer. I'll take your little one to him."

"I'll come."

"No, he's in danger. You have to trust us." She looked anxious. "Thomas will remain until we return. The Rabbi has helped others."

"Her name's Esther."

Peter crooned to her as he went, and she fell asleep in his arms. His head snapped up at the noise by the towering stone outcropping. Six men filed into his path.

"Where are you taking that child?" The speaker, taller than Peter, was an awesome sight—brawny, with massive head, a fiercely handsome face, full black beard, and intense, commanding eyes and gestures.

"To a healer."

"I don't believe in healers. Where'd you get her?"

"Uncle Barabbas!" The child had awakened, and was extending her arms. Peter handed her over.

"You're Barabbas the Zealot."

"Yes, I'm the freedom fighter."

"You'd believe in the healer I'm going to."

"Who are you?"

"Simon Peter."

"The Nazarene!" His face darkened like a storm cloud. "That man! A weakling!"

"It's clear you don't know him."

"He preaches against the sword—even the sword of righteousness!"

"That's because he's stronger than you." The words awoke no understanding in the warrior's face, but they broke his train of thought and he examined Peter.

319

"You're no weakling—and if a real Galilean, you're a patriot. Why do you follow a milksop who yields his hands to Roman chains and bids us all do the same?"

Peter showed his confusion, as he thought of what awaited them in the city. "He has a better plan," he managed weakly. The eyes that examined him cut like a knife.

"Listen!" The freedom fighter had regained his full aggressiveness. "When the moment of danger comes, and he takes the sword from your hand, you'll be unmanned. Mark my words. Men like us only know how to fight like men— not with women's words!"

Fleeting fear broke out on Peter's face before he hardened it into a mask. "There's more to a Jew's righteousness than a sword."

"More—but not less. Your own doubts are plain as rats in a pantry. Why follow him?"

"Come, and find out."

"I'm not that interested." He spat out the words with contempt. "I have more important things."

"Then come for the child's sake—because he heals. That you don't doubt."

"Where is he?"

"Come."

As they approached the lodge, Peter called, "Master!" Jesus emerged.

The man of war and the man of peace stared at one another, their life forces intensifying. The warrior's vitality flared in his face, the bronzed cheeks flaming, the eyes growing brilliant. The countenance of the Master was radiant, eye and jaw stern with authority, his stately bearing conveying the aura of the royal line from which he was descended.

"You could be king." The words were Barabbas'.

"My kingdom is not of this world."

Barabbas retreated a step. Haughtiness flared in his eyes. "Are you or are you not with me—for the glory of Israel?"

"Are you with me for the glory of the Father?"

"Occupied Israel is my concern. I'm an insurgent. You're either with us or against us."

"He who is not with me is against me."

"I hear you preach pacifism."

320

"He who takes up the sword ends with the sword in him."

"Only if he loses. I don't intend to."

"What does it profit a man to gain the world—and lose his soul?"

"You spiritual people are all alike. Of what use is your power to Israel if it helps her enemies?"

"I am come to light the world."

"We have met before."

"Yes."

"In the Temple, when we were boys. The rabbis were arguing the same way then—with my father."

"Your father was wrong."

"Are you going to help this child?"

"Give her to me."

He transferred her gently to the Master's arms. She wrapped her own around his neck. "Daddy, daddy," she lisped. He kissed her brow, laid his hands on her twisted limbs, and set her down. She began scampering about. "I run!"

"Esther, come here!" The Zealot snatched her, and turned to go.

"Does this healing mean nothing to you?" Peter thundered.

Barabbas wheeled around and glared at the Master. "Israel is more important." He swept off.

"Barabbas!" The Master's exclamation carried such imperial authority the Zealot froze. Slowly, he turned once more. "On your way, recite the Shema Israel."

The Zealot nodded almost imperceptibly, and started off again.

"I'm going with you," Peter declared. "I left Thomas with Susanna."

"No. We'll send him."

"Let them go," the Master said.

Later, when Simon the Zealot caught Peter alone outdoors, he murmured, "You endangered the Master, and all of us, by bringing her here. Miracles can't be kept secret." Peter looked distressed.

"I thought how I'd feel if she were my daughter. So I brought her." Simon said no more.

When Thomas returned, Peter filled him in.

It was dark when they heard a voice hailing the Master.

He went out, the others rushing after. The man mounting the steep path called again. "Rabbi Yeshua!"

"I am he."

"Rabbi Nicodemus sends a message." He handed over a scroll. The Master bade him enter and be fed, took the scroll to the flickering lamp, broke the seal, and read:

Rabbi Jesus:
The high priests and leaders of the people have issued the command that anyone who knows your whereabouts is to inform them or fall under censure. I have no recourse but to ask your return. The city is bursting with pilgrims, and their interest in you is unflagging. I think none will dare to arrest you before the Feast. I have devised a plan for you to consider on your return. It may secure your safety.

Nicodemus

Jesus handed the scroll to Peter. "Don your cloaks. We return at once. Lazarus, we'll go to your place."

6

A crimson and gold dawn flared in the East as the weary band reached little Bethany, which was quiet still with sleep. On the railed-in roof of Lazarus' house stood his sister Mary, watching anxiously. She ran to meet them. On her brother she bestowed a warm but hasty kiss, then turned to the Master who embraced her. "I'm afraid for you," she whispered. He nodded gently, and she gasped. He turned to the Twelve.

"Go on to the Galilee. Peter, inform Nicodemus I await him."

"My plan," Nicodemus explained, "depends on the fact that we Pharisees do not oppose your basic doctrine."

"He who is not with me," the Master said, "is against me."

Nicodemus started. "Yes. Well, my plan depends on the fact that the present conflict over your person revolves around the question of resurrection, a dogma of faith for my party. Indeed, we are gratified to see our Sadducean rivals discomfited by the issue of . . . er . . . Lazarus."

"Gratified but uncommitted."

"Yes. Well, Rabbi Yeshua, the Pharisees, having chafed much under your censures, are not well-disposed toward you. Some are jealous of your popularity."

"What is your plan?"

"To bring many Pharisees over to you by routing all doubts about the raising of your friend. Let him host a feast for the leading Pharisees, with you as guest of honor. His sisters, doctor, and other key witnesses will be in attendance." He turned to Lazarus.

"I'd be delighted," Lazarus said. Both men looked at the Master.

"Agreed," he said. "Include Simon the Leper."

"He is foremost in my thoughts," Nicodemus replied. Simon, himself a Pharisee and a friend of Lazarus, had been present at his death, and at the tomb when he came forth. A year earlier, the Master had cured him of leprosy.

"There is one other matter." Nicodemus' expression was pained. "Duty binds me to inform the authorities of your location, and we can only hope they won't act before the banquet."

"Wait!" cried Lazarus. "Send the high priest an invitation."

"What? He'll not come!"

"You don't understand. Include a guest list—among them, the Master and the most prestigious of the Pharisees. In one stroke you reveal the Master's location and hinder action."

Nicodemus smiled his thin, wary smile. "It may work. With your permission, Rabbi, I will so proceed." The Master nodded.

Baskets on their arms, Martha and her sister Mary, Mary Magdalene and Joanna the wife of Chuza passed through the massive wall of the city by way of the Fish Gate. A disorderly array of bazaars and craftsmen's shops lined the street across the whole length of the lower city.

Even before they saw the silvery ovals with the bulging eyes piled high on counter after counter, they detected the rank odor. "Phew!" Martha expelled her breath and pinched her nose. "Fish was to be my first course, but these haven't swum recently."

"Why not use salted fish?" the Magdalene suggested. "It's so tasty I sometimes served it even when I lived on the lake. Look, there's some."

Martha screwed up her nose. "Not my favorite. Does the Master like it?"

"Do you think I'd suggest it if he didn't?"

"All this fuss about fish!" Joanna snapped. "Toss a coin and let it decide." She was not much of a cook. Mary laughed.

"As well tell a general to decide his strategy that way! Tell me, how do they ever bring fresh fish all the way from the Sea of Galilee?"

"If you did your share of the shopping," Martha replied, "you'd know these are salt-water fish from the Mediterranean, half a day away."

"John the son of Zebedee used to sell fresh-water fish to the high priests," the Magdalene said. "He came on horseback, several times a year, with his fish packed in the ice he got from as far away as Mount Hermon."

"He must have charged a pretty penny!" Martha observed.

"The high-living high priests weren't deterred by that."

They passed a booth where a craftsman sat carving an olivewood tray. Martha fingered his creations, lying out on display. "I'll need some extra serving dishes," she remarked, but moved on without buying. They came to a booth featuring delicate and colorful Sidonian pitchers, glass bowls and dishes. "This will take some time," she announced. "Mary, order bread for forty guests from our favorite baker. You'd better make it forty-five. Arrange to have delivery. Then get what you think we'll need from the soap-maker's and the spice shop. Take the Magdalene with you, and meet us at the Sheep Gate in two hours."

Walking arm-in-arm, the two Marys came to a dealer in fine cloth. "Look at the beautiful linen," the Magdalene cried. "Is it from Egypt or Mesopotamia, do you think?"

"Lovely ladies, lovely ladies," the dealer chanted, "stop

324

and buy. We handle only the most treasured Mesopotamian wares. Very expensive, but for you I make an exception."

The women smiled and continued on. At The Stone, where slaves were sold, an auction was in progress. "Look at that beautiful young girl!" exclaimed Mary.

The Magdalene nodded. "She reminds me of you."

"Oh! In that scanty get-up!"

"I meant her beauty."

"But the way they make her dress!"

"Before I met the Master I didn't dress any more honorably."

"Then she reminds me of you."

"If I had the money, I'd bid for the poor thing and set her free. My two coins won't do it."

"You make me feel selfish. I have the money." Mary patted the purse hanging from her shoulder by a camelskin strap. "But my heart's set on another purchase. Oh, Magdalene, we have such hard choices, and can do so little. Slavery is such a terrible thing. Who was the rabbi who said, 'Until slavery ends, immorality will not?' "

"Even if slavery ends, immorality won't. There are women who will sell themselves, as I did."

"And men who will buy them. Oh, when will immorality stop?"

"Mine stopped when I met the Messiah." She whispered the last word. "I thought everyone's would. Now we see it's not true."

They eyed a tailor's bazaar with a beautiful display of tunics, passed stands overflowing with fresh vegetables, and stepped aside as an ass loaded with figs staggered up the lane. A crowd of shoppers jostled them, and at that moment an urchin seized Mary's purse, yanked it free, and ran off. The two women screamed. A vendor lunged at the fleeing culprit, collared him, and dragged him back by the scruff of the neck. Passers-by gaped. The Magdalene helped Mary to arrange her torn sleeve.

"Here's the little robber, lady. And your purse—heavy!"

"I'm so grateful. You'll never know." Mary reached into her cloak and handed him a silver coin, a denarius.

"Thank you, lady, thank you. Press charges and I'll drag

this bare-faced urchin to the Antonia, where they'll plant him in a dark dungeon until he trips over his beard."

"Just leave him with me for a little talk."

"Talk! Lady, the moment I uncollar him, he'll be off like a shot from David's sling!"

"No, he sees I mean him no harm." Mary looked at the emaciated face, and brushed the hair from his eyes which flashed with gratitude. Throwing up his hands, the vendor returned to his stall. "Why did you do it?" she asked.

"I'm hungry." His rotting teeth showed when he spoke. Mary opened her purse, and the Magdalene's eyes widened in surprize. It was crammed with silver coins, and several gold ones. Mary handed the child a silver coin.

"Buy what you need. And when you're hungry, come out to Bethany. Ask where Lazarus lives."

Snatching the coin, he shot her a grateful look. "I'll remember." With that, he slipped away.

"You shouldn't carry so much," the Magdalene whispered. "It's dangerous."

"I have a purchase to make. Before I tell you what, I want to say something so you'll understand."

"What is it?"

"You don't know how much I admire the way you travel with the Master."

"It's no sacrifice. I wouldn't be anywhere else."

"Oh, but it is a sacrifice. A hard life. I only wish I could join you."

The Magdalene took her hand. "Why don't you?"

Mary began to weep. "I want to. I can't. I could never stand the life—living out in the cold, with rarely enough to eat. I've heard the disciples. My health's not robust—or my brother's."

"Then he doesn't expect it."

"Sometimes I feel cowardly. Sometimes I think I have to stay and make a home for my brother. And sometimes I think the Master wants me there—it's his home, too, when he wishes."

"He loves the three of you very much."

"Oh! I'm so worried. He's in the greatest danger."

"I know. Our own authorities are looking for him."

326

"Not that alone. Barabbas is getting bolder. His assassins will certainly strike in this season. And then the Romans will seize every Jewish leader with a following."

"What can we do? The Master follows his own call."

"I'm possessed by the desire to show him my love now, before anything bad happens. I want to do something my whole heart will be in."

"What's your intention?"

"Magdalene, I heard what you did for him when you first met him—the anointing."

"Oh!"

"From John. Ever since the banquet was planned, the impulse to do something similar won't leave my heart. You won't mind?"

"Of course I'll mind! I'll be jealous! But, working in the kitchen, I won't see it."

"I quit my expensive perfumes a year ago—saving for charity."

"No wonder I detected an odor! I blamed the poor fish."

"Be serious. I've saved a good sum. And of course I had other funds to draw on. Help me select the ointment."

"That's asking the condemned to hang himself! Besides, you'll never locate what I had. A wealthy merchant brought it himself from India."

"Oh!"

"Actually"—the Magdalene thawed at the look on her friend's face—"I may be wrong. We'll look." She took her hand. "How much do you have to spend?"

"Three hundred denarii, less the one I gave the boy."

The Magdalene whistled softly. "You're not economizing."

"It's not the time. I'm looking forward to this feast."

The Magdalene's own memories shone in her eyes. "We'll go to the perfumers last. We'd better not neglect Martha's orders."

"We'd better not!" Mary laughed gaily.

When they left the spice shops, the Magdalene said, "Before we purchase the perfume, go with me to the Street of the Romans. I saw a tunic I'd like to wear to the banquet."

The Street of the Romans was in an uproar. Troops clattered by, armor gleaming, spears at the ready, sending the

327

shoppers scattering into the alleys.

"Something's happened," the Magdalene cried. "What is it?" she asked a rabbi in tall headgear as he hastened by.

"Barabbas robbed a Roman merchant to finance his freedom fighters. Killed him. He's been captured. A light of Israel going out." He hurried off.

"No shopping here, Mary. Let's go to the perfumers." The Arab was most anxious to please the lovely ladies. "All the most exotic essences of Arabia before your eyes, compounded to enchant your delicate nostrils." He bowed low, sweeping an arm toward his wares.

"And the genuine aromatic nard from India?" the Magdalene asked. The Arab's eyes widened, and he whistled.

"Ladies, ladies, very expensive!"

"We know."

He rubbed his hands together. "So rare because so expensive. But Esau will not disappoint you." He beckoned to his assistant to attend the booth, led them into its inner recesses and, reaching up to a high shelf, removed a silver casket which he set gently on the table. With a flourish he opened the ornate lid, and with loving delicacy extracted an iridescent glass phial, filmy with gold, blown in the likeness of a swan with head upraised.

"Within, the scent of Lebanon, the essence of the lily of the valley, the incense of pagan temples, the waftings of all the mystery fragrances of the East. Sealed, sealed in, to be first known by the prince or princess privileged to know its lavings." Fondly, he returned the phial to the casket, and reverently closed it. "Oh, but it is expensive, too expensive—a king's ransom."

Mary was diffident. "How expensive?"

"Four hundred denarii."

She turned pale. "That much I don't have."

"I see the love in your eyes. How much?"

The Magdalene intervened. "Two hundred and fifty."

"No, no! Impossible! Three hundred and fifty."

"Two hundred and seventy-five."

"Should my children starve? Three hundred and twenty-five."

"Two hundred and ninty-nine," Mary pleaded. "All I

have."

The Arab's face creased with suffering. "Never I stock this again. Too rich for Jerusalem! Not a penny under three hundred."

Mary of Bethany trembled.

"I have a denarius," the Magdalene said. "Buy it." She took the coin from her pocket. One silver coin remained. They were very quiet on the way. Carrying the casket pressed to her bosom, Mary spoke at last. "You think it would have been better to buy that sweet slave girl's freedom."

"Yes. But we can't always do what's better. Enough to do what's good. One day we'll know how to do what's best—like him."

"Oh! Would it have been better?"

"Sweet friend, I'm not to judge."

"My heart says no. If you could have yours back in the phial—to sell for the poor—would you?"

Tears came to the Magdalene's eyes. "No."

Weeping softly, they walked along, arms locked together.

So many accepted the invitation Martha said, "Lazarus, our house is too small. Ask Simon for his place. I'll steward."

Simon was delighted, and they awaited the morrow with great expectations. Martha loved a party, Nicodemus hoped for a mass conversion of the ranking Pharisees, and Mary contemplated her ritual of love. Judas was the exception. Was it banquets they needed? The Master was going nowhere. He, Judas, would have to continue to make plans for his own future—independently.

7

Bustling about happily, Martha directed the serving of the lemon sherbet, made possible because a local farmer had stored snow, from the one heavy fall of the winter, in a deep cave under a carpet of leaves. It had been an inspiration to rush back to the market that morning, taking advantage of the cold snap, to purchase the fresh fish which had gotten the banquet off to a lovely start. To her surprize, the salted fish was also praised. Surveying the tables to see that all needs were met, her eyes paused on the mother of Jesus who, evidently, was watching her. Reclining at the head table, next to the wife of Simon the Leper, she rose from her couch and approached.

"Martha, you look flustered. Can I help?"

"No, no. When I'm in charge of a banquet, I'm as excited as a charioteer in the Roman races! Simon's provided all the help I need. Enjoy youself." Mary resumed her place.

The guests, mostly Pharisees, had shown up to a man, with the exception of the high priest, Caiaphas. A Sadducee, he had never been expected to come. It was thrilling to see scholarly men so excited. Arriving one by one, they had stood and stared at Lazarus. "Talk to my sister," he would say when they questioned him. "I was too—shall I say indisposed?—to describe what happened." As it turned out, they delighted in prying every detail from Mary.

It's true they were treating the Master somewhat aloofly, but they stole glances at him, stroking their beards as they habitually did when especially reflective. Once they were seated and the first course was served, the whole matter was dropped. They relaxed and talked of food and other interests.

Well, she had to be thinking about food herself. Simon had accepted her offer to manage the affair, "not only because it's your brother's feast, but because your reputation as a hostess is peerless." The next course was roast duck, which she always served golden brown—but only because she hovered over the cooks. She'd better dash out to the courtyard to have a look at it and the spitted lamb. The pastries in the outdoor oven smelled heavenly. From the beautiful Sidonian pitcher, pride of her shopping spree, she replenished the wine in the Master's chalice, and almost over-poured as the sight of him distracted her—Simon wouldn't forgive her if she had. It was a flaming red vintage of unmatched bouquet, no doubt his best stock. The Master was in the place of honor on Simon's right, her brother on his left. The Master, laughing at a remark by Simon, always a humorous man, smiled at her fleetingly. Simon was a rather handsome young man of wide brow and trim beard, with ruddy cheeks and hair and eyes having the dark sheen of ebony. But of course one hardly noticed him in the presence of the Master.

Martha resented the fact that Mary was fooling around with a perfume she planned to use for some special effect, but she'd asked so sweetly for a respite from the serving that there was no refusing. Besides, the Master himself had set her straight once when she thought the only important thing at dinner was the food. She hurried into the kitchen.

Peter was flanked by Rabbi Gad on the right and Rabbi Absalom on the left. The latter pulled a scroll from his belt and said, "Rabbi Gad, I've been reading up on the fine points of the sacrifice of the red heifer. I was blessed to find this treatise."

Gad looked sympathetically at Peter before replying. "Oh, I don't know. We make too much of books."

"What else is there?" Absalom retorted, and Peter knew he was in for a dull evening.

Thomas was surprized at the congeniality of his companions. He was sandwiched between the rabbis Dan and Joseph. The moment he mentioned he had cultivated the olive, they were off and running. They touted the olive as the most precious crop of Israel, as well as the fruit of the elect and light of the world. "Why," Dan emoted, "Judean olive oil fuels lamps from here to Gaul!"

"As to my trade, I'm a master builder," said Joseph. "Though of course I carefully restrict the time given to manual labor."

"I suppose you do it for recreation," Thomas suggested.

"Oh, indeed not!" Joseph corrected. "It buys my bread. You know rabbis can't charge their pupils."

"Yes, but I hear that gifts from them provide for all your needs abundantly."

"Exaggeration, of course," fumed Dan.

"Even apart from necessity," added Joseph, "it's axiomatic among us that study of Torah without the seasoning of honest labor leads in the end to sin."

"That's why we don't understand your Rabbi," came Dan's complaining voice. "He doesn't put his hand to honest labor."

"That's explained by the urgency of his mission," Thomas defended. "He was a carpenter for many years. What's your occupation, Rabbi Dan?"

"I make, sell, and even export nails. My disciples claim I chose that occupation because I like to drive home a point. We rabbis all learn something from our trade."

"Rabbi Abel, a digger of wells," Joseph added, "says that digging into theological matters is much like digging in the stony soil of Judea."

"Yes, stones!" cried Dan, his face flushed from the rich food and the good wine. "They get into everything in Israel! I've heard it said that except, perhaps, for grapes and olives, Israel has no special product to offer. It's a pity we can't sell stones!" The three men chuckled.

"Oh!" said Thomas, "I thought Herod the Great bought them all!" His companions laughed heartily. King Herod had employed ten thousand stone masons to quarry, cut, and lay the stones to rebuild the Temple, and had also constructed massive palaces, forts, and monuments around the country.

Rabbi Joseph's expression turned serious. "I'd rather that foreigners bought our stones. Herod paid for everything with our taxes. He bankrupted us all, and left a debt that to this day impoverishes, demoralizes and degrades the populace."

"He worked wonders rebuilding the Temple," Dan reproved.

"No doubt, but the means were evil. He overdid his building program. And that, by the way," he continued, turning to Thomas, "is the danger of a trade for us rabbis. It can be overdone. My fellow rabbis have been incensed by the charges of greed your Master has levelled against us, yet greed's not absent. Other rabbis have spoken as severely."

"It's a remote danger," countered Dan.

"Remote! Look at the rapacious high priests! And some of our own rabbis are not much better." He glared accusingly at Dan, who was sputtering at the awareness that his own swollen income was a target of these remarks. "I've heard," Joseph went on, "that Rabbi Jesus says the man of God deserves to be supported without a trade."

"So now you find fault with honest labor?" challenged Dan.

332

Sizing up the situation, Thomas cut in. "Have you detected the delicious fragrance of pastries in the oven? As a boy I knew a generous rabbi who was a baker—my favorite rabbi of all time!" He smacked his lips. His companions laughed despite themselves, and the tension subsided.

Martha's sister Mary came into the room, and such was her presence that the eyes of all in the room found her at once. It wasn't just her physical beauty, for she exuded an aura of love the way some women exude perfume. She bore a filmy golden vessel in her hands, but the surprize was that her usually joyous face registered a note of distress. She went to the mother of Jesus, and crouched beside her. "Mother," she whispered, pain in her voice, "you must help me."

"What is it?"

"I want to honor your son. I don't trust my judgment. Am I presumptuous?" She raised the sparkling phial in accusation against herself.

"Can't love show affection? Do what is in your heart."

Mary of Bethany rose with a radiant smile, went to the Master, and stood over his reclining figure. She broke the sealed top from the phial, bent over him, and began pouring the liquid on the locks of his hair. The fragrance of a flower-decked meadow drifted across the room. As she continued to pour the ointment, the fragrance soared and transformed the scent from one bouquet to another, until waves of incense wafted through the chamber.

Thomas saw his friend Judas, two guests to his right, sit bolt upright on his couch, staring at Mary. His head tilted back grotesquely and he sniffed noisily, eyes bulging with concentration. He leaped to his feet and with a wild bound loomed over Mary, seized her arm, and bellowed, "Give me that!" Wresting the jar free, he examined it animatedly. Mary stared at him with open mouth, eyes wide with alarm. Inspired by Judas, Thomas hastened over to have a look.

"That's expensive stuff!" Judas barked. "The Master's taught us to live frugally—not squander money on luxuries!"

Simon the Zealot strode over. "Surely, the tax-poor deserved what was wasted on that!" he chimed in. By now every guest had riveted his attention on Mary and her detractors.

Judas waved the vessel wildly over his head, slopping out its contents in the process. He glared around, and shouted in fury. "Do you know what this cost? Almost a year's wages! We could have gotten three hundred silver coins for it, and fed thousands of the hungry!"

"Leave her alone!" The Master's injunction reverberated with such terrible force that Judas froze, every sound ceased, every eye journeyed between Jesus and Judas. Interrupting his playing, the musician set his harp down with the greatest care. It slipped, fell, and sprayed out a nervewracking cacaphony which took long to die away. When at last quiet returned, the Master spoke commandingly.

"Return it!"

Judas had recovered himself. He stood unmoving, his face a map of insolence. Then, with unnatural slowness, he restored the jar to Mary's trembling hands, glared balefully at the Master, turned on his heel, and stalked out of the room. Thomas, looking shamefaced, returned to his couch. Simon the Zealot stared at Jesus in confusion, then resumed his place. The eyes of all centered on the Master.

"You have witnessed a fair and gracious act," he said. "She has anticipated the burial anointing of my body." The guests screwed up their faces in puzzlement; Peter looked alarmed.

. "The poor will always be with you," he continued. "You'll have the chance to help them whenever you want. But me you'll not always have. What this woman did for me will be told wherever the Good News goes. You can rely on it.

"Anything done for me will not be forgotten. When the Son of Man comes glorious, the peoples will be herded in and he will separate them like sheep from goats. To the sheep he'll say, 'Come, blessed of my Father, into your Kingdom. For you fed my hunger, quenched my thirst, sheltered and clothed me, and consoled me in sickness and imprisonment.' In surprize they'll ask, 'When?' And the King will answer, 'When you did it to anyone.' And the goats he'll send off to eternal fire for doing none of these things." Here, the Master turned to Martha and signalled that he had concluded.

"Musician!" Martha cried, "Play for us!" The harpist

retrieved his instrument and filled the room with spirited music. The guests gradually renewed their conversation.

Mary was still standing by the Master with her anointing oil. Cupping it in both hands, like a sacred votive offering, she went from the head to the foot of his couch, sank gracefully to a kneeling posture, and began pouring the ointment on his feet. When she had emptied the jar, she removed her veil and bent reverently. Her long, free-flowing hair tumbled down, and with graceful motions she employed her tresses to remove the remaining ointment. When this was done, she remained where she was. Bent low, unmoving, she appeared as timeless and enduring as a figure carved in stone on some old Egyptian vase. Not simply by her arrested motion was this effect produced, but by the look on her face. It told of adventuring beyond all the shadows and forms of fleeting things, of reaching the end of the river of time and crystallizing in the eternal medium beyond.

Even Martha forgot to be in a hurry, and gazed at her sister like everyone else. Though in charge of the feast, she felt suddenly unneeded. For the first time she understood the saying of the Master that her sister had chosen the better part. Indeed, if the wafting fragrances had taken on the visible aspect of smoke and incense rising, she might have claimed witness to the epic sight of love, indefensible to the profaning eye, offered on the altar of holocaust.

Gad leaned over Peter and said, "Look at her. Already she's forgotten us all."

"You'd be grateful, too, if he'd raised your brother," interjected Rabbi Absalom, from Peter's other flank.

"It wouldn't alter what you see if she had no brother!" Gad retorted.

"Peter," Absalom said, ignoring Gad, "I understand she's still a virgin, though well beyond marriage age. About twenty, I'd say. Yet she looks presentable enough to please some man. Why hasn't she followed the way of the earth?"

"I never asked her," Peter hedged, not willing to explain the Master's teaching on the single life to one who didn't believe in him.

"If you could see what's before your eyes, Absalom," Gad rejoined, "you wouldn't ask that question."

"My theory," Absalom explained, again ignoring Gad, "is that she met your Master at an impressionable age, and became entangled in the exhortations to remain unmarried which I hear he gives. We already have too much of that misguided practice among the Essenes. Were she my daughter, she would be wasting neither herself nor her ointment on this ascetic. She'd be raising my grandchildren, like a proper and sensible woman. Judas was right."

Peter had resolved beforehand not to argue with the learned rabbis, but he found it impossible to sit by and allow such blind smugness to go unchallenged.

"Is that all you see in him—an ascetic?"

"What do you expect me to see?"

"A man who has raised the dead! A man who is . . ." He broke off. He had been forbidden to say, 'The Christ.'

"Miracles are so hard to be sure of. I prefer to judge a man by his doctrine—his adherence to tradition."

"Tradition! Did Moses adhere to tradition—or bring a new tradition? Did the prophets say nothing new? Did they not promise a new tradition—a new covenant and a Messiah? How can you hope to recognize what is to come if you admit nothing new?"

"Why bring up Moses? We're talking about a wood-worker."

"A wood-worker! What's that got to do with it? Moses was a waif born of a slave and rescued by a Gentile! David was a poor shepherd. And as to his miracles—Mary and I have no doubt he raised her brother!"

"If she believes that, she should be grateful—but not fatuous," Absalom pontificated. "He who plies his thanks too copiously is only giving bribes in disguise."

Peter gave up.

Jesus had been aware for some time of a growing clamor beating into the room from the street. Now it was drowning out the conversation and the music. He looked toward the door. Simon the Leper noticed, and said, "I'll see what's happening." He went out, and soon returned. "Master, the people have learned of your presence. A mob is clamoring for you. They won't leave and they won't be still."

"Tell them that in the morning I will enter the city, but

this night I must spend here." Simon slipped out, and the clamor began to abate.

Some time later, Jude searched for Judas. He went over and tapped Thomas on the shoulder. "Where is Judas?"

"I don't know." Thomas lifted his wine glass and took a gulp. "I noticed he was gone." He looked depressed.

"Cheer up," Jude urged. "It's not always easy to know what pleases the Master."

"Easy!" Thomas shouted. Jude breathed a prayer of thanks the guests were belting out a song under the spirited leadership of the musician. "He's exactly like those parables of his! Just when you think you've got him figured out, he eludes you. He's got me beat for good."

"Thomas, you and Judas keep trying to reduce the Master's teaching to a set of laws and ideas—and it doesn't work."

"What's wrong with laws and ideas?"

"Nothing, but Jesus teaches much more. He talks about people. Isn't that what love's about—people?"

"What about John? He keeps talking about the Master's new ideas."

"Maybe, but in the end he makes persons more important."

"You may be right," Thomas admitted dejectedly. "I'm about ready to pack up and head for home. Maybe that is what Judas did."

Jude was alarmed. "Don't do it, Thomas. The Master needs us. Besides, I think you understand a lot more than I do."

"Do you think so?" Thomas looked like a sleeper waking.

"I'm sure of it. I've learned a lot from you."

"I've had enough to drink." Thomas pushed his goblet away.

Jude was still awake when Judas entered the tent. "I missed you," he called, but got no answer. In the lamp's faint glow he was not able to make out his friend's face, but he could see him moving with those quick, violent gestures which signalled anger and depression. He whipped off his money belt with such force it flew from his hand. Jude heard the tinkle of coins on the stones.

"I'll help." He leaped from his mat and grabbed the oil

337

lamp.

"No! I'll get them!"

"Judas! These are all silver coins! I thought we were bankrupt! Where did you get them? There must be dozens!"

"Thirty, to be exact." Judas' voice was barely recognizable. "From generous benefactors. Now that you know, I swear you to secrecy—only for a few days, I expect. Say nothing until then. I have a big surprize in store for the Master."

8

Peter slept in Bethany that night. When he fell asleep the Master was kneeling in prayer, and on awaking Thursday morning he found him crouched in the same place. Had he prayed all night? Drifting into the room came the noise of an excited crowd, so he dressed hurriedly and went out.

People jammed the muddy road—it must have rained in the night—their clothes spattered, their spirits too high to care, their excited voices clamoring for the Master. The excitement set his own emotions churning, in a whirl of feelings and fears as muddy as the road. When first he had met the Master on the Jordan's wet banks, his spirits too had soared with a hope as pure as Galilee's springs, but now that hope lay prostrate and bleeding, shackled by the chains of grim reality. The Master was going into the city where all the hostile forces of the enemy were coiled and waiting. Still, who knew what surprizes he had in store for them? The thought crackled like the snapping of a chain, and he felt a little relieved. He went back inside.

In moments the sounds on the street rose to a higher pitch of excitement, the door opened, and in came the rest of the Twelve, who had billeted at the Galilee. The Master took the Iscariot aside. "Go to the trader and hire a colt for the day."

"I can't. The last of our funds went for tents at the Galilee. Shall I ask Lazarus for money?"

338

"No."

After a hurried breakfast they went out to the people. Great cheers tore the air in wave after wave.

Of the three roads leading into the city, all lined with people, the Master set out on the one which passed through Bethphage. The Twelve formed a cordon around him and hewed a way through the crowd. The people on the other routes poured after them, cheering and waving palm branches stripped from wayside trees. A little man lost in the press kept shouting, "I want to see him too!" but nobody paid him any heed. As they panted up the steep grade, the cheering waned.

Simon the Zealot, boiling with excitement, turned to Judas. "My prediction is coming true. He's entering the city like a conqueror. The die is cast. Within the hour the authorities will know what we know. The hit-and-run Zealots are needed no more. We may even rescue Barabbas!"

Judas shot him a calculating look. "You could be right. I may have to revise my plans."

"What plans?"

"I'm always full of plans. I was working to gain him access to the highest authorities."

"After today he won't need your plans!"

The trio before them were conversing excitedly, and the Zealot tuned in.

"Do you think he's really the one?" a youth was asking the two older men with him.

"I don't know," the first responded. "I was expecting great things of John the Baptizer, but he ended a disappointment."

"Well, Jashen," the other said, "this one certainly shows promise with his powerful works—and he's here on the Mount of Olives, and it's almost the Feast."

"But isn't the Messiah supposed to appear right out of a crack in the mountain?" the youth asked.

"Yes," Jashen answered, "and the bodies buried here will all pop out of the cemeteries as he passes—rising from the dead!"

"The Sadducees laugh at that," the youth said.

"Those atheists? Who cares! What do you say, Ira?"

339

"Well, Jashen, we really don't know all the details for certain."

"I don't know anything for certain," the youth confessed.

"Then why are you here?" Jashen demanded.

"There's an old priest who lives next door to me. About a month ago he waked from sleep and leaped out of bed shouting, 'The Messiah's on the way!' Every day since he's been leaning on his staff and going up to the Temple. Last night he said, 'Tomorrow's the day!' So I followed him, and he hobbled all the way up here."

"I know a Rabbi Nathan of the Pharisees," Ira confided. "Last week he ran out of his house with his hair standing on end shouting, 'He's coming! He's coming!' 'Who?' they asked. 'The Messiah!' he thundered. 'When?' they asked. 'Soon,' he replied, 'very soon.' He went in, laid out his newest ceremonial robes—he's a priest—and waited. He's been doing it every morning since. Before sunrise he vested, and came up here like he was shot from a bow."

"Is that why you came?" the youth prompted.

"No. I was coming anyway—made up my mind the moment I heard Rabbi Jesus was entering the city this morning."

The procession had reached the little town of Bethphage. Alongside the path lay a large boulder, and in its shade sprang up a little patch of Solomon's crowns, deep purple with blood-red coronets. Jesus sat on the boulder, and signalled to Peter and John. "Go into that little village," he directed, pointing to a ramshackle cluster of buildings. "Just as you enter you'll find a colt never ridden before. Untie him and bring him. If anyone objects, say, 'The Master has to have him.'"

The two fought their way through the press of the crowd. As soon as they were out of earshot, Peter grabbed John's arm excitedly. "This is it, John. The people are rising up to acclaim him on their own—not waiting for our blind leaders. And he's going along—he'll ride in on a charger snorting out the victory!"

"I wish you were right."

The leaden tone of John's words sobered Peter instantly. "What do you mean?"

"Haven't you noticed there's no gladness in him?"

"He's exhausted. He was up all night. What's your interpretation? You can't deny this enthusiasm."

"He knows something we don't—something that will dampen this enthusiasm only too soon."

"What! After the way he raised Lazarus?"

"Peter, I've been waiting the chance to ask you—have you worked out a good way to describe the raising of Lazarus on your next missionary journey?"

Peter looked deflated. "Did you notice," he hedged, "that many of the Pharisees didn't believe Lazarus or his sisters or his doctor—or any of us?"

"Of course I noticed. What's your answer?"

"We shouldn't dump everything on people at once—no more than they can accept."

"You don't intend to broadcast the news about Lazarus?"

"If anyone asks, I'll describe it. Otherwise I'll only report the healings I think they can handle. The important thing is to get them to believe in the Master."

"I'm going to tell them what they ought to believe—everything that's happened—whether they believe or not!"

"John, John, don't be such a hard charger. You're forgetting everything you learned in your fishing trade. Do you bait a hook with something hard to swallow, or with what attracts fish? And when you feel a nibble, do you yank the line right in? No, you play it patiently, trying to set the hook. Otherwise you get no fish—or men."

"We do most of our fishing with nets. We'd starve with hooks. Prance and jiggle your fancy bait all you want! I'll cast in the whole net of facts and catch them in the web of truth."

Peter stopped and looked at John reflectively. "John, you're bright. You see everything at once and your judgment snaps like a hunter's trap. Most of us aren't that way. I see facts and enthusiastically make my decision. Then I see facts I missed and I'm shaken loose, and revise my decision. The Master knows he has to be patient with me—and I have to be patient with others. You're not that way, so do what you think is best. That's what I'm going to do."

Peter saw that John looked unhappy at this. He threw

341

his arm around his companion's shoulder. "Let's be glad we'll both be fishing from the same boat. My bait'll attract a lot of fish, and your net'll pull them in." They walked the remaining distance in silence.

"Look, there's the colt!" John pointed to a handsome white colt tethered beside his mare.

"It's not a horse after all—just an ass." Peter's words were melancholy. Not until long after the final event did they recall Zechariah's prophecy, "Inform the daughter of Zion: Look, look! Your king is on the way, unassuming he is, mounted on an ass, on a colt, the foal of a beast of burden." It was, in fact, on an ass that the ancient kings of Israel rode.

They went up to the colt and untied it.

"What d'you think you're doing?" a burly fellow loitering nearby challenged, reaching for his hefty cudgel.

"The Master needs him," Peter explained, pointing to the crowd off in the distance.

"He's never been ridden," the man said.

The colt wouldn't budge. "We'll have to take his mare, too," Peter decided, looking uneasily at the man with the staff, who showed no further interest. He unloosed the animal and led her off, John following with the colt.

The Master mounted the colt, but not before Peter and John threw their cloaks over its back. As they set out again a young maiden named Abbey ran up to him with a freshly plucked Solomon's crown. He bent low, and she planted the tiny blossom in the band which circled his head covering. He smiled and rode off.

The sight of the Master on a mount made the crowd more exuberant than ever. At every muddy spot men pulled off their cloaks and threw them over the puddles. People carpeted the way with palm branches. Boys sped into the fields and returned with more, receiving a coin for their services. Smaller children were running about happily. People reclining on the roofs of the wayside buildings gawked and buzzed.

A teenager squeezed through the crowd, pressed up to Jesus, and cried, "Master, can I be your disciple now?"

"Shalom, shalom, David," he greeted the lad, laying his hand on his head. The boy, coming to him at his first

342

manifestation in Jerusalem and begging to be his follower, had been allowed to spend a few nights with his disciples, but had been too young to be called.

"How old are you now, David?"

"Sixteen."

"Would your father approve?"

"No. He's afraid of what they're going to do to you."

"Then it's too soon. But one day you'll be my disciple."

He rode on, and David stood looking after him sadly.

When they reached the summit, the city came into view across the chasm of the Kidron Valley. Morning sunlight poured down on the tawny warm blocks of the buildings which lay in undulating waves upon the rolling hills. The light flamed against the radiant gold and marble of the Temple. For one moment they fell silent and gazed, then Peter saw what awaited them.

"Lord, look!" he said wonderingly. "The road's lined with people all the way to the Temple!" Waves of pilgrims were ascending the road. On seeing the Master they sent up a tumult. When the outcry began to taper off, a man with a roar like a lion lifted his voice.

"Blessed is he who comes in the name of the Lord!" The cry was taken up and began to fly along the road in both directions. From the Mount of Olives to the walls of Jerusalem it rang. At length it began to fade, and another voice chanted, "Blessed is our father David's coming kingdom!" This chant too spread like wildfire, until it rang out across the Mount and the Valley. When it flagged, a group of men together began an orchestrated chant: "Save us now, O Son of David! Save us now, O King of Israel!"

There were gasps in the crowd, and a lull like that before a storm—and the cry was taken up, flying from mountain peak to mountain peak—from Mount Olivet to Mount Zion.

The disciples could see the catwalks along the city wall enclosing the esplanade of the Temple begin filling with priests looking no larger than ants. Floating across the valley from the Antonia came the imperious sound of a trumpet and soldiers appeared in the four towers, lining the ramparts.

Three Pharisees who had been trailing behind drove wildly up to the Master. "Teacher, silence your disciples!" He

343

looked at them in amazement.

"If they held their tongues the stones would begin to bellow." He nodded to Peter, who brought the colt to a halt, and sitting astride his mount, he contemplated the scene.

The plentiful spring rains had carpeted the flanks of the city with green grass sprinkled with flowers. Even the grave-yards strewing the valley looked cheerful. The Temple and the honey-colored stone buildings stretched away like a vision in the sunrise—except for the Antonia Fortress, which brooded over the Temple.

The Master's eyes glistened, tears began to stream down his cheeks, and he spoke, but so gently that only Peter and John heard him: "If even this late you'd recognize the way of peace: on another day, attack walls are going up to dash you down because you didn't recognize your visitation."

The procession continued, winding its way past the Garden of Gethsemane, across the Kidron Valley, and up the approach to the Golden Gate. The giant man with the lion's voice lowered his head, gored his way through the crowd, reached the Master, and shouted, "Go right up to the Antonia. Order the soldiers to throw down their arms. Strike them with fire from heaven! Save us now!" He spun on his heel, bellowing in every direction at once: "Save us now! Save us now! Save us now!" At once everyone was shouting, "Save us now!" The outcry flowed from the surging crowd like a river, poured down the narrow streets, broke against the ramparts of the fortress, and splashed up into the ears of the bowmen lining the walls high above. Their faces turned to granite, their eyes hardened into stones, and they lifted their bows to the ready.

Far below, the Master turned up the approach to the Golden Gate, reached it, and dismounted. The people fell silent, awaiting his next move. "Return the animals," he instructed Peter and John. He drew his headdress close to muffle his face, passed through the Gate onto the esplanade of the Temple, and was soon lost in the swarm of pilgrims.

The Zealot stood dumbfounded. "He's not going to do anything!" Disbelief punctuated his words.

"You saw the troops of Rome," Jude chided him, "and the hostile priests."

344

"Did you think he'd start a war with Rome—and a civil war as well?" John challenged. "He's a man of peace."

"At a time like this, he's worried about returning two asses!" Judas' words were scornful.

"He knows what to do—we don't," Peter said defensively, but he looked confused. He led the mare through the press of people, and John followed with the colt.

"It doesn't matter. I trust him," Thomas burst out, but his expression belied his words. "Maybe he's still going to do something. I'm going to find out." He went through the Golden Gate, and the other Apostles followed dispiritedly.

The crowd milled around the Gate, waiting to see what would happen next. "Who was that we were cheering?" asked a man with a traveling bag. "I'm just in from Gaul."

"Jesus of Nazareth—a miracle worker, they tell me," volunteered a man in an ornately embroidered cloak. "That's all I know. I'm just in from Mesopotamia."

"You mean you joined in the cheering without knowing why?" a Levite asked. "Did you know the chief priests have called for his arrest?" The two looked at him with hanging jaws.

"Arrest? For what?" the Mesopotamian mumbled.

"I'd say it's because they're losing power and he's gaining it," the Levite replied confidentially.

"Why haven't they arrested him, then?" asked the Celt.

"Would you like to try in front of these enthusiasts? And I'm *one,* I'll tell you. He's like the old-time prophets. I can't discount his miracles the way the chief priests have the knack of doing. I thought he'd call fire down on the Antonia, then lead us to Pilate, and demand that Rome withdraw—or face armies of angels like the Maccabees' enemies."

Many in the crowd had recently arrived in Jerusalem, and knew little about Jesus. They had joined in the clamor for immediate liberation with little thought of how their hope might be realized. When they saw the Master disappear into the crowd, they began dispersing.

The Master lost himself in the packed Court of the Israelites, and stood in prayer, cowled head bowed low. After a time, he returned to Bethany.

345

Half an hour after the concourse dispersed, the high priest fumed in his quarters. That brazen display of Messianic fervor! That brash support of Jesus—nearly an uprising! The governor would have to be in the city! But of course, that was no accident—he always scheduled his presence for the assizes to coincide with the Feast. That way, he was poised to nip sedition in the bud.

Thunder on the door startled him. A Levite burst in bellowing his message: "The freedom fighters have struck. Attacked the Roman guard at the Joppa Gate. Tried to incite an uprising. Several were captured."

Caiaphas cursed. This could cost him his post. With furious haste he dashed off a message. "Take this to the Captain of the Guard. He's to begin the investigation at once." The Levite scurried away. Caiaphas hoped for a full report before he was summoned by Pilate.

Minutes later, a mounted Roman courier clattered into Caiaphas' courtyard, dismounted, and clamored for an audience.

"Your Reverence, Joseph Caiaphas, high priest?"

"Yes, yes!"

"An urgent communique from his Excellency, Pontius Pilate, Procurator of Judea."

Caiaphas' trembling hands broke the seal and he read:

Your Reverence, Joseph Caiaphas, high priest:

I have dispatched an order for five cohorts of auxiliaries to proceed to this city by forced march from Caesarea. The legate of Syria is being advised of the situation, and petitioned to have a full Roman legion standing by.

Of the uprising at the Joppa Gate in this hour you must be aware. The terrorists have been apprehended. The charge is sedition and the murder of the Emperor's loyal troops.

I need not inform you of the provocative display earlier this day at the Golden Gate.

Arrival of the troops will be stayed only on evidence that your Reverence has taken convincing measures to contain the menace to the peace posed by the events of this day.

Pontius Pilate, Procurator of Judea
by direct appointment of Tiberius, Emperor

Caiaphas sat and wrote furiously:

Pontius Pilate, procurator of Judea by Imperial Appointment
Your Excellency:
The troops will not be needed, I assure you. The terrorist, Barabbas, whom you apprehended recently, had no great following, but only a vain hope of one, as the ease of subduing the Joppa Gate melee makes manifest.

The non-violent display at the Golden Gate was a harmless outburst of religious feeling (so common to our people) which vaporized without issue.

Jesus the Nazarene was somewhat of a figurehead there, as Your Excellency is no doubt aware. As for him, one of his closest intimates (a man numbered among those called The Twelve), having at last become disabused of his master's chicaneries, has turned informer. He will advise us of the first opportunity to seize this disturber of the peace in circumstances that will minimize the possibility of a public outbreak.

Since the peaceful resolution of this matter concerns both our administrations, I petition Your Excellency to assist our poorly-trained Levite police make the arrest, which is imminent, by providing a cohort of your superb soldiery.

Joseph Caiaphas, High Priest of the Jewish
People of Judea, Galilee and the Dispersion

9

Peter and John passed through the west wall of the city by way of the Dung Gate and stood waiting, their head coverings drawn forward to obscure their faces. From under the younger disciple's cowling came his voice, subdued and reflective.

"Peter, what was your last exchange with Jesus all about?"

"He said to expect the government to act against us after what happened this morning. The Zealot attack worsened matters. The authorities will make some move."

"Is that why he's keeping the location of our Seder secret?"

"That's my guess. If even we are in the dark until the last minute, word can't leak out."

"We may be under arrest right now."

"I know." Peter cowled his face the more.

"Persecuted for giving a dead man life. The world's gone mad."

"No," Peter rumbled, "just having its madness exposed."

"They'll be keeping a hawk's eye on the Temple—where he'll certainly go tomorrow."

"What can they do to us?" Peter blustered.

"Romans crucify rebels."

"They know we're not rebels," Peter muttered.

"The bowmen lining the Antonia weren't sure. When I first followed the Master, I was out for guerrilla action, but now he's weaned me away, and look where we end up."

"Before I met him, I thought I understood God and his ways. Now I know I don't."

"We know he's the Christ. That'll have to be enough."

"Well, he's the one who knows what to do next." Peter said it heartily enough, but John didn't miss his anxiety.

They stood watching the carts and foot traffic passing, until at length a man carrying a water pitcher entered the gate—a rare sight, as it was a woman's task. Tradesmen who sold water carried it in skins. There was, however, a settlement of Essenes near the Dung Gate; as celibates, they were reduced to transporting their own water.

It was the sign the Master had given Peter. He approached the pitcher-carrier and said in an undertone, "Conduct us to where the Nazarene is to eat the Pasch." The man examined

Peter, saw the carcass of a lamb flayed and draped in its own skin flung over his shoulder, and the baskets of food-stuffs John was carrying. He nodded, and they followed.

They were in sight of the high priest's palace when he turned a corner, pointed to a flight of stairs leading to the upper room of a spacious stone house, and went on down the street. Peter and John ascended, found the door unlocked, and entered. Peter's quick eye took in the large, handsome room in a glance—the lofty white ceiling, cedar walls, worn Arabic rug, T-shaped table appointed with couches, and the spacious southern window overlooking the Valley of Gehenna. Snowy linen covered the table, which was laid with dishes and silverware. The deep purple of the herringbone couches showed well against the warm color of the cedar wood. Two rusty old swords decorated the western wall. Unlit oil lamps hung from the ceiling, and others surmounted bronze stands. Abundant light filtered in through the window in undulating patterns, reflections from tall palm trees stirring in the wind. On the table, a medley of spring flowers showered from a silver vase. Peter recognized the white blossoms of the almond tree, the pink of the mallow, and a purple thistle.

"I did my best with the flowers," chanted an old man as he leaped up out of the shadows of one of the couches. "Apollo, your servant, in attendance, good sirs." His wrinkled face featured a cheery look that seemed as permanent a part of him as his arms and legs. His ears showed the awl marks of a perpetual slave.

"Shalom, shalom, Apollo. I'm Peter, and this is John. We'll number thirteen. Put the unneeded couches to the side."

"But you'll want an extra, according to custom, in case Elijah the prophet comes?"

"No."

Apollo stared in surprize, but said nothing.

John examined the covered dishes and other supplies on the side tables. "We won't need all the food we brought."

"Just the lamb, good sirs," Apollo announced. John saw him struggling with the couches and went to his aid.

Peter's eye spotted a cask of wine in the corner farthest from the window, and he examined it. On the barrel was the mark of a vintner of Hebron. They would not lack for good wine. He opened the tap and let a few drops spill out, but did not taste it—one took no food or drink in these hours before the Seder. Through the sour smell of the barrel he detected the rich bouquet of the spill.

The warmth and peace of the room drew Peter's dispersed thoughts together like a swarm of moths to a lamp. He felt his presence gathering itself to the quiet place until he had a heightened sense of every detail. As he went about making final arrangements, he became sensitive to the various odors—the dry smell of the raised dust as he walked, the musty odor of the rug near the window, the fresh bouquet of the meadow wafted in through the opening, the scent of the flowers, the aromas of the foodstuffs, the pungence of the cedar panels, the fresh smell of the linen. Thoughts of the happy Seders of his boyhood flickered through his mind. How he used to hope Elijah the prophet would knock and enter and take the empty couch which always awaited him. Sometimes he even opened the door a crack and peered out to see if he was coming.

A field mouse peeked in through the window, then scuttled out of view. Buzzing flies caromed off the covered food dishes.

"Peter," John called, "the utensils for the ritual footbath are over here, but with only one servant . . ."

"I know. We'll skip it."

"Tell me, Peter—why are we celebrating the Seder tonight, instead of tomorrow? Do any of the sects celebrate it tonight? And if so, is it acceptable to the high priests?"

"I don't know—but the Master always has his reasons. I do know the high priests reject the Essene dating, so I'm glad he didn't celebrate with them two days ago. You know they use a solar instead of a lunar calendar."

John nodded, surveyed the room, and said, "Everything's in order to celebrate tonight."

"Apollo, we'd better give you a hand with the lamb," Peter declared. He retrieved the carcass, and carried it out the rear entrance and down into the courtyard. A pile of branches trimmed from some hoary old grapevine lay beside the fireplace. It was prescribed that the paschal lamb be roasted over a fire of wood from the vine.

"John, put in the pomegranate skewer." Peter held the carcass while John skewered it from mouth to buttocks. Peter laid it upon its skin on the table by the outdoor fireplace. "Apollo, we're going for our baths."

John retrieved the bundles of fresh clothes from the baskets and they descended to the area near the Pool of Siloam where there were baths for hire. These were not public baths in the Roman style, but small private chambers with deep pools hewn in the rock. Tomorrow, lengthy files of pilgrims would form to use them, but this afternoon there was no wait. Peter entered his chamber, stripped, and descended the steps to the bath.

The water was chilly, but he found it refreshing. He made his ablutions, very much aware that he was performing a sacred act in preparation for sitting at the banquet of God, as his forefathers had done since their release from slavery to Egypt.

John was waiting for him when he finished. They returned to the Dung Gate. Matthew appeared first, and Peter led him to the upper room while John awaited the rest. "You'll be glad to know we have a harp, Matthew," he announced. "You can accompany our singing of the Hallel."

When John returned with the Master, the others had already gathered. The silver rim of the full moon was just peeking over the Mount of Olives and the golden orb of the sun falling below the western hills. They reclined on the couches and engaged in muted conversations. Through the south window drifted evening sounds from the Valley of Gehenna far below—the lowing of cattle, the baaing of sheep, the sharp cry of a herder.

Apollo went about lighting the lamps in the darkening chamber; each wick put forth a golden spear of fire, silent and unmoving in the still air, bathing the faces in shadowy light.

There was something inexpressibly appealing in Jesus' mood. The radiant innocence in his face seemed to enhance the light of the lamps, and his holiness charged the atmosphere like an indefinable incense. Peter's feelings were a compound of joy and anxiety, anticipation and dread, as when he sought the hand of his bride, and waited in suspense for the answer. As the moments passed, his happiness grew, and the high priests, the Romans, and all his anxieties receded. His couch was at the top of the T-shaped table, alongside John, who was next to Jesus. On Jesus' left reclined Jude, and beyond him, Judas. Thus Jesus was flanked by the two youngest members of the Twelve. Four of the other eight Apostles were on each side of the table's perpendicular.

Peter was engrossed in the music Matthew was drawing from his harp when he felt an insistent tapping on his shoulder. Turning his head, he almost bumped into Judas' lowering face. "I wasn't consulted on the selection of this hall." The low tone was angry. "Led here like a sheep—yet I'm the provisioner of this outfit."

"I only followed orders." Peter was embarrassed. Judas' complaint had legitimacy.

"If this is our Paschal feast, the Law demands we reside in the city tonight—and I've arranged no lodgings."

It surprised Peter Judas' major concern was that his services were slighted. Wasn't he bothered that Jesus was celebrating the Passover a day early? But perhaps he was more knowledgeable about the acceptable variations in the matter. Even the Pharisees and the Sadducees, he had heard, argued about the dating when Passover and Sabbath celebrations collided, as they did this year. But for the moment he had to respond to Judas. He hesitated still, then said, "I'll tell you confidentially, Judas. The Master told me not to arrange lodgings. We'll spend the night in the cave in the Garden of Olives." It couldn't hurt to tell Judas. He felt sorry for him. The Master seemed a little down on him— though not without reason, of course. There was his thievery, if Jude was right, and his mean display at Lazarus' banquet. Judas was staring at him strangely so he added, "You know that even though it's across the Kidron Valley, the rabbis have ruled it a part of the city for the purpose of paschal residency." Judas looked contemptuous.

"Of course I know it!" He returned to his couch.

Jesus had gone out to oversee the roasting of the lamb, and in his absence the disciples began complaining about the seating arrangements. Judas joined in. "By what right, John, did you put yourself next to the Master? And here's

352

Jude on his other side. Does ability count for nothing around here?"

Jesus heard them on his return, and his distress showed. He stripped off his tunic and put on a slave's apron. He took the footbath utensils, and approached to wash their feet. Peter felt terribly ashamed. It had never occurred to him to provide the service himself instead of omitting it.

When he knelt at his feet, Peter sat bolt upright shouting, "Never my feet!" He drew his feet up under him.

"Either that, or you can have no part in me."

Peter sat stunned. He saw the line of straight, fair lashes lifted high, and the clear, luminous eyes with expectant gaze. A single tear trickled down his cheek and, like a child, he extended his feet and hands and bowed his head. "My hands and head, too, Lord."

"After a bath, Peter, that's not needed." Jesus said this gently, then added more sternly, "But I can't say that of all of you." When the task was completed, he resumed his couch. There was no sound but the buzz of insects until he spoke again. "You have my example—your Master and Lord. You have to wash one another's feet too." Peter leaped up.

"Not today, Peter," Jesus said, smiling, and the rest laughed. The outbreak of jealousy was forgotten and conversation bubbled up.

The sound of a silver trumpet came slicing across the dark city, and they fell silent. High on the Temple esplanade, a priest was signalling the new day. It was now Friday, the thirteenth of Nisan (March-April), the day before the first full moon of the vernal equinox. It was officially the day of preparation for Passover. The hour was about seven in the evening.

The trumpet was just dying away when Apollo entered with an immense olivewood tray bearing the fragrant body of the Passover offering, laid with upper legs splayed out in the form of a cross. As he set it on the table, Jesus spoke with deep solemnity.

"I have desired and desired to eat this Paschal lamb with you before I suffer. Father, blessed is this day, and I bless you for this day."

He reached out with his right hand, picked up the goblet of wine mixed with water, and sipped it, and each did the same. The servant set dishes of vegetables and lettuce before them, and they ate. Then unleavened bread was distributed, and bitter herbs—their share in the bitter suffering of their forefathers. They dipped the bitter herbs in haroseth, a compound of crushed nuts and fruits mixed with vinegar.

Apollo mixed their second goblet of wine. When they had drunk it, John sat up, turned to Jesus, and spoke. "What does this rite mean? What sets this night off from all other nights?" Thus does the youngest son invite his father to explain the ancient feast. John shivered with anticipation, remembering what it was like to have Jesus recount their history.

"A wandering Aramean was your father," Jesus intoned solemnly, and went on to describe the exile in Egypt. "Then comes the night of our freedom. The blow is struck, the firstborn dies, the blood of the skipping lamb flows—a male without blemish—the enslaved flee with unleavened bread, passing to freedom through the watery walls, which become death for the racing Egyptians and their thudding hoofs and flashing swords." The doors seemed to burst in on John, the undisciplined tribes rush past, clutching their possessions, the lamb's blood on their hands, pursued, cursing Moses, bellowing to the Lord for salvation. "The Egyptians sink in the water and mud, Mount Sinai looms, the thunder and fire and smoke of the Presence close in. For the Father's great goodness to us, then," Jesus concluded, "let us glorify his name." He rose from his couch and intoned Psalm 114, "Israel came out of Egypt." They rose and joined in the singing, to the accompaniment of Matthew's harp. Jesus circled the couches in a processional dance, and they fell in behind him, singing and dancing exuberantly of their people's march to freedom—which was their march in this hour.

When they came to the words, "God turned the rock into pools of water, the flint into flowing springs," Jesus broke off the singing, and they reclined again. Turning his head from one to another, he stared at them until his eyes seemed to enter their skulls, then cried, "Long have the people

354

awaited the one coming on the self-same eve to free them from their sins forever." They stared at him wide-eyed, and he said, "One of you is stalking me to betray me." A stunned silence ensued—then pandemonium.

"No!" Peter bellowed.

"I give you my word."

Faces flowed like molten lava. Inarticulate noises squeezed out from between clamped lips as eleven men battled to control sanity, to stave off horror, to repress doubts and demons struggling to be loosed against themselves and each other.

"Not I, surely?" gasped one and another as the ground broke out from under them and the water of the Red Sea raced toward them. Peter shook his head violently, shaking away all doubts about himself. He leaned toward John, and signalled him to find out who it was. John leaned back on Jesus' chest.

"Who is it, Lord?" His voice was a whisper.

"He," Jesus said as softly, "to whom I offer the morsel of friendship still." He broke off a piece of unleavened bread, dipped it in the sauce, and with thumb and forefinger, held it out to Judas, who opened his mouth and received it.

Jesus looked around at them all. "The Son of Man now follows the path the Scriptures lay out, but terrible the fate stored up for the doer of the deed! To be unborn would be better!"

He sipped a third glass of wine, then said the benediction over the Passover offering, and they all ate of its flesh. "I no longer call you slaves; no, I call you friends."

"Lord," protested Jude, "you've long treated us as friends."

"A new mandate I give you," Jesus went on as though not hearing. "Love one another. As I have loved you, love each other. I am the vine, you the branches."

He resumed the Hallel where they had left off, and they all chanted it with him. When they came to the words, "Blessed is he who comes in the name of the Lord," he signalled for silence, took from the table a wafer of matzo, broke it in pieces, and held it out in his open hands. "Take this," he said. "It is my body." He gave each a morsel.

He took a goblet of wine, blessed it, and passed it to

355

them. "Take this," he said. "This is my blood of the new covenant, which will be poured out for the many."

Judas was sure they failed to notice when he slid from his couch and left. And no wonder. The rabbi was saying, "This is my body," and to a man they sat up, fell slack at the jaw, and bulged at the eye. All except John. He seemed to expect this latest madness. Perhaps he had been cued in beforehand. In any case, you had to hand it to him. He was shrewd; he had his angle. He planned to wring something out of the Rabbi before he finished with him. Or was his expression no more than it pretended to be—a look of simpering love like Mary of Bethany's when she robbed them of her immense contribution? Not likely, but possible. He, Judas, might be the only intelligent one. One thing he knew—he'd repay the Master, with interest. He, the most gifted among his riff-raff, treated like an untrustworthy servant! And he was gone, hurrying into the night, to put an end to it all.

"Lord," John was asking, "will you always eat and drink with us this way from now on?"

"I tell you, no more will I drink of the fruit of the vine until the day I drink of it new in God's kingdom. But you, do this in memory of me. I will not leave you orphaned. I will return to you. You will come to know that I am in the Father, you are in me, and I am in you."

"Lord," Philip cried, "show us the Father. That's what we really want."

A great weariness invaded Jesus' luminous eyes. "Have I been with you all this time, Philip, and you know me not? Whoever has seen me has seen the Father. The Father and I are one."

"I still don't understand," Philip stammered. "I wonder if I'll ever understand."

"You will, Philip, all of you. I'm going to ask the Father, and he'll send you another Advocate, the Holy Spirit. He'll instruct you in everything—bring to mind every teaching I've given you."

He stood, and one glance told them that the moment of intimacy was gone, that a new current was about to flow. "When I sent you on journeys with no provisions, did you experience a lack?"

"No!" Peter enthused, and all nodded.

"This time, take traveling bag and money—and if you lack a sword, buy one. The Scripture must be proved true where it says, 'He was counted among the lawbreakers.' One by one, the prophecies about me are becoming the facts."

John's eye sped to the two rusty weapons on the wall. Triumphantly he leaped up and pulled them loose. "Look, Lord," he said, "two swords!"

"Enough!" The sharp reprimand was lost on Peter and John, gleefully engrossed in fastening the scabbards to their waists. They were still taking literally his exhortations to spiritual armament. "We leave." It was nine o'clock.

In the darkness under the Paschal moon they began picking their way down the treacherous path and steps which drifted in a southeasterly direction into the steep declivity of the Valley of Gehenna. Out of the darkness came his voice, unrecognizably somber: "You'll all fall away tonight."

"Never I!" roared Peter.

"You, Peter, will deny me."

"No! No! No!"

"It is written, 'The shepherd I shall strike, and the sheep will be scattered.' After I've risen, I'll go to the Galilee before you."

"Not me," the big fisherman rumbled on to himself.

"Nor me," mumbled the others.

"Peter," came the Master's voice, heavy as the roll of ocean surf, "three denials before the cock crows twice."

They exited the Pottery Gate, turned into the Kidron Valley, and went east over the Brook Kidron—where David had crossed in flight from traitors a thousand years before.

Hardly had they begun the ascent of the Mount of Olives when he led them into the familiar olive garden hemmed in by cemeteries. There in Gethsemane they slumped down, but he went apart and fell on his face in prayer.

357

10

Abba, I sift the layers of my life—to no purpose. I fail. Fail to win this land of stones—stone hearts—stony eyes. And I—let not my heart lie like a stone within.

Father, what is your will? For my blood they lust—that is not your will! My *yes* you ask—not my gore.

Last Passover—the old priest—coming from the slaughter of ten thousand lambs—red hands thrown up in my face. "Does the Holy One," he moaned, "want these rivers of blood?" Came my grief, "Let it be so for now."

For how long, Father, the bleating and bleeding? Your Enemy gloats over the rivers of blood—diverts them to rivers of rebellion against you. Am even I—your Onlybegotten— to feel terror before your will?

How dam the polluted river of Adam? By my gore alone? Or by rivers of gore—by eyes vacant with hunger—bodies twisted with disease—thrust through with swords? Is there no other way?

Sinews of rebel flesh draw me. Nightmare haunts me— your Son bellowing *Non Serviam*—I won't obey!

Do you fuse me with sinners? Join me to sin? Am I to drain sin into my vitals—its sewer and cesspool?

Like this sap-laden young olive tree, I bear the fruit of life. None salts *its* roots or hews *it* down. Yet they creep here guided by my friend with bobbing lantern, axe in hand. Those gnarled old trees yonder, sapless, hoary old men squatting misshapen under the moon—still they stand! My sorrow wells up like water in a leaky boat. Fear surges like storm-tossed seas, sweeping me away like a chip on a breaker.

These arms reach out to my friends—where are they? My dear—I will no longer remember his name—the man of Carioth—I chose and called him. I failed. He trades my love for pearls, flicks me off like a maggot, grinds me like a beetle under his heel. My lonely soul calls out like a solitary sparrow on a rooftop—no answer comes.

To what you want, yes, yes! Still no answer? My terror rises up like milk boiling over. See, I lift my mouth from the dirt—go to my friends. What! Asleep, Simon, though I charged you to watch with me? On guard! Pray to escape the struggle. Spirits are willing, flesh so weak. I go back to loneliness.

Father, dissolve this nightmare. You can do anything. Bring the dawn! Decree that I am no longer the Suffering Servant, that I walked sorrow's vale too long, that my heart died of sorrow, and now is resurrected to joy. Banish the tally of sin and settlement. Undo the gore, the bleatings, the filth. Yet do only your will! There, I've said it again. Where are you? Loneliness entombs me. I am more lonely than Eveless Adam. The Spirit hovered, the ages waited with bated breath, now love has come, and they receive not—they receive not love. To the house of my loved ones I hastened only to hear the bolt shot, and within they wither. Can it be that by me the house of my loved ones is brought down? No, Father! My dear new Eve, yearning to be born, refused into life.

Peter, on hands and knees I come to you, journeying from heaven to earth, from Eternity into blood and flesh— here, a beast crawling. Is the end of my journey—death? Yes, I shall rise again, but it seems too little. Rise to condemn friends? Peter, asleep again? Awaken! What—no word? I go back, mouth to the earth, a starving child, eating loneliness.

Arms and legs, crawl not away, leaving them all behind, leaving them to hell. Obey! Stay!

Father, it's so dark, the darkness of failure. Even had I failed, been useless, I would not leave them—ever! Sinners I have loved, as you have loved me unsinning. For them I do what you do for me, join them to my life. Yes, I will let their sins pour into my vitals. I will never leave your will—ever! I have implored you to take it away—but I'll not go away. I have besought you to do my will. *Yet not what I will but what you will.* There, a third time I say it, for all time, and need say no more. A red goblet from this angel? I drink, find strength, yet in its crimson depths discover gore, vacant eyes, bleating lambs starving, filth and rebellion. Outrages, five wounds, abandonment, darkness. There! I am drunk with it.

No more delay—I go. Where? Where you send me, your

Son—*to be man.* How? By embracing your will—even dying. Obedience I have learned. Have I not walked the path of courage, shown myself Son of Man? I have kept your mandate, observed your statutes, commands, ordinances and decrees—and shall to the end, overfilling the Law.

I came as David's son and Lord, came in Moses' stead to endure rebellion and not doubt. Came as him whom Melchisedek prefigured, and Abraham, sacrificing the Isaac still in my loins, the Suffering Servant led to slaughter, carrying my posterity to the grave within me, carrying them out to resurrection. Then they will remember you confessed me your Son. And even as I learded to become your Son enfleshed, they will learn of me unfleshed. They will know that I AM, and wait in joy to share my sonship at my coming in Daniel's clouds to claim dominion.

The sages interpreted the Scriptures to promise the Messiah many helpers, sharers of his burden. But all of them together foretold only me, me alone. Alone I tread the wine press of your wrath, I, I alone. Drunk with the cup of your wrath, I stagger up and go my way—*your Son.*

11

Panting and fleeing and clung to by the dismal swamp, he was pursued by some unnameable creature projecting a lurid beam from its single orb, raying it back and forth, searching him out, when the swamp metamorphosed into the hooting of an owl (the source was actually the advance scout of the arresting force). Heavy lids lifting, he saw the figure bending over him, half obscuring the bright eye of the paschal moon. Then he became aware of the hand shaking him awake—for the third time. He was sick with shame before the words came—"So you're still sleeping, Peter, taking it easy?"

Lurching to his feet, feeling dreadfully cold, flinging his arms around his trunk, he brushed the Master's cloak.

360

It was wet. He brought hand to mouth and nostrils. "Blood!" He sounded strangled.

"No more sleep! Get up, all of you. The hour's late. The Son of Man is betrayed to sinful powers. See, the traitor's here."

The big fisherman peered about wildly, saw bobbing torches and lanterns approaching. Clumsily he tore his sword from its sheath and stood at bay. His eyes bulged. The lead lantern had lifted, illuminating the countenance of Judas.

"My Master!" The traitor ran up, embraced the Master, and kissed him. The police—Temple guards led by Malchus, a familiar slave of Caiaphas'—rushed in.

"No you don't!" Bellowing and leaping, Peter raised his sword and hewed wildly. The slave ducked. His right ear hung down, dangling against his neck, dripping. The Master called out sharply.

"No more of that!"

"*Milites Romani!*" John barked. "Behind!" Peter spun. A horde of Roman soldiers were advancing, tribune in the lead. Peter's sword dropped from nerveless fingers. The Master lifted the dangling ear into place. The bleeding stopped. The police seized him, bound his arms, fastened a rope around his neck.

"So—you treat me like a robber," the Master said. "Swords and clubs. Haven't I been in the Temple with you daily, teaching? You didn't lay a finger on me. Let the Scriptures be proved right. This is the darkness-hour."

Peter broke and ran, the others darting after. A young disciple came panting into the garden at this point and sized up the situation too late. A guard lunged at him, seized him by the linen sheet which covered him. He pulled free, ran naked through the night. "Ha! Ha!" guffawed the guard, thrusting the sheet in the Master's face. "What brave followers!"

There was no pursuit. Orders mandated only the Master's arrest. A burly guard yanked the neck-rope and led him off.

Hearing no pursuers, Peter halted. John, in the lead, stopped and returned. The rest had scattered. As he grunted,

"They don't want us," a lone figure sped toward them, and Peter grabbed for his sword. The scabbard was empty.

"It's me," a taut voice gasped, "Mark." He was naked.

"What!" The big fisherman tore off his cloak and wrapped it around him.

"A guard grabbed my sheet—all I had on."

"What brought you?"

"A nightmare—about the arrest. So I came."

"Go back home. By this path." They watched him disappear into the darkness, his glossy hair shining in the moonlight.

"Look!" John barked. Lanterns and torches were streaming out of the garden.

"I'm following." Peter's voice sounded muffled.

"Not without me."

They followed well behind. The arresting force moved as silently as it had come, across the Brook Kidron and up into the city by the Sheep Gate. Where the Antonia loomed up, dominating the sky, blackening the blackness, the Roman cohort detached and filed into the fort, and the accompanying rabble began dispersing, stripping the party down to the Temple guards and the prisoner.

"The Romans may stay out of this." Peter gulped down a hopeful breath.

The guards treaded silently through the twisting streets of the sleeping city. Tied in the courtyard of many a house was the yearling lamb which would be sacrificed in the Temple at three the next afternoon. Down into the Kidron Valley would be channeled a river of blood, to be sold to gardeners for fertilizer.

They shadowed the arresting force to the southwest quadrant of the city. It turned south just short of the Hippicus Tower and the western wall, passed the palace of Herod the Great—long since requisitioned for the Roman administration center—and entered the courtyard of Annas. As the two lurked uncertainly in the shadows near the gate, down in the Valley of Gehenna a cock crowed, and Peter stirred uneasily.

"I'll see what's going on," John announced. "I know the portress—I used to sell fish here. Coming?"

"No. What good would we be to him as prisoners?"

John left. Fifteen minutes later he hurried back.

"What's happening?" Peter croaked.

"The Master angered Annas by pointing out that he's taught in public, said all he has to say. A guard struck him hard with his rod—almost knocked out his right eye. His nose is bleeding, maybe broken." Peter swore. "We'd better get away from the gate," John added. "Annas is sending him to Caiaphas."

Dragging the Master, the police filed out, turned south, and ascended the steeply rising street. In minutes they reached the courtyard of the reigning high priest, turned in, and entered the palace. Not a hundred yards away was the upper room where this night had begun.

"Coming in?" the younger man asked. Peter saw a bonfire in the courtyard, and shivered.

"Don't think I will."

John approached the gate and waved to the portress. The slave girl recognized him and gestured him through. He made for the palace, and disappeared within. Peter fidgeted, looked longingly at the fire, and abruptly sidled through the gate. The girl stared suspiciously in the fitful glow of the bonfire, seized her lamp, and thrust it into his face. "Aren't you that rabble-rouser's follower?"

"Naw." He kept walking. She glared as he joined the circle of guards, shivering and extending his hands to the fire.

"An easy night's work," an officer chortled. "If that prisoner's a guerrilla, I'm an elephant. Why, his followers are scared lambs!" He stared at the interloper. "Where's your cloak?"

"Who knew it'd get this cold?"

A guard tossed him a sheet. "Use this till you warm up." He turned to the others. "Grabbed it from that kid who scooted from the garden naked as the day he was born! All he had on. What do you think he was up to?" His dirty laugh roared through the night, then choked off. "Say, weren't you with that prophet from Nazareth?"

He didn't answer at once—he couldn't. His trembling fingers dropped the sheet. Why so cold? It wasn't that cold. *No more of that!* the Master had charged when he used his sword. What could he use? Danger on every side, and all his

363

weapons stripped away by the Master's teaching. He couldn't smash in that leering face with his big fist and run—he wasn't supposed to hate or to fear. What had the Master done to him? He felt like the helpless little boy he had once been, coming cold out of the lake at night, alone, to find his clothes gone. He couldn't have felt more helpless issuing from the womb. But he wasn't, damn it! Inwardly he cursed in dread and frustration. He was stripped of his manhood, his identity—he didn't know this impotent Peter. Picking up the sheet, he cowled his head, obscuring his face—and knew he had to answer. Well, whatever, he wasn't caving in! He opened his mouth, and the words shocked him—somebody else babbling obscenities with his voice. "Man, what the hell are you jabbering about? I don't know any prophet from Nazareth."

"Don't give me that! Didn't you try to cleave my cousin's brain there in the garden?"

"What garden? Stir that fire. I'm cold."

Caiaphas glared at the prisoner in rage and frustration. Until now, every detail had clicked off like fate. Arrayed before him as the fruit of his consummate planning were the Chief Priests, elders of the Temple, and Temple theologians—all members of the Temple Committee, and all Sadducees. But of the score of witnesses screened from the hundreds interrogated in recent weeks, no two concurred in any significant testimony. By the Law, one mouth was worthless. And the prisoner sat boring him with the blood-shot eye, objecting to nothing, saying nothing. Nothing had been turned up to warrant the death penalty by any trick of the trade. Unless he could be induced to incriminate himself, the case was hopeless.

His head shot up—a witness was corroborating the testimony of another: "I heard this fellow bragging, 'I can destroy this hand-built Temple, and in three days raise another not built with hands.'" It was maddeningly tantalizing, but not good enough. Why didn't they say he *planned* to tear down the Temple? Then Pilate would be forced to act, since the Romans protected the temples of subject peoples to keep the peace. He was getting nowhere.

He leaped up, surged toward the prisoner. "Why aren't you answering these charges? Don't you have a shred of evidence in your own defense? What is this maliciousness of which they accuse you?" The rattling echoes from the stone walls mockingly reaccused him, but the prisoner sat as though unhearing. Caiaphas rushed over and glared eye to eye. "You are the Christ, the Son of the Blessed One?" He said, "Blessed One," because not even he, the high priest, dared to pronounce the personal Name revealed to Moses except in rare and defined liturgical instances. The court rose and strained forward in the silence, and out of it the Master's voice rang out once in the house of Caiaphas.

"I AM. Your own eyes will see the Son of Man sitting at the right hand of the Power, approaching with the clouds of heaven."

Gasping histrionically, Joseph Caiaphas wheeled so all could witness his horror. "Blasphemy!" He tore violently at his cloak. "What need for witnesses? You have heard him!"

"Blasphemy! Blasphemy!" The room swelled with the cry.

"You know the Law!" Caiaphas screamed. "Your decision?"

"Death! Death!"

The more rabid scurried up and spat on him. He had no time or patience for such childish antics. At once he was issuing orders. Return the prisoner to the guard house! Send couriers racing through the night to every member of the Supreme Council! It was nearing 3:00 A.M., and he was convoking a plenary session at daybreak.

The decision just reached was legally worthless. The Temple Committee had no jurisdiction over the case, though it did constitute a formidable segment of the Supreme Council, and gave him hope. It was feasible to press charges in the full assembly.

Feasible, but barely. When the Pharisees were seated, they would make it a divided court. Despite their jealousy of the Nazarene, many were legally scrupulous men. They would vote their consciences. To date, he had persuaded them to agree to nothing more than collecting witnesses against him. Tonight's work was, you might say, a liberal interpretation of that agreement.

Unless the plenary session concurred in the blasphemy

365

charge, the death penalty was out. Happily, all 70 members could not assemble on such short notice—and he had taken measures to see that the "right" members could. By his calculations, a quorum would be present. Would the legally sufficient majority vote for condemnation? He'd soon find out.

While Peter eyed the palace anxiously, a guard named Jehoram kept examining him hawkishly. "He's the swordsman!" he barked.

"Man, your brain's addled!" Peter bellowed.

"Ha! Fear crusts his face like mud in a wadi. And his Galilean accent's thicker than goat's cream. He's the Nazarene's!"

"Damn it, man, I don't know him. I swear it!"

Jehoram leaped up inspired. "Get Malchus. He'll settle it!"

The doors burst open and guards came clattering across the courtyard. The trailing guard gave the prisoner a vicious swipe across the back of the head. "Prophet, who struck you?" He was infected with his Sadducean masters' scorn of prophecy.

"Let's get in on the fun," Jehoram chortled, moving toward the guardhouse. The rest trailed after.

The Master's eyes met Peter's, and they gazed at one another. Up from Gehenna came a cock-crow. The guard yanked him along.

Rising from the fire, Peter felt the tears scalding his cheeks. He pulled off the white sheet and lumbered out the gate, oblivious to the portress' railings. He descended the deserted street.

In his bed behind his shutters, a father heard loud wailings and considered whether to go to the aid of that child lost in the dark.

366

12

The rivers of terror and dread pulsing through his body were backing up, as though his stifled heart were failing to make passage. When he crossed the Kidron and raced up the Mount in the darkness, it beat so wildly it must burst.

The Master, so marvelously able to win the hearts of almost everyone, given the chance, was thrust down into this dark hour when contrary forces of evil had swirled in, mysteriously carrying off the hearts of all. Even his heart was so stricken he felt nothing but horror. Didn't the people care? Didn't they know? Perhaps, if there were time . . . but there is none.

Peter lay in a drugged sleep under the little tent too small for his body. He shook him violently until he awoke.

"What is it, John?"

"Bad news. Wait 'til I call James."

He was back with his brother in moments. "It's about four, and they plan to try Jesus before the Supreme Council at daybreak. The charge is blasphemy."

"No!" Peter bellowed. The penalty was death. "For what?"

John reported what he had heard of the ordeal. "We ought to be on hand for the trial, in case we can do something."

"Wake the Eleven," Peter barked. When they were huddled under the stars on the mountain, chattering from the cold, Peter and John reported.

"What can we do?" Thomas moaned.

"I know what I'm going to do," John snapped. "The Supreme Council will meet in the Chamber of Hewn Stone at dawn. I'm entering the Court of the Israelites when the gates open." The southern edge of the Court abuts the Chamber of Hewn Stone.

"That's my plan," Peter said.

"I'll join you," James offered. The others said nothing.

Daylight was just breaking and the ram's horn sounding as the three ascended to the Temple esplanade and passed through the Nicanor Gate into the Court of the Israelites. There was only a scattering of worshippers, mostly old men. Priests were offering the morning sacrifice at the great outdoor altar amid the smoke and fragrance of incense and roasted flesh. Levites were preparing for the great slaughter of paschal lambs that afternoon.

They made their way toward the courthouse. "They're in session," John said. "Do you hear the shouting?"

"No," Peter grunted. "The priests are too noisy."

As they approached, the voices within were loud, but the echoes garbled the words. With mounting anxiety, they strained to understand the excited voices, and never succeeded. A half-hour passed.

The doors flew open and the judges swarmed out, conversing in high perturbation. There was no sign of the Master. John rushed to one of the emerging guards. "What's the verdict?"

The officer eyed him suspiciously. "Why? Are you a disciple?"

"Yes." The guard eyed him with grudging admiration. "At least you're not like the others."

"What's the verdict?"

"Let that be as it may. Scoot while you can."

"Where is the Master?"

"The accused? Led by way of the outer entrance, so as not to desecrate the Temple."

John sped back to the others. "James, would you . . ."

"They plan to pressure Pilate into condemning him to death," Peter interrupted, his face ashen. "We heard them."

"They voted the death penalty?"

"We don't know," James said. "It sounds like the referral to Pilate is being engineered by the Sadducees."

"You may be right!" John exclaimed. "Where the death penalty's involved, the vote can't be taken until the day after the evidence is heard. So they couldn't have rendered sentence."

"Not legally!" Peter snorted.

"In any case, Pilate may not go along," John said plaintively. The Jewish authorities could execute no one. When they voted the death penalty, they had to remand the case to the governor for final decision.

"John, where's the Master now?" Peter asked.

"Led off by the outer exit."

"James, follow him," Peter said, "while we find out

368

what we can. We'll meet at the Center." James vanished into the growing crowd of worshippers.

Finding they were unable to learn more, Peter and John set out for the Roman administration center. A disorderly crowd was milling about the square fronting the executive mansion. James saw them and hurried over. "The chief priests and elders told Pilate"—his voice raced—"that he's fomenting a guerrilla war to become king."

"Did Pilate swallow that?" John was incredulous.

"He's no fool. He questioned the Master briefly, apparently got nowhere, and sent him to Herod." Herod was in the city for Passover, his palace just a few minutes away.

"This is Judea," John protested. "He has no jurisdiction."

"Pilate knows he'll get no justice from Herod," Peter added. "He murdered John!"

"Maybe that's why he was sent," James said with tight lips.

"Maybe Herod won't act either," John suggested. "They all wish the Master off their hands, but none wants to brave the people's wrath."

"Cover Herod's palace," Peter directed. "I'll watch here." The brothers nodded and moved off. Peter waited with terrible anxiety for what seemed hours. Actually, it was about 9:00 A.M. The square was filling with excited people, but he learned with bitterness that few were there for the Master's sake. Most were gathering to protest the planned execution of Barabbas the Zealot, condemned for treason, robbery, and murder. Pilate was wasting no time. The dangerous firebrand was slated for execution this morning.

Peter spotted Jude entering the square with Mary Magdalene and intercepted them. He told them what had happened, and they stood waiting together.

"Look!" Peter pointed. Mary gasped piteously. The Master was coming, dragged by soldiers, his face bloodied, swollen, and disfigured almost beyond recognition, his tunic covered with a moth-eaten cape of royal purple. He was taken into the building. James and John came up well behind.

"What happened?" Peter asked.

"As near as we could find out," John replied, "Prince

369

Herod listened to the chief priests' charges, and questioned Jesus. He refused to answer or perform magic, so Herod incited the soldiers to mock him as a pretender-king. You saw how they outfitted him."

"Look." Jude pointed. "A messenger's hurrying off."

"To fetch our leaders back," John guessed. "Pilate's wary. That crowd's already in a wicked mood over Barabbas. His partisans are all over the place."

"Pilate," James observed, "wouldn't be the first of our governors that Caesar fired for failing to keep the peace."

Minutes later, the messenger returned with a cluster of chief priests, theologians, and leading laymen. "They're not going in," Mary cried.

"Not on your life!" John exclaimed. "They have to eat the Pasch tonight. They'd incur legal defilement by entering a Gentile residence. Pilate will have to come out."

Before Pilate appeared, a buzz spreading through the crowd reached them. "The chief priests are with us in demanding Barabbas. Pass the word to sacrifice the Nazarene." Peter wanted to smash in the stupid face.

Attired in judicial robes, Pilate emerged with Jesus. Ignoring the Jewish authorities, he mounted the Judgment Dais. Imperiously, he signalled for silence. "By merciful custom, I release a favorite son at Passover. Do you want the King of the Jews?" He pointed to Jesus.

"Barabbas! Give us Barabbas!" someone shouted. The cry surged through the square, drowning all dissenters. Pilate looked stunned, then angry. He marched down the steps and strode to the Jewish authorities.

"I'll listen in," John announced, moving off.

"That's dangerous," Peter cautioned.

"Life's dangerous."

Peter and the others, watching, heard the shouts and saw the wild gesticulations. Pilate spun on his heel and left, and John returned. "It looks grim. First, Pilate shouted, 'I expected you to handle this!' And they objected, 'You know we can't apply the death penalty.' 'Death penalty!' he answered. 'On what charge? You produce nothing but allegations.' 'We have a religious law,' they said, 'that demands death because he claims to be God's Son.' 'Religious law?' he roared.

'That's no concern of mine! Punish him within your competence. Scourge him, jail him!' Then they said, 'Yesterday you were concerned he's rousing the people. Isn't treason your concern—a man who would be king?' Pilate answered, 'He tells me his kingdom's in another world.' Then they laughed and pointed to the crowd: 'His followers are in this world—wards of Rome. He forbids tax money for Caesar, promises a new kingdom, and as you saw yesterday, has the people on the verge of revolution.' 'Is that,' Pilate hissed, 'why they just sacrificed him to Barabbas the revolutionary? Jealous liars!' Then they pressed Pilate: 'Release this man and you're no Friend of Caesar's.' Pilate snarled, 'He's not guilty of your charges. I'll discipline him and release him.' That's when he stomped away."

Pilate strode into the soldiers' courtyard. The orderlies dragged Jesus after him. "Scourge him—to within an inch of his life," Pilate ordered Longinus the centurion. "It may," he added loftily, "save his life. Use a team to lay on the strokes. I'm in a hurry." He watched coldly as they stripped Jesus and tied him to the pillar by his wrists, fastened high, to make him stand tiptoe. Tautening the back muscles would make the scourges dig deeper. A pair of scourgers approached briskly with two-thonged whips of hardened leather, into which lead balls were fastened. One man was tall and one short, so as not to interfere with one another's work. The clerk called out his count.

"One-and-two!" The first whip whistled and fell with a sharp crack. The body jerked under the blow—and the convulsion redoubled as the second blow fell. "Three-and-four!" the clerk chanted, and two more blows fell alongside the two red welts from which blood was seeping. By the sixth blow, the blood streamed. By the fifteenth, bits of skin and flesh flew from the bloody pulp. By the thirtieth, the body, gone limp, no longer produced spasms. From shoulders to ankles, red welts showed, and the whip ends curled around to flagellate the chest and front of the legs.

An orderly approached and reported woodenly. "A messenger with an urgent communication." Pilate left.

At forty strokes the scourgers' blows were markedly weakening. The centurion ordered fresh lash-men. At

371

sixty-four, the flow of blood was copious. No further punishment could be chanced. "Enough. Cut him down," Longinus barked. The body crumpled to the stone pavement. "Douse him with water. Cold!" The icy well-water was slow in bringing the prisoner around, but at last his eyes opened. Pilate had not returned.

Nearby, soldiers were playing the Game of Kings inscribed in the striated limestone pavement. A soldier picked up the dice for the fateful toss which would crown or condemn him. "Look," he blustered. "I'm a sport. I'll roll for the prisoner. Is it the cross or the crown?" He threw the dice. "It's king for a day!" The soldiers cheered.

"Let's crown him!" a young soldier shouted gleefully. From the pile of firewood he plucked a handful of thorny vines. Cursing each time the sharp spines stung him, he plaited a crown. He went to the prisoner, barely conscious, propped against a pillar, and drove the thorns into his skull with the limb of a tree. The head jerked as the spines pierced, and the blood ran into the eyes.

"Hail the king!" the soldiers railed, striking his head with whatever came to hand.

"Enough," growled Longinus. Even his guts couldn't stand it.

The message was from Pilate's wife. Though her quarters were yards away, she never came during office hours. "The commotion awakened me, and I learned about your prisoner," she had written. "Have nothing to do with him. He's a holy man. I was wakened from a terrible dream about him. Claudia."

With a curse, Pilate crumpled the parchment. Have nothing to do with him? How? He'd tried to pawn off the prisoner on Herod who, as tetrarch of his home district, had power of execution over him, and as a Jew by religious profession— though not ethnically—had a special interest in this matter.

Having heard that the Nazarene once dubbed Herod the fox, he had, in an upbeat mood, sent with the prisoner a message: "The game outsped the fox before, but in my realm the fox gets more. Pilate." Herod had returned the prisoner with his own message: "Did game the fox outspeed

372

before, or fox the game elude the more? Herod." He'd roared with laughter—the man was no coward about admitting his cowardice! When this was over, he'd thought, he'd have to invite him over for a few more witticisms.

The joke had turned sour. He waved to the orderly. "Conduct the prisoner to the dais." He strode out, mounted the platform, and waited, nervous and impatient. The crowd was ranting for Barabbas.

Sight of the prisoner was a shock. He was attempting to walk, and not succeeding. The orderlies were dragging him. Blood, in dark red stains, still wet, plastered the tunic to his body. His head was covered by a cap of thorny vines, around which fresh green leaves had been wrapped to imitate the laurel wreath of a conquering hero. The eyes in the pulpy face were dazed.

Pilate rose and pointed to the judge's bench. "Put him there." The orderly looked stunned, but did as told. Turning to the noisy crowd, the governor gestured imperiously for silence.

"Gaze at your king!" he shouted. A shred of pity down there would save his life—and save him, Pilate, from a dirty, dangerous business.

"Rid us of him!" the chief priests shouted, and the mob parroted the cry.

"Crucify him!" the chief priests bellowed, and their demand spread like fire in pitch. Pilate tried to speak— vainly. He waited for the uproar to wear down, then motioned for silence.

"Shall I crucify your king?"

"Our only king is Caesar!" the priests shouted, and the mob chanted the words. "We want Barabbas!" came the counterpoint.

Pilate nodded to the orderlies. They dragged the prisoner to his feet, and Pilate sat. The outcry died away. A silver basin was brought, and ostentatiously he washed his hands— twice, to mock the custom of the Jews.

"I'm innocent of this man's blood," he lied. "See to the thing yourselves."

The hue and cry went up, and he let it prevail.

373

13

A heavy beam across his shoulders, Jesus was led away as the little knot of disciples watched. Simon the Zealot saw them, hurried over, and cried, "There's a rumor the chief priest of the Temple's ordering our arrest." Peter tensed with alarm.

"Let's go. We'll meet at the Galilee and decide our next move. Coming?" He hurried off. The others trailed after him.

"I'm following Jesus," John called after them. He took the Magdalene's hand. "Come on." They hurried after the Roman soldiers.

The mother of Jesus hadn't heard. Praying in the crowded Court of Women since early morning, she had not been found despite a desperate search. Mary, the wife of Clopas, frantically threaded back and forth through the Court, at last locating her bent in worship.

"They've arrested your son," she said in a crooning, moaning voice, pressing her hand. "They've charged him before Pilate, who's beaten him terribly."

A cry of anguish escaped her. She stared wide-eyed, then turned and fled through the press. "I'm coming too," the wife of Clopas called, speeding after her. They fought their way through the narrow, crowded streets packed with shoppers carrying their voluminous bags and baskets and lambs slung over shoulders bleating laments. They came out on Market Street, which was the most direct route to the administration center.

Up ahead was a worse congestion, and an outcry which drowned out the sounds of haggling. A squad of Roman soldiers came into view waving naked swords, opening a swath through the crowd. Mary did not slacken her advance until the soldiers threatened to overrun her. At the last moment she stepped aside. Behind the lead soldiers she saw him.

It was hard even to believe it was he. He was one of three condemned men, each with a cross-beam on his shoulders. A jumble of thorns grotesquely resembling a crown was jammed on his head. His hair was matted, his face bruised and disfigured, the right eye swollen shut, his beard caked with dirt and blood. He staggered along, bent almost double under the weight of the beam.

She darted between the soldiers and ran to him. He stopped, and for one moment they looked at each other. Then she embraced him. The centurion rushed up.

"None of that! No lovers' trysts. Drag her away."

"It's his mother," the wife of Clopas pleaded.

"Oh." Longinus went to her, took her arm firmly. "I'm sorry, mother, but you'll have to move out of the way. You shouldn't have come."

John and the Magdalene, just behind, saw the exchange. John went to her. She was rigid with shock, her face and cloak smeared with blood. He took her left arm, and Mary the wife of Clopas took the other. Mary Magdalene trailed behind.

The squad moved on, followed by a procession of sympathizers, mostly women, their wailing all but drowned in the bedlam of the market place. The beam projecting from Jesus' shoulder grazed the arm of a passerby and he cursed. The hucksters continued to hawk their wares, offering the soldiers special bargains.

The most direct route to the Place of the Skull was by way of the Jaffa Gate, hard by the administration center, but Roman justice demanded this public display as a deterrent to crime. In other subject countries the centurion had followed the Roman practice of driving condemned men naked through the streets, scourging them like running dogs along the way, but these holier-than-thou Jews would not tolerate such treatment, even of their criminals.

The doomed men were led out through the Judgment Gate. For a while Longinus thought the Nazarene would never make it, but after a passer-by was dragooned to carry his beam it appeared he might not have to be carried himself after all. On they went up the steep hill of Calvary. The centurion felt dirty. He hadn't missed the political intrigue swirling around the Nazarene, and knew he'd been victimized. He thought sardonically of Pilate's brand of "mercy"— the brutal scourging to "save" him. Well, it might at least

375

end his torture sooner. Men could live on a cross for three days.

At last they arrived. The prisoners were stripped, and offered drugged wine. The Nazarene refused his. "Master," the centurion said gruffly, half in irony, half in respect, "take it. It's a damned terrible ordeal you face." He shook his head. Longinus hardened his features in a forced expression of indifference and got to the work at hand.

Judas strode toward Caiaphas' mansion, legs lashing out like whips, feeling godlike. He'd single-handedly saved Israel from disaster, conquering that messianic pretender—dashing his disruptive pretensions. Who knew what heights he might rise to for the work of this day?

From out of the crowd a familiar face detached itself, but its identity didn't register—everything seemed far away.

"Judas, what's wrong? You look terrible!"

He stopped, shocked by the assessment. "Nothing's wrong."

"Don't you recognize me? I'm David. I stayed with the Master a couple of times."

He stared at the boy. "Of course I recognize you."

"Where's the Master? Can I be of any help?"

"No, but I may find a place for you in my plans."

"Your plans? If he tells me to help, I will."

"Forget it!" He strode on angrily. Was everyone as blind as the Master to his powers of leadership? Hadn't he done what Herod trembled at the thought of, what the high priests wrung their hands with impotent desire of, what Rome was afraid of? He alone had brought the man down!

If only the man had listened to him, let him make the plans! The Master's magnetism drew people like flies to a rotting fish, but he had no sense of planning. Even the throat of Rome wasn't out of reach! Her subject peoples were ripe fruit ready to fall into the hands of a charismatic insurgent with vision and power. The Master could have reaped the glory, with only the strings in his, Judas', hands. The madness of wasting the historic opportunity!

He came to an abrupt halt. "It's not too late! If I offer to take him back, he may be in a chastened mood." He ploughed ahead fiercely, anxious to learn his fate—even to take a strong hand in moderating it if necessary. They'd have to listen to him, a principal in the action. His heart beat with wild hope, and elation seized him. A resourceful man's never defeated! His temples throbbed with the need to execute his latest plan. But there was no urgency. He effected a mechanical nonchalance.

He was soon rushing wildly again. There was some urgency, but what? At the administration center, he found an excited mob. "What's going on?" he demanded of the youth he seized by the arm.

"Barabbas has been released."

"What brought that about?"

"They traded off the Nazarene. He's on his way to Calvary."

The horror, the madness in the eyes, frightened the youth, and he hurried off. When the first shock passed, a new plan came. "Barabbas! Where's Barabbas?"

"Over there," a stander-by shouted.

He drove through the packed bodies like a raging bull and came face-to-face with the insurrectionist, who stood towering, staring at him stonily. "We've got to save the Master! Get your men!"

"You're mad!"

"It's possible! They use a handful of soldiers."

"Why should I?"

"Afterwards I'll arrange to have you meet him."

"You forget we've met. We have nothing for one another."

"Then you and I—I have plans. And pearls!" He pulled out his pouch.

Barabbas' face twisted with revulsion. "I wouldn't tend pigs with you."

The horror returned. He spun and ran. "What if he is what I thought from the first?"

He broke through the lines waiting to have their lambs slaughtered and, against the law, rushed up to the *kohen gadol*—chief priest—at the altar. "They've crucified the Master!"

"What's that to me?"

"I betrayed him to you!"

"Pilate's taken jurisdiction."

377

"I've betrayed innocent blood!"

"That's your problem."

"The money. Take it!" He extended a fistful of coins.

"I can't. It's blood money."

He hurled the coins over the altar, into the Porch of the Temple, and ran.

14

They thrust each prisoner down on his rough cross naked and still bleeding from his scourging, with one soldier pinioning each limb, and a fifth pounding home the spikes. The two condemned political prisoners screamed and cursed as the spikes tore through them. When they hammered the Master's home, he kept saying, "Father, forgive them. They don't know what they're doing."

"Hell," growled the mallet-wielder, "we know. We've done it too often not to!" He drove the spike through the right foot, and blood spurted and the body leaped and twitched. The feet were the worst—too many bones, he thought grimly. Wasn't it Cicero who'd said crucifixion wasn't a fit death for a Roman freeman? It wasn't fit for a beast!

John stood with the women at the base of the hill, stunned and gaping, a poled ox with bovine eyes glazed over. Mary's face was stricken, standing like some high priestess with the spared animals dumbly staring while the plunging knife of sacrifice went into her own bared breast. Magdalene's features were grief-stricken, seared with scalding tears. "No!" she cried up to the soldiers. "No!"

The centurion turned to her his scarred and seamy face, dull like armor plate in the gray light of the sordid sky. "Lady, tell Pilate—he's the judge. It's just our job."

The child's face of the young soldier holding the arm for the nail was full of horror. His girl-hungry heart had dreamed of snappy soldier's uniforms, not this. On the farm he'd seen animals slaughtered, but here—he couldn't look at the noble face attached to this body being so degraded. The sledge came down, the arm pressed up against all his weight. "Jupiter!" he swore in a tortured voice as the blood spurted in a fleeting fountain, and the naked body leaped and twitched.

The centurion listened in wonder to the Master repeating his words of forgiveness. If ever a man had a right to curse! He observed the athletic body, and thought, what a waste for him and for Rome. Better to put him to use as a galley slave.

Then his thoughts went deeper. He had heard that the Nazarene was condemned for making pretensions to divinity. He had no use for the whole zoo of Roman gods, but there must be one God, he had reasoned. A man wielding a little authority himself, he knew what bedlam ensued in its absence. The cosmos could never hang together without someone in charge. But that this man should be that One's son—absurd. Still, in all his life, he'd never seen such dignity in a tortured man—not to mention a forgiveness that boggled the mind. Wearied, he cast the whole matter out of his head.

"You know," the mallet-wielder was shouting, "I heard an old Jew say this is the spot where the first couple—Adam and Eve, they call them—had their pleasure garden. Things have sure changed!"

"I heard," drawled Longinus, "it was where the Temple stands."

"Listen to the Jews," a third soldier mocked, "and learn that every important thing has happened in Jerusalem!"

They jammed the foot of his cross into a rocky crevice, and walked it upright. When it jarred down into the pit, blood spurted from the wrists, and a spasm churned through the body.

When John saw the body raised against the lowering sky— it was still the rainy season, and black clouds were cascading in from the west, scraping the hills as they came—he numbly recalled Jesus' unintelligible words, which seemed like mockery now, "When I am lifted up, I will draw all men to me."

His mother started forward, and the other two Marys followed. John hesitated, then went after them. A soldier moved to intercept them. "Let her alone!" Longinus bellowed. "It's his mother." It was against regulations, but what the hell! He was beginning to respect these people.

A party of chief priests, Temple elders, and official theologians came bustling up to the foot of the hill. "Look at him now," one railed. "So busy about saving others—and he can't even save himself!" Cutting across the words came the mournful sound of the ram's horn, signal for the slaughter of the lamb offered each afternoon. It was just past noon—the horn was an hour early, as happened when Passover fell on Sabbath, to provide extra time for the slaying of the thousands of lambs for the Seder.

"Let the Christ, the King of Israel, come down from his cross," snorted an elder. "Seeing is believing!"

"Dismas, did you hear?" one of the crucified men shouted. "We have the honor of sharing the lot of our king!" His coarse laugh ended in a scream of pain.

"It's not too late, king," railed Dismas. "Destroy these Roman swine and we'll join your camp. Surely you won't fail us like Barabbas!"

A theologian peered near-sightedly at the inscription over the Master's head, citing his crime. "What's he charged with?"

His companion squinted. "Why, it reads, 'Jesus the Nazorean, King of the Jews.'"

"What?" roared a chief priest. "Are you sure?"

"I ought to be. It's in three languages—Aramaic, Greek, and Latin."

"An outrage!" The priest darted up the hill to the soldiers, who were casting dice for the prisoners' clothing. "Take down that inscription!"

The centurion eyed him insolently. "The governor ordered it."

"Then to the governor I go!" he screamed, and stormed off.

"Fat lot of good it'll do you," Longinus snarled, and turned back to the lottery. He'd like the Nazarene's seamless tunic, if he could get the blood out. Perhaps it could be dyed red. He joined the wrangling over the distribution of the convicts' clothes.

Mary looked up at her Son with a face melted in some fiery bath of compassionate love. How parched those lips, touched as with the white dust of the desert. How noble that face, and how stately, despite blood and wound.

Those outstretched arms, well-muscled in bicep and breast, recalled his carpenter's days when he worked so hard in sleeveless tunic. Lean was the body, lean as the life he had lived.The sturdy legs bespoke his endless preaching journeys across the land. The majesty of him reminded her of the prophecy of Baalam, "A star shall surge out of Jacob, a staff rise out of Israel." Truly, her heart cried, you are your Father's Son, O Original Daystar. And mine, O Adam's seed.

Her reverie was shattered by cries from below. "So you'd destroy the Temple and restore it in three days? Save yourself!"

"You bragged, 'I'm the Son of God.' Let him save you then."

Opening his eyes, he saw his mother's gaze. "Look at him," he said, his eyes going to John. "He's your son. And she's your mother." John wrapped his arm around her. She began weeping, but soon stopped. She looked up at him again, and began to count the wounds. She hadn't tears enough for each. When he was a little boy, she had kissed away his hurts. Now she could only share the pain.

"I thirst!" The behemoth cry from the cross announced the drying of all earth's rivers and the splitting of its crust into sandy, unslaked lips. His mother gasped. Those lips had in infancy sucked her breasts, and now they split and cracked and lamented that the breast of human kindness had shrunken and shriveled and run dry.

The swollen lips parted again, and a terrifying cry rent the air: "Eli, Eli, lama sabacthani?" Terror contracted John's heart and contorted his face. The words meant, "My God, my God, why have you forsaken me?" His mother remained calm. They were the opening words of Psalm 22, which foretold this terrible hour of the Messiah, and his final victory. Mary Magdalene screamed piercingly, rushed forward, and wrapped her arms around the calves of his legs and the upright of the cross. A soldier, mistaking the cry for an appeal to Elijah the prophet, cried, "Let's keep him alive, and see if Elijah comes." On a reed he lifted a vinegar-soaked sponge to his lips and he drank.

Suffocating from the terrible posture, he lifted his body by the nails in his feet to relieve the tension on chest and lungs. Muscles contracting with pain shook him, but his chest swelled. He turned his face toward the Temple, invisible through the black clouds hanging to the ground, darkening the day like night, though it was not yet three. The yearling male lambs would be dying by thousands, as they had died prophetically through the centuries. And as prophesied, they had given him his vinegar to drink, they had stared and gloated, they had sent the suffering servant toward his early grave—all as foretold. His bosom friend had done his traitorous deed, broadcast even to his forefathers, and kings and leaders had conspired as the seers saw. The cracked lips opened.

"It is accomplished!" Like a peal of thunder, the cry drowned all other sounds, dumbfounding the bystanders. It would not have been stranger to see a dove's egg splinter, and the new-born chick emerge, spread its wings and fly away with the cry of an eagle.

Dismas wondered at that victory cry. Accomplished? Achieved? He had listened to everything, but this triumphant proclamation of warrior with spoils in hand spoke more eloquently than all else to his soldier's heart. It was unmistakable. Had he gone mad? Or was he what they accused him of being—God's Son and Messiah?

"Hey, Messiah!" his fellow-terrorist shouted, "are you dead? What're you waiting for? Save us!" He shrieked with malicious laughter. This was too much for Dismas.

"Shut up! Don't you know you're dying rotten with hate? Shouldn't we fear God, with our record?" He became conscious of the faint jeering from the city wall, always lined with spectators during crucifixions. It added a sick feeling to his wracking pain, and he felt consciousness ebbing. With a fierce effort, he struggled to come to the surface. He was desperate—had he waited too long? Was the Messiah dead? At the cost of great torture, he turned his head and made out the occasional heaving of the chest. A wild joy surged up.

"Jesus! Remember me when you start reigning!"

The low-hanging head lifted and turned his way. "Accept my word: this day you will be with me in paradise."

The exchange had a powerful effect. Raucous voices fell silent, or dropped to whispers. One and another sidled away and disappeared. The rest stared at the quiescent figure. They had not long to wait. With a cry like a lion seizing his prey he spoke once more, his face to heaven.

"Father, into your hands I entrust my spirit!"

The soldiers, ignorant of Aramaic, made coarse remarks, but the young soldier, stricken by the cry, and observing the centurion's eyes go vacant as the eyes of a Greek statue, pleaded for information. "What did he say?"

Woodenly, the centurion translated the Aramaic phrase, staring at the figure, which seemed poised for something, and then—"Aiiii!" The terrible cry rived rocks, which he did not wait to see. He let his head decline gently upon the bloody breast, and was quit of mortal life forever.

Amazed by the power of that last cry, the centurion came up close and stared long at the stone-still figure. He turned to John. "That man—your Master—he really was the Son of God."

John said nothing.

"What must I do to be saved?"

"You kill him—and now you want to be saved by him!" John's voice was bitter.

Mary looked at the brutal face, a middle-aged face, shadowed by the metal helmet. The lips were thin, and trembled slightly. The shaven face was scarred and seamed, like the bark of a tree. The eyes were different. In them swam a timeless grief, ancient and comfortless as the cracked and barren mountains beyond Jericho. In their despair was a fleeting hope, fast fading. Swiftly she reached out and took the hard, coarse hand hanging by his side.

"My name is Mary; his, John. Come to us at the Galilee. We'll tell you of him, and what you must do to be saved."

At her words, John relented. "I'll welcome you."

"My name's Longinus. I'll come."

A few minutes later, just after three, a courier trotted up with new orders from the governor. Longinus read them and barked, "Break their legs, but not the king's—he's dead." He was disobeying orders in omitting the king, but it wasn't necessary. Without use of their legs, the other two would quickly suffocate, and could be taken down and buried before the feast began.

Overhearing the order, John recalled how, at their Seder, Jesus, on carving the lamb, had repeated the scriptural admonition, "Break no bone of him."

With terrible blows that evoked screams of agony, the soldiers broke the terrorists' legs. A soldier went to the central cross, and peered at the body suspiciously. "Just in case," he grunted, and before the centurion could object, thrust his lance into the heart. There were no convulsions. A stream of separated blood and water poured out after the withdrawn weapon. "He's dead, all right." Longinus looked angry, but said nothing. John did not then recall the prophecy of Zechariah, "They shall stare at the one they pierced, and mourn as over an only son."

A few minutes later a fat, dignified man in his late fifties came puffing up the hill with two slaves. John recognized him. Joseph of Arimathea, a secret disciple—from fear. As he exchanged words with Longinus, Nicodemus appeared, carrying a jar of anointing oil. He puffed up the hill hurriedly. Custom required burial before sunset on the day of death, and furthermore, the Paschal feast began within hours.

The centurion led his troops away, and the two disciples approached the mother of Jesus. "I cannot tell you my sorrow," Joseph said. "I have the governor's permission to bury your son in my tomb, which is nearby." He pointed to a garden.

John helped the two men and the slaves lower the cross to the ground, and he draped the body with his cloak. They pried endlessly at the spikes. When he was free, his mother said, "Put him here." Seated on a rock, she pointed to her lap. Joseph hesitated, then complied. Her tears melted the caked blood on his breast.

Joseph laid a hand on her arm. "We must hurry."

They carried the body down the hill. Joseph spread a linen shroud on the anointing stone, and they rested the body on it. "We can't take time for ablutions," Joseph apologized.

John removed the cloak, and Nicodemus hurriedly poured the oil freely over the body. Joseph put a small coin on each eyelid. The Magdalene fastened the chinstrap, and his mother swathed the head in wrappings. John folded the shroud over the top of the head and down to the feet, and fastened it.

They carried the body to the tomb, a cave in the rock outcropping. Crouching, they bore it through the low entrance, and laid it calmly on the burial ledge.

They emerged solemn and mournful. The slaves laid their shoulders to the head-high stone disc beside the entrance. Once dislodged, gravity carried it down its groove, and it settled across the opening. Several strong men would be required to roll it back for the next burial.

A group of mourning women who had remained for the burial now approached and offered his mother their condolences. Then the men led her away, and the women followed. Only Mary, the mother of James and Joseph, noticed the bowed figure of the Magdalene remaining behind, opposite the tomb, staring forlornly. Wordlessly she went and sat beside her in the darkness. After a while she murmured, "We must go now, dear one." Gently she led her away.

Young David, strolling along the street of the cheesemakers, was trying to put his strange encounter with Judas out of his mind. He gazed around at the stands, and enjoyed the look and smells of the cheeses, pastries, honeyed candies, dates and nuts. He thought of the feast he'd soon be enjoying at home—but how much better if he could share the *Master's* Passover!

A tear-stained band of women entered the street wailing aloud. "Something bad's happened," a vendor bawled. "I'll bet they seized another patriot."

No one asked who "they" were. It was always the Romans.

"What's wrong?" David called to the women.

"They just killed Jesus the prophet."

"O God!" came a man's tortured voice. David cried. A woman shrieked. Some fell to their knees, sobbing out prayers.

"Those Roman murderers!" the vendor spat out.

"The high priests were behind it too," a woman sobbed.

A little girl, frightened by the changed mood, clutched her father's hand and blubbered. Streets began to empty, synagogues to fill. David was among the many youthful worshippers looking stunned, and wiping tears from sparse beards.

"Go home for the feast," a rabbi admonished gently.

People were at the Seder when the earthquake struck. Longinus was stabling his mount. The animal reared wildly, snorting with fear. "I knew it," he muttered. "That Jew was God's Son."

Minutes later, Caiaphas' gatekeeper opened to thunderous blows. A Levite dragging an old man rushed past and on into Caiaphas' dining hall shouting, "The Holy of Holies . . ."

"The—the earthquake?" Caiaphas stammered.

"Tobias says not." The Levite pointed to his companion.

"Sir," came the old priest's quaver, "at three I entered the holy place to fill the lamps. The curtains tore by themselves—and there I was profaning the Holy of Holies with my eyes. Then I passed out."

"We rushed in after the quake and found him," the Levite added. "I saw no damage, but the Holy of Holies is exposed."

Next morning, the chief priests, with certain Pharisees, called on the governor. "The Nazarene claimed he'd rise in three days," they informed him. "You ought to post a guard."

"You hypocrites! You never mentioned this before!" Pilate wheeled and strode, trying to suppress his rage and fear. At last he shouted, "Take what guards you need. Guard the tomb!" As he entered his mansion, he sneered, "If you can . . ."

The guards sealed the rolling stone in place, and lounged about the garden. It was a boring duty.

Part Seven

THE FINAL SECRET

1

The night of Seder yielded to dawn, and the high holy day wore away without incident, save the one south of the city, in Gehenna, the Valley of Hell. Once the site of pagan rites of human sacrifice, and now of refuse always burning, the place and its name had been loaded with meaning by the curses of the prophets—it was to be yielded up to the buried and unburied dead, and to a fire never to go out.

High on a bluff above the valley, a stunted tree overhung the ledge. Hanging down into empty space, swaying in the morning light, a body was discovered at dawn. Grotesquely arrayed in a magnificent silver robe flapping loosely in the breeze, the figure was capped by a towering gold turban so askew it hid the face. The ornate fastening from which it hung was the sash missing from the midriff. The effect was of some pagan high priest fallen victim to his own unspeakable rites.

Perhaps by reason of the high holy day, the authorities were slow to act, and the body remained swaying in the hot sun. It would not be until the next morning that the effort was made to take it down, and in the process the sash broke and the swollen body plunged into the valley and disembowled. The body was recognized. It was Judas Iscariot. The priests were informed and, after a hasty consultation, they bought the place of impact with the thirty pieces of silver, and buried the body there in the potter's field, in the Valley of Hell.

News of the tragedy was hushed up as far as possible to avoid casting a shadow over the festive season.

389

On the holy day the city, aglow in the bright warm sun of spring, was festive with its hundred thousand promenading pilgrims gathered from all Israel and the diaspora. Jews from Babylon glided past in long black robes, Persian Jews in silk, Phoenicians in striped drawers, Romans in togas.

The strollers, taking care not to exceed a Sabbath day's journey, complained of the long-winded homily of the family patriarch at the Seder, laughingly recalled the children's antics, glorified Barabbas the freedom fighter, and argued heatedly over the strategy of sacrificing the wonder-working Nazarene to facilitate the patriot's release.

Twilight fell, three stars appeared, and the ululations of the ram's horn floated across the city. The great feast day and the Sabbath had ended. Hucksters appeared at booths, shoppers materialized, and the bustle of business supplanted the festive mood.

Mary Magdalene wandered among the shoppers like a lost soul. Trancelike, she found and bought ointments to anoint the body of the Master with the shekels she had borrowed. Cradling her purchase on her bosom like a loved one, she roamed in confusion through the maze of streets. A tender-hearted old man noticed, and guided her to the Fish Gate. From there she found her way to the Galilee. Before her tent she sat, gazing at the city across the Valley. As the pale sky blackened behind the pinpoints of the brightest stars, the sounds floating across the Kidron died away. Lulled into a kind of stupor by the sleeping city, she at last retired.

John sat hunched down on a couch, alone in the Upper Room. Darkness had fallen, but he lit no lamp. He was in hiding. After the burial yesterday he had accompanied the mother of Jesus and the other women to the Galilee. They had implored him, and prevailed on him, to conceal himself.

He had, however, returned to them this afternoon, seen that they were managing sufficiently well, and departed again, telling none but the mother of Jesus and the Magdalene where to find him.

Thoughts and feelings were numb. He was like a man alone in a small boat who had witnessed all the continents sink below the waves, and could only wonder if there was any

390

land left on earth. Jesus was the Messiah, he thought, but we killed him as we killed the other great prophets. Will God abandon us now? Without him, I don't seem to care.

He hadn't eaten since it happened. Thought of food turned his stomach. It was so hollow that when he tried to lie down it seemed to press against his backbone, so he sat up again.

Jesus loomed up now not as the great hope of the ages, but as the crushing memory of the whole history of illusory Jewish expectations. Seeing him that first time was like seeing a new land which he did not think existed or could exist, a land where light shines even when other regions fall into darkness. And his teaching! When he heard him exhort people to the very imitation of God, he almost staggered with desire to do it, as one inebriated with the sense of being already half a god—or else, he thought now, half mad. In any case, without the Master, the incentive was gone, the help dissolved, and the aspiration was madness.

What was he going to do? He and all of them? The thought of going back to fishing turned his stomach too. He had no wife, no children. That made sense while he shared Jesus' mission. But now? He thought of Mary of Bethany, and warmth suffused his cold body. He pitied her, but he also loved her. That might have new meaning now, since she too would have to rethink her decision not to follow the way of the earth. But it didn't seem right to be throwing over the Master's teaching almost before his body was cold. Yet, he thought, can I live it now that he's gone? O Father in heaven, you've got to give me light! I don't know what to think or do!

Long he sat staring out at the stars. A quiet knock sounded, and he tensed. It repeated, just as softly. A good sign.

"Who's there?"

"Simon Peter."

He slipped the lock-bar and his friend entered. "His mother told me where to find you." He didn't add that she had urged him to go. The two men embraced silently, then sat facing one another in the dark. "I heard you saw it," rumbled the big fisherman.

"Have you ever seen one?"

"No."

"I hope you never do. He was degraded like an animal. Hanging, gasping for breath like a fish out of water " It was evident he was still in shock.

He described the last hours, and how he had been entrusted with the Master's mother. As an afterthought he added, "When the centurion saw how he died, he thought he was a god."

"He doesn't know how a Jew dies."

"He's seen a lot of Jews die. He just had more faith than we." The words were bitter.

"What does that mean? He's a pagan."

"Who knows? Forget it. Peter, what are we going to do?"

"What do you suggest?"

"We have to take the women back to Galilee."

"Not yet. We'll wait until the pilgrims leave. When there's no danger of rioting, they'll lose interest in us fishermen."

"Peter, there are other problems. The Magdalene has spent all her money."

"She can live with my wife and me if she likes."

"I'll make a home for his mother."

"Some of the other women will need help too."

"Peter, what of his work?"

"We can't just let his teaching drop."

"His death—it changes everything."

"John, don't rush things. We'll see more clearly as the days go by."

"The centurion believes. He wants to know how to be saved."

Peter whistled softly. "Maybe he does see more clearly than we right now."

"Dismas—one of the two crucified Zealots—pleaded with Jesus to save him, and he promised to do it."

Peter sat long in silence. "I was right when I said we'd see more clearly with time. We'll have to reflect on his teaching and see where it leads us. Is there any food? I haven't eaten today."

"The staples we brought for the feast are still here." Rummaging about in the dark, they located unleavened bread, dried dates, and a skin of wine. Peter began eating, but John took nothing.

"Peter, I'd like to ask your opinion."

"Ask."

"Because of the call, I didn't marry. What about that now?"

Silence was the only answer. Then, "John, you're moving fast."

"Jesus said the single state was for his sake and the good news. He's gone, and we may break up. I'm lonely already. Life alone . . ."

"I thought you said you were going to care for his mother? I'd feel greatly honored if he had entrusted her to me."

"Maybe he would have if you were there!" Peter didn't answer the outburst. After a long silence, John spoke again. "I'm sorry. I'm ashamed to admit it, but I was forgetting her, thinking only of myself—and Mary of Bethany."

"Oh." Peter tried to see his face, but it was too dark. He reached out and laid his hand on his friend's shoulder. "I've always admired your understanding, but you've been through too much. You're trying to move in the dark. Wait for a little light." As an afterthought he added, "Have you eaten today?"

"I'm not hungry."

"Eat!" He handed him a piece of the matzo. The youth took it and ate. He accepted the skin of wine, and drank deeply. Peter spoke slowly, as though waiting for each word.

"It's hit us all hard, John, but you hardest. You were there."

"It was like seeing our port of destination sink below the waves. What good's the cargo?"

"You'll find a new direction."

"I feel like the only direction is down."

"He loved you very much, John. Loved and admired you. Never more than at our last supper. He put you right beside him."

"Because I was youngest."

"Because of how much he loved you."

A sob rent the darkness. Peter went to him, sat beside him, and laid his arm on his shoulder. "Grieve, John. You lost more than any of us. He gave you the most. Even if I'd had the courage to be there, he'd have given his mother to you."

Peter felt the youth's body shaking with sobs. He could

393

see only his luminous eyes, glistening with tears. He breathed a prayer of thanks. Now he would be faithful as ever. "We believe in everlasting life, John. We'll see him again."

When John had recovered himself he said, "You always give support, Peter. I feel a little better."

Peter got up then. "I'll leave you with your thoughts. You need time to sort them out, and when you do, you'll have something to tell us all. Besides, it's best to split up, so they can't trap us together. I'm staying with an uncle, on the Street of the Pines." He described the house. "I'll drop in again after dark tomorrow." With that he was gone.

In a little while, John stripped down to his undergarment, a sleeveless tunic of coarse linen, reaching to the knees. He made a pillow of his outer garment, covered himself with his cloak, and settled down. Peter had helped, but he doubted he could sleep. It was hard to believe Jesus was really gone. In the dark, it seemed he must be nearby, as always. With that he fell asleep.

2

The Magdalene rose from her mat and groped for the door flap. At the touch of the goatskin, Judas surged up in her imagination. He it was who had rented the tents and had seen that they were well pitched. Bitterness and grief coursed through her—and the image of the Master's shrouded body disappearing into the tomb.

She peered out. Across the valley the watch fires still burned in the courts of the Fortress and the Temple. Slipping from the tent, she turned and looked toward the east. The horizon was dark, but the morning star heralded approaching dawn. Hastening into the tent, she crouched down beside Mary, the wife of Clopas and mother of James and Joseph, and gently but firmly shook her awake, softly calling her name. "It's time to anoint the body."

"It's dark."

"It'll soon be light."

The wife of Clopas sat up languidly. She was a big, cheerful woman with small, twinkly eyes, and round, fat cheeks that shook when she laughed. As she dressed, she recalled how she had sat with the forlorn Magdalene before the tomb. That girl would need support. Every one of them was devoted to the Master, but she had sunk all her roots in him, like a plant on a rooftop, and had no one else.

The Magdalene roused Joanna next. Young and lively, her eyes always dancing with mischief, she had a face at once appealing and a little too pointed, as though it had been sniffing into things so long it had set in an inquisitive mode. Joanna was wide awake at her first touch, and leaped from her mat.

Next was Salome, wife of Zebedee, mother of James and John—a woman to be reckoned with. Her husband, though he talked like a firebrand about Israel's plight, was rather indolent, a mere armchair general, while she was a woman of action. It was more from her that her sons got their thunder. She was no raving beauty, but she was attractive with her full cheeks and communicative eyes. She had a habit of raising her right eyebrow quizically, as if to say, "What's this crazy world up to now?" Her ambitious nature lost her some friends, but her reliability and generosity attracted others. Nobody could control her except Zebedee, and he rarely cared to make the effort.

Finding her awake, the Magdalene whispered, "It'll be light soon." She went on to Ruth, a dumpy little woman with expressive black eyebrows, wide mouth and full lips, and an excitable nature. In her eyes, every molehill was a mountain—usually in the throes of an earthquake. It made for a strenuous life. She redeemed her faults by her sweet and genuine concern for everyone.

"Time to get up, Ruth," the Magdalene announced. "We're going to the tomb."

"How are you feeling, dear?"

"Like I can be of some use to him—after three days."

The three others in the tent, Cora, Tamar and Eve, had awakened and were rising. From a corner, the Magdalene retrieved the ointment and winding sheets she had purchased.

395

"Joanna, don't forget the water," she called. She saw that Salome too had a jar. "Is that more water?"

"It's anointing oil. Mary of Clopas and I bought it last night."

"Oh? I bought some too."

"Bring it, then. Better too much than too little."

They left quietly. Looming up nearby was the massive banquet hall which was rented out to pilgrims gathered for the feast. They took the path south, reached the Roman road, and followed it down into the dark Kidron Valley.

"To think we attended him here hardly a week ago," Joanna recalled, "with our palms and our hopes. It's like a dream." The Magdalene began to sob, and Joanna repented of the thoughtless words. She wracked her brain for something to distract her. "Mary, look up," she urged. "How many stars do you see?" The colorless tint of first dawn showed in the east, but stars were still visible.

"Quite a few. Why?"

"Once a wise man asked, 'When is it dawn?—when there are less than four stars? No,' he said, 'not yet. Is it when you can see the face of an approaching stranger? No, not yet. When is it dawn? When in every strange face you recognize a brother.'"

A cry of pain escaped her friend. "Then I've known only one man who brought the dawn!" Joanna put her arm around her.

They were nearing the Sheep Gate. "Which way—through the city or around the wall?" Ruth asked. They could cut through the city to the Judgment Gate and Golgotha, or skirt the north wall and follow the west wall south.

"Around the wall," Salome decreed. "Use the gates at this hour and the guards will ask questions."

"One thing I don't understand," Eve murmured. "Magdalene, why didn't you anoint his body before burial?"

"Those men! They hurried so, they poured on oil without washing his body."

"You know there wasn't time," the wife of Clopas chided.

"It's bitter cold," Ruth moaned. "Magdalene, you could have waited for the sun to come up."

"The body—I was afraid to wait." It was 36 hours since

396

the burial.

"The truth is, she wanted to go last night," Joanna cried. "I wouldn't go with her."

"I wish I'd gone alone. It may be too late."

"In this cold weather?" Joanna was incredulous. "There's nothing to worry about."

"There is one thing to worry about," the wife of Clopas said. "How are we going to get at the body?"

"What's the problem?" Ruth was anxious at once.

"The tomb's fitted with one of those gigantic rolling stones. The men closed it before leaving."

"Oh no!" lamented Cora. "Why don't we get some of the Twelve?"

"They're scattered to the winds," Eve snapped with scorn.

"Of course they are," Salome fired back, "with the rumor circulating that there's a warrant out for their arrest. My sons wanted to stay with us, but I made them go. The authorities couldn't care less about us. It's the men who are in danger."

"Where are they hiding?" Joanna asked.

"I wouldn't let them disclose it. What I don't know I can't be made to tell."

"John told me," the Magdalene said, "in case we need him."

"Well, we're almost there. What are we going to do?" Ruth demanded. Golgotha loomed up ahead. The sun had yet to rise, but the crimson of dawn was flaring above the Mount of Olives.

"We could hire men in the city," Joanna suggested.

Ruth was alarmed. "They might report us. They execute grave robbers. Who owns this tomb?"

"The noble Joseph of Arimathea," the Magdalene said.

"I suppose you have no proof of permission to use it," Ruth sighed.

They topped a slight rise. Golgotha now lay fully exposed. On its northern ascent, the trees of the garden signalled the location of the tomb. They hastened their step.

"Look!" shrieked Cora. By the trees fronting the cliff face, sprawled in grotesque postures, lay the bodies of several soldiers. It was just light enough to make out the color of their brown cloaks. Salome was the first to recover.

"Let's see if they need help." She ran and bent over one of the bodies. Joanna crouched alongside.

"Is he dead, or wounded, or drunk?"

"He's breathing," Salome reported, "and I see no wounds and smell no liquor."

"Maybe he's drugged."

"There!" exclaimed the Magdalene, pointing toward the cliff. The massive stone looked bright next to the black hole. The stone had been rolled back. She flew to the opening.

"What do you see?" Joanna called. No answer came. "Come on!" she urged, and ran, the others close behind. They pushed the Magdalene aside and peered into the cave. The body was gone. A radiant youth sat on the burial ledge, his face shining in the dark, his long white robe glistening. The women froze.

"Calm yourselves!" The resonant voice reverberated through the cave. "You're in search of Jesus of Nazareth, the crucified one. He has risen. You won't find him here." He tapped the blood-stained ledge where the pierced feet had rested. "Go quickly, alert the disciples. Tell Peter he goes ahead of you to the Galilee. You'll see him there as he said."

The women fled. Joanna fought panic, ground to a halt, and looked around. Salome came up and stopped. Cora, Ruth, and the wife of Clopas were stumbling toward her, gasping for breath. There was no sign of the youth. Up ahead, Eve and Tamar were moving fast, and the Magdalene, running wildly, was already disappearing in the distance.

Despairing of the latter three, Joanna and Salome collected Cora, Ruth, and the wife of Clopas. They were shaking with fear. Taking command, Salome led them to a clump of trees down toward the Joppa road, away from the city. Insensible to the brambles, they drove through to concealment, and dropped down exhausted.

When her breath came, Joanna spoke in a taut voice even she didn't recognize. "What are we going to do?" The others returned vacant stares. She felt equally stunned but fought it. "We can't sit here the rest of our lives! What do we do?"

"What can we do?" Ruth gasped, her eloquent eyebrows raised rhetorically.

"We should go to the Antonia and tell them about the soldiers, shouldn't we?" Cora asked. She was still in shock.

"The soldiers!" Joanna exploded. "Forget the soldiers! Their trouble is exactly the same as ours—only worse!"

"Shh!" chided Ruth, looking around fearfully.

"All right," Joanna whispered, "but when they get themselves together they'll trot off and tell their own story. Do you want to try to explain to some centurion—or to Pilate before it's over—what just happened?" Her indignation was clearing her head.

"We're supposed to tell the disciples," Ruth lamented, "but who'd believe us hysterical women?" No one replied, so she repeated, "We are hysterical. I'm hysterical." She began to weep.

"We could tell the Twelve—or just Peter," Cora suggested, "and let him handle it."

"We could if we knew where they were!" Salome cried. "They're hidden away just like us." She examined the tall cedars.

"The Magdalene knows where to find John," Cora recalled, looking around. "Where is she?"

"Running south—fast!" Joanna reported. "A real scared rabbit!" She tried to repress a sudden impulse to laugh. Since forcing her legs to abandon flight, she had been battling panic, cultivating sanity and sweet reason, taking firm hold of presence of mind, and holding on for dear life. But the uncontrollable message of the angel was a wild ocean battering away her everyday life, a new mountain range rising up before her eyes, ascending to the clouds, sweeping out of sight on either horizon, spewing vapors ascending in intoxicating waves through her brain, generating an exhilaration bubbling up like wine. As the image of her fleet friend came back, she burst into necessary laughter. The others looked at her with disapproval, but then Ruth tittered, the wife of Clopas' cheeks rippled with mirth, and Salome's voluminous lungs belted out gales of laughter.

"I thought I could run," Joanna gasped, "but did you see her? She mustn't have waited for the angel to finish!" She broke into another peal of laughter, until the tears came.

"Shh! Someone will hear you," Ruth cautioned.

With a snicker, Joanna gradually subsided, then said, "Any ideas?"

"Until we talk to the Twelve, tell no one," Salome decreed. The others nodded, and she went on. "Since we need the Magdalene to take us to them, we'll return to the Galilee and wait for her."

"Let's go by way of the Joppa Gate," Ruth suggested. "If I don't shop, we won't eat."

"You think of food at a time like this!" Joanna cried. "Do as you please—I'm going to the tents to pry out the Magdalene."

"No, please," Salome said. "We need one another."

Joanna fidgeted, then—"I suppose you're right. I'll stay." She was glad she did.

3

Not an hour ago she had left her bed to seek in a burial chamber the sole meaning left in her world. Now, stooping and peering into that cave, she saw an untenanted space crammed with emptiness into which she stared vacantly and tumbled deeper and deeper . . .

Shocked back to herself by her companions thrusting against her to peer into the tomb, she was seized by one thought—go to John! She ran frantically for the Joppa Gate. She had not seen the angel.

Even as she ran panting, the roseate glow of full dawn crimsoned the East, and the orb of a red-orange sun peeped above the Mount of Olives. She flew south along the city wall's great stone blocks. Seeing the wall angle west some distance on, she twisted across the open field to meet it near the Joppa Gate.

John had named and described as contact point the Upper Room of the last supper, in the southwest quadrant of the city, on its highest ground, in the newest and most affluent neighborhood. Should she approach it by way of the Joppa

Gate and the twisting streets, or proceed along the outside of the south wall? The latter route was longer, but avoided the city traffic. A thicket lay before her, but she drove straight ahead, the shrubs and tall grasses swishing against her robe. An exposed root snared her foot, throwing her to the ground. Leaping up, she stumbled on, smeared with grass and dirt.

At the Joppa Gate she hesitated an instant. The burly Roman guard clamped her arm in a bruising grip. "What's the rush, pretty lady?" His raucous voice beat against her ear as he glared down at her. "What're you up to?"

Bosom heaving, she panted for breath. "I just learned . . . a dear one . . . missing! Have to tell his friends!"

He scrutinized her dirt-and-tear-stained face. "Sorry, lady. You looked wild." Before he had fully released his grip she was running, on up the steep path along the west wall, close to the yellowish-brown lichen which crept from the cracks. The rising sun played on a patch of mountain lupin, paired petals lifted like open palms. Of these things she saw nothing.

Hurtling around the corner of the wall, she caromed off two men in the peculiar dress of Essenes exiting the Dung Gate, and sped through. Panting desperately, her step flagging, she pushed on—only another block! When at last she saw the house she panicked. Had she remembered rightly? Her heart thundering, she clambered up the steps and made a wild effort to tap out the prearranged signal.

Within, John awoke to the thumping, leaped for the one sword hanging on the wall, and hurtled toward the door calling, "Who is it?"

"Me! Magdalene! Open up!"

He tore the bar clear out of its socket and flung the door wide. She looked wild-eyed, her bosom heaving, her face and clothes smeared and stained.

"John, where's Peter? He's disappeared!"

Seizing her arm, he pulled her into the room. "Whom have they taken now?"

"The Master! He's disappeared!"

"What're you talking about?"

"Where's Peter? I have to tell him!"

401

In silence he took her arm, guided her to a couch, sat her down, and looked at her. Her whole face conspired to grief. Her eyes were wide and staring, the corners drawn down in sadness, the brow darkened by little valleys above the contracted nose. Her normally generous mouth was pinched and small, the lips compressed and hidden, the chin rumpled by muscular contractions, the dimple in her chin nearly gone. Hanks of hair hung from under her headdress and lay in loops half across her eyes. She looked as though she wanted to weep, but felt beyond the redemption of tears. Her shoulders were hunched and her whole body sagged. She exuded a damp exhalation laced with the fragrance of her hair. He was moved with pity and wanted to put his arms around her, but she gasped again, "I have to see Peter!"

"He's not here. It's unsafe to congregate. He's nearby."

"Take me!"

"Stay and catch your breath. I'll get him." He unrolled his outer tunic, pulled it on, wrapped his cloak about him, stepped into his sandals, and bounded down the stairs.

Feeling as if she were suffocating still, she pulled off her headdress, and her hair fell in long tresses across her face and shoulders. She collapsed onto a couch and sat slumped, gasping, staring . . .

Peter ran in, shouting, "Mary, what's happened?" Seeing she was in a state of shock, he sat beside her, wrapped his arms around her, and drew her to his chest. Gasping sobs burst from her and tears began to fall, but almost at once she recovered herself. "Peter, his body's gone."

"Who told you?"

"We went to the tomb."

"It's been sealed!"

"It was open. It's empty."

"You went to the wrong tomb."

"No! John knows I saw where they put him." John nodded. "So did the wife of Clopas." John nodded again.

"Did you see anything else?"

"No."

"We heard they posted guards."

"We saw them—sprawled on the ground!"

"John—come on!" They flew out the door.

"Wait for me!"

Showing no sign of hearing, they took the steps in bounds, raced around the corner, and sped past Caiaphas' palace and down into the business section of the narrow street. Vendors and hucksters were setting out their wares. Out of a narrow alleyway a cart laden with early figs nosed suddenly. Peter crashed into it, figs flew, the vendor spewed curses, but he kept running.

They raced out the Judgment Gate with the swifter John in the lead. He circled the hill of Golgotha to where the garden lay on the slope above him. Through the ordered lines of palm trees he could see the row of caves in the cliff. He spotted the mouth of the one where Jesus had been laid. It was open. There was no one in sight, neither soldiers nor women. Heart wild, lungs bursting, he raced up the hill to the rectangular hole, little more than a yard high, cut into the rock. He bent and looked in. On the burial ledge lay nothing but the shroud, stretched out in just the way the body had lain.

Simon Peter came panting up the hill and, doubling over, rushed right in. John laid his hand on the cold, rough stone of the cliff, bent low, and crept into the dank chamber. He stepped aside so the light could penetrate. In utter silence the two men stood and took in every detail. The shroud was lying full length along the burial shelf, as though the corpse had evaporated, allowing the top fold to drift down and rest on the lower one. Still rolled up, shaped like a helmet, the head covering lay by itself. Both helmet and shroud were stained with blood.

"I don't understand." Peter's voice sounded eerie, as though it were drifting back from some strange and fearful world. "Let's get out of here!" He bent low and hobbled out. John followed. Peter set out briskly.

"Wait, Peter." John re-entered the tomb, rolled up the shroud, and returned with it tucked under his arm.

"I don't understand, " Peter repeated.

"I think I do." John's voice was unnaturally still and faint.

"Who would rob the body and leave the linens?"

"Didn't you notice how the linens looked—as though the

body left them without disturbing them?" The words pulsed with restrained excitement.

"What are you talking about?"

"He's been raised up!"

"Get a grip on yourself!" Peter was bellowing.

"He raised Lazarus."

"There's no one to raise him!"

"No one but his Father." Peter had no answer. John went on. "The shroud—it brought back his words—he had to die and rise."

"We never took that literally! We agreed it was a parable."

"Why? Because he wasn't clear?"

"Because we thought the Messiah would never die . . . "

"Exactly!"

"That's what a great many think."

"They're wrong—about that and a lot more. That's why they killed him."

"I'm not convinced."

"Then listen! Didn't he explain his parables to us?"

"Yes."

"How many times?"

"Once. We weren't stupid."

"But he repeated the saying about his death and resurrection several times and never explained it—because it was plain talk. And now it's happened!" John ended with rising excitement, but Peter threw out his hands in a downward movement.

"Don't let an empty tomb rush you into a fantasy you'll be ashamed of."

"Rush me! Peter, can't you see how stupid we've been? He spoke plainly and we twisted his words! Why? Because we couldn't face the facts."

Peter kicked a stone out of his path and started walking again. John followed. At length Peter spoke. "It'd be great to believe, but I'm not going to let my emotions color my judgment."

"Is that right? Your fear of going wrong again is blinding your judgment! You trusted, and ended on your face. You're not risking that again, are you? No matter what the evidence!"

"Calm yourself. The Master must have trusted my good

sense—he made me leader, not you."

"You need to be led right now!"

Peter said no more. They walked back in silence, this time by the route Mary had followed. At the Dung Gate Peter said, "I'll see you later, John. I'm going off to think."

"What if Mary's still waiting?"

"Thank her. Tell her about our disagreement if you like."

"All right, Peter, but stay where I can find you, because I'll tell you something else—this isn't the end. It's the beginning!"

4

"Wait for me!" she called again, more desperately, but they were gone. Her sterile cry dissolved in the silence. Moaning softly, she slumped down in the big, quiet room and stared, the emptiness of the place and of her soul flowing in and out of one another in soundless waves of despair. She tried to rise, to run after them, but bone-deep weariness gripped her. She must leave this forsaken place, search for him, anoint him, before it was too late. Where? Her benumbed brain found no answer.

Implacable instinct settled it. As though fated to be driven on a hopeless quest forever, she rose like a sleep-walker to return to the last point of contact—the grave. At this crawling pace, how ever reach it, a place too distant? Beyond the dark cliffs of her grief lay the smoking fens and bogs of her total disaster. Neither wife nor mother, she had no home, no income, and no means of earning one.

The hucksters opening their stands stared. Her sensuous beauty of two years past was gone, worn away by hardship, but like the soft glow of embers, a subdued radiance was in the thin cheeks and glistening eyes of the stricken face. An appealing hunger parted the lips, and the languor of her movements was belied by a banked energy that flared her nostrils.

A street urchin, crouching in a corner shivering from the

cold, saw her, examined her suffering face, felt a kinship, and knew for certain that he had found a benefactor. He ran to her, touched her hand, and spoke in a piping voice.

"Give me money."

She stopped and looked at him. He was a gaunt little creature, dressed in a thin, ragged tunic hardly reaching his knees, which were knocking together with the cold. The gray garment was dirty and splotched with stains of many colors. The dark eyes below the thatch of coal-black hair were sunken and sad, and the lips were set in a straight, expressionless line. The apparition seemed a long way off, and did not penetrate her paralyzed heart.

"I'm hungry." He held out a thin palm, blue with cold.

Her hand went to her belt—she hardly aware of it—fished in the little pocket, and drew out its contents, one silver coin, a day's pay. With both hands she pressed it into his icy palm. He cast on her an eloquent look of gratitude, and ran off. She resumed her crawling pace.

In the garden there was no one, not even Peter and John. She was like one alone on the earth. Her senses took no note of the air sweet and rich with the fragrances of burgeoning new life, and vibrant with the happy twittering of birds. Her soul registered only the rank decay of death, and the stillness of the grave.

Unable to take another step, she was sinking to the ground when, instinctively, her gaze sought and found the black pit yawning. At once, a moth drawn to flame, she began to weave her way toward it.

Her fingers brushed a patch of purple-headed thistles. A few, gone to seed, were swollen with soft, white thistledown. One tuft, nearly blown loose, hung along the edge of the larger mass, its shiny black seed dangling. Preoccupied, she freed it and cast it upon the gentle spring breeze. It drifted only a few feet and fell heavily to the ground. A stab of pain pierced her childless womb. Bending double, she wrapped her arms around her abdomen, cradling it forlornly. Her last ounce of strength abandoned her; she slipped to her knees and sank forward on the ground. She wanted to die.

O God, she grieved, does no love bring lasting happiness?

Her sad nights with that cold stone of a husband dragged across her imagination, and prancing behind came the sordid tangles of flesh she had called making love—but who can *make* love? Oh no, it is a meteor flying out of heaven and burrowing into the heart. Solemnly it promises to go on forever, and cannot be doubted. But always love is incarnated in the flesh of another—and with a flash and a clap of thunder that flesh lies mangled and dead, and the heart stops and grows numb.

Even that mangled flesh upon which to rain her tears was gone. Heavy as a pregnant woman, she struggled to her feet and went to the tomb. She did not go in, did not look in. She fingered the cold, wet stone of the entrance, and the touch loosed wet tears and a wild sobbing. Crying out in pain, she bent and peered in.

The tomb was not empty. The burial ledge was bereft of its precious burden, but two youths sat there. She took no notice of the glory in their faces, their thick golden locks, the radiance of their alabaster tunics. Confirmed in hopelessness, she was turning away when one of them called to her.

"Woman, why such broken-hearted weeping?" His words swept her back to the time her tears had run in a torrent, washing those warm feet to which she was clinging. Now she could not even wash them cold in death. Her voice came thick with sobs.

"They've carried off my Lord, and I've no idea where." She turned away to weep in private, only to find swimming in her tears the feet of another man—no doubt the gardener.

"Woman, why such broken-hearted weeping?" Thus repeating the youth's words, he added, "Who are you looking for?" At these words, a new idea registered.

"Sir, if you carried him off, tell me where! I'll take him away."

"Mary."

In the familiar tones and cadences of that one word spoken, she found her life again. Dying in her, it had been living on in another—and there was only one other in whom it lived. It was he! She knew it before she could make him out through her tears—before her head speared up, wet

407

lashes lifting, eyes opening wide, lips parting in the wondrous cry, "Rabboni, my teacher!"

What she ever remembered in after years, and never could successfully describe to John, was the oneness-with-her in that noble face. She *saw herself there*, not as in a mirror, but as the loved one in the lover. Every feature expressed recognition, relationship, communion. It made love well up in her like some sacred liquid, warm and pure, filling the chalice of her body to the brim.

The next thing she was aware of was the sound of his voice once again. "You can't keep caressing me. I have not yet gone up to my Father." She unwrapped her arms from the calves of his legs, and saw the wounds in his feet still wet with her tearful kisses. She began to rise, gangly as a newborn calf. He took her hand and lifted her. "To my brethren carry this message—'I go to my Father and your Father, to my God and your God.' Hurry now."

One last adoring look, and she spurted off.

The same burly soldier who had apprehended her earlier watched as she flashed past. "Do you see the running lady?" he asked his companion. "Graceful as a doe."

"That I see for myself. Do you know her?"

"If only I did! She ran by earlier, wild with grief, carrying bad news about her lost lover to her friends. Now she's wild with joy. She must have found him, and can't wait to tell them. I'd like to be one of them."

Back to the Upper Room Mary flew, fleeter than the first time, before the sun had risen, before the last Adam had appeared on the earth.

5

Sounds of the valley awaking below drifted in the south window with the full morning light. John was lying back on a couch, attending to a bird trilling sweetly, when the excited knock came. Before the door was fully open the Magdalene flew into his arms.

"He's alive!"

John held her for a moment and released her.

"I saw him! He sent me!"

"Where?"

"At the grave!" The experience cascaded from her lips in a thrill of recall. He listened attentively to the end.

"I'll contact Peter—the Eleven! We'll meet here. Go, tell his mother, and hurry back—alone."

Peter was out. John left word and hurried to the haunts of the others. Each in turn was enlisted in the search for the rest. When he located Matthew, the two jogged back to the Upper Room, Matthew puffing mightily, and found them in animated conversation. Peter was pacing like a caged lion.

"John!" he roared, "What's this all about?"

John poured out Mary's account. Peter looked skeptical. He turned to Matthew. "Has John filled you in?"

"About the dazed soldiers, empty tomb, and shroud? Yes."

"Did he add any propaganda of his own?"

"What do you mean?"

"Forget it. We're all here but Thomas. Any news of him?"

"James of Nein saw him speeding toward Jericho," Matthew reported. "That was just after the arrest."

"We'll discuss this matter without Thomas," Peter decided.

"Wait for the Magdalene," John urged. "She'll be here any moment." Peter nodded assent and resumed his pacing. In minutes the coded knock sounded, the door was unbarred, and Mary rushed in with her companions of the morning.

"I told you to come alone," John snapped.

"We saw him too!" cried Salome.

"What!" barked Peter, running over.

"Yes, after we saw the angel," added Joanna.

"Not the angels I saw," clarified the Magdalene. "Or at least, not at the same time."

Peter threw up his hands. "Try to make sense!"

"You see," the Magdalene went on, "when I saw his body was gone I ran off to tell you."

"And we who stayed behind saw an angel," Salome declared.

"Stop!" Peter shouted. "You're confusing us. Take it from the beginning."

"Peter, keep it down," John cautioned. "They can hear you in the high priest's mansion."

"When we set out we could still see the stars," the Magdalene began.

"Right," agreed Joanna, "because I told the story about dawn."

"And we wondered whether it was too late to anoint the body," the wife of Clopas added with a delicious shudder. "You know, because of decay."

"Please, no blow-by-blow account," Peter cut in. "Get to the tomb."

Salome described the dazed soldiers, the open tomb, the flight of the Magdalene, Eve and Cora, and the angel's message that Jesus had risen, which they were to carry to Peter with the promise that he would meet them in Galilee.

"I have to add," Ruth reported, "that I saw two angels. I was slower than the rest, you know. They were staring into the cave when I got there and saw an angelic youth in a brilliant white robe sitting high on the closing stone. I wanted to thank him for rolling it back, but he didn't speak to me first, and besides, I was anxious to see what the others saw— and I did. When I looked, the first angel was gone. I thought they'd all seen him."

"Then we all ran," Joanna went on, "but Salome and I stopped, and collected all except the Magdalene, Eve and Tamar. We haven't seen Eve or Tamar since. We hid in a thicket and talked it over. We couldn't find you except through the Magdalene, so we planned to return to the Galilee, but first we rested. Some were badly shaken up."

"We must have stayed half an hour," Cora estimated.

"Then we saw him." Joanna's voice sank low with such a cargo of memories she could not go on.

"Suddenly he was in front of us," Salome took up the account, excitement mounting. "We clasped his feet. 'Don't be afraid,' he said. 'Go, bear the news to my brothers. They're to go to the Galilee where they'll see me.'"

"And now your story, Mary," Peter directed.

Mary described her experience. "He told me," she concluded, "to give you this message—'I am going up to my Father and your Father, to my God and your God.'"

410

"Nothing about Galilee?"

The Magdalene shook her head.

"That's weird," Philip mused. "First he says he's going to meet us, then he says he's going up to the Father."

"It was the other way around," John objected. "Long before Salome's group completed their half-hour in the thicket Peter and I were at the tomb, and the Magdalene was there minutes later, because she returned to me shortly after I got back."

"Either way it sounds visionary," observed Simon the Zealot. "And confused. They're terribly excited." He looked at the beaming women, who couldn't refrain from making little comments to one another. "Maybe excited enough to see what they'd like to see."

Salome leaped to her feet. "Simon, don't you know me? My whole family joined the Master in the hope of results we could lay our hands on, just like you. I didn't spend Zebedee's hard-earned money to buy visions!" She turned to her sons. "James! John! You know better!"

"I believe you, mother," John said.

"Yes," Peter agreed, "but he believed before he heard about any visions. Tell them, John."

While John explained his deductions from the lay of the grave clothes, Peter examined the women critically. Their joy was irrepressible, undimmed by the men's disbelief. The Magdalene was no withdrawn visionary, but a woman bursting with energy. Salome was a practical woman, and so was Joanna. The others were every-day types, too unimaginative to dream dreams. He wasn't ready to say what had happened, but it was no use pretending these women had lost their wits.

"What bothers me," James put in, "is that we are his chosen leaders and key apostles. If he is alive, wouldn't he come to us first?"

"Son, maybe he would have," Salome snapped, "if you'd been around!"

"Mother, you're the one who pressed me to leave."

"Maybe you shouldn't have listened!"

"We could argue all day about what to believe or not believe," Peter rumbled. "What we have to decide is what to do. Are we going up to the Galilee where he said he'd meet us?

411

I want to hear you on that."

"Is it safe?" Bartholomew asked. "They're looking for us."

"If Jesus intends to meet us there, it's unsafe not to go," John retorted. "If you know what I mean."

"I do!" Peter barked. The others laughed. "Is there more to be said?"

"I have a question for the women," Matthew said. "Are you certain the appointed place is the Mount of Olives' Galilee and not the province of Galilee?"

"That's the meaning we took," Salome replied.

"This might help," Ruth cried. "The angel said he would meet you in Galilee *as he told you*."

"Do you see what I mean, Peter?" John exclaimed. "Peter and I," he explained to the others, "were discussing the times he told us he would suffer, die and rise again." He recounted their exchange, and added, "It was then he said he'd precede us to Galilee."

"Wouldn't that mean Herod's Galilee?" Jude asked.

"No. He was foretelling that we wouldn't be together where we ought when he came—that we'd be acting from fear, not faith."

"Your interpretation doesn't carry weight with me," growled the Zealot.

"Here's something that does carry weight," barked Peter. "The Mount of Olives is close by. If it's the wrong place, we can correct it a lot faster than the other way around. So up to the Mount of Olives we go. Any objections?" There were a few grumbles but no objections. "The next question is where to stay up there. If we don't advertise ourselves, the authorities may leave us alone."

"The banquet hall's empty now," Salome reported. "You could hide out there. The owner is one of us."

"All right," Peter agreed. "Try to arrange it. Give Salome a few hours, then start drifting up in pairs."

"What of Thomas?" Bartholomew asked anxiously. "We can't leave him out of this."

"Matthew, you're a man with connections," Peter observed. "Scout out someone to find him, even if he has to go all the way to Jericho. But I doubt he went that far."

"Matthew, that's not permission to visit Three-a-day,"

Jude smiled. "If I were Thomas, that's where I'd be."

John drew the Magdalene aside. "Did you tell his mother?"

"She wasn't about. She went to the Temple early, but I couldn't find her in the crowd."

"Be sure to tell her the moment you return."

"She'll have heard, but I want to tell her myself."

At the Galilee she ran to Mary's tent and flew into her arms. "Mother, we've seen your son and he's alive!—but they don't believe us."

"I believe you. I saw him."

"Where? When? Were you at the tomb?"

"He came here. At sunrise."

"Then you saw him first! Didn't he send you to the apostles?"

"For that he chose you. That I saw him is not for the others."

"They won't believe me because I'm a woman. It's unjust— sinful."

"There's been so much sin. O happy sin, that brought us such and so great a Messiah!"

They looked at one another triumphantly, tears of joy on their lashes. "Tell me of your meeting," the Magdalene pleaded.

"I have no words to describe it."

"Oh! Please tell me."

"I won't refuse, but understand that the words I use will be strangers to my experience. When he embraced me, time lost its hold and swept by under my feet, the light of the sun entered me, the stars gathered round, and the twelve largest circled my head. Joseph was there, and Adam and Eve, and all their children and mine." A look of pain seared her radiant face, and the Magdalene grasped her hand.

"Say no more."

"I have said too much already—because too little."

"Oh! I can't wait for the Eleven to see! They will, won't they?"

Mary smiled, and nodded.

413

Like sparks on the wind, fragments of the resurrection account flew from believer to believer. Cleopas of Jerusalem got the news while in the Upper Market buying food for a journey. Turning his moon face to the bearer in full absorption, he attended with those oversized ears which, by some trick of the way he held his head, seemed to lift to right angles from their moorings when a communication engrossed him. Then he ran home puffing, and before he reached the house was shouting, "Theo, have you heard what's happened now?"

The door was kicked open, and a sturdy little man with protruding eyes burst out flourishing his walking stick, his mustache twitching as he exploded into speech. "I know what's going to happen next! You're ready in two minutes, or off I go without you! Look!" He pointed his staff at the westering sun. "It must be . . ."

"The women went to the tomb—saw an angel—he said the Master's alive!"

"And caterpillars fly! Come on, let's go."

"Theo, didn't you hear me?"

"Oh, I heard you! Do you believe them?"

"Well . . ."

"Well then! Do you want to go earn your living, or stay and starve?" The two were tentmakers.

"What's your hurry?" Cleopas hedged. "Something more might happen."

"My hurry! Brigands roam that desert road, and we can just make Emmaus before sundown! Who was your source?"

"John Mark's house servant, Rhoda."

"That hare-brained woman!"

Cleopas looked startled. "I have to admit she was in a state. She heard it from Tamar and Eve, who were at the tomb with some others. Before she had the whole story, she ran off to spread the news, so she could only give a garbled account. She's been making the rounds since early morning."

"That settles it. Let's go. The way he died's enough to make any woman hysterical. They have their visions—we have our living to earn. Coming or not?"

"I'll get my gear. But I'd prefer to run up to the Galilee and learn more—talk to Salome. She was at the tomb too, and she's a sensible woman." As he went inside, he called back, "Oh, Rhoda bumped into Peter. He and John were at the tomb. It's empty all right."

On the road, as Cleopas talked about the report, Theo interrupted—"When I think of all his miracles! Why didn't he escape? That I could believe."

"Miracles? His presence was a miracle! Only he did die, and I'm talking about his resurrection!"

Cleopas took up the thread of Rhoda's report again, but was repeatedly interrupted by caustic comments. The state of his companion's soul was as barren as the desert road they traversed. Cleopas finally cried in exasperation, "You're down on everything today!"

"That," Theo cried with satisfaction, "is because I've been meditating on those reliable words of Isaiah, 'Cursed be the man who lodges his trust in a man.' Isn't that what we did?"

"What do you propose—waiting for God to appear in person to save us?"

"Now *you're* getting sarcastic! Let me remind you that many of the Sadducees don't believe in a Davidic Messiah."

"Sadducees! Since when are they your shining light? I'm not sure they even believe in God."

Their heated exchange slowed them. A solitary traveler came up behind. They paid no heed until he broke into their conversation. "What are you two arguing about so heatedly?"

They stopped dead and stared at him with sagging eyes, their faces elongated with sadness. They had entered a springfed little valley, and the silence was broken only by birds twittering in the mustard tree and yellow bumble bees buzzing among the fragrant white and pink blossoms of an asphaltus shrub. Theo discharged his incredulity.

"Are you some out-of-towner living like a hermit in the city? Aren't you aware of the things happening these days?"

"What things?"

"What things!" Theo shouted in disbelief. "The things the whole city's stewing about—what they did to Jesus the Nazarene! The man was a prophet. His word and works were powerful before God and the people."

415

"Don't you know," Cleopas asked as Theo gulped for breath, "how our chief priests and leaders sentenced him to death and crucified him?"

"We were hoping he was the very one who was on the verge of liberating Israel," Theo lamented.

"And that's not the end of the story," Cleopas confided. "In addition to everything else, it's now the third day since then—and would you believe it . . ." The poke in the ribs from his companion was meant to silence what he saw coming, but Cleopas only gasped and barged on: "Would you believe that certain women among us, out at the tomb early, not finding his body, came back startling us, babbling about a vision of angels saying he's alive! Two of our men went to the tomb. It *was* empty—but they didn't see him."

"How slow-witted you are!" At this surprize remark of the stranger, the two halted and stared dumbly. "What undiscerning hearts! What lack of faith in the prophets!"

Theo's temperature boiled to the flash point, and he turned to tongue-lash this interloper—until he looked into that face. The eyes flamed, and energy livid and incandescent as molten lava descending a mountain played from brow to beard. His later recall of that countenance never seized hold of a single feature, only of the naked, vital force of life it exposed. He could only gulp and murmur, "What do you mean?"

"The Christ could not do other than pass through those foretold fires of pain to emerge in glory. Moses and all the prophets prepared the way. Their words prophesied him and their lives prefigured him."

"Prefigured him?" Theo protested weakly. "Moses was a man of glory!"

"Moses fled for his life. Stood against rebellion after rebellion. Was all but killed. Do you realize how far they had their way with him?—he was never able to lead the people into the promised land. That was left for Jeshua."

"Just yesterday," Cleopas recalled, "his mother told us not to despair. She said God would bring good out of what happened—we'd see. Told us of an old man named Simeon, who held the Master as a baby, and prophesied that controversy would engulf him, but said he was the Messiah."

416

"Of course! Was there ever a prophet the people did not persecute? Nor was it different with the Lord's Anointed. David made it plain in the second psalm—our leaders would join pagans to plot against him."

"Yes, but David says they'd fail!" Theo found he could argue with the stranger by not looking at that terrible countenance. "But the plot against the Master succeeded!" He cried the last words triumphantly. He would teach this stranger!

"No! You overlook Isaiah's forevision. His Suffering Servant led lamb-like to slaughter. Cut off from life. It seemed the end—then, lo, he returns to see his far-flung offspring and bring salvation to the whole earth."

"But if he died—how?"

"What did the women tell you of him?"

"That he's alive . . ." Theo froze, thunderstruck. His thoughts were out of control, plunging down the cataract of the stranger's irresistible words.

"David prophesied it even earlier!" The stranger's voice was slashing the air like thunder. "'Never shall you let corruption seize your Holy One!'" The familiar words made the hackles rise on their necks, and still he rushed on. "Amos too foretold this raising of the fallen dwelling of David. Could it be otherwise since the Lord's love is everlasting? God of the living is he!" The molten river of Scripture continued to erupt from him. Prophecy after prophecy flamed up like dawn, driving their hearts to thunder against their ribs. Cleopas was walking with his head turned sideways, ears extruded, to catch every nuance of word and tonality— but with head deflected downward to avoid staring into those burning eyes and that face with its contrary qualities. It seemed so totally strange and so altogether familiar that it bewildered and frightened him because he seemed poised on the edge of some mental precipice from which he was in danger of falling.

Theo nearly missed the fork which led to the inn.

"Dear friend, I hesitate to interrupt," he apologized, "but that inn is our destination." He observed the sun, setting golden in the west, and the moon rising silver in the east, and added, "Look, it's late. It'll soon be dark. Do stay with us

417

for the night."

"My plan was to go on."

"Sir," cried Theo, "it's dangerous to travel this road after dark."

"Please, sir," begged Cleopas, "eat with us, be sheltered the night in our tent—and continue to lead us. We were two travelers wandering about lost within, and you've brought us so far. Lead us a little further and we'll have our bearings."

"You've persuaded me." The man's voice smiled, but still they feared to look at him.

When they had pitched their tent in the courtyard, they unpacked their foodstuffs and made for the inn. The sound of drunken partying emerged as they approached the weather-worn stone building. Cleopas pulled the sagging door ajar. The dark interior, lit by a few oil lamps, had the capacity to seat about forty. It was half full. The air was heavy with the odors of unwashed bodies, lamb stew, spilt wine, rancid oil, and acrid smoke from the outdoor oven.

The sound of revelry faded as the guests turned to peer at them, and stare hypnotically at their chance companion. Theo made for a dark corner. He sat against the wall with Cleopas, and their companion took a seat facing them. Thus deprived of the sight of him, the guests resumed their partying, shouting for a tune from the harpist. A waiter sidled over, saw their food, and turned away.

"Waiter," Cleopas called, "bring us three goblets." He was soon pouring the wine into three battered metal cups. "Sir, please bless our fare."

Their guest took a wheaten loaf into his hands and looked up to heaven. "Blessed are you, Father, King of the world to come. You bring forth food."

Cleopas froze, staring at Jesus hypnotically in the dark room. He fell to his knees. Theo gaped at his friend, turned to the stranger, and saw him breaking bread, extending the pieces, and saying, "Take and eat." He too was on his knees, his eyes bulging. Reverently they reached out, took the bread from his hands—and he was gone from their sight. Theo stuffed the fragment of bread into his mouth and chewed. His tears were moistening it—he could taste the salt. Cleopas ate his morsel with streaming tears.

418

The people in the room were staring at them in silence. The proprietor shuffled over. "Are you some kind of religious nuts?" He peered at them. "What's going on?"

"We were lost and are found," replied Theo.

"What? There were three of you. Where's the other man?"

"He left suddenly," Cleopas said.

"Left, did he? I didn't see nobody leave, and I don't miss much. Look, don't disturb my customers or I'll ask you to leave."

"Come on, Cleopater," Theo urged, "we've got to tell the others. Do you think they'll believe us?"

"They have to believe!"

"If they don't I have it coming!"

7

The Zebedee brothers leaped down the steps of the Upper Room flashing lightning remarks to one another about the women's report. For once, they were not of the same mind. James was not ready to believe.

Instinctively they strode toward the Temple without having to discuss their destination—both felt an urgent need to pray. Their stay was prolonged. Like hidden logs freed from some underwater snare, Jesus' prophecies of death and resurrection broke loose one by one and floated up to the surface of John's consciousness, confirming his faith.

It was late afternoon when the two brothers descended into the Kidron Valley. "He told us beforehand," John summed up his reflection, "but we couldn't grasp it then." He held up the burial shroud. He was taking it to the Master's mother.

"I still can't grasp it," James reported sadly.

"I wish you'd been to the empty tomb with us," his brother exclaimed, and began citing the prophecies he had recalled.

419

They trudged up the slope of the Mount of Olives through the groves of olive trees. A spanking evening breeze was tipping up the light undersides of the oblong leaves, setting them gleaming like a thousand golden flames in the light of the westering sun.

At the ridge of the Mount they took the path leading north, and soon abandoned it for the footpath swinging west. In minutes they reached a spacious plain carpeted with green grass and graced with stands of cedars and palms. A few carob trees clustered together on one hillock, their scimitar pods hanging darkly from the branches. Tents dotted the plain. This was the Galilee, the area frequented by Galilean pilgrims.

The western extreme of the plain plunged into the canyon-like Kidron Valley. At about the same height as the Temple Mount across the divide, the plain provided a splendid panorama of the city and a privileged view of the Temple.

Rearing up on the edge of this lookout point was the fieldstone banquet hall which Salome had been appointed to engage. The brothers made for it now, their head coverings drawn forward to obscure their identity and discourage unwanted attention.

At the entrance stood the Magdalene. She recognized them from a distance and tapped out the appointed signal. "The rest of the Eleven are here," she informed them, "except for Peter and Thomas."

The portal swung open to Andrew's greeting. He closed the thick oaken door behind him and slid the heavy timber lock-bar into place. "You'll find it cold," he said, "but we don't want smoke to signal the building's in use."

The brothers scanned the dimly lit room. Beside the Eleven and the resurrection witnesses, there were other disciples present. John saw the mother of the Master, embraced her, spoke with her in low tones, and presented to her the burial shroud, which she took reverently.

"The Eleven were supposed to gather here alone—secretly!" snapped James to Andrew. The latter waved his hand in a brushing motion.

"We couldn't keep the others out. Each time one of the Eleven arrived, someone smelled him out and followed,

420

excited by the women's report. We have refused to admit most."

When James sat at the table of the Eleven, Matthew said, "We'd like your brother to describe more in detail the lay of the shroud and what it means."

"Peter ought to be in on that," James replied. "Where is he?"

"We don't know," the Zealot answered. "We thought you might."

John joined them, and was asked to repeat his observations at the tomb and his discussion with Peter. "As I told you," he wound up, "the look of things there reminded me of Jesus' prophecy of dying and rising, and I believed it—before the women reported it."

"What we still can't understand," lamented Bartholomew, "is why he appeared to them and not to us."

"He couldn't find us," drawled Jude, to the humor of all but the man from Cana, who was ready with his own retort.

"He always knew where to find us before! Would he know less in resurrection?"

" 'Would?' " John challenged. "You mean, 'would if he'd risen?' "

"I want to hear more before I mean anything definite," came the evasive reply. "Call the Magdalene in. We haven't really sat down and grilled her."

They were plying Mary with questions when a thunderous knock interrupted the exchange. "It's the signal," Andrew observed, and opened the door. Peter catapulted in, his face aflame with triumphant joy.

"I've seen the Lord!" His bull voice reechoed off the stone walls, and they began to crowd around him, but he saw the Eleven and made for them. John pulled out the chair at the head of the table and he sat down. The others flocked around.

"I went up to the Temple to pray," he began, "and I did, long and hard, for I was very troubled. 'What are you praying for?' a voice asked. 'Faith,' I answered. I thought it was one of the priests, but when I turned to look, he wasn't in priestly vesture. He seemed familiar, but I couldn't place him. 'What else?' he asked. 'Understanding—like John's,' I told him,

421

then explained, 'A close friend of mine.' 'I know,' he said. That's when I recognized him! He extended his hand to grasp mine. His showed the nailhole. He led me into the Chamber of Hewn Stone and gave me a mission. I'll tell you about it when the time's ripe. Then he explained the Scriptures the way he used to—only this time I understood everything. But now," he concluded, "I'm hungry. Have you eaten yet?" At this question, hubbub ensued.

"Forget food!" Matthew shouted above the others. "We want to hear more!"

In a commanding voice, Andrew exclaimed, "No, Peter, but the women have food ready."

Peter looked around. "Salome, serve the meal. We'll talk more later. Little by little is better." He looked at the varied expressions around him—very much like his had been.

As they ate a staccato burst shook the door. It was not the signal. Fear flared on many faces. The knocking grew more imperious, and then a voice—"Open up! It's Theo and Cleopas. We've news!" Andrew unbarred the door.

"We've seen the Lord!" Cleopas' moon face shone, and his awed voice, low and gentle, reached every ear. A chill played along Jude's spine; Bartholomew's mouth fell open.

"He's alive!" cried Theo, his face radiant. The grating of the heavy lock-bar sliding into place punctuated his words.

"We know," Peter replied. "He appeared to me."

"Praise God!" Cleopas sang out. "When?"

"Several hours ago. Tell us about yourselves."

The two told of their meeting with the wayfarer, of his words of fire, of their failure to recognize him until the breaking of bread. Their faces glowed with greater and greater joy and exaltation as they relived the experience. When they concluded, Theo gazed around with his bulging eyes, and his countenance changed. "When we entered, you said you knew he'd risen. But many of you still don't know—you don't believe!"

"Why would he appear to you two?" Simon the Zealot growled.

"Why didn't you recognize him right off?" Philip demanded.

"How would we know?" Theo shouted. "He's different risen, but it's him. I'd stake my life on it!"

"Did you hear that the women saw him?" asked Matthew.
"I heard they saw an angel who said he's alive," Cleopas responded.

"Did you believe it?"

"Not exactly," Cleopas hedged.

Theo put three fingers across his lips. "You make your point."

"You must be hungry," Peter observed. "Salome, what about it?"

"We can manage." She set food before them, and they ate at the table of the Eleven, who kept firing questions. Theo lost his temper repeatedly.

"You can believe or not, but we did see him," Cleopas concluded when the questions ceased. His moon face beamed on, but Theo glared around angrily.

"You ooze doubt like serum from a sore!" Theo shouted. "Are we liars?—or just plain stupid? What then? What about jealousy? That's blinding!"

"Stow it, Theo!" Peter barked. He turned to the mother of Jesus by his side. "Mother, we're divided over him who brought us together. You know him best. Tell us what to do."

"What did he advise you when in need?"

" 'Ask and you shall receive,' " John quoted.

"Peter, lead us in prayer."

"Our Father," Peter intoned.

"Who art in heaven," the brotherhood continued.

8

It was while they continued in prayer together that the disciples first felt the streaming fog of unbelief dissolving. There was as yet no full-fledged dawn, but at least sadness, division and obstinate disbelief were dissipating.

"Father in heaven," the mother of Jesus prayed, "your children are saddened, not knowing the great things you have done. Help them to reach the faith in my Son which this day calls for, and gladden every heart."

A stillness and sweetness entered the place. Then Peter's voice rumbled through the room: "Lord Jesus, you promised to be with us, even two or three, gathered for your sake. We didn't understand. Yet today you came to the women who went to care for your body. You joined the two wayfarers as they dwelt on you. You visited us singly—the Magdalene weeping with broken heart, me in my troubled faith. Come now to us all. End division, give faith as gift, restore union. Amen."

Peter opened his eyes. Those at table stared beyond him unheeding. Outstretched arms were pointing, jaws hanging slack. Peter leaped up and wheeled around. Jesus stood there. Only the sound of night insects played in the air. Mouths hung open in silent screams, hands reached up to shield eyes, or clamp across mouths. The big fisherman fell on his knees.

"Shalom! Shalom!" The words were the ancient greeting of his people, the promised gift of prophets, the hunger of all human hearts. Like fireflies upon the dark, one face lit with joy, and then another, but doubt and fear constricted many.

"What's upsetting you?" the familiar voice demanded. "Why are you still questioning and doubting? Haven't you had enough of doubt? You made up excuses for not believing the women, but you didn't believe the men either. What's wrong with you?"

"Help us Lord!" Matthew's voice came like the cry of one disappearing in stormy waters.

"Then renounce blindness. Look at me!" The words came with such force that they stared still harder, some moving crabwise to gain an unobstructed view. He raised both hands above his head, the nail-holes still red. "See my feet too." Balancing on one foot, he raised the other high. The wound was clear to see.

"It's him all right!" cried James the son of Alphaeus.

"Now feel me—as the women did—and see for yourselves I'm no ghost. Ghosts have no flesh and bones as you see I have. You Eleven, come here, lay your hands on me!" The tone brooked no delay. They went to him. Jude gently touched his hand, and he clasped Jude about the shoulders.

424

John put his hand over Jesus' heart, waited, and announced, "It's beating again—I saw it pierced." He knelt and bowed low.

The rest slipped to their knees, took the hand he offered them one by one, and looked at him. Their faces registered the turning of the tide. Doubts and questionings were no more.

"Now sit and relax." When they had done so—he took Peter's seat, and the latter sat beside him—he asked, "Do you have anything to eat?" They looked surprized and delighted. Salome pattered about, and set before him the remains of one large fish and a dish of wild honey. He broke off a piece, picked out the bones, dipped it in honey, and began eating. They watched intently. "Share a morsel with me." He handed each a bite. "Is this all you have?"

"I'm afraid so," Salome apologized.

"We'll save a little for Thomas."

"He's not here," Jude lamented.

"Soon." At this one word, Peter broke into a grin, Jude laughed with delight, and the rest smiled. Jesus rose, fixed his gaze on each in turn, then spoke solemnly.

"Didn't I keep hammering at my coming suffering, death, and rising?" The apostles nodded. "Moses foretold it, and the prophets and psalms did as well. I assured you their word would come true. The Father's Son had to be snatched from death. David's Lord couldn't undergo decay. Jonah came forth on the third day in prefigurement. The Suffering Servant, laid unjustly in the grave, must reappear when human hope was gone—and have his uncounted children."

"What comes next, Lord?" blurted out Simon the Zealot.

"You, my witnesses, and all the believers must spread the good news to the nations. Teach repentance and the forgiveness of sins. Start with Jerusalem."

"Right now?" Jude bounded to his feet.

"No. Stay in the city until you receive the divine power I plan to give you. My Father promised it, and I'll send it down."

The conversation went on for some time before he rose from his chair and beckoned to the Eleven. "Come here." When they had clustered around him, he repeated the ancient words, "Shalom, shalom." Then, breathing on each one, he said, "Receive the Holy Spirit. When you forgive people's sins, they're forgiven. When you hold them bound, they're held bound."

Stunned, they saw he was gone. Peter fingered the half-eaten fish, and then they found their voices. The hubbub had not abated when the signal was beaten out on the door, it was opened, and in bounded Thomas—with Malachy, dispatched by Matthew to find him. "Welcome, Thomas!" Peter roared, and gathered the tall, gangly youth in massive embrace.

"Glad to be back," Thomas growled. He looked around in surprize. "I expected to be welcomed, but didn't expect so many smiling faces." He looked sad.

"The Master came—here!" Peter exclaimed. "Minutes ago."

"He's alive again!" Jude cried. "You just missed him."

Thomas turned his head to survey each one before he spoke. "I don't believe it." He etched the words on the air the way men inscribe them on monuments and emboss them with lead to preserve them for posterity.

"He took my hand." Matthew said the words like a plea.

"He put his arm around my shoulder," Jude whispered.

"I don't believe—not until I see." He looked ready to wheel and go back out the door.

"Are your five senses better than ours?" John challenged. "Is your exalted intelligence despising ours? Is your judgment . . ."

"As to judgment, you're suicidal—staying here with your secret silly knock! When the Temple guards charge up, they'll knock as they please—then knock down the door!"

"You're beginning to sound like Judas!" someone charged.

"Shut up!" Jude shouted.

Peter commanded silence, then spoke. "Thomas, the Master told us to meet him here."

"Don't be stubborn," Jude pleaded. "We just told you . . ."

"Let me tell you and have an end to it! Until this finger of mine"—he held up his right index finger—"goes through the nailholes in his hand, and this hand goes into his side, you won't find me gullible. Is that clear?"

There was stunned silence. Out of the silence came the voice of the Master's mother. "Children, be patient. Be

426

grateful you weren't left out." Thomas went to her and took her hand. He looked ready to cry.

"Thank you."

"Are you hungry?" she asked.

"Do you have anything to eat?"

"Yes!" The way John intoned the word made Thomas stare at him. "The fish Jesus was just eating. He saved some for you—said you'd be right along." He pointed to the dish in front of him, drew the chair out, and held it for him. Hesitantly he sat.

"Have some, Malachy."

"No! No!" Malachy fended it off with both hands straight out. They watched Thomas in silence. He approached the fish the way one handles food dangerously hot from the oven. Reverently, he began to eat. When only the bones were left, he looked up. Tears shone in his eyes.

"What happens next?"

No one answered.

9

Walking into the rising sun that Monday morning, young David kicked a pebble with such force it hurt his toe and he didn't care. It took his mind off that other pain. Four days ago they killed Jesus. Judas' terrible face as he last saw it swam up, and he shivered with horror. Now it was no mystery. He'd learned of the betrayal.

The boy was unaware of the reports flying since yesterday. With his father away and his mother unwell, he had been confined to the house tending his young sister. She was cute though. When he said he was off to visit his girl, Abbey, she sang out, "Are you going to marry her?"

To think he'd not been with the Master at the end. That turncoat Judas! Actually, he felt a little like him, not being there—but father forbad it.

Feeling warm, he pulled off his head covering and ran his fingers through the heavy fall of thick brown locks. The

427

youth had strong, full features, and a well-developed body. His face was as pleasing as some pastoral scene with easy sweep of wood and hill and two dark shining lakes.

Maybe Abbey could cheer him up. He pictured her, face fresh as a budding windflower, head and tresses caressed by that orange cloth which fell down her shoulders, accentuating the inward curve of her body to the tiny waist. She was sixteen like him, and had blossomed before his eyes, with wide hip and full bosom and a new light of tenderness in the luminous eyes shaded by lashes that could almost talk. Only the high holy days and the family need could have kept him away like this—four days!

His thoughts drifted affectionately to the followers of Jesus, especially Peter, and he wondered what had become of them. Would the big fisherman go back to fishing? He'd be glad to join him if Peter would have him, but his father wanted him to take up his own merchant's trade. He liked the women disciples too, and above all the Master's mother. She was so sweet to him that he wished she were his mother too—and felt guilty about it.

His father had been growing more willing to let him join Jesus—until a week ago when he learned how really dangerous the Master's position was, and tried to "talk sense" to him. After that failed, he called in his influential friend, Counselor Joseph of Arimathea. The counselor spoke of prudence and gave tiresome reasons for not following the endangered Master openly, and David responded with, "I don't care! If he's the Messiah, none of us should."

"There's no reasoning with you," Joseph snapped, "so I quote the Law—'Honor your father and your mother.' Obey them!"

That was when the boy had decided to ask a better counselor. He had put his question to the Master during his triumphal entry, and been promised he'd be his disciple one day. Only, what did that mean now? It was over.

Abbey's mother looked surprized to see him so early, but seemed pleased. Abbey ran out crying, "Did you hear the news? Some women saw Jesus alive!"

"What?"

"He's been raised up! An angel said so!"

428

"An angel? Where did they see him?"

"In the Master's tomb—near Golgotha."

"I'm going!" David spurted off.

"Wait! The guards are looking for him!"

"Then I have to warn him!"

"I'm coming too!"

David stopped dead. "Come with me unescorted and your father may never let me come again." He looked at her hungrily.

"If not with you, I go alone."

"Come on!" He took her hand and they ran, skidding down the steep path from the Ophel Ridge—the oldest part of the city—into the Valley of the Cheesemakers, and on north into the quarter known as the Maktesh. At the esplanade fronting the Huldah Gates leading into the Temple grounds they slipped through the crowds entering the triple gates and swung west into the quarter Mishneh. Zigzagging along the twisted market streets, they reached the Judgment Gate and shot out to the cemetery garden.

Hundreds of people were milling around, Levite guards were shouting to them to go home, and nobody was listening. Abbey pointed. "That's where he was laid—they described it to me." Guards fronted the tomb with spears and clubs in hand.

"Half the city's here!" shouted David in high excitement.

"They closed and sealed the tomb!" Abbey exclaimed.

"It's all a fairy tale," a guard shouted.

"Ha! Show us the body," the crowd mocked.

"The high priest forbids your presence!" thundered a Levite guard. "Go home!" He waded forward with swinging club. The people shrank back, but one man, struck a glancing blow, fell and lay still, his head bleeding. Others rushed to assist him, and the guard backed off.

A thunder of hooves sounded, and a detachment of Roman cavalry rounded the corner of the north wall. "When the Romans get here you'll go fast enough!" raved a guard. Helmets flashing, the horsemen swept past the wood market and bore down on them. The crowd dispersed in all directions. He took her hand and ran. A horseman drove straight at them. He pushed her forward just as the mount struck him

429

and he went flying. She ran to help. Blood was seeping from his scraped forehead and nose.

"You're hurt." Her eyes were wide with terror.

"I'm all right. Let's get out of here!" Hand in hand they sped east across the city.

"Where are we going?"

"You'll see." They ran out the Golden Gate, across the Kidron Valley and up through the orchards of the Mount of Olives. Gasping beyond endurance, she staggered and threw herself on the ground. "The Master used to come here," he gasped. "Lots of caves. Maybe he's hiding. Have to warn him."

They crept into the caves that honeycombed the area. "Jesus," he would whisper, "it's your friend, David. I won't betray you. They're looking for you. Can I get you food?" There was never any response except the scurrying of small animals until one unseen occupant growled, "What're you jabbering about? Beat it!" Then they sprawled on the ground, exhausted and defeated.

"I don't know where else to look." Despair glazed his eyes.

"Maybe he went to Bethany, to Lazarus."

"You're right!" They bounded to their feet, he grasped her hand, and they hurried off.

Martha opened the door, and her sparkling happiness changed to concern. "David! You look like you fell off a cliff. Come in. What happened?"

"This is Abbey. Is Jesus alive? Have you seen him?"

Mary burst into the kitchen happier than anyone they had ever seen. "He's alive! He is!" she kept saying as she embraced them, and didn't even remark on his bloody scratches.

"Mary, you're making a mess of yourself," Martha spouted. "David, sit down!" She dabbed at the blood and grime with a wet cloth, but no one was paying any attention to her.

David pulled free. "Then take me to him. Where's he hiding?"

A peal of laughter rang from Mary. Martha threw down her washcloth and sat. He looked hurt. Abbey looked from one to the other in wonder.

"I'm sorry, David," Mary apologized, "but I'm just too

430

happy. It's not the way you think. He's in no danger any more."

"What're you talking about? The guards are looking for him and so are the Romans!" Martha laid a hand on his flailing arms.

"Quiet down, David."

"I don't understand," he moaned, and sat down.

"It's not easy to explain," she admitted, "but Mary's telling the truth. He isn't in danger." David looked bewildered.

"You heard how he walked on water once," Mary said. "You might say he lives that way now. Times and places can't hold him any more."

"He comes and goes at will." Martha snapped her fingers. "Like that!"

He shook his head like a fractious horse. "He's still a man, isn't he? And why can't Lazarus do what you say?"

"Our brother returned to the life he had," Mary replied gently. "He'll die again. Jesus won't. He's entered the final age—the final Adam." Abbey nodded, eyes gleaming, but David bounded up in frustration.

"Then why's he hiding? Anyway, take me to him."

"Now listen!" Martha barked, then added more sympathetically. "He doesn't live with us in the old way."

"Not until we rise," Mary explained.

"For now," Martha added, "he only appears to those he's chosen as witnesses. Last night he visited the Eleven."

"Take me to them."

"David, they're the ones in danger."

"You mean my part in all this is ended?" he asked in grief.

"It's just beginning for us all!" Mary exulted.

"Have patience," Martha urged, and laughed. "What's the use of telling a young man that? I don't have much myself." Then she added, "When they've made their plans, you'll hear, I promise."

"But there's something they should know. They sealed the tomb, chased the crowds, and called the Romans. That's how I got hurt."

Martha looked at her sister. "I'd better take him."

"David, we know of these developments," said Peter. "Two of the women who were there have been held for

431

questioning."

"How can I help?"

"Tell your family the good news, and then wait until we preach in public again."

"They'll arrest you —kill you!"

"No. We've been promised power from on high—in God's good time. After we've received it, we'll tell you what to do."

"That's fair enough. I hope it's soon."

He dragged Martha along in his eagerness to get back to Abbey. Repeating what he had heard, he cried, "Come on, let's tell our families!"

Abbey's mother listened with her fingers over her mouth. Her soul had been stirred by the prophet and grieved by his execution, but she had never dreamed of this. Then it was not over . . .

The youngsters' rush of words ceased, and the boy looked at her with concern. "Are you angry with me for running off with Abbey like that?"

Anne's face melted. "Not under the circumstances. Now I have to find my husband and tell him the good news."

"And I have to tell my family!"

"Then come back," Abbey urged, "and we'll sit and talk about it. When it sinks in, we'll know a lot more."

"Talk'll have to do until we see him. I just hope it won't be long."

10

After a volcanic eruption has changed forever the aspect of the land, the people of the region try to restore order and return to their accustomed life—though in fact it will never be the same. So it was in Jerusalem. On the surface, affairs so resumed their normal course that the new reality seemed not to exist. The tomb remained sealed and guarded. Brutal tactics discouraged pilgrimages. Thousands of pilgrims had streamed from the city after the Passover week. Temple

432

guards kept searching ostentatiously for the Eleven, with secret instructions not to find them. The real objective? To drive them into hiding. What the authorities least wanted was more publicity for the alleged resurrection.

Dispersing into their secret shelters, the Eleven had agreed to meet in a week. Thus it was that Thomas dragged his sandalled feet up the Mount of Olives. Any alert passerby could make out his turned-down mouth and sagging eyes even in the twilight. He was thinking in horror and grief of what had happened to Judas. Stories of Judas' last hours had been pieced together from eye witnesses. The most bizarre thing—after the way he died—was the garment he was wearing. A merchant shed light on that. Judas had glided up to Gomer's garment display trance-like, and haughtily demanded the most regal vesture money could buy. When he saw the ornate silver robe with pearl-grey sleeves and majestic golden turban, he seemed hypnotized by the interminable golden sash which circled the midriff. Robing himself in his new acquisition, for which he paid in pearls, he had thrown his head high and marched on through the bazaar.

Others remembered the imposing figure, towering in the great turban, gliding through the city like some conquering foreign potentate or alien high priest—and they remembered the terrible look of the eyes.

When the Seder had commenced and the streets were dark and deserted, a Roman officer had espied the figure, wandering still, abruptly departing by the Judgment Gate.

The reminiscence darkened Thomas' mood the more, and he tried to cast it from him, but it adhered like some tunic shrunken and clinging with sweat. At the thought of meeting the others, Thomas felt worse still. Who needed further harassment for refusing to be gullible? Still, they were a good bunch, and he was terribly lonely. If only they knew how to let him work this out in his own way. It wasn't that he didn't think their claim might be true—he had to *know* it was true. Hadn't his former faith raised his hopes to treacherous pinnacles which collapsed under him and roared down in an avalanche which buried his self-esteem? He was ashamed of his defection, but angry about it too. It wasn't an act of cowardice, but the disintegration of a system of faith that had made him instinctively run to firmer ground.

Resentment, too, plagued him. If the Master had come last week, why hadn't he waited for him? That was hard to forgive.

As to faith in the possibility of the Master's rising, he had plenty! In Jericho he hadn't even gone to his wife. He'd holed up in Three-a-day's, refusing food, thinking, going deeper than ever into the mystery of the Master, and coming up with a stunning possibility which, if so much as mentioned, would shock the others—who thought they had so much faith! Although his idea was too brazen to come right out with, it remained the only explanation that tied together the ancient prophecies, the Master's startling teachings and works, the disaster, and even the claimed resurrection. In fact he, Thomas, should have predicted the resurrection on the basis of his insight. He had plenty of raw material for faith. He just needed more evidence.

His crawling pace finally carried him to the great oaken portal. He delayed there, trying to heap up still higher his protective wall of indignation. This Sunday more than last, he suspected, he would be pressured to turn in his brain for a believer's badge. Raising his fist to the coarse grain, he belligerently hammered out the code. The lock-bar grated and the door opened.

"Shalom, Thomas," Andrew greeted him fondly. "You're the last." The rest welcomed him cordially enough too, but they glanced at him oddly.

"We were exchanging news," Peter informed him, and reported that they were still being hunted. "We've had no further contact with the Lord." Peter turned to the others. "Have I overlooked anything?"

"Just that the authorities have an official story now," Bartholomew responded. "They're saying we robbed the body."

"They probably believe it," rasped Thomas.

"It's easier than believing the truth, isn't it?" James snapped.

"Don't start that," Jude chided. "In his shoes I'd be feeling bad too—and maybe just as stubborn."

"Who's stubborn?" Thomas bristled.

434

After a discreet pause, Peter spoke. "Twin"—he used Thomas' nickname—"you've had a week. Has your position changed?"

"Nothing's happened, nothing's changed."

"Nothing's happened!" Bartholomew was indignant. "You've now talked privately to each of us. We wouldn't lie to you."

"This kind of thing you have to see for yourself."

"See for yourself?" James raised his eyebrows. "You never do see! Take the time the Master suddenly announced that Lazarus had died and he was going to him. I was amazed—how did he know? But all you saw was the danger— 'Let's go and die with him!' "

"How wrong was I? He was killed, and if we weren't, it's because we're a bunch of cowards."

John leaped in with, "Still, my brother's right. When Jesus said he was going ahead of us but we knew the way, do you recall your reaction?"

"I had the courage to speak up and say that since none of us knew where he was going, we certainly didn't know the way."

"Your words were a prophecy about yourself."

"What are you talking about?"

"The way is by resurrection. We all know but you."

"I know what's reasonable. You've been charmed by hysterical women into visions. I haven't. Someone has to keep his head in the midst of disaster."

"Look who kept his head in disaster!" the Zealot bawled. "The only thinking you did was with your legs!"

"Stop it, all of you!" Jude reprimanded.

"The truth must come out," John insisted. "Twin, you're not just unbelieving—you're allergic to belief. Because you were left out of our experience, you have no intention of sharing our faith."

"You have all the answers, don't you?"

"I have this one."

"For two copper coins I'd pull out for good."

"Simmer down, John," Peter admonished. "Are you satisfied, now that your 'truth' has eaten away our bond? The Master's own mother told us to be patient with one

435

another."

"She has some concern for others," grumped Thomas, touched by Peter's intervention.

"I'm sorry, Thomas," John said. "You know I'm with you."

"Twin, we've been telling *you* why you don't believe," Peter said gently. "Won't you tell us?"

"Because I haven't seen him."

"Shalom, shalom." At the sound of that familiar voice behind him, Thomas froze an instant, then catapulted from his seat and spun around. The Lord stood before him.

"Thomas." They looked at one another. Tears began to slide down the Twin's cheeks.

"Bring that finger of yours here." Out of the silence the words came gentle but firm. "Investigate these hands of mine." So saying, he reached for an oil lamp, raised his right arm, and held the lamp behind the hand so that the light passed through the nailhole. Slowly, the Twin slipped to his knees.

"Bring that hand of yours here and thrust it into this side of mine." He bared the deep wound, red in the lamp's streaming rays. "Stop disbelieving and begin believing."

Thomas' parched lips opened. The others strained to hear the words he gasped. "My Lord and my God!" They looked stunned, but none spoke. Jesus gazed at them during a long silence.

"Thomas, now that you have seen, you have believed. Blessed are those who believe without seeing."

Then he was gone. None stirred until at length the Twin arose. On his bearded young face played a beatific smile. Peter went to him and they embraced wordlessly.

"Praise God, we're one again," Jude rejoiced, and they all gathered around the Twin with thumps on the back and words of friendship.

John laid his hand on Thomas' shoulder and said in a voice reverent with respect: "Just when we were doing all the teaching, you gave us a lesson—and what a lesson!"

Peter looked troubled at the remark, but only said, "Thomas, tell his mother the good news, and come right back."

"Now that we're reunited," the big fisherman began when Thomas returned, "I'm planning a speedy trip to Galilee, to confirm the reports the disciples there will have heard."

"We're to wait in the city for heavenly power," Philip objected.

"This mission," Peter explained, "I received from the Lord when he came to me in the Temple. I told you then I had something further to say when the time was right. Andrew will take charge here."

"Take Thomas along," Jude suggested. "He travels fast—he was halfway to Galilee an hour after he left Gethsemane." They laughed, but the Twin grumped.

"Be a good sport," Matthew urged. "It was only Jericho you made in an hour." Jericho was a six-hour trip.

"Let him be," Peter chided, unsuccessfully repressing his own smile. "I wish I'd done nothing worse than make it to Jericho in the shortest time ever. You didn't really go all the way to Jericho, did you?"

"Yes, all the way! Now do you want to call the town crier?"

"How did Malachy fetch you back so soon?"

"He didn't fetch me. I was returning when we met."

"I will take you along because I have a bone to pick with you—and with you, John, since you saw fit to pat him on the back."

"I go gladly," said John.

"James and Nathanael will come too. Now let's put supper under our belts and get some sleep. We leave before dawn."

11

The lock-bar grated in the morning stillness, the oaken door swung out, and the five men emerged under the canopy of stars, slipped silently onto the path to the Roman road, and strode toward Jericho.

They traveled in silence, Peter preoccupying himself with the white stars in the black firmament. Suddenly, one flared ruby red, flamed burning emerald, flashed a radiant amethyst, and sedately settled once again into a luminous white dot lost among a thousand others. How far beyond comprehension were even such daily experiences—and now the Twin had plunged him into the bottomless depths of an outrageous mystery.

The blackness began yielding to a faint light in the East, and the stars were snuffed out one by one. When but three remained, he intoned the first words of the Shema Israel, and the others took it up, "The Lord is our God, the Lord is unique," and continued on to the end. The last cadence was still ringing when his troubled voice cleaved the air.

"Twin, I got little sleep last night because of you."

"I didn't sleep at all."

"When you said, 'My Lord and my God,' my first instinct was to stone you." The others pressed in closer. Rising a crimson ball behind diaphanous clouds, the sun's dramatic hues played on his solemn face and massive beard, lending an awesome look. "I hope you can explain yourself."

"You know I'm not good at words. I doubt I'll be able to explain."

"One thing is sure—you're going to try!"

"I am trying! I can tell you this—if you think I was spooked into saying it to make up for everything, you're wrong."

"I don't think that. Why did you say it?"

"There really wasn't any one thing."

"Then start somewhere."

"I'll start at Gethsemane. When they seized him my faith fell apart. I ran, and kept running long after it had meaning. When I couldn't run, I walked. My arrival in Jericho came as a surprise—I had no plans. I explained to Three-a-day, got a room, and fell asleep.

"When I awoke, I lay and thought. I couldn't accept that we'd gone completely wrong—he's given us too much proof. My only food was my thoughts and my prayer. I was determined to work it out—I felt we'd missed something. I took hold of every Scripture about the Messiah I could remember, and followed it up word by word, climbing the mountain on that whole chain. Every time I got higher I could see farther into the strangeness of it all. I recalled our discussions about the Master, and the strange ideas of Judas—God have mercy on him!

"The Lord promised through the prophets to come himself and shepherd us, and I tried to fit that in. Malachi marches to that tune, where he has the Lord say, 'Lo, I send my messenger before me, and he shall purge my way.' The Baptizer purged the way for Jesus—who must then be the Lord!"

"I didn't see it till now," John rushed in, "but Jesus did take Malachi's text to himself."

"Stay out of this, Son of Zebedee," Peter admonished.

"The idea," Thomas resumed, "made sense of all the impossible things the Master said and did, and the way he called God his Father. Now you know why I couldn't believe you. If I bought your story, I'd have to accept the rest, and I was afraid. I'm an Israelite."

Peter aimed his massive head at him. "Not very helpful."

"Who can explain?" the Twin despaired. "You suddenly knew—he's the Messiah. You never explained."

Peter's words flew like sparks from an anvil: "That was different. We expected the Christ. It was in all our minds it might be he. But you scandalize my Jewish blood."

"Right!" Nathanael interrupted. "How can he be God when his Father is God—and there is only one God?"

"Why didn't you tell the Master that," Thomas asked, "when he kept calling God his Father?"

"When I heard Thomas," John injected, "things fell together for me as well."

"You owe us an explanation too!" Peter burst out.

"You know Psalm 45 calls the Messiah, 'the comeliest of the sons of men,' and then goes on, 'Your throne, O God, stands forever.' So in one psalm the Messiah is called both man and God."

"Poetic exaggeration!" Nathanael bellowed. "Like Moses being told he'd be god to Aaron!"

Said Thomas, "When in Jericho, I remembered Isaiah's prophecy of the son to be given us—to be called mighty God. I feared I understood." His voice broke.

439

Peter spoke next. "Look over there." He pointed to the wildly beautiful disarray of precipitous cliffs and mountains lying before them, concealing the mighty chasm of the Jordan rift. "Hidden down there is Bethany-beyond-Jordan where the Lord called me. If there were any truth in what you say, he'd have given us hints."

"Hints!" exploded John. "He gave us revelations! We were too stupid to take them in."

At this, James spoke in excited words that crackled like thunder over the lightning of his flashing memories: "John and I used to discuss those revelations. We couldn't accept them, so we'd explain them away."

Peter faced the pair of brothers. "What are some of those 'revelations?'"

"When we were last at the Feast of Tabernacles . . ." James began, but John cut him off.

"Wait." John gripped Peter's arm with fingers of steel and turned on him a burning look. "Son of John, it's time for you to give witness to the *bath kol* on the mountain. Or must I do it?"

Peter looked thunderstruck, James froze with the wonder of sudden recall, and the others moved in closer.

"How did I *not* remember?" Waves of realization rolled across his face as he described the event. "And then the voice from heaven said, 'This is my only Son. Listen to him.'"

"At the time," John added quietly, "we couldn't take it in. We could only think of it in the sense of a holy relationship."

In silence, in searching thought, they went on. The chill of early morning had passed. They reached a wadi swollen by spring rain, singing its rushing song of encounter with rock and stone and curving bank. Peter and Nathanael stooped, cupped the water in their hands, and drank. The others knelt and sank their lips in the sparkling flow.

When the Twin rose, he turned to the others and spoke in gentle tones: "Dear friends, the Master used to correct our blunders. Just last night he hit at my obstinacy. Yet when I confessed him my Lord and God, he didn't correct me."

"I'm still not convinced," declared Nathanael in a tone unutterably sad and desolate.

"Maybe none of us is, fully," conceded James. "Ants don't climb Tabor in an hour."

"I," said the Twin, "am fully convinced."

"Brothers, listen to me." The big fisherman's voice was laced with iron. "The Master said no one could come to him without help from the Father. Now that we've discussed the matter, let's pray to the Father for help. In time, perhaps we can agree. Now I have to think."

He took the lead, walking alone. More and more, he needed these times of meditation when the clutter was left behind and heart and mind could wander freely, in the medium of eternity, pursuing their own pace. Then he realized he was doing what the Master used to do—walking alone in prayer. It seemed that the more deeply he entered into the kingdom of heaven, the more he felt out of place in time, like a creature in the wrong medium—like a gasping fish out of water, or a frantic fly mired in syrup. It was only by slipping for a while into eternity that he could find refreshment, and return renewed to carry on.

Hours later, as they strode along in a happy mood, chatting pleasantly, the big fisherman suddenly stopped. "Twin, I don't know how you did it."

"You mean came to know?"

"I mean came to Jericho in an hour."

"Peter, you're a card! You ought to turn comedian! What I did is nothing to joke about."

Peter gripped Thomas' arm. "Look at me!" There was no laughter now. There was a haunted, tortured look. "We've shared nightmares together. If we don't dig out the lode of humor, we'll break—we'll split wide open like a ripe melon, dropped hard, on rock!"

"All right, but why do I have to be lode?"

The big fisherman backed off, poking a finger at his own massive chest. "Make a joke about what I did. Please! Then it might not seem so bad. Because if you're right, do you know whom I denied? No wonder Judas hanged himself!"

"Yes," John whispered. "He had the first inkling."

In one giant step, Thomas was at Peter's side, putting his arm around his shoulder. They walked on together. The others heard them sobbing.

441

On reaching the cliff lowering over the city, they rested on a shattered boulder, gazing down on the houses nestling peacefully in an island of green. To the south gleamed the Dead Sea's steely dark waters, rimmed by high mountains.

"We'll eat here," Peter announced.

"We'll be at Three-a-day's soon," Thomas objected. "We don't have time to stop in the City of Palms."

"He must have heard by now. I have to confirm it." When the Twin saw the refusal in that face, he rushed on. "I owe it to him. You've joked about my long legs—now let me use them. You eat, I'll go—and be waiting for you beyond the city."

"Off you go," he agreed affectionately. Before the last word was formed, the youth was speeding down the road— and soon out of sight.

"Maybe he did make Jericho in an hour," Nathanael marveled.

When they met Thomas, he was carrying a sack and devouring a fistful of dates. "Three-a-day believed me. He's happy as a lark, already trumpeting the good news. He pressed some fresh fruit on me." He held up the sack.

"I'm glad you're as fast as we thought," Peter said. "You remember we have to carry the message to the whole world. I'm going to keep you in mind for the distant places."

"That's all right with me. I like to travel."

They continued north all that day. Whenever they fell silent, Peter's mind gnawed at their earlier conversation. Once he took John aside and asked quietly, "Any further thoughts?"

"Just this—that in time we'll remember too much to doubt."

Later, Nathanael sidled up to Thomas looking sheepish. "I just want you to know," he murmured, "that it's beginning to make sense. Sorry."

"About objecting? You had a right to—a duty to. I was tortured too when I first began to realize . . ."

The sun began dropping swiftly below the western mountains. Peter gazed across the Jordan rift, watching the liquid flow of ebbing light stippling the naked mountains rising in an indescribable medley of towering gray rock and pale

442

white sand interspersed with elements of subtler, iridescent hues. Hills and mountains issued from one another in an involuted pattern of originators and originated that defied the mind. It was like a forbidden glimpse into a world where beauty and chaos were wed in some primal union. He turned away, overwhelmed.

What mysteries still remain, towering above the grasp of man!

12

Fading light from an overcast sky played luridly on the leaden waters as Peter descended to Capernaum with his companion, Nathan, a local disciple. He looked at the man in admiration. Two weeks they had been traveling, carrying the good news—and meeting incredulous stares—and yet Nathan maintained more the look of a self-possessed gladiator than a defeated preacher. He was known as a man with a compelling need to climb mountains. Once every year he would scale the icy peaks of Mount Hermon, to teeter in the winds of heaven at its pinnacle. There was a stratospheric aura about his person, especially his far-seeing look. His face appeared haggard, the eye sockets shadowed, but the gleam of his gaze was undimmed, and the set of the jaw as firm as rock. Lean and tough of body, lean and strong of character—his faith unshaken by their desolating experience. Though half a head taller, the big fisherman felt dwarfed by the man. They were about the same age, but Nathan had a temperament seasoned like the hills, and was shaken by events no more than a mountain by wind. His loyalty was like old, fire-tried, beaten gold. It was a privilege to know him, and a humbling experience to be his leader.

Peter was anxious to learn how the others had fared. Since their arrival two weeks ago, each Apostle had been touring an area of Galilee with a companion, carrying the news of the resurrection to the local disciples. Humbling as it might be, he hoped the others had done better than he.

They had agreed to meet on this Sunday evening at his house before sundown. He found the four Apostles already assembled in his courtyard. Of their companions, however, only Thomas' partner, Stephen, was present. These two were old boyhood friends, and the Twin had long since won him over to Christ. He was as lanky and long-legged as his friend, but of an opposite temperament—sedate and unchanging of mood.

"How did it go?" Peter queried. The silence was eloquent. He turned to John. "Where is Saul?"

"He saw the disciples in town after town setting their jaws in obstinate disbelief, and I saw his faith shriveling like a raisin. Wednesday I woke to find him gone."

"Ahithophel abandoned me for a like reason," James said.

"And Benjamin me," Nathanael added mournfully.

"And you and Stephen, Thomas?"

"Peter, they had ears of stone, so in desperation I began recounting how the Lord had raised Lazarus before his own rising. It only made matters worse. After my conduct, I didn't even have a comeback."

"Not many received our testimony," Peter confessed. "Now let's eat." They ate in silence, munching their rations with bovine slowness, staring into the twilight.

"What do we do now?" James barked when the snail's pace got under his skin. Peter, who had been toying with his walking stick, rose and threw it to the ground.

"I'm going fishing."

"I'll come along," James said, and the others nodded. With food and money low, it would be more than a diversion.

The seven men lumbered down to Peter's boat, checked the fishing gear, and launched the craft. It was dark—not a star in the sky. A smudge of light was all that betrayed the crescent moon, and the smudge appeared to be roaming among the clouds. Black water swirled past as they rowed, and there was the occasional plop of a leaping fish unseen in the darkness.

"Take her down by the submerged boulders near Seven Springs," directed Peter. "That spot never fails me. Over a fresh-netted breakfast we'll decide our next move."

He watched the patches of fog lying heavy on the surface, drifting slowly. Thick as the darkness on those Galilean minds, he thought. We went out to change their lives with the good news, and left no more trace than we do on these dark waters—a splash and a gurgle, a momentary wake, then the sea flows back and it's as though we'd never passed. If they only half-believed the Master, how will they ever believe us?

The dark thoughts seemed to congeal the night into a shroud lying heavy across head and shoulders. Never had he found this beloved lake so cheerless and unfriendly. After the brilliance of the resurrection experiences, the blackness around struck him as nightmarish—some prehistoric grave-yard of eons past which had no right to keep clinging to existence. Didn't it know it was banished to extinction now that the light of Christ had flared in the world? Didn't the people know?

An emaciated moonbeam broke through the cloud cover and feebly lit a playing wave and it annoyed him—as if, turning miserly, nature was offering to placate him with crumbs when he wanted bread.

He stripped for work. It was growing chilly and he shivered. He hurled the slimy net with unwonted violence, and drew on it impatiently. Even the fish had grown elusive—mocking his failure to catch the evasive disciples in the net of faith. Bitterly, he thought of his own refusal to believe, and it further blackened his despair. If, after seeing so much, he had not believed, how would those believe who had seen so little, or had seen nothing?

At last the Lord's Anointed had come—and now, was the human race to behave like starving madmen, refusing to feast on the banquet set out because, without making trial, they had deemed it a mirage, a thing too good to be true? Never had he felt so helpless.

The night dragged by, wasted. What fish they took were inedible, thrown back in disgust. His stripped body felt encircled by a tangle of clammy snakes crushing out his soul—cold, hunger, discouragement, fatigue, and others too many to mention.

The figure on the near shore became visible as a clear

445

dawn blushed crimson along the skyline across the lake. He paid no attention until the man hailed them.

"My little ones, you haven't caught anything to eat, have you?"

He overcame the impulse to ignore the annoying question. "No!"

"Cast your net to starboard, and you will."

"Another dry-footed fishing expert," Stephen commented. The big fisherman showed no sign of complying.

"What can we lose?" the Twin asked. Peter growled something about hard work, but hauled in the net and hurled it out to starboard, whereupon the boat lurched. "Snagged!" he muttered.

Thomas the landlubber tugged at the net in exploratory fashion. "Feels anchored in lead."

John took hold and held it a moment. "It's quivering." Peter tested it.

"Then it must be a whale!" He hunkered down and squinted into the water. "Start drawing it slowly. Not so fast! You'll tear it." They peered into the water as the net began to emerge. It was swollen with flashing, wriggling silver bodies.

John leaped to his feet and stared at the figure on the shore, the hackles climbing his neck. In a strange, tight voice he announced, "It's the Lord."

Peter shot bolt upright, sending the craft into a wild rock. Stripped and shivering, he stood for a fleeting instant staring at the shore-bound figure, then seized his tunic, knotted it round his midriff, plunged into the lake, and began swimming.

"You'll disembowel yourself!" John warned. A horde of volcanic rocks, ragged and razor sharp, lurked just below the surface about fifty feet closer to shore. None dared swim in that water. Ignoring the warning, the swimmer struck on with powerful strokes that sent up plumes of water and drove him surging toward the beach.

On board, they seized the oars and rowed wildly, thrusting the lurching craft erratically toward the shore, dragging the fish-gorged net. The prow grated on the beach, and they leaped out and waded ashore.

He was standing by a midriff-high outcropping of table rock, with bread laid out, and fish sizzling gently on a charcoal

446

fire. "Bring some of the fish you caught," he said. The compelling voice was intimately familiar and chillingly unknown. The big fisherman, standing alongside him clad in his dripping tunic, ran to the boat, unfastened the net, and dragged it ashore. It was crammed with large fish—when counted, there would prove to be 153—but the net showed not the least tear. It was a marvel that it had not been shredded by the inescapable rocks.

Seizing several fish, he cleaned and scaled them without a wasted stroke, and took them to the Lord—he knew it was the Lord—who removed the baked ones from the gold-vermilion embers, and laid on the others.

Nathanael was gawking. When his gaze was returned, he sheepishly looked away, only to steal another glance at once. The others were not behaving much better—except Nathan, who comported himself as if he were eating with the Master just as in the old days. Stephen was the worst, staring with protruding eyes, incapable of adjusting to the unearthly experience. They knew it was he, but their eyes simply could not confirm or deny that knowing. It was like returning in manhood to some familiar old landmark of childhood, a foothill up which one had often scampered as a boy, and to be touched by the sight, yet confounded to see, unremembered in the background, a towering, windswept peak lost in the clouds. And so none asked him, "Who are you?" because they knew they knew—and did not dare the question.

"You're hungry?" he inquired, and they nodded dumbly. "Come, have breakfast." He broke the bread, gave each a portion, and likewise portioned out the steaming fish.

The big fisherman examined for bones, and devoured his. "Delicious," he thought. "Our netful couldn't be fresher. Where did he get it?" It seemed a silly question, but there it was.

In silence they finished that ordinary yet awesome meal, the Master partaking with them. Often, afterwards, they were to describe it to hungry-eyed believers when celebrating the Eucharist.

After the meal, he turned and gazed long at Peter before he spoke. "Simon, offspring of John, do you love me—more than these others?"

That comparison with the others struck like a blow. It opened a door in his memory, and out blared his own voice bragging, "If they all fall away, I won't!" He'd believed it then, but events proved the lion's heart was John's, not his. So how answer? He'd best reply only to the first part of the question.

"Yes, Lord, you know I love you."

"Feed my lambs," the Master said, and then, after a pause, he repeated the question, but without the incriminating part. "Simon, offspring of John, do you love me?"

Peter breathed a sigh of relief—and choked it off as it hit him that the word for love now twice used was one he'd heard expounded by a learned rabbi, a scholar who treaded air intellectually, and was wafted to higher regions by every breeze of his reflections until he disappeared from mental sight. The word signified a love reverent, noble, spiritual, exalted, other-worldly. He'd wanted to slink out and lumber back to his nets where he belonged. And now, worse still, throbbing up like an unearthly drum, beat the Twin's fateful words, "My Lord and my God." Was such a love indispensable then? Desperately, pain registering in the sudden wrinkles around his eyes, he doggedly repeated his first reply, in which he had instinctively used a different word for love— "Yes, Lord, you know I love you."

"Tend my sheep. Do you love me?"

The relief was soothing as a plunge into cool water. *His* word was being used now, and he could ring out his yes! Then the sledgehammer hit him—three questions, to match his three denials? The large mouth opened into a raw wound. "Lord, you know all. You know I love you."

"Feed my shearlings." The Master regarded him until the gaze seemed to penetrate his bones and marrow. "As a youth, you buckled your own belt and went your own way. Once old, you'll stretch out your hands, have your belt buckled for you—and be led by a way not of your choosing.

"Follow me." The Lord walked away, and his first in command followed. Boldly, John trailed after, as if knowing instinctively he was welcome anywhere Jesus went. They passed out of earshot, and then out of sight beyond a stand of trees.

448

The two returned alone. "He's gone," Peter said.

"Peter, what's wrong with me?" Nathanael burst out. "My eyes wouldn't work! I recognized him and yet I didn't."

"I too," James acknowledged.

"I suspect we all did," Peter said. The others nodded—except Nathan. Nathanael pressed on.

"What does it mean?" No one responded. After a time Thomas volunteered an answer.

"He's changed now." He spoke slowly as each word was new-forged on some inner anvil. "He's the Christ we so long awaited—the one who can't die. His risen body is—different."

"We recognized him in Jerusalem," James objected.

"Can it be," John proposed, "that he's accustoming us to his gradual withdrawal from our sight?" At this they fell silent again. A look of intense concentration crinkled Peter's brow.

"I have another explanation. When he called to us from the shore, what was our first reaction?"

"We weren't interested," Stephen recalled. "He was just a meddling stranger."

"Exactly. But when we recognized him—what then?"

"We weren't interested in anything else!"

"Peter, you've hit on it!" John's face flamed. " 'What you do to others you do to me'—his words!"

"Yes."

"That means that now we find him everywhere—in others! We've got to do it by faith."

"Something like that," Peter agreed. "The two on the Emmaus road recognized him only after they offered him hospitality. We, only after we did what he said."

"You," Thomas whispered, "are into a mystery almost as big as the one I had to wrestle with."

"Perhaps they're connected. Nathan, a question."

"What is it?"

"When we were all staring at him, you weren't."

"I knew it was he."

"Could you see him clearly, recognize him clearly?"

"No."

"Then what do you mean?"

"I saw and I believed."

"But surely you wanted to confirm it with your eyes!"

"No. It can't be done. He provides hand-holds in the mountain to be scaled, but won't level it for those who fear to climb the heights of faith. He was a mystery to me since I first met him. Why not more so now?"

"It's only natural to want to see and recognize!"

"Maybe too natural. But don't think I didn't take him in. While you stared at his face, I was at home with his every gesture, tone, attitude—his whole temperament. That I did recognize—the whole cluster. I knew him all right—as he'd know me by the way I act, even in the dark."

"I'd never deny that." Peter spoke with profound respect. "So would I. You're inimitable."

While this exchange went on, John, though listening intently, picked up a twig and drew on the ground.

"What are you up to, John?" Peter asked.

"I was just drawing two shepherds. One is the Good Shepherd. The other is you—watching over his flock."

"Amen to that," Peter said, and they all said amen. "It's high time to start shepherding. We leave for the Holy City at once, to wait there for the Power from heaven. We learned here how little we can do without it—and, thanks to you, Thomas—how little we can understand without it. Nathan, take care of things here. We'll keep you informed."

They embraced in solemn parting, and traveled south.

13

On the third day of travel, the five disciples saw the Mount of Olives coming into view, marking their journey's end. In the days just ahead they were fated to witness the close of the first leg of their greatest journey, and to set out for their final destination.

They ascended the Mount, crossed the grassy field thick with wild flowers, and laid eyes on the homely lodge where they would gather with the others once again. Peter's heart leaped and all his fatigue washed away. Within that place all the hopes of his people had come to fruition. The prophets and priests must be hovering over it in their invisible hordes, chanting, "Here it all happened as we foretold." Across the valley, all the Holy City should be singing with joy, sending its glad songs cascading up to this sacred place, consecrating its triumph in glad thanksgiving.

The pale gold wands of grain clustering around the lodge in the brilliant sunshine turned Peter's thoughts another way. Uncultivated, drying, bleaching in the wind, the stalks spoke to him of the long-abandoned Gentiles waving their distress signals from afar. He, Peter Shepherd, had much to think about, much to do.

A figure lounging by the portal espied them and ran up, sending a long-eared rabbit bounding into the brush.

"Shalom, Jonah," Peter called.

"Andrew posted me here," he said. "They vacated the hall. I'm to take you to his tent."

As they approached the goat-skin frame pitched by a bed of mountain lilies, Peter's brother emerged. Calling the peace, he ran to embrace them. "Welcome back! Peter, the Lord appeared to his cousin, James."

"When?"

"Two days after you left."

"Jonah says you moved out of the hall."

"We're back in the Upper Room."

"Isn't that dangerous?"

"No longer. A minority of the Pharisees are pressuring the Supreme Council to investigate the Lord's resurrection seriously."

"We're not under arrest?"

"No. Rabbi Gamaliel insisted that none of us be harassed. Some of the priests are supporting us. A few have come over. The hands of the chief priests are tied. How did you fare?"

"We saw the Lord in Galilee. The rest of the Eleven must be told. We leave for the Upper Room at once."

The Apostles bent round as their leader recounted the failed missionary journey, the great haul of fish, the Lord on

451

the shore, and what followed. "Any questions?"

"You mean," Jude queried with a grin, "you finally made a catch big enough to turn brag to fact?"

The big fisherman laughed with the rest.

"Peter, doesn't the failure in Galilee concern you?" Philip asked anxiously.

"It did until the Lord came."

"Don't you see?" Thomas exclaimed. "We accomplish nothing without him—but with him, everything!"

"The haul of fish was his latest parable," John pointed out.

"Now we wait for him to redeem his pledge to send the Power from on high," Peter declared. "But we don't just wait. Since the danger has passed, we arrange an assembly of the disciples. They shouldn't be left prey to rumors and doubts."

"Which disciples?" Andrew asked.

"The seventy-two, the devoted women, and the most committed of the others."

"It will take time. Some are dispersed, some still hiding."

"Tomorrow's Thursday. Say a week from tomorrow."

"That should do it. Can we crowd them all in here?"

"We'll meet at the Galilee, to attract the least unwanted attention."

A brilliant sun rising in blue skies ushered in the appointed morning. The gathering place was an open field near a stand of palm trees and a few evergreen myrtle, which were in fragrant bloom.

When the Apostles arrived an hour after sunup, Thomas cried in happy surprize, "A whale of a crowd! They've multiplied like scarab beetles! How many believers do you think we have here?"

Peter, recalling the many sceptics in Galilee, replied whimsically, "Oh, about half."

The laughter this evoked was knifed through by the Twin's voice. "Simon, take it from me, it's not easy to believe if you weren't in on it from the beginning."

"Don't I know that? Ask the Magdalene."

"Peter, by your estimate," Jude declared, "we have here about 250 believers."

Simon Peter joined the cluster of devoted women disciples, found the mother of Jesus, and embraced her. Greeting the others affectionately, he said, "Join the Eleven at the center. We want you as witnesses." Then he addressed Mary. "Mother, we need your prayers. It's not going to be easy for some to believe."

She took his hand. "Just do as you saw him do."

"It's time to begin," Peter announced to the Eleven. "Be seated, and rise when I call for your witness." He rotated, arms outstretched, powerful voice raised over the hubbub, calling the encircling crowd to silence.

"Faithful friends of Jesus, Servant of the God of Abraham, Isaac and Jacob, we have assembled you for one reason—to witness that God has raised him from the dead. We have seen him, conversed with him, touched him with our hands." A roar of approval went up, but his practiced eye spotted the doubting glances. Vigorously, he called for silence.

"His love and truth, which bonded us when he was with us, must unite us still now that he has left us. We who walked with him most closely—the Eleven—have been appointed to confirm your faith and join you together in him."

"Tell us about Jesus!" a raucous voice interrupted, loosing a burst of excited cries. Peter called impatiently for order.

"Listen! The good sense the Master always showed we must show. Everything in due time. Each of the Eleven will give his witness. After that, we will circulate among you—we and the women who first saw him risen—and you can ask us what you like. John, begin with the shroud and the empty tomb."

The accounts of the witnesses were punctuated with cries from the crowd. Interruptions mounted with the growing excitement. When Peter described how Jesus came to him in the Temple, the outcries took over.

"Praise God!" "His wonders can't be numbered!" "Jesus is the Christ!"

A tall, stringy man of emaciated face and glaring eye bounded up beside Peter and screamed, "To the high priest! Action against the murderers! Down with Caiaphas and Pontius Pilate!"

An uproar ensued. Peter labored to restore order. "Disciples

453

of Jesus the Christ," he exclaimed, "do not yield to every spirit, every self-appointed leader. You know that he himself appointed the Eleven. He has come to us risen. He guides our course still. We are led by his will and purpose, nothing else—least of all, vengeance!"

"Are you afraid—afraid to die?" shrilled the stringy man. A hushed silence fell.

"Afraid?" the big fisherman repeated, puzzled. "Afraid of the resurrection?" He stared straight ahead. "No. Ashamed." His eyes fell—a posture in which he looked a stranger. "Until I've done my work, so that, like him, I leave the earth a man."

These words produced a sober calm, providing the Eleven a chance to recount their Easter experience—but not for long.

"I see him, I see him!" a large, wild-eyed woman shrieked. "Clothed in a golden robe, borne by angels, crowned with a silver crown with shining rays, appointing me spokesman because they doubted."

"Where? Where is he?"

"Silence!" thundered Peter. "Woman, be quiet or be removed. Yours is not the spirit of Christ. He does not contradict himself. He does all things in order." She muttered and fell silent. The testimonies continued, and concluded with the Sea of Galilee experience.

"So you see," Peter summarized, "we Eleven await the Power to be given us from on high. Now we will share the food the devoted women have prepared for us—but be considerate. We didn't expect so many. After we have eaten, Mary Magdalene has a surprise for us."

They gathered into little groups and sat about in the lush grass of springtime, the butterflies drifting about their heads, eating and conversing in high spirits. Circulating among them, the Eleven spoke with one and another, assuaging doubts and confirming faith. Young David and Abbey flew up to Peter and plied him with questions. Longinus the centurion spoke with John and the mother of Jesus. Many others, too, were eager to converse with her—causing to resonate like a caroling of bells in her heart those prophetic words from the days of her child-bearing, "Every race and every age will cry, 'Blessed Mary!'"

At length Peter asked Mary Magdalene to stand forth.

"Sweet friends," she began, "I will sing of the Man. I have known him. I will sing of the Savior. Our twelve tribes have journeyed toward him, and I sing of their pilgrimage. I celebrate the fellowship in him which makes us one. May you find good pleasure in my words." And with a gracious bow, she began her song.

Ages past was tale begun
Of men offending God the One.
Abram heard the call afar
And came with faith for guiding star.
Moses sent to lead the flock
Did stir high wrath, and doubt the Rock.

Guides and sheep repeated sin
And made the Lord's restraint wear thin.
From the land he drove them then
But promised he would come again.
Flesh of David, Abram's son,
One day would be the Chosen One.

Sing we now our happy song,
For all of us to him belong.
Mary's womb brought him to us,
He is her Son, we saw him thus.
He for whom the world so longs,
He is the theme of all my songs.

John named him by Jordan's side
And called his people for his bride.
Tears I used to wash his feet,
My soul he washed to make me meet.
All he told their sins to shun
To join the Kingdom one by one.

Twelve he called the word to preach.
They were the first he had to teach.
Months passed by before they knew,
Then Peter cried *The Christ are you!*

Rock I call you, Jesus said,
With power o'er the quick and dead.

Jealous leaders did not know
They worked the plan of long ago.
Seeing Christ, they failed to see,
And bled the Lamb slain on a tree.
Took we fruit of Mary's womb
And weeping laid him in the tomb.

Women friends of his we went,
To wash his body our intent.
Empty tomb and angels fair
Revealed to us he was not there.
Him I saw before my eye
Alive again whom I saw die.

Ten locked in saw him that day.
When Thomas heard he said fierce nay.
Heart must first receive my hand
And until then I take my stand!
Christ struck him with word as rod.
Said Thomas then, *My Lord, my God.*

Shore of Sea became the place
Where they next saw his holy face.
Peter's love withstood the test
And so he shepherds all the rest.
Now we all in joy and love
Wait Power promised from above.

The gathering gave her its devoted attention. When she came to the last words, about "Power promised from above," on lifting her eyes to heaven, she heard cries of wonder. Surprized, she looked at the people. Every gaze was fixed on a point behind her, and she knew even before she turned.

"Shalom, shalom!" He extended his pierced hands with the greeting.

Most sat frozen. A few slipped to their knees. Doubt commandeered some faces. "Shalom, shalom," a few returned;

456

Jesus came forward.

"Know," he said in a voice that rang clear in every ear, "that I have received total power over the affairs of heaven . . ."

"Then Daniel is fulfilled!" John burst in, aflame with excitement. He was coming to feel so at home with his risen Master that his old, uninhibited way of friendship was reasserting itself.

"And over the affairs of earth," Jesus continued.

"Lord, will you send the Romans packing now," Simon the Zealot blurted out, "and restore Israel's glory?" Gone completely from his head was the terrible prophecy made over the Temple and the city.

"The Father has not chosen to reveal the time of the restoration," came the answer. "I have come to commission you."

"What are we to do, Lord?" Peter shouted.

"Delay until you receive from the Holy Spirit the Power I promised. Go then and give witness to me."

"Even to Samaria?" Andrew called.

"To Jerusalem, Judea, Samaria, and the ends of the earth— to all creation. Make disciples of all nations."

Stunned silence followed. Then Jonah cried out in the words of the psalmist: "His enemies shall bend to him, kings shall honor him. All nations shall serve him!"

"How can we *make* them believe?" That anguished cry could come only from Thomas.

"You will work signs—exorcise demons, speak in tongues, pick up serpents, be unharmed by poison, and heal the sick with the laying on of hands."

"And if they're obstinate?" the Twin asked anxiously.

A long silence held sway, a lifting and tuning of ears, before the answer came.

"He who refuses to believe will be condemned. He who believes and receives baptism will be saved."

"Praise God!" "Halleluiah!" "Justice and mercy!" the assembly cried. He beckoned to Simon Peter, who went to him. They turned, and together walked the path to the peak of the Mount of Olives. The rest of the Eleven fell in behind, and then the others.

On the highest elevation of the Mount, with Bethany

lying behind in the valley and the city before him in the distance, he addressed them again.

"I am going home to the Father now, to prepare a place for you. I shall return, take you with me, and we shall be together always."

He raised his hands and blessed them. A bright cloud began to form around him, and rise slowly, and he with it.

"Are you going to leave us alone?" The piping cry of sorrow, a mournful note of a shepherdess' flute on midnight stillness, emanated from Mary of Bethany, lips parted, face tragic.

From the cloud, his voice descended. "I am ever with you, until time enters eternity."

Her heart leapt with joy—this was not a parting! A new and deeper union with him was beginning for his disciples. Each must attend it in his or her own way. In this she heard her call confirmed. Her contemplative life must go on, to keep the awareness alive in his people.

"Come back soon!" the Magdalene cried, and her earnest plea was taken up in a symphony of longings. "Lord Jesus, return quickly!" "Come, Lord Jesus!" "Maranatha!"

They watched until he was lost in the sky, and even then they stared blindly after him.

"You Galileans, why stand here gaping at the heavens?"

Simon Peter heard the commanding voice, and peered at its source, a lordly young man in a glistening robe. A second youth with him could have been his twin.

"Didn't you see what happened?" Peter asked in astonishment.

"Yes—and when the time comes, he will return just as you saw him go." With that, the two vanished.

The big fisherman called the multitude to attention. "It is time to go, as the Lord commissioned us in your hearing. The Eleven, the seventy-two, and the chosen women are to come with me to the Upper Room, to await the Holy Spirit and Power."

"What of the rest of us?" a forlorn voice cried.

"Return home and await further word." Peter turned to the mother of Jesus. "Mother," he said simply, "you know him best. Come, guide us in his footsteps until his Spirit descends."

"Thank you, Peter. I, too, want to be with all of you."

On the way, John said, "Mother, I'm concerned. The Eleven are divided in their understanding of your Son."

Mary laid her hand on his arm. "John, you told me what he said at that last supper. Recall the part about the Paraclete." John's eyes opened wide.

"That the Father will send the Paraclete, the Holy Spirit, and he will instruct us in everything."

"Isn't that our purpose now—to await him? When he comes, you will all know and understand—and be of one mind about the Son."

"About your Son. Mother, would you like to pay a visit to Bethlehem, where it all began?"

"That's not necessary." She laid her hand on her cloak, beneath her heart. "It all began here." She smiled. "We'll go with the others to the Upper Room. There it will continue."

The End

ABOUT THE AUTHOR

Herbert Francis Smith began working on his first novel thirty years ago, but abandoned it to enter the Society of Jesus. As a priest, he turned to non-fiction, and produced books, articles, and an occasional script for TV and film.

The inspiration to write a novel so many years later came welling up out of a far-reaching search to portray in the most compelling way what he has given us in *Hidden Victory*.

Born in Buffalo, N.Y., on December 31, 1922, he is the fifth of nine children. He had wide-ranging experience as a factory worker, technician, electronic service engineer, entrepreneur, and radio and TV instructor.

These experiences left his inner search unquieted until he joined the Jesuits in 1951. He earned his M.A. from Fordham in 1961, and was ordained at Woodstock College, where he received the bachelor's degree in Sacred Theology.

In October, 1979, Fr. Smith flew to Israel and remained almost a year traveling, researching, consulting scholars, and beginning the novel. Thirty years of living close to dedicated religious men and women gave him a wealth of insight into the biblical characters he portrays.

When not writing, he travels widely, conducting retreats and other spiritual programs. He hosts a weekly radio program, and is a speaker on International Sacred Heart Radio. He is listed in Gale's *Contemporary Authors*.

Fr. Smith resides at The Jesuit Community, Saint Joseph's University, 5600 City Ave., Philadelphia, PA 19131.

FROM THE AUTHOR

Why did I write this novel? Creative springs run deep and fast, but let us scout out what we can. When I was a boy, my avid interest in Admiral Byrd and his polar explorations was observed, and I was asked, "Are you going to be an explorer?" Later, outer space beckoned: that so-called "last frontier." Yet the human race, deeper than space, is still on its own frontiers. And deeper still, the Son of Man is the true final frontier. To him my interest turned.

I saw today's theologians wrestling with the question of Christ's consciousness, but their explanations are a jungle as impenetrable to

460

most people as their subject.

In my work as a priest I met the resulting confusion in believers who assumed that, since Jesus was God, he didn't have to struggle as human beings do, when he became a man. I'll always remember counseling one belabored Christian to try to be more like Jesus, who himself struggled to cope. She retorted, "Oh, but he was God!" She had just undone the Incarnation.

A frontier was beckoning. I longed to hack my way through the jungle and let out the light of Christ. I decided to attempt a commentary on his life. Then it came—make it a novel! Skirt the need to justify every insight! Let the story pour out in all its human grip and drama. The idea took hold, but one step remained: I sought the divine will and guidance. And found it. That's the origin of *Hidden Victory*. May it be a window letting the light of Christ into our hearts until we all stop undoing the Incarnation, and learn to be as human as he.

INDEX OF SCRIPTURAL REFERENCES

References are by page number-line number, scriptural source. Thus, 19-17 Is 7:10-14 signifies: page 19, line 17—see Is chapter 7, verses 10 to 14 (See right margin of this page for a Line Yardstick, which can be photocopied or cut out).

When a whole episode is based on one scriptural passage, both the starting page and line, and the ending page and line, are given. Other major scriptural passages used within those pages are given in closed parentheses, without page or line number.

The references are not exhaustive. For example, only one Gospel may be cited for a given episode even when parallel accounts in the other Gospels are also used as sources (The parallel passages can be found in any cross-referenced bible).

ABBREVIATIONS

Am	Amos	Jer	Jeremiah	Mk	Mark
Cor	Corinthians	Jl	Joel	Mt	Matthew
Dn	Daniel	Jn	John	Phil	Philippians
Dt	Deuteronomy	Jos	Joshua	Ps	Psalm
Ez	Ezekiel	Lk	Luke	Ru	Ruth
Ezr	Ezra	Lv	Leviticus	Rv	Revelation
Gn	Genesis	Mal	Malachi	Sm	Samuel
Heb	Hebrews	Mc	Maccabees	Zec	Zechariah
Is	Isaiah	Mi	Micah	Zep	Zephaniah

1
2
3
4
5
6
7
8
9
10
11
12
13
14
15
16
17
18
19
20
21
22
23
24
25
26
27
28
29
30
31
32
33
34
35
36
37
38
39
40

461

462

463

467

469

ORDER FORM

(Order from your bookstore, or write the distributor, address below):
Send me **Hidden Victory**, A Novel Of Jesus, by H.F. Smith:

_____ copies of hardcover at $11.95   Total $ _____

_____ copies of paperback at $5.95   Total $ _____

(N.Y. State residents, add sales tax: 7%) $ _____

Add shipping/handling charge:
1 copy $1.50; EACH ADD. COPY $.50; less in bulk $ _____

My check (or money order) is inclosed for total $ _____

    SEND TO: NAME_____

    STREET_____

    CITY_____ STATE _____ ZIP_____

    Send a gift copy—*with author's autograph if possible*— (and gift
card bearing my name _____) to:

    NAME _____

    STREET_____

    CITY _____ STATE_____ ZIP _____

_____ Mail to *arrive* by the following date: _____
       (in time for Christmas, birthday, etc.)

_____ Send trade discount list (business firms only).

_____ Send discount prices for fund raising or educational use (Send
your name and parish or organization's name).

_____ I'm interested in being a sales agent for **Hidden Victory**. Send me
information.

(MAIL YOUR ORDER TO: Bonny Books, Inc., 180 Sweeney St., North
Tonawanda, N.Y. 14120)

Price subject to change without notice.